More praise for

Bad Things Happen

"[Harry Dolan] has a gift for storytelling . . . the narrative comes with startling developments and nicely tricky reversals. There's also something appealingly offbeat about the wry, dry tone of its academic humor . . . [David Loogan is an] interestingly enigmatic hero."

—Marilyn Stasio, *The New York Times*

"[A] droll and delightful first novel . . . *Bad Things Happen* works perfectly well as a straight murder mystery, but it isn't pure realism; there's an air of make-believe here, of fun . . . Even as Dolan enmeshes us in his intricate crime story, he's playing with the foibles of writers and giving us a witty sendup of the crime genre itself . . . ingeniously put together . . . as well plotted as Agatha Christie at her best . . . It's witty, sophisticated, suspenseful and endless fun—a novel to be savored by people who know and love good crime fiction, and the best first novel I've read this year."

—*The Washington Post*

"[A] brilliant first novel . . . I could go on for pages about the amazing amount of trust that Dolan generates from page one, letting us know that he won't make a false move. But I don't want to spoil your pleasure."

—*Chicago Tribune*

"With writing that's as tight and finely crafted as the plot, the book is equally deserving of accolades as a literary thriller and great beach book, and marks Dolan as an emerging talent . . . Dolan never passes up an opportunity to twist the plot in unexpected directions . . . *Bad Things Happen* is good news for fans of intelligent, well-written murder mysteries."

—*Detroit Free Press*

"From the astringent first sentence—'The shovel has to meet certain requirements'—*Bad Things Happen* by Harry Dolan builds like a midwestern thunderhead into an atmosphere of darkness, dread and impending doom. It is a hypnotically readable novel, with richly wrought characters, a corkscrew plot and dialogue worthy of Elmore Leonard. What a breathtaking debut." —Douglas Preston, author of *The Monster of Florence* and *Blasphemy*

continued . . .

"Dolan's neatly symmetrical plot is tight, his dialogue is crisp and his humor wry . . . A twisty whodunit with a thriller's pace."

—*Booklist* (starred review)

"Harry Dolan has written a wonderfully moody and atmospheric story reminiscent of the masters of the noir mysteries. *Bad Things Happen* is a tightly plotted, sophisticated and engrossing debut novel. Dolan has a fine ear for good dialogue and an uncanny sense of how people think and act, and why they do what they do. This is a winner."

—Nelson DeMille

"Dolan gets everything right in his debut, a suspense novel that breathes new life into familiar themes . . . Pitch-perfect prose and sophisticated characterizations drive the noirish plot, which offers plenty of unexpected twists. Fans of Peter Abrahams and Scott Turow will find a lot to like . . . [Dolan] has a bright future."

—*Publishers Weekly* (starred review)

"*Bad Things Happen* is a tense read that keeps you tightly in its grip until the very last page. Harry Dolan has written an incredibly rich, smart read reminiscent of *A Simple Plan* or *Presumed Innocent*—not to mention that it's just a damn good story. Readers are in for a breathless ride."

—Karin Slaughter

"For a debut novelist, Dolan . . . is unusually skilled in narrative. His humor shows not only in the fiction-versus-reality theme but also in the twists and turns of the plot and language that keep the characters and the reader guessing—and engrossed. Highly recommended for readers who enjoy twisty and witty crime thrillers."

—*Library Journal* (starred review)

"Dolan has provided a seven-course banquet for readers with a taste for deliriously overplotted pulp with just enough polish to keep them from feeling guilty."

—*Kirkus Reviews*

Bad Things Happen

Harry Dolan

BERKLEY BOOKS, NEW YORK

THE BERKLEY PUBLISHING GROUP
Published by the Penguin Group
Penguin Group (USA) Inc.
375 Hudson Street, New York, New York 10014, USA
Penguin Group (Canada), 90 Eglinton Avenue East, Suite 700, Toronto, Ontario M4P 2Y3, Canada
(a division of Pearson Penguin Canada Inc.)
Penguin Books Ltd., 80 Strand, London WC2R 0RL, England
Penguin Group Ireland, 25 St. Stephen's Green, Dublin 2, Ireland (a division of Penguin Books Ltd.)
Penguin Group (Australia), 250 Camberwell Road, Camberwell, Victoria 3124, Australia
(a division of Pearson Australia Group Pty. Ltd.)
Penguin Books India Pvt. Ltd., 11 Community Centre, Panchsheel Park, New Delhi—110 017, India
Penguin Group (NZ), 67 Apollo Drive, Rosedale, North Shore 0632, New Zealand
(a division of Pearson New Zealand Ltd.)
Penguin Books (South Africa) (Pty.) Ltd., 24 Sturdee Avenue, Rosebank, Johannesburg 2196,
South Africa

Penguin Books Ltd., Registered Offices: 80 Strand, London WC2R 0RL, England

PRINTING HISTORY
Amy Einhorn Books hardcover edition / July 2009
Berkley trade paperback edition / July 2010

Berkley trade paperback ISBN: 978-0-425-23440-2

The Library of Congress has catalogued the Amy Einhorn Books hardcover edition as follows:

Dolan, Harry.
  Bad things happen / Harry Dolan.
  p.   cm.
  ISBN 978-0-399-15563-5
  1. Periodical editors—Fiction. 2. Women detectives—Michigan—Fiction.
3. Murder—Investigation—Fiction. 4. Ann Arbor (Mich.)—Fiction. I. Title.
  PS3604.O424B33   2009   2008054628
  813'.6—dc22

PRINTED IN THE UNITED STATES OF AMERICA

10 9 8 7 6 5 4 3 2

FOR LINDA

(She knows why.)

Bad Things Happen

Chapter 1

THE SHOVEL HAS TO MEET CERTAIN REQUIREMENTS. A POINTED BLADE. A short handle, to make it maneuverable in a confined space. He finds what he needs in the gardening section of a vast department store.

He stows the shovel in his cart and moves unhurriedly through the wide aisles, gathering a few more items: D-cell batteries, a bag of potting soil, a can of weed-killer. Leather work gloves, two pairs. In the grocery section he picks up four deli sandwiches wrapped in plastic and a case of bottled water.

The checkout lanes are crowded. He chooses a line and the fluorescent lights flicker overhead as he considers how he's going to pay. His wallet holds a credit card in the name of David Loogan. It's not the name he was born with, but it's what he calls himself now. He's not going to use the credit card.

He does some calculations in his head and decides he has enough cash.

The line moves and he thinks he'll get out quick and clean, but he's wrong. The cashier wants to talk.

"I think I've seen you before," she says to him.

"I doubt it."

She's tall, broad in the hips, attractive, though the stark light accentuates the lines under her eyes and around her mouth.

"You look familiar," she says.

The man who calls himself David Loogan doesn't want to be familiar. He wants to be nondescript. Unmemorable.

"Maybe I've seen you here in the store," the cashier suggests.

He offers her a lukewarm smile. "That must be it."

He busies himself loading things onto the counter. The cashier takes the shovel and holds it with the blade pointing skyward so she can scan the bar code on the handle.

"You must be a gardener," she says.

He ought to agree and leave it at that, but he gets flustered. He starts to say, "I'm an editor," but stops himself. The truth won't do. He goes with the first lie that comes into his mind.

"I'm a juggler," he says.

It's a mistake. She decides to find him charming. She smiles and sets the shovel on the end of the counter and reaches for the potting soil in a leisurely way.

"You must be very good," she says lightly. "I've never heard of anyone juggling shovels. But one's not enough, is it? You ought to have three."

Go with charming then. "I've already got three," he says. "Anyone can juggle three. The real trick is juggling four."

"It must be dazzling," she says. "Where do you work? Kids' birthdays?"

He waits a beat and answers in his most serious tone. "Garden parties."

"Ha. Are you sure we haven't met before?"

She's flirting, Loogan decides. He looks at her fingers as she scans the sandwiches. She's wearing a wedding ring.

"I could swear I know you," she says. "Maybe we went to school together."

"I never went," he says. "Everything I know about juggling is self-taught."

"I'm serious. I think we went to high school together."

"I didn't go to high school around here."

"Well, hell, neither did I," she says. "And it's been quite a while. But you remind me of a boy in my class. I'll think of your name in a second."

She bags the gloves and the batteries together, the weed-killer separately.

"Dennis," she says suddenly, looking up at him. "Or Daniel?"

David Loogan picks up the shovel from the counter and is troubled by a momentary vision. He sees himself stabbing the blade into the base of the cashier's neck.

"Ted," he tells her. "My name is Ted Carmady."

She smiles and shakes her head. "Are you sure?"

"I'm sure."

She lets it go with a shrug. "Well, then I was way off, wasn't I?"

He puts the shovel in his cart, and she reads off his total and takes his money. He thinks she has turned shy on him, but she scribbles something on his receipt before she hands it over. He scans it on the way out, sees her name (*Allison*) and a phone number, and crumples the paper discreetly.

Out in the parking lot, Loogan adjusts the collar of his black leather coat and checks his watch. Nine-thirty on a Wednesday night in October. A mist of rain is falling and the cars in the lot glow in the yellow light of tall arc lamps.

The lamps reassure him. He is not exactly afraid of the dark, but he often feels uneasy going out after sunset. And parking lots unnerve him. The echo of footsteps in a parking lot at night can set his pulse racing.

Loogan moves steadily along a row of cars, pushing the shopping cart before him. He has an uncomfortable moment when he sees a figure coming toward him. A thin man with a weathered face, hollowed eyes. A hooded sweatshirt, pants torn at the knee. Right hand resting in a pocket of the sweatshirt.

Loogan is suddenly aware of the humming of the arc lamps, the turning wheels of the cart.

You're fine, he tells himself. Nothing's going to happen.

As the thin man gets close, his hand comes out of the pocket of his sweatshirt. Loogan sees a glint of silver. Metal, he thinks. Blade. Knife.

Reflexively he reaches out to grab the thin man's wrist, but he stops himself in time. The thin man flinches away from him and hurries past, clutching a silver-gray cell phone to the front of his sweatshirt. He mumbles something Loogan doesn't catch.

Then he's gone and it's over and Loogan comes to his car. He loads the shovel in the trunk, and the potting soil, and all the rest. He shuts the trunk and pushes the cart into an empty parking space.

The hum of the arc lamps has receded into silence. Everything is normal. David Loogan is an ordinary shopper. No one would think otherwise. He opens his car door and slides in behind the wheel. He looks nothing at all like a man heading off to dig a grave.

The man who called himself David Loogan had been living in Ann Arbor since March. He rented a small furnished house on the west side: a sharp-roofed wood-frame place with a porch in the front and a little yard in back wound about with chain-link fence.

He spent his days in the vicinity of Liberty and State streets, reading newspapers in cafés, watching movies at the Michigan Theater. He observed the comings and goings of university students, listened in on their conversations. He was not out of place in a university crowd: he might have passed for an older graduate student, or a young professor. He was thirty-eight.

The house he rented stood on the corner of a tree-lined street and belonged to a professor of history who was on sabbatical, doing research at a think tank somewhere overseas. He had left a neglected garden in the backyard, and for a few days in April Loogan tried his hand at planting flowers. He bought seeds and poked them into the dirt. He watered, he waited. The flowers showed no sign of growing.

On an afternoon in May, he found a short-story magazine that someone had abandoned in a coffee shop. The title was *Gray Streets*. He ordered a cappuccino and found an overstuffed chair and read a story about an innocent man framed for murder by a beautiful and enigmatic woman.

The next day he set up camp in the professor's home office, clearing books and papers from the desk. He turned on the computer and started to compose a story about a killer with a fear of parking lots. It took him three days to finish a draft, which he printed and read through once before tearing it in half and burying it in the wastebasket.

The second version took him four days, and he considered it barely passable. He let the pages sit on the desk for a week, until one evening he put them away in a drawer and began to click away at a third version. He kept at it for several more nights until he had worked out a plot that satisfied him. The killer turned out to be the hero of the piece, and there was a twisted villain, and a woman the killer saved from the villain. The climax took place on the top level of a parking garage. Loogan went back and forth on whether the woman would stay with the killer after he saved her, but he decided it would be better if she left.

When he had the ending the way he wanted it, he printed a clean copy with a title on the first page and no byline or contact information, and then consulted his copy of *Gray Streets* for the magazine's editorial address. The address was a dozen blocks away, on the sixth floor of a building downtown. He walked there on a Saturday and the lobby doors were locked, but in the back he found a service entrance—a steel door propped open with a brick. A dingy stairway brought him to the sixth floor. He passed the offices of an accountant and a documentary production company, and there it was. Neat black letters on the pebbled glass of the door: GRAY STREETS.

He had the manuscript in an unmarked envelope. It was too thick to slide under the door but there was an open transom above, and he slipped the envelope over and heard it drop to the floor on the other side.

In the days that followed he returned to his routine, going to movies and lingering in coffee shops. Then, on a night when he couldn't sleep, he went down to the professor's office and sat before the computer screen, reading the story again line by line, tinkering with it as he went along. Trimming words and phrases and finding that the sentences were stronger without them. The next day he printed a new copy and after business hours he walked downtown and climbed the narrow stairs and slipped another envelope over the transom.

He was sure that would be the end of it. He made himself busy, branching out in his wanderings: to museums, to art galleries, to public parks. But it wasn't the end. His memory was sharp; he could recall sentences and paragraphs; he could rewrite them as he walked along a path or stood before a painting. On another sleepless night he descended to the professor's office, intending to delete the file from the computer; he stayed there for an hour, for three, mulling every word choice, fussing over every bit of punctuation.

He thought he would leave it there, a file on a hard drive. What would it matter if he printed it again? At twilight two days later he found himself in the hallway once more, holding the manuscript in an envelope under his arm. He stood before the door with the transom and tried to see beyond the pebbled glass. There might be nothing on the other side, he thought. Maybe just an empty room with two envelopes on the floor, gathering dust. And now a third to join them.

The door opened.

The man who opened it wore a dark blue suit with a powder blue shirt and a silk tie. He paused in the motion of putting on his hat—a black fedora with a band that matched the suit. He saw Loogan and his eyes went to the envelope and the hat came down, the door swung open wide.

"It's you," he said. "Come in."

He retreated into the dimness of the room and after a few seconds a light came on in an inner office. From the lighted doorway he beckoned to Loogan with his hat.

Loogan took a few tentative steps. "I can't stay," he said.

"Why not?"

There was no answer for that. The answer that occurred to him— *Because it's going to be dark soon*—would sound ridiculous.

"You're not going to make me drag you in," said the man in the blue suit.

His voice had an oddly formal quality, the voice of an actor running lines. He directed Loogan to a chair and went around behind the desk. Among the papers on the desktop, Loogan saw his own two envelopes, each one sliced open along the edge.

"I've been waiting for you to come by," said the man in the blue suit. "That was clever, leaving your name off. It sparked my interest."

He tossed his hat onto a filing cabinet. Loogan said nothing.

"Is this the same one again, or a new one?"

Looking down at the envelope in his lap, Loogan said, "It's the same one. I've made some improvements."

"You ought to be careful. If it gets much better, I won't be able to publish it." The man took a seat at the desk. "The reason I've been waiting for you—I wanted to make you an offer. I want you to work for me."

This was unexpected. Loogan frowned.

"I'm not really a writer."

"I don't need another writer. I've got writers scrabbling between the walls here, gnawing on the wiring. What I need is an editor."

Loogan shifted in his chair. "I don't think I'm qualified. I don't have the training."

"Nobody does," the man said. "It's not like people go to school for it. No one sets out to be an editor. It's something that happens to you, like jaundice or falling down a well." He pointed at Loogan's envelopes. "I like what you've done here," he said. "There's a clear improvement from one draft to the next. The question is, could you do the same thing with someone else's story?"

Loogan looked to the window, where the twilight was deepening. This isn't a problem, he thought. You can always refuse.

"I suppose I could," he heard himself saying, "but I'm not looking for a job. I don't know how I feel about coming into an office every morning."

The man in the blue suit leaned back. "You won't have to come in. You can work from home. You won't have to follow a schedule. You'll only have to do one thing."

"What's that?"

"You'll have to tell me what your name is."

A moment's hesitation. Then: "David Loogan."

"Tom Kristoll."

Chapter 2

Tom Kristoll owned a house on a wooded hill overlooking the Huron River. It was a sprawling affair of thick wooden beams and broad panes of glass. There was slate on the roof and a patio paved in stone, and wide stone steps that led down to a pool.

On weekends in the summer Kristoll hosted parties for the staff and writers of *Gray Streets*. The first time Loogan was invited he decided he wouldn't go, but Kristoll phoned him in the early afternoon. They had everything they needed for a barbecue, Kristoll said, but no barbecue sauce. Could Loogan pick some up on his way? Loogan could and did. He arrived to find Kristoll, dressed in white from head to toe, overseeing the preparation of the grill. Kristoll's wife scolded him for making their guest run errands. She took charge of Loogan, gave him a tour of the house, and was on hand to introduce him to a series of writers and interns.

"This is David Loogan," she told them, "Tom's new editor."

Laura Kristoll wore a silk blouse and capri pants. She was sleek and blond and had a degree in English literature, which she taught at the university. Most of the interns were her students. She saw to it that Loogan always had a drink. She offered him towels and swim trunks in case he wanted to go in the pool. When he wandered off toward the edge of the woods to get away from the crowd, she let him alone.

Later, as he was leaving, she approached him and said quietly, "David, I'm afraid you haven't had a good time."

"Sure I have," he told her.

"You'll come again then."

"Of course," he said, though he hadn't intended to.

Through the summer Loogan had a steady stream of editing assignments from Tom Kristoll. He worked on more than one story at a time and soon the manuscripts littered his rented house, the pages dotted with revisions in his fine, clean handwriting.

One evening in July, Kristoll called him and asked to meet him for a drink. Loogan drove to a restaurant downtown and a waitress led him to a booth paneled in dark wood and illuminated by a single bulb in a fixture of gray steel. Kristoll had ordered him a glass of Scotch.

"I didn't think you'd agree to come," Kristoll said. "I thought I'd have to drag you. I had it all planned, the dialogue written. 'When I offer you a drink, you'll have a drink and like it,' I was going to say."

Loogan made a show of relaxing. He sat sideways, his back to the wall, his left leg bent, the other stretched along the cushioned seat.

"You're a closemouthed man," Kristoll said, "but I like a closemouthed man about as much as any other kind. I'm not going to make you tell me your secrets."

"I don't have any secrets, Tom. Ask me anything."

"All right. Where are you from?"

"Portland."

"How long have you lived in Ann Arbor?"

"Four months."

"And what were you doing, before I hired you?"

"For work?"

"For work."

"I was with the circus."

"Do I need to point out that Ann Arbor doesn't have a circus?"

"This wasn't in Ann Arbor," Loogan said. "This was before I came here."

"So you ran away from the circus and came to Ann Arbor?"

"More or less."

"A lot of people go the other way. What did you do, in the circus?"

"I was a juggler."

"Is there any point in continuing this conversation?" Kristoll asked.

"Call the waitress, Tom. Have her bring some dinner rolls. I'll prove it to you."

"And your hometown. Portland. Would that be in Oregon or Maine?"

"Which do you like better?"

Kristoll laughed quietly and tended to his drink. Loogan reached up and with his fingertips set the steel shade of the lamp swaying gently above the table. After a while the waitress brought them fresh glasses and they talked about other things: about the quality of the writers in *Gray Streets,* about writers generally, about the heat of the Michigan summer.

It was a pleasant conversation and it was followed by others on other evenings in the same booth, or in Kristoll's office. Once, Kristoll came un-announced to Loogan's rented house. "Tell me to go to hell, David, if you don't want me to come in," Kristoll said. "Come in, of course," said Loogan. Kristoll inspected the furniture in the living room, the stonework of the fire-place. He admired some of the paintings and prints that hung on the walls. "None of them are mine," said Loogan. "Naturally," Kristoll said.

Unlike Loogan, Kristoll showed no reluctance to talk about himself. He had been raised in a middle-class suburb of Detroit, had moved to Ann Ar-bor to attend the University of Michigan. He had met his wife there and with a small group of friends they had founded *Gray Streets* as a student publication. It was a modest success for four years, though it faded when Kristoll and his wife departed for graduate school out of state. When Laura Kristoll returned to Ann Arbor to teach at the university, Tom Kris-toll set out to revive the magazine, gently prying it away from the students who had taken it over.

In the years since, the magazine's circulation had grown to a respectable number, and the rise of the Internet had brought it a new audience. Kristoll had designed the original *Gray Streets* Web site himself, as a way of resur-recting stories from issues that had gone out of print. Bloggers had discov-ered the site and reviewed it. It had been mentioned in magazine articles about electronic publishing. More people read *Gray Streets* online than had ever read it in print.

"I'll let you in on a secret," Kristoll said to Loogan one evening. He had the window open in his office, his feet resting on the sill. A bottle stood on the desk. "In the early days, when Laura and I were in college, most of the stories we published were written by students. We wrote some of them ourselves, published them under pseudonyms. But when I started building the Web site, I left off most of those old stories. Only the best ones went onto the site. None of mine are on there. I have enough judgment to know they don't belong there. Do you know what that makes me?"

Loogan hadn't expected the question. "What?" he said.

"An editor. Nobody sets out to be an editor, but here we are, you and me." Kristoll picked up his glass from the desk and held it in his lap. "Now I've turned maudlin," he said. "You'll forgive me. You can attribute it to the Scotch."

"I think you drink less Scotch than you let on," Loogan said.

"That's a good line. I can tell—I'm an editor."

A breeze from the window lifted a letter from the desk and carried it to the floor. Loogan reached for it but Kristoll told him to leave it there.

"Go home, David," he said gently. "The sun's gone down. It stays up forever this time of year, but now it's gone down."

"You're not leaving?"

"I'll stay awhile. Turn off the lights out there, will you? Good night."

Loogan's steps were silent on the carpet of the outer office. He paused at the door to the hallway to press the light switch. Looking back, he saw Kristoll sitting in profile, his head tipped back, eyes closed. The doorway of his office framed the image, a composition in black and white: dark hair, close-cropped; crisp white dress shirt; gray gunmetal desk.

The light of the desk lamp gleamed on the rim of his glass. It made the skin of his face a pale white. It gave his expression a purity and a calm that Loogan hadn't seen in him before.

Loogan would remember that calm, and he would remember the gentleness, the fondness in Kristoll's voice when Kristoll told him to go home. He would remember both these things later, when he started sleeping with Kristoll's wife.

In a museum in late August, Loogan stood looking up at an immense photograph of a leaf. The leaf was lush and green but it lay amid stones and sand, and grains of sand had drifted over its surface. Loogan stepped to his right and there was a series of smaller images: dead leaves trampled into dry, cracked mud. The leaves had split with the mud as it dried; black grooves ran through them like veins.

He heard someone speak his name and turned to find Laura Kristoll beside him.

"It's all leaves," she said. "There are two more rooms of leaves. Come on, I'll show you."

The parties at the Kristoll house had gone on through the summer, and Loogan had put in a few appearances. He had talked to Laura only a handful of times, but now she seemed at ease taking his arm and leading him through the exhibit. It was, as she had said, all leaves: Leaves after rain, leaves on the bottom of a stream, leaves on country roads. Leaves blackened by fire. A close-up of a single withered leaf, so thin and brittle that it seemed on the verge of crumbling into dust. She kept her casual grip on his arm as they stood before this final image. After a time he told her he had better go. He had work to do. Her hand traveled down his arm, to his wrist, to his palm. Their fingers intertwined. "All right, David," she said.

She called him the following week. There was another photography exhibit, this one at a gallery downtown. "The photographer is local," she said. "He does something with paper and broken glass. But secretly I'm hoping there'll be leaves."

They went the next day. They had the gallery mainly to themselves and they took their time. Most of it looked to Loogan as if someone had thrown the contents of a china cabinet through a stained-glass window and then taken pictures. But Laura was delighted to discover a photograph of flower petals and broken glass mingled with bits of paper torn in the shape of leaves. She bought it on the spot and arranged with the gallery owner to have it delivered at the close of the exhibition.

She led Loogan from the gallery to a used-book shop, where they spent half an hour browsing. Then she suggested coffee, which morphed into a late lunch. She was quiet when she drove him home. The car rolled slowly along his street in the sunlight and in the shadows of trees. She brought it to a stop and shifted into park and turned to look past him at the house.

"David," she said. "Ask me in."

She followed him up the walk, pressed the palm of her right hand between his shoulder blades as he unlocked the door. In the kitchen she paused to read a few lines of a manuscript he had left on the counter. She stepped through an archway into the living room and surveyed the space. There were more manuscripts on the coffee table, but she didn't look at those. She turned to find him beside her, touched her fingers to the base of his throat, and said, "I'll be right back."

She found the downstairs bathroom on her own. It was down a hallway off the living room. Loogan went around closing curtains. He scanned the history professor's CD collection, discovered it was terribly impoverished, and tuned the stereo to a Detroit station that played instrumental jazz. When Laura returned, she had left her handbag behind. Her hair, which had been pinned up, was down around her shoulders. Her lips were a shade redder. Her linen blouse was two buttons more unbuttoned than it had been, revealing tanned and freckled skin. Her breath, when she turned her face up to his and curved her palm around the back of his neck, was flavored with mint.

He kissed her, extensively. First standing, then sitting, then lying on the sofa, with the length of her body pressed against him. They undressed by degrees, without urgency, and he discovered when her skirt came off that she had left her underwear behind with her handbag. They made love on a bed of sofa cushions on the living-room floor.

After, they went upstairs, and in the coolness of the history professor's sheets they fell asleep. When Loogan woke it was dark and he was alone. He reached reflexively to the night table for his watch. He had left it on the floor of the living room. He went down and found that the cushions had been restored to the sofa. His clothes were on a chair, his watch on the mantel of the fireplace. It was after nine o'clock.

The phone rang as he was dressing. He picked it up and Laura said, "You're dangerous."

"I will be, when I get my socks on," he said.

"You sleep beautifully. It's a natural wonder, how you sleep. I couldn't bear to wake you."

"Sleeping is one of my best things."

"I just called to say everything's grand. Nothing to worry about. You're not the sort to worry, are you, David?"

"Not me."

"But I wanted to touch base. So we know what story we're telling, if any story needs to be told. I've stuck with the truth, as far as I could: You and I went to the gallery today, and the bookstore, and lunch. After that, we parted ways."

"All right."

"Better than saying I never saw you, I don't know you, I never heard of you."

"Sure."

"So everything's grand," she said. "I should run. We'll talk again soon."

"Yes."

"Good night, David."

"Good night."

Loogan saw Tom Kristoll two nights later. He thought it might be awkward, but they were just the same as they had ever been. They drank Scotch in

Kristoll's office after hours. They discussed manuscripts, briefly. Kristoll talked about a trip he had taken to Europe with his family as a teenager.

Laura was mentioned only once. "I'm learning more about you, David," Kristoll said. "I'm scoping out your secrets."

"Is that so?" Loogan said.

"Laura filled me in. You like to spend time in galleries, and you have excellent taste in photographs. Two more facts to add to the dossier on David Loogan."

In the weeks that followed, Loogan saw Laura regularly. Usually she came to his house. Once they met at a hotel, once in her office at the university.

She rarely mentioned her husband, never talked of being unhappy with him, never complained about his habits. Loogan was alert for any slight, any disparaging remark. He told himself he would end it, if he thought she was motivated by malice. But when she spoke of her husband, it was usually in connection with Loogan himself. She would pass along something Kristoll had said: a bit of praise for Loogan's work, or an idle comment.

One afternoon she stood naked by the window of Loogan's bedroom, looking down into the yard. "Tom thinks you've got some dark secret," she said. "You're a man with a past. He thinks you might have spent time in prison."

She said it lightly, carelessly. Loogan was lying in bed, watching her.

"Really?" he said.

"Yes. Tom has a certain respect for criminals, you know. *Gray Streets* goes out free to a lot of prison libraries. He's even published a few stories written by convicts."

"And what does he think I did, that landed me in prison?"

She turned away from the window and crossed to the bed. Pulled back the sheet and climbed in beside him.

"Oh, nothing terrible," she said. "Something white-collar, probably. Defrauding people. Embezzlement or passing bad checks. Have you ever defrauded anyone?"

"I've never been to prison."

"I don't think it's anything like that," she said, tracing her finger along his collarbone. "I think if you were to go to prison, it would be for something violent. A crime of passion. It's always the quiet ones."

"Is it?"

"And they'd interview your neighbors on the news, and they'd say, 'He was such a nice man. He never gave anyone trouble.'"

He smiled faintly. Closed his eyes. "And what would you say?"

Her lips brushed his cheek. "I'd tell them I always knew you were dangerous."

The weeks passed by—September and the beginning of October. Loogan's days revolved around Laura Kristoll and Tom Kristoll and *Gray Streets*. Then, on a Wednesday night, as he sat in his kitchen with a manuscript on the table before him, his phone rang. The caller was Tom Kristoll. He wondered if Loogan could do him a favor. He needed a shovel.

Chapter 3

THE ROAD CURVED AND A LINE OF TREES CURVED WITH IT. SOMEWHERE behind the trees was the dark course of the Huron River. Loogan drove at the posted limit and his car's headlights washed over bark and branches and leaves. A light rain speckled the windshield. He slowed, looking for the turn, found it, and climbed slowly up the long driveway.

Moonlight touched the slate roof of the house. Two slivers of light escaped from a pair of curtained windows on the ground floor. The rest were dark.

Loogan turned off the engine, got out, and followed a stone walkway to the house. He left his purchases behind—the shovel, the groceries. The front door opened as he approached. Tom Kristoll let him inside.

"It's after ten," Kristoll said. "I don't think I've ever seen you this late in the evening. I half believed you wouldn't be there when I called. That you ceased to exist after a certain hour."

"Here I am," Loogan said.

"I'm rambling. Don't pay any attention. Thank you for coming. Do you want a drink? No, you don't want a drink. I wanted a drink, and I had one. But one was enough."

They had moved into the living room. There was an empty glass on the arm of a leather sofa. Wooden beams crossed overhead, and a table lamp threw the shadows of the beams onto the ceiling. The floor was paved with stones and in a corner stood an antique furnace, a fire burning behind its iron grate.

Kristoll paced across the floor in his sock feet. He wore dress pants, charcoal gray, with a faint stripe. His white shirt was wrinkled and partly untucked. There was a hint of a shadow of stubble along his jaw. It made his face look haggard.

"Maybe you should sit," Loogan said.

Kristoll froze. He seemed suddenly conscious of his appearance. He tucked in the tail of his shirt, rubbed his face with the palms of his hands.

"There's no time for sitting, David."

"All right. Then you'd better show me."

Kristoll led Loogan through the darkened house. They arrived at the doorway of the study and Kristoll reached in to find the light switch.

Loogan had seen the room before, and in the moment when it was still dark he visualized it: at the far end, a desk with a high-backed chair. Three arched windows behind the desk. Bookshelves lining the walls, right and left. Four upholstered chairs in the open space between the lines of shelves. The chairs faced one another, two on either side, forming the corners of a perfect square.

The light came on. Kristoll stood back. The first thing Loogan saw was that one of the chairs had toppled over. The second thing he saw was the body.

"There are things I need to ask you," Loogan said.

He stood with his hands in his pockets, looking down at the body. Kristoll was in the doorway.

"Ask," Kristoll said.

"Start with the obvious: Are you sure he's dead?"

"He's dead."

"It'd be a hell of a thing if he wasn't."

"No breathing. No pulse. He's dead."

He looked dead. He was on his back, his face tipped toward his left shoulder. Eyes open, staring. Blood at his temple. Left arm extended, palm open; right arm at his side. Pale fingertips touched the dark wood of the floor. Left leg bent; right leg straight. All that remained was for someone to draw an outline in chalk.

"And you don't know who he is," Loogan said. "You never saw him before tonight."

"Never," Kristoll said.

"And he broke in. He was a thief."

"He didn't literally break anything. The patio door was unlocked. But yes, I assume he was a thief."

He might have been a thief, Loogan thought. He looked to be in his early thirties, trimly built, with thinning blond hair. His face was clean-shaven. He wore a black turtleneck, appropriate attire for a thief. He wore it with tan khaki pants and a pair of brown loafers. There was a tattoo on his left wrist: a pattern of interlinked rings.

"How did he get here?" Loogan asked.

"He had a car," said Kristoll.

"I didn't see a car."

"He left it down the hill, by the side of the road. I moved it into the garage."

Loogan stepped around the body in a half-circle.

"Are you sure you want to . . . do what we're going to do?"

"He can't stay where he is," Kristoll said.

"It's not too late, though. To call the police. It was self-defense."

"Of course it was."

"They'll want to know why you didn't call immediately," Loogan said. "But you can answer that. You were rattled. It's understandable."

"I don't know if I want to gamble on what the police will understand."

Kristoll's voice was soft. He leaned against the door frame, staring at the floor.

"Tell me how it went," Loogan said. "You were in here. At the desk?"

"Yes. I heard someone in the hallway."

"So you got up."

"Yes. He saw me. Maybe he didn't realize anyone was home. He rushed at me."

"So you hit him. What did you hit him with?"

Kristoll pointed to a bottle of Scotch—Glenfiddich, nearly full—that rested on a low table between two of the chairs.

"Where did it come from?" Loogan asked.

"From the desk. I brought it with me."

"You heard someone prowling. You wanted a weapon in hand. How many times did you hit him?"

"Twice. Maybe more. I'm not sure."

Loogan brought his right hand out of his pocket and rubbed the back of his neck.

"It would be better if you were sure," he said. "And if there were a witness."

"I was here alone," Kristoll said. "Laura has been gone all evening."

"Where?"

Kristoll looked off in the direction of the front door. "She went in to her office at the university. She had papers to grade."

"When do you expect her back?"

"I'm not sure," Kristoll said. "That's another reason not to delay. I want him gone when she gets home." He stepped into the room and the overhead light made a hard line of his jaw. "Look, I've thought about this, David. If I go to the police, the very least that can happen is it gets written up on the front page of the paper. It gets talked about. I have to explain it to everyone I know. I can only imagine how miserable it would be. How could people look at you the same after something like that? And that's the best case."

He glanced down at the body. "The worst case is the police are skeptical. Maybe this guy's got no record. Maybe he volunteered at church, he had a tragic childhood, some goddamn thing. So somebody in the prosecutor's office decides he has to bring it to a grand jury. And two out of three people on the grand jury decide they don't like the look of me. I get to spend the next year of my life talking to lawyers and sitting in courtrooms. I can't imagine twelve sane people voting to convict, but who knows?"

Kristoll paused for a moment, his eyes intense under dark brows. Then: "This guy's nothing to me. He should have stayed the hell out of my house. I'm not sorry for what I had to do to him. He's not worth one minute of my life. I intend to drive him out to a field somewhere, plant him in the ground, and forget I ever saw him."

He looked away from Loogan toward a row of books along the wall. "Now I'm making speeches," he said. "Listen, David, you can go if you want. I shouldn't have called you. I'll deal with this. You don't need to get involved."

"I'm already involved," Loogan said.

"It's too much to ask."

"You already asked."

"There's still time to come to your senses."

"That's what I've been trying to tell you," Loogan said. "And I still think you'd do all right if you went to the police. But if you've made up your mind, I'm with you."

Kristoll was quiet. His shoulders, which had been raised, seemed to relax.

"Thank you, David."

His manner seemed to change then. He stood casually with his arms resting on the back of a chair, the sleeves of his white shirt rolled up.

"I suppose you've already been shopping," he said to Loogan. "You found a good shovel."

"Yes."

"I've got three in the garage, but all of them have handles that are five feet long. They'd be useless in a . . . narrow space."

"This one should work."

"We'll have blisters before we're through. I should have had you buy gloves."

"I did," Loogan said. "Also water and sandwiches. And some potting soil and a bottle of weed-killer."

"What for?"

"Camouflage. The cashier wanted to know if I was a gardener."

Kristoll laughed quietly, a single exhalation. "I made the right choice, calling you."

"We'll see," said Loogan. "For now, we need to think about the plan. You mentioned a field, but I don't like the sound of that. Too exposed. A wooded area would be better."

"Not around here."

"No. Somewhere across town. Let's give it some thought. In the meantime there's one thing you'll need to do for me."

Kristoll made a puzzled face. Loogan touched the sleeve of his dress shirt.

"You'll need to change your clothes."

The curtains of the study were closed, but when Kristoll was gone Loogan switched on a reading lamp beside one of the chairs and switched off the overhead light. He brought the lamp closer to the body and got down on one knee. He patted the man's pockets, felt coins, no keys—Kristoll would have taken them in order to move the car. He shifted the body slightly so he could reach the back pockets. Found a handkerchief, no wallet.

On impulse he held the back of his hand close before the man's nose and mouth. No breath reached his skin. He laid two fingers on the inside of the man's wrist. The flesh was neither warm nor cold. There was, of course, no pulse. Gingerly he picked up the man's right hand and peered at the fingertips. There was red beneath the white of the nails. He lowered the hand to the floor and stood up. Realized he was trembling, his heart was racing.

He scanned the body again, thinking there should be something more to look for. The man's sock had fallen down around his right ankle. A patch of pale skin showed beneath the cuff of his pant leg. Loogan knelt and lifted the cuff. There was an indentation in the skin, a line that wound around the man's calf, too deep and sharp to have been made by a sock.

Loogan stood. He heard footsteps on the stairs—Kristoll had put on a pair of heavy hiking boots. He appeared now in the doorway of the study, wearing jeans and a flannel shirt, unbuttoned, a white T-shirt underneath, a denim jacket open at the front.

"I've thought of a place," he said.

Chapter 4

THE THIEF'S CAR WAS A SKY BLUE HONDA CIVIC WITH A HATCHBACK. It had rust on the fenders and a crack in the windshield, but the suspension was good and the engine ran smoothly. Loogan drove it east and south toward the city, winding along beside the river. The rain had stopped.

He reached the edge of the city and crossed the river and pointed the car northeast. Soon there were lights around him, shopping centers, gas stations. He could still change his mind, he thought. He owed nothing to Tom Kristoll. He could pull into any one of those parking lots. Abandon the car. Find a pay phone, call a cab, let it take him to the history professor's house. Gather everything he needed—it would fit into a single suitcase. Another cab to the airport, the first flight out. In the morning he could be in a new city.

He drove on, leaving the lights behind. Eventually he turned north, slowed, watched for a break in the trees. There were two wooden posts, a gravel drive between. After a short distance the drive widened out into a lot. Railroad ties marked the edges.

He cut the engine, doused the headlights. The supplies were beside him on the passenger seat, and in the back were the shovel and a rake he had brought from Kristoll's garage. He broke out a bottle of water and drank half of it sitting in the car. He noticed that the door beside him was unlocked, reached absently to lock it, and then felt foolish.

He got out of the car and waited in the dark, sipping water, getting used to the idea that he was alone, that no one was going to charge at him from out of the trees at the edge of the lot.

The moon was high above him, three-quarters full. He let his eyes adjust and after a while he could see, off to the right, a dirt path leading up into the woods. A sign stood at the foot of the path—he couldn't read it in the dark, but he knew what it said. MARSHALL PARK.

Ten minutes later, he heard the sound of another car's engine. A pair of headlights jounced along the gravel drive and a long dark Ford sedan drew up alongside the Civic.

Tom Kristoll's steps were energetic. The gravel crackled beneath his boots as he came around to where Loogan was standing.

"This is going to work," Kristoll said. "I was right about it, wasn't I? You can't see the lot from the road."

"No."

"And nobody's going to be around, this time of night." He pushed a button on his watch and the face glowed in the darkness. "Sorry I'm late," he said. "As I was heading out, I realized Laura would come home to an empty house and your car in the driveway. So I dashed off a note. Told her you and I had gone to see a late movie, maybe have a drink afterward. It's not the best lie, but it'll have to do."

Kristoll locked his car and they took the shovel and the rake and went scouting along the path. Kristoll played the beam of a flashlight over the ground ahead. When the path leveled off, they struck out into the woods and after twenty or thirty yards came to a clearing. Branches on the ground, a scattering of autumn leaves. They left the shovel and the rake and made their way back to the path. Arranged a fallen tree limb to mark the turnoff.

They had removed the body of the thief from the study using a folding cot from Kristoll's basement as a stretcher. They used it again to carry the body from the trunk of Kristoll's Ford up the hill and to the clearing. It was rough going, but they took it slowly. Kristoll had covered the thief's head and upper body with a white plastic bag. It glowed faintly in the moonlight.

They laid the cot on the far edge of the clearing, in the space between a pair of birch trees. Loogan shrugged off his coat and dropped it on the ground. Kristoll had already picked up the rake and begun sweeping away the leaves and branches from the center of the clearing.

The moon descended beneath the treetops. Stars revealed themselves. David Loogan sat on a patch of moss, his back against a tree trunk, drinking the last of a bottle of water. He listened: for voices, for footsteps, for the rhythm of an engine. He heard nothing but the sound of Kristoll's breathing, the blade of the shovel cutting into the earth.

They were making good progress. Kristoll had taken the lead, marking out a rectangle on the ground, carving out hunks of turf with the shovel and laying them aside, to be replaced later. After that, he and Loogan worked in shifts, piling the dirt on one side of their excavation, raking it back from the rim when the pile rose too high. Kristoll's flashlight, tied to a tree branch with a handkerchief, illuminated the scene. The grave descended, so deep now that only Kristoll's head and shoulders were visible above the ground.

Loogan got up and drew on his gloves. His arms were streaked with dirt and there was dirt in his hair, and his clothes had taken on the color of dirt. Kristoll had stripped off his denim jacket and flannel shirt; his white T-shirt was black.

Loogan stepped to the rim and Kristoll looked up. "Rest, David," he said. "I'm good for a few more minutes." But Loogan shook his head and Kristoll relented. They traded places: Loogan sitting on the edge, sliding down, making a step of his hands to boost Kristoll out.

"We're close," Kristoll said. "Another foot and a half should do it."

It went on. They traded places once again. Eventually Kristoll tossed the shovel over the rim, declared the job complete. Loogan helped him scramble out.

They retrieved the cot, carried it to the side of the grave. By unspoken agreement, they paused and stood silently for a moment over the body of the thief. Then, because there was no graceful way to do it, they dragged the cot closer to the grave, lifted one side of the frame, and dumped the body in.

"Something's not right," Loogan said.

Kristoll had picked up the rake and started filling in the grave.

"What do you mean?" he asked.

"This has all gone too smoothly," said Loogan. "Two men set out to bury a body in the woods, and they succeed. There's no tension. You see what I'm saying?"

"Not really."

"If this were a story for *Gray Streets,* you'd reject it out of hand."

Kristoll smiled. He dragged the rake slowly along the ground. "If this were a story for *Gray Streets,*" he said, "I would have gotten a flat tire on the way here. And a helpful cop would have come along as soon as I pulled over. If this were a story for *Gray Streets,* there would be a mysterious blonde involved, and she would probably knock me over the head and push me down a flight of stairs."

Kristoll pointed the handle of the rake down at the body of the thief. "If this were a story for *Gray Streets,* he would only be pretending to be dead. The two of you would be in league, and the whole point of this exercise would be to lure me into the woods and make me dig my own grave." He spread his arms out casually at his sides. "If you're going to kill me, use the shovel. All I ask is: Not in the face."

Loogan shook his head. "I haven't got the energy. But you've made my point for me. If this were fiction, things would be something other than what they seem. So what are we missing? Let's go over the plan. We bury the body in the woods. We gather our tools, pick up the empty water bottles—no evidence left behind. Down the hill to the cars, a quick cleanup, a change of clothes. I drive the thief's car, you follow along. We take the car to a questionable neighborhood, leave it on the street. And that's it. The body's taken care of, the car's taken care of. What are we forgetting?"

Kristoll gripped the end of the handle of the rake, holding it upright. He rested his chin on the back of his hand. "Well, you've gotten sloppy," he said. "You forgot to wipe the steering wheel. Now you've left your prints."

"Fair enough. I'll wipe the wheel. What else?"

Kristoll seemed to consider the question for a moment, then shrugged his shoulders.

"What about the gun?" Loogan said.

The flashlight was aimed at the grave, but in its light Loogan could see Kristoll's face well enough. It went blank for a second and then life returned to it. To the eyes first. They were the eyes of a man making calculations.

A trace of a smile formed itself in the corners of Kristoll's mouth. "You've been waiting to ask me that, haven't you? You've been very patient."

Loogan said nothing.

"How did you know about the gun?" Kristoll asked him.

The question hung in the air of the clearing. Off to the side, the branch that held the flashlight swayed. The clean edge of the circle of light shifted over the ground.

"The thief had a mark on his ankle," Loogan said, "the kind of mark made by a leather strap."

Kristoll laughed quietly. "You're a detective."

"No. I just read a lot of stories. What do people strap to their ankles? Holsters. What do people keep in holsters?"

"Elementary."

"So he had a gun," Loogan said. "That's an interesting fact. And here's another: You took the gun. I can think of a couple reasons for that. You felt threatened. Your home had been violated. You planned to go out, in the night, to dispose of a corpse. Having a gun would be reassuring."

Loogan studied Kristoll's face in the dim light. "There's another reason," Loogan said, "but maybe it's best left unstated. You don't want me to go into it."

"Go ahead."

"It's all right, Tom. You can keep your secrets."

"Sounds like it's too late for that. Say what you want to say."

"All right," said Loogan. "You took the gun because the gun was inconvenient. Your story was shaky in the first place, but the gun makes it laughable. A man breaks into your house, presumably to rob you. If he's any kind of thief at all, he has to realize that someone could be in the house. He's brought a gun with him; he ought to keep it in his hand until he's sure no one's home. But he doesn't. If he did, you wouldn't be able to kill him with a bottle of Scotch."

Loogan shifted his gaze from Kristoll to the grave. "And that means you knew him. He wasn't a thief. You let him in the house. He felt safe. He didn't need to hold the gun. It was enough to have it in the holster on his ankle. That's the only way it makes sense. That's why we had to bury him. If he was a stranger, we could have dumped his body somewhere. What would it matter if he was found? No one would suspect you. But we had to bury him, because you knew him."

Kristoll took a long breath, let it out. "I'll tell you who he was, if you want to know."

"You don't have to tell me," Loogan said. "But you need to think about the gun. It's *his* gun. There's probably a way to trace it to him. If you keep it, then it connects you with him."

"You're right, David. I'll get rid of it."

"Do it now. You've got it here, don't you? If I had to guess, I'd say it's on your ankle."

Kristoll let the rake fall to the ground and stepped his right foot forward. The denim of his pant leg rose, revealing in the light of the flashlight first the brown leather of the holster, then the nickel finish of the pistol's grip. Kristoll got down on one knee and worked the strap, then stood up and drew the pistol out. He handed the holster to Loogan.

"It's a small-caliber, obviously," Kristoll said, weighing the pistol in his hand. "A twenty-two or a thirty-two, I suppose. I ought to know more about guns than I do."

Loogan wiped the holster with his shirt and dropped it into the grave.

"I don't know if it's loaded," Kristoll said. "Or even how to check if it's loaded. I imagine it is."

"There should be a catch on the side, to release the clip," Loogan said. "But it doesn't matter whether it's loaded or not, unless you plan to use it. There's nobody here but us. Are you going to shoot me?"

Kristoll's hand closed around the grip. He aimed the pistol at the ground.

"I haven't the energy."

"Then wipe it down and toss it in," Loogan said. "Let's finish this and get the hell out of here."

Chapter 5

"You were wrong about one thing, David. He was a thief. I wasn't lying about that."

They were driving west in Tom Kristoll's car: Kristoll behind the wheel, in a fresh T-shirt and fresh jeans; Loogan beside him in a borrowed gray jogging suit. They had left the blue Civic on the street in front of a run-down apartment building.

"His name was Michael Beccanti," Kristoll said. "I met him three years ago. 'Met' isn't the right word—we corresponded. He read some things he liked in *Gray Streets* and wrote in to say so. I wrote a polite reply. Then he sent a story. The spelling was awful and it was scribbled out longhand on a legal pad, but the basic idea was sound—a revenge story, as I recall—a drug dealer kills a man's wife, and the man stirs up a war between the dealer and one of his rivals. I worked with him on it, and we knocked it into shape. I published it.

"He wrote two or three others. They needed a lot of work, but he had plenty of time for rewrites. He was in prison. They got him on a string of burglaries. He was rather good, to hear him tell it. He would go in at night when the weather was warm. People would leave their windows open and he would slice through the screens. It didn't matter to him if someone was home—he was quiet, and he went in and out fast. Then one night someone woke up—a bruiser of a man, drove a garbage truck, I think—and he snuck up on Beccanti with a baseball bat. So then the police had him. He'd never been caught before, so he thought he might get away with probation. But the cops knew all about him. It turns out he always cut the screens the same way—he'd slice them along the top, then along the bottom, then once diagonally, like a Z. So they had a thick file on him. They had him for thirty-one break-ins. They even had a nickname for him. They called him Zorro."

Kristoll stared straight ahead as he spoke. Loogan watched him from the passenger seat.

"He got out of the state prison in Jackson a year ago. Came back to Ann Arbor. He called me, very respectful, asked if we could meet. We had lunch. He talked about how hard it was, adjusting. His parole officer had found him a job stocking shelves somewhere, which he hated. I got the sense he wanted me to help him find something better. I liked him, but I wasn't going to hire him, and there was no one I felt comfortable recommending him to. He didn't press it. I saw him after that occasionally. Once he came to the office with a new story. I gave him some money for it, though we never published it.

"Then tonight he came to the house. He was sorry to bother me at home, he said, but he needed to speak to me about something important. I let him in. It didn't seem like a risk. We went into the study and he started talking about this woman he'd met. He took a while to come to the point, but the point was he'd gotten her pregnant. Now there were medical bills. He needed money. Five thousand dollars, he said. I don't know how he came up with that figure. I think he was just trying to see what he could get. I told him I didn't have five thousand to give him. He smiled at that, as if he was genuinely surprised. Living in a house like mine, on the river? I couldn't put together five thousand dollars?

"Well, the truth is the house is mortgaged, and most of the income from *Gray Streets* goes right back into the business. Laura brings home more from her job at the university than I net from the magazine. I didn't go into this with him. I just made it clear there wasn't going to be any five thousand. I was sorry about his situation, but there was nothing I could do for him. He never got agitated, never raised his voice, but he wouldn't let it go. It could be a loan, he said. I refused. I made some suggestions about public assistance, Medicaid. But by then it had dawned on me that his whole story was probably a lie. He didn't need money for medical bills. In the end I called him on it. 'There's no woman, is there?' I said. His manner changed then. He laughed.

"It was a short burst of a laugh, a momentary loss of control. He clamped down on it quickly, and after that he said nothing, as if he had decided the time for talking was over. He was sitting in a chair in the study and I was across from him. He leaned over and started pulling at his pant leg. I saw the leather, the metal. My mind made the relevant connections. Holster. Gun. The bottle was on the table beside me—I had offered him a drink when he came in. Then I was on my feet. He was fumbling around at his ankle, I think the gun might have caught on something. The bottle was in my hand. I drew my arm back, swung it at the side of his head. I thought the bottle would shatter. It didn't shatter. I held it up in front of me, looking at the label upside down, marveling at it.

"He was on the floor, on his hands and knees. The gun was under his hand. It wasn't pointed at me. It didn't matter. I don't know if you've ever faced anything like that, David. Something primitive takes over. Now, after the fact, I can reflect on how far he might have gone. He wanted to threaten me with the gun. He didn't want to kill me. Maybe hitting him once was enough, maybe I could have kicked the gun away. I don't know. I know I hated myself for letting him in the house. I hated him for making me afraid. I wanted him dead.

"I drew the bottle back again, swung. It was a glancing blow, unsatisfying. The next time I was more careful. I took aim at his temple and swung with my whole body. Felt the bottle connect. He went down. I picked up the gun, stood over him with it. He didn't move. After a while I nudged him with my foot, then turned him over onto his back. I went through the motions of checking for a pulse, but I knew he was dead."

Kristoll fell silent. They had passed through the city and were driving alongside the river north and northwest. Wind stirred the leaves of the branches that hung over the roadside. Loogan leaned his head against the glass of the passenger window and closed his eyes.

"You're quiet over there," Kristoll said after a while. "What are you thinking?"

Loogan let his eyes come open. "I've just been going over your story," he said. "It's not bad. If that's the way you want it, it's all right with me."

"I'm glad to hear it."

"Purely as an exercise, I've been trying to figure out how much of it is true. I'd like to think some of it is. I'd like to think you're at least working your way toward the truth."

Kristoll's thumbnail picked at something on the steering wheel. He wiped dust from the dashboard. "I'd like to be able to tell you the truth, David."

"I believe you would," Loogan said, sitting up straight. "Maybe we should leave it at that. It's late and we're both tired. I meant what I said before: You can keep your secrets."

With infinite care, Kristoll guided the car through a gradual curve.

"I appreciate that, David. I wish things were different but . . . I have my reasons."

"Of course you do. I don't need to know what they are. A man gets himself killed in your home, that's a heavy burden to bear. The details hardly matter. It's a burden. Even if he had blood and skin under his fingernails, and you don't have a scratch on you. Even if he struggled with somebody, but it wasn't you. Even if you didn't kill him."

The next day Loogan woke at two in the afternoon. His back ached as he sat up in bed; his legs ached as he climbed down the stairs; his shoulders ached as he filled a glass with water and reached for the aspirin on the high shelf of a kitchen cabinet.

Though he had showered the night before, he showered again, and dressed. By three he had driven to the campus of the university. He left his car in a lot where he had no business parking and walked across the quad. The sun was out. He sat on a bench within view of Angell Hall. Students went by on the sidewalk, and a few of them gathered and passed around a pack of cigarettes. At twenty after three, Laura Kristoll came down the steps of Angell Hall. There were two students with her: a girl with long auburn hair and a boy with a black mustache and goatee and a shaved head. Loogan recognized them from parties at the house on the Huron River.

Loogan rose from the bench and Laura spotted him. She said something to the students and they went on across the quad without her. The girl with auburn hair looked back at Loogan and then leaned in to whisper something to the boy with the shaved head.

Laura Kristoll wore a long woolen coat and a silk scarf. Her blond hair fell over the silk. Loogan stood by the bench and let her come to him.

"Hello, David," she said. "I understand you and Tom hit the town last night."

"We did."

"A movie and a drink," she said. "I suspect it was more drink than movie. Tom slept like a bear this morning."

"Me too."

"You too. But not like a bear. You slept beautifully, I'm sure. And then you woke up and came here." It was a statement, but her eyes made it a question.

"I needed to see you," Loogan said in a low voice. "I hope it's not . . . indiscreet."

"Don't be silly," she said. "You're always discreet."

"I need . . . a few minutes of your time." He made his tone mischievous. "Can we go to your office?"

"You're sweet, David. But I have a committee meeting."

"You can be late. Let's go to your office. I need to see you."

She wavered for a moment, then turned without a word and went back up the steps of Angell Hall. He followed her to her office on the second floor. She locked the door and walked casually to the window to close the blinds. Slipped out of her coat and threw it on a chair.

Then she spun around and pressed herself against him. He kissed her, fiercely: her mouth, her neck. He tore away the silk scarf; his fingers worked the buttons of her blouse. He turned her around and pulled the tails of the blouse out of her skirt. His right hand ran over her stomach, his left stroked her neck.

She let out a long breath. "I really don't have time, David. I'll be missed."

"I just need to see you," he said. "Let me see you and then you can go."

He pulled the blouse down along her arms and off. Unhooked her bra in front and drew it off the same way. He raised her arms so they were parallel to the floor, and with his index fingers he traced two lines from her wrists to her shoulder blades, then a single line down the center of her back. He turned her around to face him and traced another line over the freckles at the base of her neck, down between her small breasts.

"This is what I wanted," he said.

She leaned against the edge of her desk. Her blue eyes locked on his.

"You're perfect," he said. "Your skin is flawless."

She reached up to grip the collar of his coat and pulled him close. He felt her lips on his neck, heard her whisper a single word: "Dangerous."

A week went by before Loogan saw Tom Kristoll again. It happened in the evening. Loogan had spent the afternoon downtown watching a pair of foreign films whose plots he would have been hard-pressed to describe. The day before, he had driven to Toledo to view an exhibit on the history of glassmaking. In the days before that, he had attended a play in Chicago and a concert in Detroit.

Now he sat in the swing on the porch of his rented house watching rain fall from a cool gray sky. He had a pen in his hand and a notebook open on his knee. He was jotting notes on the subject that had occupied his thoughts in Toledo and Chicago and Detroit.

Someone Tom Kristoll identifies as Michael Beccanti was killed on the night of October seventh in the study of Tom's house on the Huron River.

The dead man had a pistol strapped to his ankle—why?

He had traces of blood and skin under his nails, indicating a struggle with his killer. Most likely he would have scratched his killer on the face, neck, arms, or hands. Tom has no scratches in any of these places. Laura Kristoll has no scratches anywhere on her body. It seems unlikely, though not impossible, that she would have the strength required to kill a man with a bottle of Scotch.

If neither Tom nor Laura killed Beccanti, then he was killed by someone else. That person left after the killing. He didn't stick around to help dispose of the body—why?

Tom may be lying about the dead man's identity. It may not be Michael Beccanti. There may be no such person as Michael Beccanti.

Rain fell on the railing of the porch, on the toes of Loogan's shoes.

The dead man, whoever he was, was killed in the Kristoll house. The killer was most likely acquainted with Tom and Laura Kristoll.

Loogan paused. Who did he know that was acquainted with Tom and Laura? There were interns and writers from *Gray Streets*. There were a few friends he had met at parties over the summer. There would be parents, brothers, sisters—but he had never met them.

He would stick with what he knew. He wrote the heading WRITERS and listed several whose stories he had edited. None of them lived in the area. But there were two local writers he had met at the Kristoll house: A tall man with a ridiculous name—Nathan Hideaway. A woman—Bridget something—who wrote books about a lady detective and a dog. He added them to the list. Under another heading—INTERNS—he wrote: *The girl with the auburn hair—Valerie? The boy with the goatee and the shaved head. I really ought to learn people's names.*

At the bottom of the page he added: *I know next to nothing about Tom and Laura Kristoll.*

Loogan looked up and saw a car parked at the curb—Tom Kristoll's Ford. Kristoll, raincoated and fedoraed, jogged up the walk and climbed the steps. He had a package under his arm: rectangular and thin and wrapped in brown paper. "What are you doing?" he said.

Loogan closed the notebook and laid it on the seat of the swing. "Making notes for a story I'll never write."

"I don't like the sound of that," Kristoll said. "If you've got an idea, you ought to write it up. If it's giving you trouble, I could have a look."

"It's too soon, Tom," Loogan said, rising. "Why don't we go in?"

"I can't stay long," Kristoll said. He bowed his head and beads of rain rolled down the brim of the fedora. "I never thanked you properly for your help the other night," he said. "I thought a gift would be in order. Any other time, I would have gone with a bottle of Scotch. But I knew that wouldn't do here. The symbolism was all wrong. So I went with this instead."

He handed the package to Loogan. The brown paper was dotted with rain. Loogan tore through it and underneath was a framed photograph— shards of broken glass, and flower petals, and bits of paper in the shape of leaves. The photograph Laura had bought on the day of their visit to the gallery.

"Laura picked it out," Kristoll said. "I told her I wanted to get you something. She didn't know the reason, of course, but she thought you'd like this. I don't know where you'll put it. It's not big enough to go over the fireplace, I suppose. Maybe in your office. Do you like it?"

"It's marvelous," Loogan said.

Chapter 6

HE HEARD FROM KRISTOLL AGAIN THE FOLLOWING WEEK, ON FRIDAY afternoon. He was lying on his stomach on the living-room carpet, the pages of a manuscript spread before him. He was stuck on a line of dialogue—he had written seven variations on a yellow legal pad when the phone rang. Distracted, he picked it up on the fifth ring.

"I thought you weren't going to answer," Kristoll said. "What are you up to?"

"Trying to figure out what a blackmailer would say to a money-launderer," said Loogan.

"I see. . . . Is this the new story?"

"What new story?"

"The one you were making notes on the other day."

"No. It's someone else's story. That's what I do. Edit other people's stories."

"Hell, David, you ought to be working on something of your own."

"As it happens, someone's paying me to do this."

"That could change," Kristoll said. "Maybe I should fire you."

"Is that why you called? To fire me?"

"No, but maybe it's the best thing I could do for you. What are you doing later?"

"Depends on whether I'm fired. What are you doing?"

There was a delay before Kristoll answered, and when he did his tone was thoughtful.

"Making notes for a story I'll never tell," he said. "Isn't that what you called it?" Another delay. "Only maybe I will tell it."

"What do you mean?" Loogan asked him.

"Maybe I made the wrong decision the other night."

"Which night would that be?"

"Don't be dim," Kristoll said. "Look, why don't you come in later. To the office. We'll have a drink. Maybe I'll run something by you."

"All right."

"'All right,' he says. You're very matter-of-fact about it. You don't have to come, you know. I've asked a lot of you already. You're allowed to refuse."

"I'm not going to refuse," Loogan said. "What time should I come?"

"Around seven."

The story of the blackmailer and the money-launderer occupied Loogan for much of the afternoon. His revisions grew to fill the spaces between the lines of type. At five-thirty he stood in the middle of the living room. The pages of the manuscript were spread out at his feet—twenty-four of them. The letters of his fine, dark handwriting were as clean as the type. Viewed from a height, they were virtually indistinguishable.

He stood over the pages longer than he had intended. He was about to kneel and gather them together when he heard a tapping sound. Turning to the window, he saw Laura on the porch. She smiled and tapped her knuckles again on the glass.

He met her at the kitchen door and took her coat, and a moment later she was in the living room looking down at the manuscript.

"I've wondered what it would be like," she said, "catching you at an unguarded moment. I think I've always had it in my head that you're not like other people. I can't picture you doing mundane things—watering plants or taking out the garbage. Or at a desk, with a pencil, editing a story. Turns out I was right—you don't use a pencil. You just stare at the manuscript until the words burn themselves onto the paper."

She slipped out of her shoes and got down on one knee, lifted the first page, and began to read. Her legs were bare beneath her skirt. Loogan switched on a lamp, and the light was silver on the silk of her blouse, golden on the strands of her hair. She got through six pages and would have gone through the whole thing, Loogan thought, if he hadn't interrupted her. "I'll make you a copy," he said. She picked up the seventh and eighth pages, glancing over them.

"This is good," she said. "This is better than it has any right to be." She stood and held the papers up to the light. "You've done a lot of work on this."

"It's not difficult," he said, "when all you have to do is stare at the pages."

"Sometimes I think it's better when they need work," she said. "When you can see at once what's wrong and how to fix it. And you make a change and you know it's right. And you give it back to the author and he can't argue, not if he has any sense."

She laid the eight pages on the mantel of the fireplace and sat at the end of the sofa.

"I wonder if Tom realizes what a good choice he made, hiring you," she said.

Loogan let that pass. He watched her pat the cushion beside her.

"Come sit with me, David," she said. "I didn't come here to talk about editing. I came to see what you'd done with that." Her gaze went to the framed photograph that hung above the fireplace—glass and flower petals and paper leaves. "It's not quite right for the space, but I like it just the same. I can't remember what was there before."

"Some awful painting of sailboats," Loogan said.

"That's right. This is much better. I didn't know if you'd approve. Tom wanted to buy you a gift, and I meant to give that to you anyway. You're not angry, are you?"

"I'm not angry."

"I like seeing it there and thinking about that day." She turned toward Loogan, rested her arm on the back of the sofa, stroked his hair with her fingers. "And it was right here . . ." She didn't need to say what was right here. "I think we should put these cushions on the floor, David," she said softly. "I think you should build a fire. We didn't have one then, but it might be nice on a day like today."

"I don't think that's a good idea," Loogan said.

"We don't have to have a fire."

He said nothing. Her hand drew back. It went to the front of her blouse. "You're not talking about the fire," she said, studying him. "I should have known. You've stayed away from me these past two weeks."

Loogan's face held no expression. He stared at the photograph over the fireplace.

Finally he said, "The thing is, I like him."

"Yes, it would have to be that," she said in a small voice. "I knew you liked him. If you didn't, it wouldn't have worked. If you hated him, I wouldn't have had anything to do with you. But he's your friend. And I should have known—David Loogan is a loyal man."

She sighed. "You and Tom, you're like that fable. What's the name of it?"

"I don't know—"

"Androcles," she said. "Androcles and the lion." She paused to brush a strand of hair behind her ear. "Androcles is an escaped slave, wandering through the woods. He finds a lion with a bleeding paw. The lion has stepped on a thorn. Androcles pulls it out."

"I thought it was a mouse who pulled out the thorn."

"That's a different fable," she said. "Androcles removes the thorn, and after that the lion befriends him. He hunts for him and brings him food. Then both of them are captured, and Androcles the slave is sentenced to be thrown to the lion in the Colosseum. But instead of tearing Androcles to pieces, the lion lies down at his feet."

Loogan leaned back against the sofa. "Am I Androcles in this scenario?"

"You're the lion," Laura said. "The lion is grateful. He's not going to attack Androcles. He's not going to let any harm come to Androcles at all." She smiled faintly. "He's certainly not going to sleep with Androcles' wife."

She moved close to him, let her head rest in the hollow of his shoulder. "Poor David. You were afraid to tell me, weren't you? You thought I'd cry."

"I thought you'd make me change my mind," he said.

"I feel like doing both, but I won't. I'll leave if you want."

He put his arm around her. "You don't have to leave."

"I don't want to. I want to sit here for a while and not say anything. Is that all right?"

"Sure."

Loogan woke in the semi-dark. Laura Kristoll was standing over him. He seized her wrist and sat up sharply.

"Easy, David. It's only me."

"Dark," he said.

"I turned off the lamp. I'm leaving now." She had her coat on.

"What time is it?" he asked.

"Twenty after seven. What's the matter?"

He got to his feet. "I forgot about Tom. I'm supposed to meet him."

"Comb your hair first. You look like you've been sleeping. Don't frown, David. We haven't done anything wrong."

She kissed him on the cheek and then turned and went out without saying anything more.

He went to the phone and dialed Kristoll's number at the office. After three rings he got Kristoll's voice mail. He left a message saying he was on his way.

He put on a fresh shirt, brushed his teeth, and got his coat. His car was on the street. He walked around to the driver's side and the tires caught his eye immediately. Both of them were flat. Someone had scratched an obscenity in the paint of the driver's door. He felt a wave of anger, looked up and down the street. Saw no one but a white-haired lady walking her dog.

Standing in the cold, he deliberated. He would need to have the car towed, but that could wait. He could call a cab, but that would take time. It was twelve blocks to the *Gray Streets* office. He would walk.

Gloves from the car, one last look around, he set off eastward. He walked in the street, avoided the shadows of the sidewalk. A brisk pace warmed him. Houses with lighted windows. Gutters full of leaves. Traffic picked up as he got closer to downtown. He moved onto the sidewalk.

Near Main Street he heard sirens. Ahead, a police car crept through an intersection, red and blue lights flashing. Another followed a few seconds later.

Loogan reached Main and turned north. Flashing lights in the distance, two blocks away. Northbound traffic crawled. People milled in front of restaurants. A man in a long knitted scarf played saxophone, the instrument case open at his feet, a few dollar bills in the bottom. A border collie nearby, its leash tied to a fire hydrant. The collie and the man with the saxophone were the only ones not looking north.

Some of the restaurant people drifted toward the flashing lights. Loogan started to jog. The two police cars he had seen were latecomers. There were three others on the street. Cops at the intersections, directing traffic.

The flashing lights surrounded a building on the corner. The building that housed the offices of *Gray Streets*.

A barrier of sawhorses held back the crowd. Loogan insinuated himself among the people. A woman with a cell phone at her ear. A balding man with rimless eyeglasses. The woman with the cell phone broke her connection and dialed a new number. "You're not going to believe where I am," she said.

Loogan pressed through to the barrier. Beyond it, there was a tree growing out of an opening in the sidewalk. A wrought-iron bench beside the tree. A man's shoe had found its way underneath the bench.

Trailing off from one end of the bench: a line of uniformed cops. Four of them, hats off, hands behind their backs. Stone-faced. Between the cops and the building, a blanket had been spread on the sidewalk. The cops stood facing the crowd, as motionless as sentries, but their presence could do nothing to conceal the shape beneath the blanket.

Loogan thought he should ask them the name of the man beneath the blanket. He was sure they wouldn't answer. It was a formality in any case. He knew the answer. Looking up, he could see that every window in the face of the building was closed—every window except for one on the sixth floor.

Chapter 7

ELIZABETH WAISHKEY NODDED TO THE OFFICER IN THE HALLWAY AND went on through. The outer office of *Gray Streets* was unoccupied. The air was cool.

The door of Tom Kristoll's office stood open. Carter Shan was inside taking photographs. Elizabeth paused for a moment in the doorway—a tall woman with raven hair. Her clothes were unassuming: tan overcoat, gray blazer and slacks, pale blue blouse. Her only adornment was a necklace of glass beads.

Carter Shan turned and aimed the camera at her. He didn't press the button.

"Pushed," she said to him.

"You're dreaming, Lizzie," he said.

Elizabeth stepped into the room. "You think he jumped, I suppose. That's why you're taking pictures."

"I'm covering the bases."

"The pictures'll come in handy," she said. "We'll need all the evidence we can muster, when we put him on trial for killing himself."

She crossed to the open window and looked down. A small crowd lingered on the street below. The medical examiner was kneeling beside the body. The blanket had been cast aside.

"Whose bright idea was the blanket?" Elizabeth asked.

"It wasn't one of our people," said Shan. "The woman who called it in, she covered him with a blanket from her car. She had her kids with her."

Elizabeth nodded and silently watched the scene below.

Shan put the digital camera in the pocket of his coat. "All right, Lizzie," he said. "Don't be so inscrutable. Why do you think he didn't jump?"

She walked away from the window. "Maybe it's just a feeling."

"I know better than that."

"The west wind brings me tidings."

"Fine. Keep it to yourself."

She surveyed the room, from the bookshelves to the desk to the rack by the door that held a long coat and a black fedora.

She said, "Have you ever thought about killing yourself, Carter? Never mind. It doesn't matter. Just imagine you *have* thought about killing yourself, and you're here in your office and you decide today's the day. You look around, and you don't have a gun handy, or a rope, but there's the window. Would you jump through it?"

"Why not?"

"That's the spirit," said Elizabeth. "Why not? But it's not an ideal window for jumping. You throw up the sash, and the opening is—what?—two feet square? You can fit through, but it's going to be awkward. How do you go about it?"

Shan studied the window. "I don't know. Headfirst or feetfirst—I suppose it wouldn't matter much. I'd want to get it over with."

"Would you?"

He looked thoughtful. "No, you're right. I'd want to put it off a little. Get used to the idea." He bent to open the deep drawer of the desk. There were two tumblers and a bottle inside. "I'd want a drink," he said.

Elizabeth touched the glass beads at her neck. "Yes. You're a man who's fond enough of Scotch to keep a bottle in your desk—you're going to want a taste."

"Maybe he took a hit from the bottle, and put it back when he was done."

"Maybe he did. Eakins'll be able to tell us." Lillian Eakins was the medical examiner. "So you've had your drink, or not, and the window's still beckoning. You didn't answer me. How do you go through?"

"Not headfirst," Shan said. "It's too scary that way. You'd want to go feetfirst. You'd sit on the windowsill with your legs dangling out and then sort of lean back and slide through— No, that's too awkward. What you'd really want to do is climb out onto the ledge and stand there for a minute to get your bearings. But there's no ledge out there."

"No," Elizabeth said.

"If he wanted to jump, he wouldn't have jumped out this window. He'd want a place where he could stand."

"Yes."

"He would've gone to the roof," Shan said. "But maybe he couldn't. Maybe there's no way to get up to the roof. You're smiling. That's your inscrutable smile. You've been up there."

"The stairs at the north end of the building go all the way up," Elizabeth said. "There's a door with a lock, but the lock is broken. People go up there and smoke. There's a low wall. You could stand on it and work up your nerve. If you wanted to jump, that's where you'd go."

"Suppose that's where he went," said Shan. "He decides he's going to jump, opens this window, sees that it's no good. He leaves the window open and goes up to the roof."

"And jumps from a spot that happens to be directly above this window."

"Why not?" Shan said.

"You haven't been up there. The wall at the front of the building comes to a peak. It's part of the design. The wall at the rear of the building is level—much better for jumping."

Elizabeth paused, shaking her head. "He didn't go from the roof. He went through this window. But if I'm right, he was pushed. Killed first, or rendered unconscious. You'd have a rough time getting him through if he was awake and resisting. You'd hit him on the head and hope that the damage from the fall would conceal it. With any luck, it would pass for a suicide."

The two of them stood quietly. Street sounds came up through the open window. The cool air turned colder. Shan said, "Who is he?"

Elizabeth looked up. She had been staring at the tumblers in the drawer. "You know as much as I do. He's the publisher of a magazine."

"Not Kristoll. The man who killed him. Assuming it's a man, because a woman would have a harder time wrestling him through the window. You've got the M.O. worked out; I thought you might have a suspect in mind too."

"No," she said. "I haven't got that far."

"I might be able to tell you something about him. I think he's a fan of Shakespeare." Shan pointed to a book on the desk. "That's *The Collected Works*. It's open to the final scene of *Hamlet*—the one where everybody dies. Before you got here, I assumed Kristoll was reading it before he jumped. But if he was murdered, the killer might have put it there, open to that page."

Elizabeth leaned over the book. "Did you get a picture of this?"

"I got half a dozen."

"And this pen was here. You haven't moved it."

"Give me some credit, Lizzie."

"The way it's placed—it's underneath a particular line."

Shan nodded. "I saw that. It's something Horatio says. 'I am more an antique Roman than a Dane.' I read the thing in high school. I suppose I ought to know what that means."

Elizabeth stood back and smoothed away the strands of raven hair that had fallen into her eyes. "We're supposed to think it's a suicide note."

Chief Owen McCaleb of the Ann Arbor police was wiry and handsome and fifty-four years old. He had a bag of golf clubs in a corner of his office, but no one in the department had ever seen him on a golf course. Everyone had seen him jogging. He was the sort of jogger who always kept moving. At a crosswalk, waiting for a light to change, he would jog in place. Even indoors, he was never quite still. Sometimes, talking to subordinates, he would bounce on the balls of his feet.

He was doing it now, as Elizabeth Waishkey and Carter Shan filled him in on the scene at Kristoll's office. Shan had gotten to the part about *Hamlet*.

"So in the play, Hamlet's dying," he said.

"I know that much," said McCaleb.

"His uncle, the king, has plotted to have him killed. The king has Laertes challenge Hamlet to a duel. He gives Laertes a sword with a poisoned tip. But if the sword doesn't do it, the king has a backup plan—he'll offer Hamlet a cup of poisoned wine."

"The details aren't that important," Elizabeth said.

Shan continued. "So Laertes stabs Hamlet with the poisoned sword. But Hamlet stabs Laertes too. And Hamlet's mother drinks the wine, not knowing it's poisoned. Then Hamlet stabs the king—"

"The details aren't important," Elizabeth said again. "The point is Hamlet's dying. He asks Horatio—"

"Horatio's his friend," Shan explained.

"He wants Horatio to tell his story," Elizabeth said. "But Horatio reaches for the poisoned cup. And that's when he says, 'I am more an antique Roman than a Dane.'"

"He's not literally a Roman, he's a Dane," Shan said. "Hamlet's a Dane too. They're all Danes."

"It's his way of saying he wants to kill himself," said Elizabeth. "It's a matter of loyalty. When a Roman nobleman was killed, his followers sometimes committed suicide. It was a point of honor. Horatio feels the same kind of loyalty to Hamlet."

Owen McCaleb nodded. "So he kills himself?"

"He tries to. Hamlet stops him. But that's the meaning of the line. It's Horatio's way of declaring his intention to kill himself."

"So the open book is supposed to be a suicide note," McCaleb said, pacing the office. "But you don't think Kristoll killed himself. So what we have is a murder made to look like a suicide. And a murderer who quotes Shakespeare."

McCaleb reached the doorway and turned back. "And the victim is a man who published a literary magazine. A man who, we have to assume, knew plenty of people capable of quoting Shakespeare. A man who lived in

Ann Arbor—a city where, if you order a mocha latte, it gets handed to you by someone who's read *Hamlet*." He stopped suddenly. "Let's not get ahead of ourselves. Eakins has the body?"

"Yes," Elizabeth said.

"We'll see what the autopsy tells us," said McCaleb. "In the meantime, Kristoll's office stays sealed. And no one talks to the press. I've already heard from a reporter at the *News*. She wanted to know if there was a note. Let's keep the Shakespeare theory to ourselves."

At home, Elizabeth shed her coat and her gun and her cell phone. She boiled water and fixed a cup of herbal tea. She took it into the living room, where the television was on low. Her daughter, Sarah, lay asleep on the couch—a lanky girl of fifteen with sleek black hair like her mother's. She slept like a girl in a painting, on her side with her hands palm-to-palm beneath her cheek.

Elizabeth set her cup on an end table and switched off the television. She reached for a quilt to cover her daughter, but just then the girl stirred.

"You should be in bed," said Elizabeth.

"I was waiting up for you."

Elizabeth took a seat at the end of the couch, and Sarah turned onto her back and laid her legs across her mother's lap.

"I was watching the news," the girl said. "They had a story about a guy who fell out a window. Is that why you're late?"

"That's why."

"He fell six floors. It must have been gross."

"You should be in bed."

"They were cagey about it. They wouldn't come out and say he jumped."

"They don't know. There weren't any witnesses."

A pause. Elizabeth tasted her tea.

"Defenestration," Sarah said. "That's what you call it when somebody gets thrown out a window."

"It's not for sure he was thrown."

"But he could have been. Do you think he was?"

"I'll tell you, but you have to promise not to talk to the press."

"I promise."

"It's possible Tom Kristoll was defenestrated."

"Do you have suspects?"

"It's too soon to say."

"What about his wife? Does he have a wife?"

"Yes."

"Have you talked to her?"

"I saw her tonight, very briefly," Elizabeth said. "She came in to identify the body."

"But you didn't question her."

"It wasn't the right time. She was in no condition to answer questions. And she had her lawyer with her."

"That's two strikes."

"How's that?"

"She's the wife, and if a man gets killed, you have to suspect the wife. And now she's hired a lawyer."

"I don't know that she hired him," Elizabeth said. "Mrs. Kristoll is a professor, and her husband was a publisher. Some people don't need to go hire lawyers—they already have them, like they have dog walkers or accountants."

"Still, it's two strikes. The only way it could be worse is if she's having an affair. That would be three strikes. Is she having an affair?"

"That's something I'll have to ask her, if I can pry her away from her lawyer."

Elizabeth sipped tea. Sarah rose from the couch and stretched, arms reaching for the ceiling. *Lanky* was the wrong word, Elizabeth thought. *Lithesome* was closer to the truth.

"Are you having an affair?" she asked.

"Mom," the girl said. She gave the word an extra syllable.

"There are two soda cans on the counter by the sink," Elizabeth said. "One Pepsi and one Mountain Dew. Billy Rydell is a known consumer of Mountain Dew."

"I'm not having an affair with Billy Rydell."

"Billy Rydell is sixteen," Elizabeth said. "He's a roiling sea of hormones. If teenage lust were a crime, it would be my duty to lock him up."

"Billy Rydell was here for twenty minutes. We talked about a project for school. Then he asked me to go with him to a movie."

"Ah."

"A matinee, tomorrow afternoon," Sarah said. "I told him I'd have to clear it with you. I said you might be able to drive us. He turned pale at the thought. I think he's afraid you might shoot him."

"I might. We'll have to see about whether I can drive you. It depends."

"What does it depend on?"

"Whether Tom Kristoll was pushed out the window. If he was, it's going to fill up my afternoon."

Sarah went up to her room around one o'clock. Elizabeth followed suit a short time later. She showered, washed and dried her hair, and went to bed. She stared for a while at the window of her bedroom. A streetlight cast the shadows of branches on the curtains. When she slept, there were windows in her dreams.

She walked down a long corridor with a window at the end, and as she approached she saw the silhouette of a man outside, but when she reached the window he was gone. Through the night, she had variations of the same dream. Once the window was in Tom Kristoll's office. Once it was in her own room and the man at the window began to climb through. She assumed it was Kristoll, though in the dream his face was hidden in shadow. He beckoned to her as if he wanted to tell her something, but when she got out of bed he began to climb back out through the window. She stepped through to follow him and at first her feet found solid ground on the other side, and then the ground gave way.

She woke suddenly, her legs jerking the way legs do in dreams about falling. She sat up and looked around. Gray light. Her bedside clock read 7:40. Her cell phone rang on the night table.

It was McCaleb on the line. "I just heard from Lillian Eakins," he said. "She won't have anything official till later, but you better come in. You were right. It wasn't a suicide."

Chapter 8

"I KNOW WHAT YOU'RE GOING TO TELL ME."

"Is that right?"

The house on the Huron River was thick with solemn young men and women in their twenties. The majority wore black, though whether it was a matter of style or of mourning would have been difficult to say. Laura Kristoll had her lawyer with her—a pudgy man with weak lips and thick gray hair that swept back from his forehead. She left him behind and invited Elizabeth into her husband's study.

"I knew Tom," Laura said. "I've never believed that nonsense about not being able to really know another person. Are you married?"

"I was," Elizabeth said.

"I knew Tom. I know he wasn't depressed or guilt-ridden or whatever he would have to be to decide to throw himself from the window of his office. So what you're here to tell me is that you've come to the same conclusion."

They sat in upholstered chairs and the afternoon sunlight came through the arched windows at the far end of the room.

"That's true," said Elizabeth. "We believe your husband was the victim of an assault. The medical examiner found an injury that wouldn't have been caused by the fall—a fracture of the skull at the back of the head that can't be accounted for, given what we know about the impact and the position of the body. There was swelling at the site of the injury, and that means blood had to have been circulating, his heart had to have been beating—"

"And it wouldn't have been, after the fall," said Laura.

"No. So we believe your husband received a blow to the head, maybe more than one, at some point before the fall."

Laura Kristoll looked away toward the windows. Her golden hair was gathered up and pinned, but a few strands hung free. She trembled and Elizabeth saw the trembling in those strands.

A tear rolled unobtrusively down Laura's cheek, and she rose abruptly and crossed the room. There was a box of tissues on the desk. Elizabeth would have liked to let her alone. She thought about looking away; it took discipline to watch. Laura wiped her eyes. She braced herself, head low, elbows locked, palms flat on the surface of the desk. Elizabeth observed nothing false in her movements.

She came back to her chair. "I apologize," she said.

"There's no need." Elizabeth nodded toward the closed door of the study. "Do you want me to call for someone?"

"No. You'll want to ask me things," Laura said. "You'll want to know if my husband had enemies. He didn't. I can't think of a reason why anyone would want to kill Tom."

"Had he been experiencing any financial trouble? Any large debts?"

"Nothing like that. The magazine's doing well."

Elizabeth lowered her voice. "Forgive me for asking, but did he have any bad habits? Gambling? Drugs?"

"He drank. Moderately. Once in a while he drank immoderately."

"Was it common for him to be at the office late on a Friday night?"

"He kept his own hours."

"Who else has access to the office?"

"There are interns going in and out during business hours," Laura said. "One or two of them have keys. There's a secretary, Sandy Vogel. But she would have left by five."

"I'll need to talk to her. Anyone else?"

"Cleaning people. Sandy can give you their names. And I have a key, of course."

Elizabeth shifted in her chair. "I have to ask: Where were you yesterday evening?"

Laura examined the backs of her hands. "Now we come to it," she said. "Rex wanted to be here when I answered that question." Rex Chatterjee was the pudgy lawyer. Elizabeth waited.

"I was at the home of David Loogan," Laura said. "He's a friend of mine, and of Tom's. He's also an editor for the magazine."

"And how would you describe your friendship with Mr. Loogan?" said Elizabeth.

Laura smiled faintly. "That's an artful way of asking the question," she said. "David Loogan and I were intimate. We were having what I suppose you would call an affair."

Elizabeth took care not to react. "How long had that been going on?"

"Not long. Since the end of August. But when I went to see him yesterday he told me he wanted to end it."

"Why was that?" Elizabeth asked.

"He didn't feel right about it. He was fond of my husband."

"Was there something in particular that prompted his decision?"

"Not that I know of. I see what you're saying. If that was how he felt, why not break it off sooner?"

"Why start it in the first place?"

"He didn't exactly start it," Laura said. "I pursued him."

"Did your husband know about the affair?"

"I don't think so."

"But he might have. What would his attitude have been if he knew?"

"You're being artful again," Laura said. "We weren't swingers, if that's what you're getting at. I wasn't in the habit of sleeping with my husband's friends. If he knew, he would have reacted as any man would."

"He would have been jealous? Wounded?"

"Yes."

"Angry?"

"Possibly."

"Would he have confronted Mr. Loogan?"

"I think he would have confronted me. But he never did." Laura closed her eyes for a moment. "If you think he confronted David and David threw him out a window—well, you don't know David Loogan."

"You don't believe he's capable of murder?"

"I imagine he is. But he wouldn't kill Tom. He liked Tom."

"He might not have set out to do it," Elizabeth said. "They might have argued—"

"I don't believe it."

"Because you know David Loogan."

"Yes," Laura said. "I'm sure that's difficult for you to understand. All you know about David is that he had an affair with his friend's wife, and now his friend is dead. You can spin any number of scenarios out of that. He argued with Tom and things got out of control. Or he killed Tom to get him out of the way, so he and I could be together."

"That possibility has occurred to me."

"Or David and I conspired to kill Tom, so we could be together."

"I haven't suggested that."

"No. That would be a crude thing to say at a time like this. You're not crude. You're artful." Laura's blue eyes were locked on Elizabeth's. "It doesn't matter. David didn't kill Tom. I'm sure of that—and not just because of my judgment of what kind of man David is."

"No?"

"No. It's because of the timing. They told me last night that Tom died at around twenty after seven."

"That's right," Elizabeth said. "A driver passing on the street called 911. The call came in at seven twenty-two."

"At twenty after seven, David was at home. That's when I left his house."

Chapter 9

DAVID LOOGAN HAD COFFEE BREWING WHEN ELIZABETH ARRIVED AT HIS house on Sunday evening. She took the seat he offered her—in the living room on the sofa with the wall at her back. He sat in a chair with the front window behind him.

A floor lamp stood near the chair and outside was the street and the night coming on. Through the window, Elizabeth could see the shape of an elm tree on the front lawn. A few stubborn leaves clung to the branches. The sight was strangely familiar. She had an elm on her lawn at home.

She turned her attention back to Loogan and saw that he was watching her. He was clean-shaven and his copper-colored hair was trimmed and he had on a blue Oxford shirt and khaki pants. He looked like a man who would never be out of place. Put him anywhere, Elizabeth thought, and he would blend in. Put him in an office or a laboratory—or on a construction site, loping along with a wooden beam balanced on his shoulder.

She reached for her bag and took out a pen and a notebook.

"It's an unusual name," she said. "Loogan."

"Yes," he said.

"Sounds like it might be Dutch."

"It may very well be Dutch."

"The people I've talked to," she said, "seem to know very little about you."

"Really?"

"Sandy Vogel, for instance. The secretary at *Gray Streets*. She said you were a cipher."

"I haven't gotten to know Sandy as well as I probably should."

"Laura Kristoll—well, she's a different story. She knows something about you."

On the coffee table between them, their cups were untouched. Loogan's right hand rested on his knee. He raised it and looked at his palm in the light of the floor lamp.

"I've never heard the name Waishkey before," he said. "What sort of name is that?"

"It may very well be Dutch," Elizabeth said dryly. "Where were you last night?"

"Last night?"

"I stopped by here, hoping to speak with you."

"I went to visit Laura Kristoll." Loogan's attention was focused on his palm. He curled his fingers into a fist.

"That's interesting," Elizabeth said. "What's the matter with your hand?"

"It's nothing. I have a sliver."

"Does it hurt?"

"It's a distraction."

"How did you get it?"

"From taking apart a picture frame this morning."

"Why were you taking apart a picture frame this morning?"

"It's not important," Loogan said. "I'm sure there are other things you'd like to ask me."

"Indulge me."

He looked up at a framed photograph above the fireplace. "Tom gave me that," he said. "I took it apart this morning, then put it back together."

The photograph was of flower petals and bits of paper and colored glass. The glass reminded Elizabeth of the beads around her neck.

"Why would you do that?" she asked him.

"It's irrational. I was looking for something."

"What?"

"A message, I suppose. Tom is gone. That's the only thing I have from him."

"You thought there might be a note concealed in the frame?"

"I told you it was irrational."

"Did you find a note?"

"All I found was this sliver."

"You should take it out."

"There aren't any tweezers in this house."

Wordlessly, Elizabeth dug through her bag for a pair of tweezers. She crossed to where Loogan was sitting and bent over his open palm. In the lamplight she worried at the sliver with her thumbnail. After a moment she was able to get a grip on it with the tweezers and draw it out.

Loogan rubbed his palm. "Thank you."

She returned to the sofa and dropped the tweezers in her bag. A scent lingered in her memory, the scent of soap and fresh-scrubbed skin.

"You visited Laura Kristoll last night," she said. "How long were you with her?"

"An hour, maybe ninety minutes," he said.

"What did you talk about?"

"We talked very little. She cried a good deal."

"She must have told you that her husband didn't commit suicide. He was killed."

"Yes."

"Yet this morning you were looking for a note from him."

"I'm not saying it makes sense."

Elizabeth looked again at the photograph above the fireplace. "When did he give you that?"

"More than a week ago now."

"What was the occasion?"

"There wasn't an occasion. It was a token, I guess you'd say. Of friendship."

"You were friends."

"Yes."

"Yet you slept with his wife."

Loogan smiled slowly. "You're very direct."

"Some people say I'm artful. Laura was here on Friday. The two of you were together."

"Yes," said Loogan. "She came here around five-thirty. Left around twenty after seven."

"Tom Kristoll died around twenty after seven," Elizabeth said softly. "So you couldn't have pushed him out his office window."

"As it happens, I didn't."

"I know. I wasn't sure yesterday. I had only Laura's word then. But we were able to listen to Tom's voice mail. You called him Friday evening from your home phone. You left him a message at seven twenty-one."

Loogan frowned. "I'd forgotten about that."

"I believe you. A less innocent man might've kept a tighter grip on his alibi." Elizabeth fanned the pages of her notebook with her thumb. "In your message to Tom, you said you were on your way. You were supposed to meet him?"

"He had invited me to stop by the office for a drink. I was supposed to meet him at seven."

"But you were here at seven, with Laura. Did you know she was going to be here?"

"No. She just stopped by."

"And you lost track of time."

"I fell asleep."

"Is that right?"

"We talked, and then we sat for a while on the sofa, and I fell asleep."

"And when you woke up?"

"Laura was leaving. She had her coat on. I intended to drive to Tom's office, but when I got outside I found my car had been vandalized. Two of the tires were slashed and the driver's door was keyed—scratched with a key."

"I know what 'keyed' means, Mr. Loogan," said Elizabeth. "When you saw the damage to your car, who did you think had done it?"

"Neighborhood kids, I imagine. Who else?"

"Keying is what jilted girlfriends do to their boyfriends' cars," Elizabeth said. "You had just broken off your affair with Laura. Did you wonder if she was the one who vandalized your car?"

"I thought about it, for all of ten seconds."

"Is it so implausible? She had her coat on when you woke up. She could have gone out and come back in."

"If she was eighteen, I might believe it," Loogan said. "If she was more flighty, less sophisticated. Do you really think she might have done it?"

"No, but I'm not sure it was neighborhood kids either." Elizabeth turned to a blank page and made a note. "So, what did you do? Your car was undrivable."

"I walked."

"You were already late. It was a cold night. For all you knew, Tom had gone home. Why not call it off?"

"It was only twelve blocks. When I got to Main Street, I could see something was happening. It must have been nearly eight o'clock by then. There were police cars, barricades. I got as close as I could. The body was covered with a blanket, but I think I knew right away. I saw the open window on the sixth floor, and then I was sure."

Loogan's eyes were downcast. "I borrowed someone's cell phone and tried to call Laura, but got no answer. I found a cab to drive me to their house. But Laura had been notified by then. She'd gone in to identify the body."

"So you didn't see her again that night?"

"No."

"And when you saw her last night and she told you her husband's death wasn't a suicide, what was your reaction?"

"I wasn't surprised," Loogan said. "I never thought Tom was suicidal."

"Do you think he was happy?"

"I think he was content. He had a good life. He had work he enjoyed."

"And his marriage—was he content with that?"

"He never gave me reason to think otherwise."

"But you wouldn't have called him happy."

Loogan hesitated, as if searching for the right words. "Tom had regrets. He told me once that no one sets out to be an editor. That's what he ended up as, but it's not what he wanted to be, when he was young. He wanted to be a writer."

Loogan fell silent and Elizabeth put her notebook away. She got up and went to the window and looked out at the elm tree and the street.

When she turned, he was standing by the fireplace watching her.

"Who do you think killed him?" he said.

"I'm supposed to ask you that," she said.

Loogan ran his palm over the stones of the fireplace. "It must have been someone he knew. Someone he trusted."

"Why do you say that?"

"He was struck on the back of the head. He wasn't on guard. He didn't feel threatened."

"Go on," Elizabeth said.

"I'm just speculating."

"You're doing fine."

"It was someone strong enough to wrestle a body through a window. Someone confident, someone daring. Whoever he was, he couldn't be sure there would be no witnesses—someone could have looked up from the street at just the right time. But that didn't stop him."

"Go on."

"It was someone who had been in the office before, who knew the building," Loogan said. "If there's a body on the sidewalk, you're not going to want to go out the front door. He would have used the service entrance in the back."

"You've got his escape route worked out. You've given this some thought."

"If he knew Tom and he knew the building, he was probably someone with ties to *Gray Streets.*"

"We've got a list of people associated with *Gray Streets*," Elizabeth said. "Sandy Vogel gave it to me this morning. She had it ready before I requested it. She said you asked her to prepare it."

"It should include the writers," Loogan said. "Tom sometimes published stories by people in prison. People in prison get out of prison. That's worth looking into, isn't it?"

"It is," said Elizabeth.

"I want him caught," Loogan said quietly. "I should have been there, at the office, at seven. I fell asleep. If I had done what I said I would do, this wouldn't have happened."

Loogan bowed his head and his eyes were lost in shadows. "If this were a story in *Gray Streets*, I'd catch the killer myself. It would be my responsibility."

"This isn't a story in *Gray Streets*, Mr. Loogan."

"It would be my responsibility. Tom was my friend. I should have been there."

On Monday morning Elizabeth spoke with Carter Shan. In the squad room of the Investigations Division, she filled him in on her conversations with Laura Kristoll and David Loogan.

"I'd like it better if they denied the affair," Shan said.

"They're wily," said Elizabeth.

"If they denied the affair, we'd have something to work on. We could show their pictures to waiters and hotel clerks."

"I know how you love showing pictures to hotel clerks."

"There's nothing easier than proving that a man and a woman are having an affair. It's wrong of them to come out and admit it."

"We could bring them in," Elizabeth said. "Put them in a windowless room. Get them to change their story."

"They still could have done it," Shan said. "If they wanted Kristoll out of the way, they could have hired someone to ease him out a window."

"I'd believe it, if it wasn't for the timing. If a woman hires someone to kill her husband, she knows she'll be a suspect. She needs an alibi. Laura Kristoll managed to be alone with her lover when her husband was killed—not the alibi I would have chosen."

"Suppose Loogan hired the killer," Shan said, "and Laura knew nothing about it."

"It makes even less sense that way," said Elizabeth. "If you've hired someone to kill your friend, you don't call your friend and tell him you're on your way over. If you want to establish an alibi, you call anyone but the man you're having killed."

Shan thought it over. "Maybe David Loogan is a criminal genius."

"I don't think he's a criminal genius."

"He's got you convinced he's innocent."

"I never said he was innocent. I think he knows more than he's saying."

"Let's bring him in. Put him in that windowless room."

"Not yet," Elizabeth said. "There's something I want to look into first. A crime that could be linked to Tom Kristoll's murder."

"What crime?"

"A bit of vandalism."

Alice Marrowicz had an office in a storeroom on the second floor. Her hair was mousy and she wore blue eye shadow and dressed like a spinster in thick sweaters and flowered frocks. Yet Elizabeth knew for certain that she was twenty-eight years old. The department had hired her as a tactical crime analyst, which meant she kept a database of information on every crime committed in the city of Ann Arbor.

Her workspace consisted of a laptop computer and a table and chair and very little else. She had the contents of a case file spread out on the table and was tapping on her keyboard when Elizabeth knocked on her open door.

"Hello, Alice."

"Hello," the woman said. She finished typing and spun her chair around.

"I wonder if you could do me a favor," Elizabeth said.

"You're working on the Kristoll murder."

"Right."

"There are limits to what I can do with just a database."

"I know."

"I've already had a go at the Kristoll murder," Alice said. She spoke sedately, but there was a glint of humor in her eyes. "I typed in 'publishers pushed from sixth-floor windows.' Nothing came back."

"Is that right?"

"Of course, the data I use only comes from the local area. There could be publishers being pushed from windows all the time in other cities."

"I don't doubt it," Elizabeth said. "But I'm interested in something more prosaic right now. Vandalism, particularly against cars. Slashed tires, scratched finish. Keying."

"I can give you that," Alice said. "No sweat."

Elizabeth handed her a sheaf of papers. "Whatever you come up with, I need it cross-checked against this list. These are people associated with Kristoll's magazine, *Gray Streets*. They could be victims of vandalism, or perpetrators."

"Doesn't matter," Alice said. "If they're either one, they'll be in the database."

"Can you get me something by this afternoon?"

"Give me an hour."

Chapter 10

VALERIE CALNERO WORE EYEGLASSES WITH BLACK PLASTIC FRAMES. They were an ineffective disguise, a device to make a beautiful girl seem plain.

The woman had the figure of a starlet, the legs of a showgirl. She had a smooth high forehead and long auburn tresses. She had a nose that was slightly too prominent—a nose that a plastic surgeon might have been tempted to fix, though he would regret it afterward. Her skin was pale and clear, her lips generous.

She met Elizabeth and Carter Shan at her door, led them into a modest apartment. She wore a powder blue skirt and a simple white blouse.

"I've seen you before," she said to Elizabeth. "On Saturday at the Kristoll house. You came to talk to Laura." She sat on an overstuffed sofa and offered Elizabeth a chair. Shan took up a position on one of the sofa's arms.

"You were alone then," Valerie Calnero said. "Now there are two of you, and you want to talk about my car. Is this a trick?"

"I'm not sure what you mean," said Elizabeth.

"Tom Kristoll is dead. But you're not here about that. You're here because, months ago, somebody scratched the paint on my car. So I have to wonder: Is it a trick? You do that sometimes, don't you? You tell someone you want to talk about one thing, when you really want to question them about something else."

Shan put on a disarming smile. "We're not trying to trick you. I might be tempted, but Detective Waishkey would never stoop to something so low."

"You're the bad cop, then, and she's the good cop?"

He laughed easily. "You've got us figured out."

"Let's go over a few things, if we could," Elizabeth said. "You're a friend of the Kristoll family."

"I'm a student of Laura's," said Valerie. "She's my adviser. But I'd like to think I'm a friend too."

"And you were an intern at *Gray Streets.*"

"I was, last spring."

"And last spring someone vandalized your car."

"They scratched a word on the hood. 'Bitch,' I think it was."

"At the time, did you have any idea who might have done it?"

"I assume you've read the report. The officer I talked to asked me that question. I told him no." The woman's posture was defensive. She sat with her shoulders hunched, knees tight together, hands in her lap.

"Here's what we're thinking, Valerie," Elizabeth said. "Suppose you never wanted to file a report. You just wanted to get your car repainted. But the insurance company wouldn't pay without a police report. So you went along. When the officer asked who might've done it, maybe you weren't sure, but you had your suspicions. You didn't want to get anyone in trouble. So you said you didn't know."

Valerie's fingers fussed at the hem of her skirt. "If that's the way it went, why would I want to say anything now?"

"We need to know," Elizabeth said.

"I see. So this does have something to do with Tom's murder. But if I didn't want to get anyone in trouble then, the same would be true now."

"You don't need to worry about that," said Shan. "If you tell us who it was, we're just going to talk to him. We're not going to haul him in for murdering Tom Kristoll."

Valerie laid open her palms. "The thing is, I was never sure. He might not have done it."

"Who was he?"

"Someone I dated back then. Well, it was never really dating. We had lunch, we went to movies. He wanted it to be more than that. When I told him I wasn't interested, he reacted badly. He never got angry—he was just sort of brooding. It was a few days later that the thing happened with my car."

"What's his name?"

"I don't know that it was him," Valerie said. "Afterward, I convinced myself it wasn't. He's been all right since then." She took off the black-framed glasses. "If I tell you, are you going to let him know I told you?"

"Not unless we have to," Shan said.

"That's not what I wanted to hear. You ought to lie and tell me he'll never know."

"We need his name."

"It's Adrian. Adrian Tully."

Adrian Tully lived in a dumpy apartment. The furniture was secondhand, the bookshelves made of cinder blocks and wooden planks. Books overflowed the shelves and were piled on chairs and sofa cushions. Tully himself was neat enough. He had a shaved head and a close-trimmed mustache and goatee. His polo shirt and slacks were unwrinkled. He sat Elizabeth and Shan down at his kitchen table.

"I'm afraid I never had much to do with Mr. Kristoll," he said. "I don't think I'll be any help to you."

"That's all right," said Elizabeth. "We have to talk to everyone who worked at Gray Streets. I'm sure you understand."

"I've wondered how the investigation's going," Tully said. "Do you have any leads? I guess I shouldn't ask. You can't really tell me, can you?"

"Not really."

"It's always fascinated me—how someone goes about solving a crime. I mean, do you go strictly by the evidence? Do you have hunches?"

"I have hunches," Shan said. "Detective Waishkey has theories. Hypotheses."

There were groceries in the middle of the table: cans of soup, boxes of macaroni and cheese. Tully moved them off to the side.

"I've been reading a book that says you can solve anything, answer any question, if you just ask enough people," he said. "The idea is that we know things collectively that none of us know individually. It's not as strange as it sounds. Researchers have done experiments. Take a jar of jelly beans and have random people guess how many beans are in the jar. If you take their answers and average them, you'll get a number that's very close to the actual number, probably closer than any one person's guess."

Carter Shan seemed to listen eagerly. Elizabeth, who knew he was acting, was half convinced that he was fascinated by Tully's conversation.

"I never thought of that," Shan said appreciatively. "You're saying we should ask people to guess who killed Tom Kristoll."

"Well, it sounds frivolous when you put it that way," Tully said.

"No, it makes sense. We ought to try that," Shan said. "Maybe we could start now. Who do you think might have killed him?"

"I don't know. Anything I tell you would be a guess."

"That's fine."

"I don't know. I suppose—David Loogan."

Shan looked surprised. "Now why would you pick him?"

"It's only a guess."

"It must be based on something."

"Well, I don't like to talk out of turn, but I think he may be having an affair with Laura."

Elizabeth broke in. "Is that right? What makes you say that?"

"Just the way they act around each other."

"Do you spend a lot of time with them?"

"No."

"But you've observed how they act around each other," Elizabeth said.

Tully shrugged his shoulders. "During the summer, Tom and Laura had parties at their house. David Loogan came to some of them. He would go off with her alone sometimes and talk. And I saw him with her once on campus."

"Did you ever ask Laura about it?"

"She's my dissertation adviser. It's not my place to ask about her personal life."

"Of course," Elizabeth said. "Do you think Tom Kristoll suspected his wife was having an affair?"

"I couldn't say. I didn't know him that well."

Shan had gotten up from the table unobtrusively. From an open cabinet over the sink he took a glass and filled it from the tap. Carrying it with him, he wandered into the living room.

Elizabeth asked Tully about his work in the English department. She let him ramble on a little about the subject of his dissertation.

Then she said, "You were an intern at *Gray Streets* this past spring."

"That's right."

"What does an intern do, at a magazine like that?"

"Some light copyediting, some proofreading. But mostly you read slush—manuscripts that come in unsolicited."

"You worked there in the office?"

"Usually I brought things home."

"So you never saw much of the boss."

"Not really. Like I said, I'm afraid I can't be much help."

"Just a few more things," Elizabeth said. "When was the last time you saw Tom Kristoll?"

Tully considered the question. "It would have been at one of those parties they had at the house," he said. "Early September, I think."

"When was the last time you went to the *Gray Streets* office?"

"I haven't been there since May, when my internship ended."

"We're trying to nail down Kristoll's movements in the days leading up to his death. You didn't see him in the past week, or talk to him?"

"No."

"And for the record, where were you Friday afternoon and evening?"

"I was here," Tully said. "I graded papers and worked on a chapter of my dissertation. I'm afraid there's no one to vouch for me. I live alone."

Shan had wandered back in from the living room. He emptied his glass into the sink and left it on the counter.

"That's fine," Elizabeth said. "I think that's all we need."

A drizzle of rain spotted the sidewalk in front of Tully's apartment building. The sky was darkening. Shan started the car and pulled away from the curb.

"Well, you've had a look at him now," he said.

"I have," said Elizabeth.

"What do you think?"

"I think if we asked a lot of random people if Adrian Tully is a weasel, they'd say yes, yes, yes."

"He was eager to steer us toward David Loogan," Shan said. "But he didn't want to seem eager. You figure he has a thing for Laura Kristoll?"

"She's an attractive woman," Elizabeth said. "And she's his adviser."

"Hot for teacher. And he has it in for Loogan because Loogan was having an affair with Laura Kristoll?"

"Suppose he wasn't sure about the affair. So on Friday he followed her to Loogan's house. His suspicions were confirmed. He was angry. He slashed Loogan's tires and keyed his car."

"Did he go beyond that?" Shan said. "Did he kill Tom Kristoll? It seems like a stretch. If he was mad at Loogan, why would he kill Kristoll?"

Elizabeth wound a finger through the string of beads around her neck. "Try it this way. Tully feels rejected. If he can't have Laura Kristoll, at least he can ruin what she's got going with Loogan. He goes to her husband's office to tell him about it. But Tom Kristoll doesn't buy it—his wife and his friend having an affair. So he tells Tully to go to hell. Tempers flare. Tully knocks Kristoll over the head. Now Kristoll is unconscious. Tully panics. He didn't mean for this to happen. He eases Kristoll out the window and tries to make it look like a suicide."

Beside her Shan was nodding. "With a suicide note courtesy of Shakespeare," he said. "'I am more an antique Roman than a Dane.' Tully had a copy of *Hamlet* on his bookshelf."

"Is that right?"

"I paged through it. There were a fair number of lines highlighted—including the one about an antique Roman."

The light on the porch was glowing when Elizabeth got home. In the kitchen she found a casserole warming in the oven, a bowl of salad covered in plastic in the refrigerator. Two soda cans—Pepsi and Mountain Dew—at the top of the recycling bin.

In the living room her daughter was sitting on the floor with her back to the couch. A math text and a notebook were open on the coffee table.

"I should be cooking *you* dinner," Elizabeth said.

"That's true," said Sarah. "Sometimes I tell people I come from a broken home."

"I should be helping you with your homework too."

"I don't know about that. It's trigonometry."

"I wouldn't be any use then. We didn't have triangles when I was in school."

Sarah got up and together they set the table and sat down to eat. The salad was elaborate: three kinds of lettuce, tomatoes, slices of onion and carrot and apple, cashews, and shredded cheese.

"You could have invited him for dinner," Elizabeth said. "I bet he would have been impressed."

"Who would that be?" Sarah asked.

"The boy you're having an affair with. Billy Rydell."

"Oh. You saw the Mountain Dew can."

"I did."

"You know, I told him we could live a secret life, if only we were willing to give up soft drinks."

"When was he here?"

"He came by after school. We sat on the porch for a while." Sarah went to the oven and brought out the casserole. Rice and broccoli and chicken— she spooned it onto their plates. "What did you do today?" she asked.

"Talked to people," Elizabeth said.

"You can tell me who. I won't squeal to the press."

"One of them was a man who might have killed Tom Kristoll."

Sarah speared a piece of broccoli with her fork. "Tom Kristoll is the publisher who got defenestrated."

"Yes."

"And you talked to his killer. Was it the man with the sliver in his palm?"

Elizabeth had told her daughter about her encounter with David Loogan.

"Not him," she said. "We ruled him out."

"I thought you might have ruled him back in."

"No. The man I talked to is a student of Kristoll's wife. His name is Adrian Tully." She sketched the theory that she and Shan had worked out.

"How do you prove it?" Sarah asked.

"Tully gave us an alibi. He said he was home Friday afternoon and evening. We'll try to prove he was lying. We'll show his picture to people in David Loogan's neighborhood and in the area around the building where Kristoll was killed."

"What if no one remembers seeing him?"

"It might mean he didn't do it, or it might just mean no one remembers him."

"Maybe he'll confess."

"It would be nice if someone would."

"Maybe he'll be racked with guilt," Sarah said. "When will they have the funeral?"

"I don't know if it's been scheduled. The medical examiner hasn't released the body yet."

"Tully—if he's the murderer—he'll go to the funeral."

"He'll probably go either way."

"If he's the murderer, he'll feel compelled to go," Sarah said. "You should be there. He'll stand with the mourners at the grave, and he'll feel tormented. If you're there, he might confess to you."

Chapter 11

Nathan Hideaway was a tall man, broad of shoulder, thick of neck. His face was all strong features: piercing eyes, formidable nose, wide mouth, square jaw. A lined forehead and a crown of curly white hair. David Loogan had seen the face before: in photos on the jackets of mystery novels. And he had met the man once, at a party at the Kristoll house on the Huron River.

At a few minutes past eight on Tuesday night, Loogan knocked on the door of the Kristoll house. The door swung inward and there was Nathan Hideaway, extending a great mitt of a hand in greeting. He was dressed in a suit that might have been black or might have been a very deep blue. His face betrayed no sign of recognition. He said, "Mr. Loogan, I presume."

He led Loogan back through the house and into the study. Laura Kristoll came forward as if she might embrace Loogan, but in the end she only trailed her palm down his arm. She said, "Thank you for coming, David."

There was another woman with her—a woman Loogan had met before, at the same party where he had met Nathan Hideaway. Her photo had also appeared on the jackets of novels. She was scarcely over five feet tall. Loogan estimated her age at forty, though she dressed as if she were fifteen years younger. Her white blouse hugged her slim form, and her skirt ended well above her knees. Her brown hair was cut short and disheveled, pixielike.

"This is Bridget Shellcross," Hideaway said. "Bridge, meet David Loogan."

"We've met," Loogan said. "It's a pleasure to see you again."

Bridget's smile made slits of her eyes. It revealed small white teeth.

"Of course," she said. She plainly had no idea where she was supposed to have seen Loogan before.

The room was as Loogan remembered it. The desk at the far end, the rows of bookshelves, the four upholstered chairs. Three weeks ago he had stood here with Tom, and they had talked about disposing of a body.

The same bottle of Scotch, or one very much like it, stood on the side table.

Nathan Hideaway settled into a chair, gesturing for Loogan to do the same. Laura and Bridget followed suit.

"Well, let's begin," Hideaway said. "I think I speak for us all—"

Bridget Shellcross interrupted him. "Before you start speaking for us all, Nate, maybe Mr. Loogan would like a drink."

"Certainly," Hideaway said. "By all means."

"I don't need a drink," said Loogan.

"You ought to have something," Bridget said. "We've been drinking Chardonnay."

There was a half-spent glass on the floor by her chair.

"Maybe I'll have a Scotch."

Laura stood up. "I'll get some ice."

"I'll take it just as it is," Loogan said.

She retrieved a tumbler from a cart beside the desk and poured Loogan three fingers from the bottle on the table.

"I think I speak for us all," Hideaway said again, "when I say that Tom's loss is a terrible blow—"

"He means Tom's death," said Bridget. "It's Tom's death and our loss. Christ, Nate, you always needed a good editor."

Hideaway seemed to take no notice of her. "Tom was a vital man," he said. "He has passed away from us far too soon, and with his passing it falls to us to look after his interests."

"I believe that's true," Loogan said quietly.

"We must attend to the things he cared about," Hideaway said. "One of those is *Gray Streets*. Tom was the wellspring, the prime force, the motive power—"

"Get the man a thesaurus."

"—the architect of the magazine's success. *Gray Streets* was the central project of his life. If it were allowed to decline, or to cease publication—"

"Nate's point is, we don't intend to let that happen," said Bridget.

"It's our understanding," Hideaway said to Loogan, "that Tom thought highly of your abilities as an editor. Laura shares that view. No one can take Tom's place, of course. But we'd like you to consider taking over some of his responsibilities."

Loogan felt a wave of something like nausea pass through him.

"I don't know what to say."

"What we have in mind," said Hideaway, "is for you to continue to do the sort of editorial work you've been doing, and to take a hand in the selection of stories for publication. You needn't worry about being on your own. We would advise you."

Loogan tipped his glass side to side, watching the light play over the amber liquid. Several moments passed in silence.

"You're reluctant," Hideaway said.

"Yes."

"There are details to be worked out. You'll have your own thoughts on how things should be managed. I'm sure we can come to an accommodation."

Loogan rose from his chair. "I don't think I want to talk about this now."

"It's all right, David," said Laura, rising in turn.

"Let it rest, Nate," said Bridget. "He'll want some time to think about it."

Hideaway stood up and Bridget followed suit.

"Perhaps I could speak to Mr. Loogan alone," Hideaway said. "Just for a few minutes. You don't mind, do you, Laura?"

Laura's face was unreadable. "I guess not," she said.

Bridget shook her head in disapproval, but she followed Laura out and closed the door of the study behind them. Hideaway got a glass and poured himself some Scotch.

"I handled this badly," he said. "There are some things it's easier to talk about one-on-one than in a crowd."

He sipped from his glass. Loogan said nothing.

"Also, it's too soon," Hideaway said. "Tom has been gone for four days and we bring you here to talk about commerce. That's my fault. The others wanted to wait. When I see something that needs to be done, I don't like to delay. But it's too soon. You think it's unseemly."

"It was certainly unexpected," Loogan said.

"Was it?" Hideaway said. "You must have wondered what would become of *Gray Streets*. When we asked you to come here tonight, you must have assumed we had some motive. What did you suppose it was?"

"You wouldn't believe me if I told you."

Hideaway swirled the Scotch in his glass. "Now I'm intrigued."

"I thought you wanted to hire me to find out who killed Tom."

The lines of Hideaway's forehead crinkled. "Why would you think that?"

"Don't you want to know who killed Tom?"

"Naturally," Hideaway said. "But I'm afraid I'm at a loss. Laura was vague about your background. She hinted that you had a checkered past. She even suggested that you might have been a criminal. I took that as a piece of whimsy."

"That's the way it should be taken," Loogan said.

"So you were never a criminal. Am I to understand you were a policeman?"

"No."

"Then why would I want to hire you to solve a murder? Isn't that a job for the police?"

"Is that what you believe? I've read some of your books."

"That's fiction."

"In a Nathan Hideaway novel, the police are never quite up to speed. They're always a few steps behind."

"Fiction, Mr. Loogan."

"In a Nathan Hideaway novel, the protagonist is always an amateur detective," Loogan said. "And he's always a man who can be trusted with secrets. Secrets you might not want to share with the police."

"I don't think I'm following you," said Hideaway.

"Now that Tom's gone, we have to look out for his interests. That's what you said. But that's not an easy job, is it? Tom had his secrets. Is it better now we should keep them or reveal them?"

"Now I'm sure I'm not following you."

"I wonder. Did you really ask me here to offer me a job?"

"Why else?"

"I think maybe you wanted to get a sense of me. To see if I was going to be trouble."

"You really should listen to yourself, Mr. Loogan. You're sounding very peculiar."

"Maybe I'm wrong and you're exactly what you seem to be. You're just looking for someone to edit *Gray Streets*."

"I thought I'd made that clear."

"Maybe you're guileless."

Hideaway spread his arms out at his sides. "I'd like to think so."

"I can almost believe it," Loogan said, looking around at the chairs, at the bookshelves, at the desk. "If you had any guile, you would have picked a different room. You would have talked to me anywhere else but here."

Chapter 12

THE WEB SITE OF *GRAY STREETS* DISPLAYED PHOTOS AND BIOGRAPHIES of the magazine's interns. The online images were too small to be of much use, but the original photographs were kept in a file in the outer office of *Gray Streets*. The secretary, Sandy Vogel, showed Elizabeth the file on Tuesday morning. The photos were in no particular order, but it didn't take Elizabeth long to find Adrian Tully's.

She had duplicates made that morning, and by the afternoon she and Carter Shan and a handful of other detectives had fanned out through David Loogan's neighborhood and through downtown Ann Arbor, searching for anyone who had seen Adrian Tully on the day Tom Kristoll was killed.

The canvass continued on Wednesday. The results were disappointing. Elizabeth found a waitress in a diner who thought she had served Tully breakfast, but couldn't be sure what day it had been. There were a few other sightings of similar uncertainty. Then, on Wednesday afternoon, Shan spoke to the girl who delivered the newspaper in Loogan's neighborhood. She recognized Adrian Tully. She had seen him on Loogan's block on Friday evening.

Shan took the girl's statement, and he and Elizabeth met with the chief the next morning to bring him up to date. Owen McCaleb stood by his office window, listening. He was fresh from a jog and hadn't yet changed his clothes.

"It's slim," he said when Shan finished.

"I know."

"I mean, what we have is Adrian Tully on Loogan's street," McCaleb said. "Not even near his car, right?"

"He was walking along the street near Loogan's house," said Shan. "That's what the girl said. But we also know the time. Around quarter to six. Tully claimed he was at his apartment all afternoon and evening."

"The timing fits with what Laura Kristoll told us," Elizabeth added. "She arrived at Loogan's house around five-thirty. Tully could have followed her there."

"And then he could have punctured Loogan's tires and keyed his car," McCaleb said. "But the papergirl didn't see him do it."

"No."

"And then he could have gone downtown to the office of *Gray Streets*," McCaleb said. "And out of jealousy, or just to be a prick, he could have told Tom Kristoll about his wife's affair. He could have quarreled with Kristoll and hit him over the head and pushed him out the window. But no one saw him in the building, or even in the vicinity of the building."

"No."

"So right now," McCaleb said, "what we've got on Adrian Tully is that he lied about where he was on Friday. I don't see how we have enough to charge him with the vandalism to Loogan's car, much less the murder of Tom Kristoll. We don't have enough to get a warrant to search Tully's apartment, and even if we did, there's nothing to search for. Do we even know what Kristoll was hit with? What did the M.E. say?"

Shan smiled ruefully. "A blunt instrument."

"Lovely."

"That's what Eakins wrote in her report," Elizabeth said, "but when I talked to her she ventured a guess. She thought it might have been a book. In fact, it might have been the book on Kristoll's desk—Shakespeare's *Collected Works*. That one was hefty enough to do some damage. And the dust jacket was missing. The killer might have taken it with him. It might have been easier to take it than to wipe it for prints."

"And if he took it, he's had time to get rid of it," McCaleb said. "So where does that leave us? Tully lied. You want to talk to him again?"

"That's what we were thinking," Shan said. "We tell him we've got a witness who saw him on Friday evening. We don't say where the witness saw him. Let him wonder. The point is, we know he lied to us. See if he changes his story."

"Elizabeth?"

"It's worth a try. I'd like to see what he says."

McCaleb nodded. "All right. Do it."

On the sidewalk across the street from Adrian Tully's apartment building, two pigeons danced around a scrap of bread. One of them caught it up whole in his beak and then the other hopped in, wings fluttering, and made him drop it.

Elizabeth watched them from the car, with Shan in the driver's seat beside her. They had gone up and knocked on Tully's door, but there had been no answer.

Shan had his cell phone out. His thumbs moved rapidly over the keys. He had an ex-wife and a son who lived in a suburb of Detroit, and he kept in touch with them frequently through text messages. Elizabeth had met the boy, a twelve-year-old with his father's slim build. The child's mother taught voice lessons, and there was a rumor in the department that she and Shan had once been in a band—she had been the lead singer, he had been the drummer. It was a rumor that Shan would neither confirm nor deny.

Elizabeth watched him grin at something on the cell phone's screen. Then he typed a final message, put the phone away, and tuned the car radio to an all-news station. She turned her attention back to the pigeons on the sidewalk. The pair of them skipped along the concrete, trading the scrap of bread off between them. A dog appeared at the corner, an Irish terrier straining at its leash. The pigeons scattered. The terrier snapped up the bread as it passed. Elizabeth kept an eye out for the pigeons, but they didn't return.

"It's the third way," she said.

Shan turned down the radio. "What's that?"

"That's how this is going to go," Elizabeth said. "The third way."

"What do you mean?"

"It's just something I've noticed," she said. "You're waiting for something to happen, and you expect it to go one of two ways. But you're wrong, because there's always a third way."

The air in the car felt stale. She pressed a button at her side and lowered the window.

"Say you've applied for a job," she said, "and you're waiting to find out if you got it. Then the call comes, and you're expecting a yes or a no, but it turns out the person you interviewed with is in a coma, and the board of directors resigned, and the new management wants you to come in and interview again for an entirely different job that you didn't even know about before. That's the third way."

Shan lowered the window on his side. "And you think that's going to happen with Tully?" he said. "We tell him we know he's lying, and we expect he'll either come up with a new story or he'll break down and confess to murdering Tom Kristoll—"

"And it's not going to be either of those."

"What's the third way, then?"

"That's just it. You never know." She nodded in the direction of a car coming down the street. "But we're going to find out. Isn't that him?"

"That's him," Shan said. "That's his crappy little car. There he goes, turning into the lot of his crappy apartment building. Shall we let him go up first?"

"Sure. We don't want to seem too eager."

A few minutes later they were in the hall outside Tully's door. Elizabeth knocked. Shan put on a pleasant, distracted expression—a bit of performance, Elizabeth knew, in case Tully looked through the peephole. There was no answer and no sound from within.

She knocked again. After a delay they heard Tully's voice, as if from far off. "Who is it?"

"Detectives Waishkey and Shan," Elizabeth said. "We need to speak to you."

Tully took too long to answer, and when he did it was, "Just a minute, please."

Shan was frowning. He unsnapped the holster at his belt and rested his hand on the grip of his pistol.

"Come on, Adrian," Elizabeth said. "Open the door."

"Just a minute." Again, the answer seemed to come from far off.

Shan stepped to the left side of the door and drew his pistol.

"Is this the third way, Lizzie?" he said quietly.

"Easy, Carter," she said. But she reached to her hip for her own pistol.

"Open the door, Adrian."

The silence inside stretched out, and then there was the sound of a dead bolt being turned. Elizabeth held her pistol down at her side.

The door opened a few inches, then swung wide. Adrian Tully, grinning, showed them the palm of his right hand. His left hand held the receiver of a cordless phone. Shan said something under his breath. Elizabeth thought it was the word "idiot."

"Sorry," Tully said. "It's my lawyer on the phone. He advises me not to talk to you. He says if you have any questions you can go through him. If you plan to shoot me," he added, looking at Shan, "you ought to maybe wait." He held up the phone and wiggled it in the air. "Witness."

Shan scowled and holstered his pistol. Tully held the phone to his ear, listening, and then said: "My lawyer wants to know if he should meet us here, or if we're going to the station."

"The best we can hope for," Carter Shan said, "is the third way."

Elizabeth sat at her desk in the squad room of the Investigations Division, sorting through her mail and her messages. Shan, in a chair across from her, stared at the closed door of the chief's office.

"The first way," Shan said, "is if Tully walks out of there with his hands cuffed behind his back."

They had driven Adrian Tully from his apartment to City Hall. He'd been silent during the trip. Tully's lawyer—Rex Chatterjee—had been waiting when they arrived.

"The second way," Shan said, "is if he skips out of there scot-free."

Chatterjee had calmly and politely requested to speak with the chief. Lawyer and client were in McCaleb's office now.

"The third way," Shan said, "is if he walks out of there and I punch him in his smirky, goateed face. I think I like the third way."

Elizabeth came to a pink message slip from Alice Marrowicz. *Kristoll body released,* it said. *Funeral scheduled for Friday.*

"You're quiet, Lizzie," Shan said. "What are you thinking?"

"Do we think Tully is smart?" she said.

"Not especially."

"Yet apparently he knew we were looking at him."

"Someone probably tipped him off. My guess is Valerie Calnero. She felt bad about giving us his name in the first place."

"It could have been Sandy Vogel," said Elizabeth. "She showed me the file of intern photographs. I didn't let her see me take Tully's, but she could have looked in the file afterward and seen which one was missing."

"Either way," Shan said, "it's someone from *Gray Streets.* People in the *Gray Streets* crowd seem to look after their own."

"Tully's lawyer is Rex Chatterjee. Laura Kristoll's lawyer is Rex Chatterjee. What does that suggest to you?"

"Laura Kristoll doesn't want us to question Adrian Tully. Maybe we were wrong about him. We assumed he had a thing for her, but maybe it went both ways. They could have been involved, and they could have decided to get rid of her husband."

"That's one possibility," Elizabeth said.

"Or it could be she wasn't involved with Tully, and doesn't know for sure that he killed her husband. But maybe she suspects he did, and it's all right with her."

"You're a cynical man, Carter."

"Or it could be she thinks he's innocent." Shan picked up a pen from the desk and tapped it against his knee. "And maybe he really is innocent, and we're on the wrong track."

"That's too many possibilities," Elizabeth said darkly. "We don't know enough yet. We haven't talked to enough people."

Just then the door of the chief's office opened. Rex Chatterjee emerged, brushing with pudgy fingers at his thick gray hair. Tully came out next and cast an airy look around the squad room before following Chatterjee out.

Owen McCaleb watched them leave and then approached Elizabeth's desk. "The upshot of that," he said, "is that Adrian Tully is represented by counsel. He's made all the statements he's going to make. If we think he's guilty of a crime, we should charge him and see how it stands up in court."

McCaleb rolled his eyes. "Beyond that, it was a lot of bluster. Chatterjee was shocked and disturbed that the Ann Arbor police would come to a citizen's door with guns drawn. He was expansive on that point. Before long he had you waving your guns in his client's face."

"Nobody waved anything," Shan said.

"I know," said McCaleb. "He was just making noise. We're supposed to have it in the back of our minds that there could be a lawsuit. That's supposed to deter us."

"Are we going to be deterred?"

"No," McCaleb said. "We're going to get something more on Adrian Tully. Or failing that, we're going to get something on someone else. It would be nice if we had a plan."

"Elizabeth was just sketching one," Shan said. "It involves talking to people and finding things out."

McCaleb turned back toward his office. "Let me know how that goes," he said.

Sifting through the papers on her desk, Elizabeth came to a green file folder and a typed note from Alice Marrowicz. Beneath the folder was a sheaf of papers clipped together: the list of writers and staff associated with *Gray Streets*.

"These people we're going to talk to," Shan said. "Any thoughts on where we're going to start?"

Without taking her eyes from Alice's note, Elizabeth tossed him the *Gray Streets* list.

"I've got a copy of this," Shan said. "There must be two hundred names here."

"We ought to be able to narrow it down," said Elizabeth. "Not all of them are local. And Tom Kristoll's funeral is tomorrow. It'll be interesting to see who shows up. You'll want to wear a nice suit, and try not to wave your gun around."

"And in the meantime?"

"In the meantime, Alice Marrowicz has done some of our work for us. Tom Kristoll published stories by convicts. I asked Alice to weed out their names from the master list. She found nine altogether. Seven are still serving their sentences. Of the two that are out, one is in California and the other is in a trailer park down in Saline."

"A local boy," Shan said. "What's his name?"

"Zorro."

"Dresses in black. Good with a sword."

"Michael Beccanti," Elizabeth said, opening the green folder. "It wasn't my case, but I remember him. He did residential burglaries in the summertime, and got in by cutting through window screens. He always cut them the same way, in the shape of a Z. He got out of Parnall Correctional in Jackson a year ago."

"Let's go talk to Zorro then."

"I don't think it'll take two of us." She handed him Alice's note. "Why don't you get started on our friend from California. After that, you can look at the ones who are still inside. See what sort of contact they had with Kristoll and the *Gray Streets* crowd."

She saw him frowning and added, "Don't worry, Carter. I'll call you if I need you."

———

The drive to Saline took her past fields of houses, places where prosperous young families would live. The trailer park was tucked away out of sight, but it was clean and well tended. The grass was trimmed, the cars were in good repair.

Elizabeth drove around to lot 305. The door of the double-wide was a cheery red. The woman who answered to her knock wore sandals and sweats and a tank top. The tank top had been ironed. It was stretched tight by her swelling stomach.

"I'm looking for Michael Beccanti," Elizabeth said.

"Who are you?"

Elizabeth showed her badge. "Detective Waishkey," she said.

"Mike's not here."

"What's your name?"

"Karen."

"Does Mr. Beccanti live here?"

"Sometimes he does."

"When was the last time you saw him?"

"It's been a while. What do you want from him?"

"I need to speak to him."

"So I gathered. He's not here."

Elizabeth put on a friendly smile. "How far along are you, Karen?"

The woman rested her hand on her stomach. There was a ring on her finger with a very small diamond.

"That's a personal question, isn't it?" she said. "I don't think you should be asking me personal questions."

"You're right," Elizabeth said. "It's hardly my business. Are you engaged to Mr. Beccanti?"

"That's another personal question."

"I'm just trying to get the lay of the land. Mr. Beccanti lives here sometimes, and it's been a while since you saw him. Seems like a very casual arrangement."

The woman crossed her arms over her stomach. "Is there anything else I can do for you?"

"You could tell me where to find Michael Beccanti," Elizabeth said.

"I don't know where he is."

"I find that hard to believe."

"I'm not going to lose sleep over what you believe. Mike served his time, he did his parole. He's free of you people now. I've got a cousin in law school. I know how things work. I don't have to talk to you, I don't have to tell you anything about Mike, I don't have to show you pictures—"

"I haven't asked for pictures."

"No, you haven't. I guess I should be grateful."

"Did someone else come around here, asking for pictures?"

"Another cop," the woman said bitterly. "He seemed like a cop, anyway. He had a name like a gun. Luger."

Elizabeth blinked. "Loogan."

"That's right."

"And he wanted to see a picture of Mr. Beccanti?"

"I didn't show him one. He got about as much out of me as you have."

"Serves him right. Look, Karen, do me a favor. The next time you hear from Mr. Beccanti, tell him to call me." Elizabeth dug a card from her pocket. "All I want to do is ask him some questions."

The woman accepted the card wordlessly. She was still holding it, still standing in the doorway, when Elizabeth drove away.

Chapter 13

"The tall one," Loogan said, "with the white hair. That's Nathan Hideaway."

Elizabeth shaded her eyes against the noonday sun. "I've heard the name," she said. "He's an author."

"He writes thrillers. All of his books have a month in the title. *January Rain. Dying in September. The Longest Night in June.*"

"And the woman beside him?" Elizabeth asked.

"Bridget Shellcross."

"Is she an author too?"

"She has a mystery series about an art dealer who solves crimes with the help of her golden retriever."

"Really?"

"It takes all kinds."

The sky was clear and the weather mild for late October. Loogan had kept himself apart from the crowd of mourners who stood clustered around Tom Kristoll's grave. He had taken up a position by the cemetery fence. Elizabeth had joined him there.

She had been at the funeral service earlier. A great lot of people had been at the funeral service. When Loogan arrived at the funeral home that morning, he had seen Laura Kristoll alone in a hallway, in a black dress with long sleeves and a high collar. They regarded each other from a distance, and then she walked to him and embraced him, her hair soft against his neck. She spoke a single word. "David." Then they were joined by others in the hall: Laura's sister and father, Tom's brother and sister from out of town.

As more guests began to arrive, Loogan let himself fade into the background. He stood against the back wall of the viewing room as the rows of chairs filled up. He saw Elizabeth Waishkey enter with a dark overcoat draped over her arm. She wore a gray silk blouse, a long skirt. A short necklace of glass beads at her throat. She took a seat in the last row.

The minister was in her sixties, a gaunt woman with thick eyeglasses. She stood beside the closed casket with sprays of lilies at her back and rambled on about traveling and searching and coming to rest. Tom's sister delivered a brief eulogy. His brother read a Kipling poem in a voice never far from breaking.

Near the end of the service, a slim, well-dressed Asian man came in and sat next to Elizabeth. Loogan saw them leave together and later, at the cemetery, he saw them again. He watched them walk across the lawn of stones and leaves and grass. The Asian man turned aside to linger with the mourners, and Elizabeth joined Loogan by the black iron fence. She stood quiet beside him as the minister read psalms over Tom Kristoll's grave.

The crowd at the graveside was smaller than the one at the funeral home had been. Many of them stayed after the minister intoned a final blessing. They formed themselves into groups and talked in hushed voices. From the cemetery fence Elizabeth surveyed them curiously, and Loogan pointed out Nathan Hideaway and Bridget Shellcross. The two were talking with another man: medium height, fortyish, with short, thick hair and a closely trimmed beard.

"What about him?" Elizabeth said.

Loogan touched his temple absently. "He looks familiar."

"Where have you seen him?"

"On the flap of a book jacket, probably."

As they watched, Nathan Hideaway put a hand on the bearded man's shoulder and bent close as if to pass on a confidence. The bearded man glanced in Loogan's direction. After a time, Hideaway turned to face Loogan and Elizabeth, sketched a bow, and took his leave, heading off at a slow pace along a row of stones.

"What was that about?" Elizabeth said.

"It's like watching a show," said Loogan.

Bridget Shellcross and the bearded man had linked arms and were walking toward them across the lawn. Bridget wore a close-fitting tunic of black leather and a pair of black leather pants. Her eyes were hidden behind the black lenses of her rimless sunglasses. She removed the glasses as she approached.

"David, may I introduce Casimir Hifflyn?" she said. "Cass, this is David Loogan."

The bearded man offered his hand and Loogan shook it.

"And this," said Loogan, "is Elizabeth Waishkey."

There were greetings all around. Hifflyn said, "Mr. Loogan, would it be presumptuous of me to offer my condolences for the loss of our mutual friend?"

"Not at all."

"What did you think of the ceremony?"

"Honestly?"

"Of course."

"I found it . . . inadequate."

"I know what you mean," said Hifflyn. "Words fail at times like these. The twenty-third psalm is the standard, I suppose. 'The Lord is my shepherd.' But it's overly familiar. If it had been up to me, I might've chosen something else."

Loogan looked up at the clear sky. "I might've chosen silence, and a smaller crowd."

"I won't disagree," Hifflyn said. "Grief is a fiercely private matter. I'll let you be, Mr. Loogan. I only wanted to meet you, since I missed the gathering the other night. I hope we'll have a chance to speak again."

"Certainly."

"I'll leave you then," Hifflyn said. To Elizabeth he added, "It was a pleasure meeting you."

Bridget stood on tiptoe and kissed both of Loogan's cheeks, and then she and Hifflyn departed. When they were out of earshot Elizabeth said,

"So that's Casimir Hifflyn. The writer. He's on a different plane from the others, isn't he? His books are more highbrow."

Loogan leaned back against the cemetery fence. "Some of them are. He got his start writing literary crime novels. *The Emperor's Tailors. The Man Who Paved the Road to Hell.* But he also has a detective series: *Kendel's War. Kendel's Rumor. Kendel's Key.*"

"What was that he said to you—about a gathering the other night?"

"That was Tuesday," Loogan said. "I was summoned to the Kristoll house. Laura was there, and Bridget Shellcross, and Nathan Hideaway. They offered me a job."

"Is that right?"

"They asked me to take over as editor of *Gray Streets.*"

"Did you accept?"

"I haven't given them an answer."

"Maybe you should," Elizabeth said. "A job like that would occupy your time. It would keep you out of trouble."

Loogan stared down at the withered grass around his feet. "Have I been getting into trouble?"

"You tell me. Why did you go looking for Michael Beccanti?"

"Oh. Is that going to get me into trouble?"

"It might. Why did you do it?"

"Tom mentioned his name once. Said he was a burglar."

"You think he might have had something to do with Tom's death?"

"I don't know. I guess I thought it would be worthwhile to talk to him."

Elizabeth put on a serious expression. "You're not a detective, Mr. Loogan. This isn't a story in a magazine. You're not investigating the murder of Tom Kristoll."

"I know."

"You asked Beccanti's girlfriend if she had a picture of him. Why?"

Loogan shrugged. "I was looking for him. I thought it would help to know what he looked like."

"What would you have done if you found him?"

"I guess I would have improvised. Can I ask you something?"

"Go ahead."

"That necklace you're wearing—the beads are made of glass, aren't they?"

The question caught her off guard. "Yes. Why—"

"The last time I saw you, you were wearing another necklace. Similar, but not the same."

"My daughter made them both. Why are you asking me about them?"

"I've wanted to ask you since I saw you this morning," said Loogan. "And here we are in a cemetery. Cemeteries remind us that our time is short. We shouldn't put off doing what we want to do."

Elizabeth looked at him sideways, the hint of a smile forming on her lips. "Mr. Loogan, I think you're trying to charm me."

Across the lawn, groups of mourners were drifting toward their cars. At the graveside, Laura Kristoll was engaged in a muted discussion with her sister and father. She waved them away and turned to walk toward Loogan. Loogan left the cemetery fence to meet her halfway. Elizabeth trailed behind.

There was a scattering of yellow leaves at the place where Laura stopped. Leaves rustled under Loogan's feet.

"Well," Laura said. "That's done."

"Yes," said Loogan.

"They're telling me I should go home."

"That's not a bad idea."

"I've got a house full of guests. People want to look after me."

"Sure."

She looked over her shoulder. Her father and sister were still at the graveside. The funeral director hovered nearby.

Turning back to Loogan she said, "You ought to come. I'd like to have you there."

"I will if I can," he said. "There's something I need to do."

"All right." She nodded to Elizabeth, who stood a little distance away. "Detective," she said. Then she left Loogan and headed back.

He watched her join up with the pair at the graveside, watched them move off toward the cars with the funeral director in tow. There was no one left now at the grave, nothing there but a low metal framework that surrounded the opening and a mound of earth half-concealed by a tarp.

From behind him Elizabeth spoke in a low voice. "You don't have to be circumspect for my sake."

Loogan turned toward her. "I don't know what you mean."

"There's no reason you shouldn't go see Laura Kristoll. It's not really the business of the Ann Arbor Police. I'm not going to write it up for the file."

"That's good to hear. But I meant what I said. There's something I need to do. Someone I need to find."

Elizabeth sighed. "I thought we had that settled, Mr. Loogan. You're not a detective. You're not going to go looking for Michael Beccanti."

Loogan offered her a fleeting smile. "Not him."

"Then who?"

"I can't tell you his name, but he's the caretaker, the groundskeeper"— Loogan made a sweeping gesture with his arm—"whoever's in charge of this place. When I find him I intend to question him at length. He's going to tell me how this works."

He tipped his chin in the direction of the grave. "I have an idea of what happens next. I think they lower a steel enclosure into the ground, over the casket. Then they shovel the dirt on top of that. I'm not sure if they'll do it now or later. I aim to find out."

"Why?"

"Because I intend to help bury Tom." He looked into Elizabeth's eyes. "That probably sounds ridiculous."

"No," she said. "But I'm not sure you can do it."

"I know how to work a shovel."

"I'm not sure it's allowed."

"I imagine it isn't," Loogan said in a quiet, weary voice. "But what is and isn't allowed might not matter when it's just me and a work crew and I ask them for a favor."

A breeze pushed the yellow leaves over the grass.

"Someone's going to bury him. I don't see why it should be strangers."

Carter Shan was waiting in the car—a black Crown Victoria. Elizabeth got in on the passenger side. Through the window she could see Loogan standing alone by Tom Kristoll's grave.

"What's he doing?" Shan asked her.

She found herself reluctant to answer. What Loogan was planning was his own business.

She said, "I suppose he's doing whatever people do. Saying good-bye. Saying a prayer."

"You talked to him a long time."

"He introduced me to some writers. He acknowledged that he went looking for Beccanti. Did you find anything out?"

"Adrian Tully never showed his face. Not at the funeral parlor, not here."

"What else?"

"I talked to Sandy Vogel. She was the one who revealed that we were investigating Tully. I don't think she meant any harm. She told Laura Kristoll."

"That fits. We assumed that Laura Kristoll got Tully his lawyer."

"It also lets Valerie Calnero off the hook," Shan said. "She didn't warn Tully. She's still one of the good guys."

"You seem pleased about that," said Elizabeth.

"I've always gone for redheads. She's got nice legs too."

"God, Carter."

"Well, she does."

"You didn't hit on her at a funeral, did you?"

Shan turned the key in the ignition. "I know better than that. I'll wait for another time."

In the distance, David Loogan was striding across the cemetery lawn.

Shan's fingers drummed the steering wheel. "Do you want to stick around, see where he goes?"

"No," Elizabeth said. "We've got work to do."

Chapter 14

THAT NIGHT THE MAN WHO CALLED HIMSELF DAVID LOOGAN DREAMED in the darkness of his rented house. In his dream, Tom Kristoll was alive. The two of them were in the clearing of the woods of Marshall Park, with the grave of the thief at their feet. Tom weighed the silver-gray pistol in his palm and dropped it into the earth. But in the grave something stirred. Loogan glimpsed a pale hand closing around the pistol's grip. He heard the sharp knell of gunfire. Two shots.

The shots woke him. He stared at a black shape like a grave and couldn't move. He panicked for a moment, until he realized he was staring at the open doorway of his bedroom.

He rolled onto his elbow, swung his legs off the bed. His pants rustled against the sheets; he had fallen asleep in his clothes.

Down the stairs in his sock feet. He turned on the light in the kitchen, sipped tap water from his cupped hand. There on the floor his shoes were coated with the dust of Tom Kristoll's grave. On the table was a Montblanc pen that had belonged to Tom, a token that Laura Kristoll had wanted Loogan to have.

Leaning against the counter he looked into the dimness of the living room and felt a chill. He listened for a sound of movement, but there was nothing. Slowly he pulled open a drawer beside him.

He made his way to the living room armed with the longest knife from the drawer. He sorted out the black rectangles: one was the opening of the fireplace, one was the doorway of the history professor's home office. He switched on a lamp and felt the chill again. The air grew colder as he approached the window that looked out on the front porch. The sash was raised about an inch. There was a screen on the outside. There were two long cuts in the screen, corner to corner, forming an X.

Loogan heard movement and felt sure someone was behind him. He spun around, slashing with the knife. The blade whistled faintly in the air. It struck nothing; there was no one for it to strike. He lowered the knife until the blade pointed at the floor.

Just then the figure of a man seemed to materialize in the doorway of the office.

Elizabeth woke on the couch, a quilt twisted around her, the muted television tuned to a late-night talk show. Her daughter stood over her, holding the receiver of the phone.

"Call for you," said Sarah. "It's Carter."

Elizabeth yawned. "Tell him I said hello."

Into the phone Sarah said, "She's loopy, Carter. Give her a minute."

Sitting up, casting off the quilt, Elizabeth took the receiver. "You're calling me on the wrong phone," she said.

"I tried your cell and got kicked to your voice mail," said Carter Shan.

She picked up her cell phone from the coffee table and flipped it open. "The ringtone's off. I shut it off for the funeral."

"I'm glad we got that settled," Shan said. "I'm taking a drive to the country. North Territorial Road. Thought you might want to come."

"What is it?"

"Body in a car. White male. Gunshot wound to the head. I think you'll be interested."

"Who is it, Carter?"

"Can't be sure yet, but the car belongs to someone we know."

The man was slim and shy of six feet tall and dressed in black. His face was a pleasant oval framed by dark, tangled hair and three days' growth of beard.

He stepped into the living room and said, "I have a gun."

"Do you?" Loogan said. "Let me see it."

"I don't really. But I thought it might make you think twice about using the knife."

Loogan had brought the blade up automatically. His fist was clenched around the handle.

"You're not going to need it," said the man dressed in black. "If I wanted to hurt you I could have done it already. I'm here to talk. I'm—"

"Michael Beccanti, I know," Loogan said. "I saw the damage you did to my window screen. Cutting an X instead of a Z—I suppose that's the equivalent of a disguise."

"The Z was what got me into trouble," said Beccanti. He gestured at the sofa and chairs. "Maybe we could sit."

Loogan made no move. "How long have you been here?"

"Maybe an hour. You were asleep." Beccanti looked at his watch. "You turned in a little early for a Friday night. It's barely one o'clock."

"I've had one of those days."

"The chair in the office is comfortable," Beccanti said. "I almost dozed off. But I'm glad you woke up. I thought I might have to wait here till morning."

"You didn't think to wake me?"

"Some people react badly when you go into their bedroom and start shaking them. Some people, you break into their house, they get hysterical. You've handled things pretty well, apart from the knife. Tom said you were a levelheaded man."

Loogan's breath caught in his throat. "Tom talked to you about me?"

"Sure. He was always talking about his friends. Didn't he ever mention me?"

"Just once. Do you have any ID? A driver's license would do."

"Why?"

"Did Tom ever tell you I was in the circus?" Loogan said. "I was a knife-thrower."

Beccanti chuckled and took out his wallet. He flipped his license through the air and it landed at Loogan's feet. Carefully, Loogan picked it up. The name was right: MICHAEL ERIC BECCANTI. The photo was a good likeness.

He ran his thumb along the edge of the license, considering what to do. The sensible thing would be to call the police, but he had stopped being sensible quite a way back.

He thought of Elizabeth Waishkey and the conversation he'd had with her earlier that day.

Why did you go looking for Michael Beccanti? she had asked. *What would you have done if you found him?*

I guess I would have improvised, he had told her.

Beccanti stood expectantly with his arms at his sides, palms forward. Loogan tossed the license back to him and decided to improvise.

"Tom mentioned you once. He told me you were dead."

The patrolman stood in the road and tapped a flashlight against his thigh. His breath was visible in the night air.

"Couple of teenagers called it in," he told Elizabeth and Shan. "Boy and a girl. They drove up behind the victim's car and couldn't get around it. Honked like hell, trying to get it to move. Eventually the boy got out and walked up to the driver's side—and saw what he saw."

Shan had picked up Elizabeth and they had taken Route 23 to North Territorial Road. After five or six miles, they had turned onto a narrow side road that ran between stubbled cornfields. A patrol car and an M.E. van were already on the scene.

"Teenagers," the patrolman muttered, shaking his head. "You can imagine what they were doing out here. Maybe that boy'll think twice before he takes some girl cruising again, this time of night. Anyway, he saw what he saw and he backed out of here fast. Took the girl home and called 911 from her house. I've got their names."

"Good," said Elizabeth.

"I opened the car when I got here. I wouldn't have, but you never know. It didn't do that fellow any good. He didn't have a pulse. Once I knew that, I backed off."

"That's fine," Shan said.

"Medical examiner's looking at him now," the patrolman said. "Eakins."

Lillian Eakins was in her indeterminate fifties. She was sturdy and unstylish, her brown hair liberally streaked with gray. She had both doors of the victim's car open and was squatting in the road on the driver's side when Elizabeth and Shan came up to her.

"Ugliness," she said, without looking up. "Just plain ugliness."

"Hello, Lil," Elizabeth said.

"I suppose you'll want to know who he is."

"We have an idea."

"I haven't dug his wallet out yet. I haven't wanted to move him."

"Don't worry about it. I'll come around and look."

"Ugliness. I'll get his wallet. You stay put."

"Never mind, Lil. I can see him well enough from here."

"What's his name then?"

"Adrian Tully."

Loogan said, "He told me you tried to rob him, and he had to kill you."

"Tom had a sense of humor," said Beccanti.

Though Loogan's pulse had been racing, he felt it begin to slow. He lowered the knife, holding it by his side.

"I helped him bury you," he said quietly. "In a clearing in the woods."

Beccanti let out a short, sharp breath that might have been a laugh. "You're serious."

"Yes."

"Maybe you'd better explain that."

Loogan rocked on his feet. He brought the knife up distractedly and trailed the end of the blade along his shirtsleeve.

"Three weeks ago, Tom called me to his house and asked me to help him bury a body." The blade clicked against a button. "Now that I've seen you, I can tell you that the man we buried didn't look like you at all. He was shorter; he was blond; he had a tattoo on his wrist. But Tom said he was you. He said you had come to ask him for money. Five thousand dollars. And when he refused, you drew a gun. He slugged you in the temple with a bottle of Scotch."

"That's a realistic touch—the Scotch."

"Sure," Loogan said. "Tom was spinning a story, but there were elements of truth in it. He said you needed money because your girlfriend was pregnant. He went into some detail about how he met you, about the stories you wrote for *Gray Streets.*"

Beccanti lowered his eyes thoughtfully. "Why would he lie?"

"That's the question, isn't it?"

"I'd say he didn't trust you—but he asked you to help get rid of a body. I'd call that a sign of trust."

"He wanted a story that would satisfy me," Loogan said. "But he didn't want to reveal the dead man's real identity."

The yellow lamplight left Beccanti's face half in shadows. "They're connected," he said, "Tom's death, and this other man's."

"They must be," Loogan said. "I might be able to figure out how, if I knew who he was—the man we buried."

Beccanti's eyes gleamed through the shadows. "I think I can tell you that."

Carter Shan had his camera out. The flash lit the night periodically, like slow, patient lightning.

Lillian Eakins stood with Elizabeth at the roadside behind the car. "Looks like one shot," Eakins said, "just in front of the right ear. Contact wound. Gun's on the seat there, thirty-eight revolver. A smaller caliber'll bounce around inside the skull, but this went right on through. Punched a hole in the driver's window."

"You think he shot himself?" Elizabeth said.

"First impression—yes."

"Strange place to do it. He's pretty far from home."

"There's no telling what people'll do. It's a quiet spot anyway. Not a bad night for it."

Shan called them over. He lifted the revolver from the seat and opened the cylinder so all three of them could see.

"Six rounds," he said. "Only one spent."

He dropped the rounds into an evidence bag.

To Elizabeth he said, "Do we think Adrian Tully was suicidal?"

She made a noncommittal noise through closed lips.

"If we were right that he killed Tom Kristoll," Shan said, "then maybe he was overcome with remorse."

Staring in at the body slumped behind the steering wheel, Elizabeth said nothing.

"You don't look convinced," Eakins said, "either one of you."

"Three weeks ago. That's when you buried him."

Beccanti sat in the chair with the lamp beside him. Loogan was on the sofa, the knife resting on his lap.

"Yes," he said, "it was on the seventh. A Wednesday night."

"That sounds right," said Beccanti. "It was the Friday after that when Tom called me. He had a job for me. He seemed embarrassed about asking. He wanted someone's place searched—a condo on Carpenter Road. No one would be home, he said, and I wouldn't need to break in. He had a key."

Beccanti slouched in the chair, relaxed. "I went in that weekend, on Saturday night. Tom never told me whose place it was, but once I got there I found bills, credit card receipts. All in the same name. Sean Wrentmore."

"Sounds familiar," said Loogan. "I think he's on the list."

"What list?"

"The *Gray Streets* list. I think he's a writer."

"That fits," Beccanti said. "Tom wasn't interested in cash, or jewelry, or Sean Wrentmore's stamp collection. He said if I found anything like that, I should leave it be. He wanted discs, CDs, flashdrives, any kind of storage media. But there was nothing like that in sight. There was no computer either, no laptop. Tom had already searched the place himself, I think. I was his backup. He needed me to look in places where he wouldn't have thought to look.

"That was never my strong suit, looking for secret hiding places. In the old days, I'd climb through your window and grab your wallet and your cell phone and your camera and I'd climb back out. But it's amazing the things you learn in prison. I turned the key in Sean Wrentmore's door at eight o'clock Saturday night and didn't leave till Sunday morning. I unscrewed light fixtures, I peeled back rugs to look for loose floorboards, I took the fuse box and the telephone jacks out of the wall. I looked for things taped to the underside of drawers, the underside of furniture, the underside of just about everything.

"When I was through inspecting the contents of the freezer and digging into the dirt of the potted plants, I had exactly one thing to show for all my efforts. I found it early on, behind the faceplate of an electrical outlet: a flashdrive, about as big as your thumb. I delivered it to Tom the following Monday in his office and collected my fee, and we never talked about it again."

Loogan laid the knife on the cushion beside him. He leaned forward, elbows on his knees. The house was quiet. Outside, there was a faint sound of rustling leaves.

"I don't suppose you know what was on the flashdrive?"

"No," Beccanti said.

"I wonder if it's still in his office."

Beccanti's smile was mischievous. He reached into his shirt pocket and came out with a sleek plastic cylinder, the size of a cigarette lighter. He set it upright on the coffee table between them.

"I did some searching this afternoon," he said. "The office was closed, out of respect for Tom, but the cleaning staff still had to show up. I walked into Tom's office like I belonged there, sat at his desk, and started reading a book. No one questioned me. When everyone was gone, I poked around a little. There's a false bottom in one of Tom's desk drawers. The drive was in there, and so was this." Beccanti produced a key from another pocket and tossed it onto the coffee table.

"That'll get you into Wrentmore's condo," he said, "if you care to go there."

Loogan picked up the drive. "You said you didn't know what was on this."

"I don't. It's a secure drive. You need a password."

Loogan slipped the drive into his pocket. He picked up the key, balanced it on the back of his index finger, and then walked it across the back of his hand. He passed it to his other hand and kept going, end over end, finger to finger. He stopped when he saw Beccanti grinning at him.

He dropped the key in his pocket with the drive. "Is that why you came here, to give me these?"

"That, and to see what you were like," Beccanti said. "To see if we could help each other."

"Help each other do what?"

"Find out who killed Tom."

"Shouldn't we leave that to the police? That's what I keep hearing."

Beccanti made a sour face. "I don't intend to sit back and do nothing. Tom did me a lot of favors. He didn't have to. That story he told you, about me asking him for five thousand dollars? That part was true. Only he didn't refuse. He gave it to me, without a second thought. I owe him."

Loogan leaned back and propped his feet on the coffee table. "Still, maybe you'd be better off going to the police and telling them what you know."

"I have an aversion to dealing with the police," said Beccanti. "And look who's talking. I bet the police would be interested in hearing about how you helped Tom bury a body in the woods. They might decide it's relevant to their investigation."

Loogan let that pass. He stared at the ceiling—white stucco turned yellow in the lamplight. Eventually he said, "How thoroughly did you search Tom's office?"

"Not very," Beccanti said. "I turned up the trick drawer pretty easily. I didn't look much further."

"Maybe you should try again. See if you can find anything else that has to do with Sean Wrentmore. I can get you in this time. They offered me Tom's job. I imagine it comes with a key to his office."

"All right."

"And I'll pay a visit to Wrentmore's condo. If nothing else, maybe I'll find a picture of him. I'd like to be sure he's the one we buried."

"Does this mean we're not going to the police?" said Beccanti gently.

"Not yet. It's like that rule that lawyers follow: When you're questioning a witness in court, you never ask anything if you don't know what the answer's going to be."

"Is that what it's like?"

Loogan's voice dropped low. "Tom had his reasons for what he did, for the secrets he kept. I don't want to go to the police without knowing where it might lead."

Chapter 15

ADRIAN TULLY'S PARENTS LIVED IN GRAND RAPIDS. THEY RECEIVED the news of their son's death at three A.M. Saturday, from a Grand Rapids detective who had once been a classmate of Elizabeth Waishkey.

They drove to Ann Arbor Saturday morning, arriving a little before noon. They had their daughter with them, a sullen girl of seventeen. Elizabeth spoke to them in Tully's apartment. They were bewildered. Adrian had never talked about being depressed, had certainly never talked about suicide. Elizabeth got the impression that Adrian hadn't talked to them about much at all.

It was one o'clock when she left them. There was nothing more to be learned at Tully's apartment. She and Carter Shan had searched it in the early morning. They had found nothing out of the ordinary, no evidence linking Tully to Tom Kristoll's murder. No suicide note.

By one-fifteen, Elizabeth was back at City Hall. She waved at the desk sergeant in the lobby, took in the bare details of her surroundings: a janitor pushing a broom across the floor, a woman on a bench with her head bowed. She was opening the gray steel door to the stairway when she heard a voice call her name.

"Detective Waishkey."

She turned to see the woman from the bench approaching. A woolen coat covered her figure; her hair was in a ponytail; she wasn't wearing her glasses. It took a moment for Elizabeth to recognize Valerie Calnero.

Her face was pale. She had been crying. She said, "I need to ask you something."

"Come up to the squad room," Elizabeth said. "We can talk there."

"I'd rather talk here," the woman said. "I heard about Adrian. Did he shoot himself?"

"You should come up."

"The news reports don't say. They call it an apparent suicide. But I'd like to know, one way or the other."

"I'm afraid I can't tell you," Elizabeth said gently. "It's not clear yet."

"Did Adrian kill Tom Kristoll? Can you tell me that?"

Elizabeth let the steel door close. "I don't know," she said.

"Because less than a week ago you came to ask me about graffiti scratched into my car. I pointed you toward Adrian. I didn't want to—"

"I can understand why you're upset," Elizabeth said.

"I didn't want to," Valerie repeated, "but you were only going to talk to him, you said. And now he's dead."

"I can understand—"

"Adrian's parents are in town now. They want to talk to Adrian's friends. What am I supposed to tell them? Should I tell them I drove their son to suicide?"

"Valerie—"

"Or that I got him murdered? I'd like to be able to nail it down for them."

Elizabeth put her hand on the young woman's shoulder. "Come upstairs, Valerie. I know it's a lousy time for it, but there are things we should talk about. You might know something that could shed light on Adrian's death. Maybe something he said, or something about the way he acted."

Valerie Calnero's mouth was set in a stern line. She shook her head slowly and began to back away.

"I don't have anything to say to you."

Upstairs, Elizabeth brewed some coffee and typed a report on the Adrian Tully crime scene, and another on her conversation with Tully's family.

The squad room was largely deserted. When she finished her paperwork, she took out the case file on Tom Kristoll's murder and began to page through it.

The sound of a soft voice made her look up.

"I don't want to bug you."

It was Alice Marrowicz, her mousy hair in a ponytail, the sleeves of her sweater enveloping her hands.

"You're not bugging me, Alice."

"You were out late last night, that's what I heard."

She dragged a chair toward Elizabeth's desk and sat down.

"I'm not snooping around or anything," she said. "I want you to understand that. But I've heard things."

Elizabeth closed the Kristoll file. "What are you getting at, Alice?"

"Adrian Tully."

"What about him?"

"I heard he was found dead in a parked car by a cornfield in the middle of nowhere."

"That's been on the news," Elizabeth said.

"I heard he died of a gunshot wound to the head. There was stippling around the wound. Tests turned up gunshot residue on his hand and on the sleeve of his coat. The gun was on the seat beside him. A box of ammunition in the glove compartment."

Alice paused for breath and then continued. "So there's every indication of a self-inflicted wound. But then there are one or two things that don't fit. I heard, for instance, that Tully's prints are on the gun, but not on the bullets. And not on the ammunition box either."

She leaned forward in her chair, her voice growing more animated. "So on the one hand, it seems like a suicide," she said. "But on the other hand, it wouldn't be that hard to fake. If you knew him, if you were in the car with him. If you were fast with the gun. One shot to the head, point-blank. Then you put on a pair of latex gloves and wipe your prints from the gun. You remove the spent shell, put it in your pocket, and replace it with a fresh round.

You roll down the passenger window, put the gun in Tully's hand, fire a second shot out into the field. Now he's got residue on his hand and there's still only one spent round in the gun. You stash the ammo in the glove compartment, leave the gun on the seat. You've planned all this in advance, so you've got another car waiting nearby to make your escape."

She looked at Elizabeth expectantly. Elizabeth obliged her with an encouraging smile.

"It's not a bad theory, Alice. I've had some thoughts along those lines myself—"

But Alice was shaking her head. "You're missing the point. It's not my theory. I didn't work it out. I read it in a mystery novel."

Elizabeth's smile faded. "What novel?"

"The question you want to ask is: Who wrote the novel?"

"All right. Who?"

"Bridget Shellcross."

"It's a cliché," said Bridget Shellcross. "A murder staged to look like a suicide. Every mystery writer uses it sooner or later. I used it in my second book."

The door to Bridget Shellcross's townhouse had been answered by a woman with a pageboy haircut. She was tall and athletic and dressed for a workout; her bare arms were well toned. She led Elizabeth to a sitting room decorated with designer furniture: squarish shapes in leather with bands of dark wood and burnished metal.

Bridget rose from a divan to greet Elizabeth. She wore a stylish black suit fitted to her sprightly frame. The tall woman—whose name turned out to be Rachel Kent—left and returned with bottled water and a tray of raw vegetables and hummus. Then she slipped off to sit in a corner.

Bridget had resumed her place on the divan. "In my first book," she was saying, "I used a different cliché altogether. One of the cops investigating the crime turned out to be the killer. No offense."

"None taken," said Elizabeth.

"I wrote the first one when I was twenty-three. It was based on a short story I'd done, something Tom Kristoll published in *Gray Streets*. He encouraged me to work it up into a novel."

She shook her head thoughtfully. "Poor Tom. His death was a cliché too—another murder made to look like a suicide." Her eyes locked on Elizabeth's. "You think they're related."

"Do I?"

"Adrian Tully was under suspicion for killing Tom," Bridget said. "That's the gossip anyway. So maybe whoever killed Tom also killed Tully, as a way of deflecting suspicion. If you think Tully committed suicide out of guilt over killing Tom, you'll stop looking for Tom's real murderer. You know what that means."

"It must mean something," said Elizabeth.

"It means someone wants to make Adrian Tully a fall guy. There's another cliché. How many are we up to?"

"I've lost count."

"Not to mention that Tully's death resembles a murder in a book, thus casting suspicion on the author," Bridget said. "That's a cliché all on its own. I suppose you'll need to hear my alibi."

Elizabeth lifted her shoulders almost imperceptibly. "If it's no trouble."

"Let's see. You saw me at Tom's funeral. After that, a lot of us went over to the Kristoll house to keep Laura company. I left there around five and met Rachel at Palio downtown for an early dinner."

"Rachel didn't attend the funeral?" Elizabeth asked.

"No. She didn't really know Tom," Bridget said. "After dinner, we did some shopping along Main Street, and then went to a café. Crazy Wisdom. There was a folksinger." She turned to Rachel. "What was her name?"

"Angela something."

"Right. She wasn't very good. We were home by nine-thirty or so and stayed in the rest of the night."

"The two of you were here alone then," said Elizabeth.

"That's right. Rachel is my only alibi for after nine-thirty. Aren't you, Rae?"

In a tone that was light, amused, the woman answered, "Sure, Bridge."

"Of course, she's desperately in love with me. She'd lie for me. Wouldn't you, Rae?"

"Absolutely."

"But you're not lying now, are you?"

"Nope."

"So there you have it," Bridget said to Elizabeth. "What else can I tell you?"

Elizabeth studied the woman in silence for a moment, then asked, "Did you know Adrian Tully?"

"I met him once or twice," said Bridget, "at those parties Tom and Laura were forever throwing."

"What was your impression of him?"

"I thought he was gay. But then I realized he was just socially awkward."

"Did he ever make a pass at you?"

Bridget hesitated. "Now why would you ask me that?"

"I believe he may have had a thing for attractive older women."

"Notice how she tempers 'older' with 'attractive,' Rae. She's tactful," Bridget said. "The answer is yes, he made a pass at me once. I pretended not to notice, and he went away and pouted."

She sat up straight on the divan and planted her feet on the floor. Her tone became more serious. "Still, I don't think he was very bright. So if I tried to lure him out to a cornfield with the promise of sex, he might have gone along with it."

Elizabeth's fingers brushed the arm of her chair dismissively. "I haven't suggested any such thing."

"No. But that's the subtext," Bridget said. "That's the problem with the whole scenario: If Adrian Tully was murdered, whoever did it must have either driven out there with him or arranged to meet him there. Either way, there must have been some pretext, some reason he went along. I couldn't tell you what it was, because I'm not the one who killed him."

She picked up a square black pillow from the divan and held it in her lap. "I'm not the one who killed Tom either, if you want to know. Rachel is my alibi for that one too. We were here the night he died. We cooked dinner together—lasagna with eggplant and tomato-basil sauce." In the same sedate tone she added, "I believe I was laying out the napkins and the silverware right about the time when Tom smashed into the sidewalk."

She put the pillow down and stood. "I'm afraid I've lost interest in continuing this conversation," she said. "If there's nothing more, perhaps I could show you out."

Chapter 16

"You missed the sunset," Casimir Hifflyn said.

"I didn't mean to," said Elizabeth.

"I can sum it up for you. A few wisps of cloud, and behind them the sky glowing pink over the branches of those trees, and the pink deepening to red."

Hifflyn lived in a sprawling ranch house shielded from the road by tall hedges. He had a flagstone deck in the back and a broad, terraced lawn. A fire burned in a shallow copper bowl set on the flagstones. Hifflyn and Elizabeth were sitting in deck chairs drawn up close to the fire.

"Have you read any of Bridget's books?" Hifflyn asked.

"I'm afraid not."

"I suppose one shouldn't judge," he said. "They're not intended to be serious literature. Realism is not their forte. The one you've mentioned— with the faked suicide in a parked car by a cornfield. It doesn't hold up, not if you look at it closely. First, you've got to convince your victim to drive out into the wilderness in the middle of the night."

"Bridget mentioned that problem herself," Elizabeth interjected.

"But that's only one difficulty," Hifflyn said. "Another is witnesses. Because you're not really in the wilderness. You're next to a cornfield. That means a farm. That means a farmhouse. In her book, I think the farmhouse was supposed to be abandoned. But still, what about neighbors? Is this supposed to be the only farmhouse for miles around? The sound of gunfire can travel far on a calm night. And to make it work, there have to be two shots, one to kill the victim, and one to get residue on his hand. If anyone hears the second shot, the whole thing breaks down."

"We're looking into that," Elizabeth said. "Some of my colleagues are out there now, questioning people who live in the area."

"Then there's the bullet itself," Hifflyn said. "The second bullet. When you fire it, it has to end up somewhere. In the field, probably, or—are there trees at the edge of the field?"

"I believe there are."

"In a tree trunk, then. Either way, the bullet can be recovered. And if it is, that's evidence of a second shot. It no longer looks like a suicide. Our murderer is out of luck." Hifflyn added a stick of wood to the fire. "Incidentally, that's how the crime is solved in Bridget's book. The second bullet is recovered. The heroine's dog fetches it from the field. Dusty or Rusty or whatever his name is. That's the way her books always end. The dog saves the day."

"It takes all kinds," Elizabeth said.

"I suppose it does. If it's not too presumptuous, I'll suggest you try a more conventional approach. A grid search of the field with metal detectors, for instance."

"We've thought of that too. I believe it's being organized now."

"There you are."

The two of them fell silent. Elizabeth watched the fire crackle in the copper bowl. Then she said, "What can you tell me about Adrian Tully?"

Hifflyn took a moment to consider. "He was a quiet young man. Meek, I would say."

"He copyedited a manuscript of yours—a short story for *Gray Streets*. This past spring."

"You have excellent sources of information."

"The secretary at the magazine keeps track of everything."

"Yes, Adrian edited my story," Hifflyn said. "But bad editing is a weak motive for murder, Detective—though in the heat of the moment it can often seem otherwise. And Adrian's editing was good. He found a few typographical errors, questioned a few word choices. He didn't change things for the sake of changing them."

"Was that the first time you met him," she asked, "when he edited your story?"

"Yes, we got together over coffee and went over what he'd done."

"Is that common—for an author and an editor to meet in person?"

"Probably not," Hifflyn said. "But I'm something of a curiosity, especially for students. A published novelist. Sometimes they want to see for themselves if such a thing really exists."

"And you oblige them?"

"When I can. For Tom's sake, more than anything else," he said. "Tom and I went to the university together. We founded the magazine together—with Laura and a few others. My part in that was modest, though, and my motives entirely self-interested. I saw *Gray Streets* as a way of getting some of my own stories published. But I'm straying into personal history now, and you want to hear about Adrian Tully."

"How often did you see him, after that first meeting?"

"Not often. Our paths crossed a handful of times, usually at the Kristoll house. The last time I saw him was after Tom died. Those first few days, there were always students hovering around Laura. Adrian was one of them. I remember speaking to him, but only in passing."

"You can't shed any light on his mood then."

"I'm afraid I can't."

"Were you aware that he was under suspicion in Tom's murder?"

Hifflyn pushed at a stick of firewood with the heel of his shoe. "That's something I heard, though I never heard why."

"We believe that he followed Laura on the day Tom died and that he discovered she was having an affair with David Loogan. We were working on the theory that he went to Tom's office to tell him about the affair and the two of them had an argument that got out of hand." Elizabeth observed Hifflyn's face in the glow of the firelight. "Did you ever get the impression that Tully was attracted to Laura Kristoll?"

He shook his head slowly. "I can't offer you any insight on that."

"Let's put Tully aside then," she said. "Let me ask you about Tom. You went to school together."

"Yes."

"Then you started getting books published, and he had the magazine. Did that ever put a strain on your friendship?"

"I'm not sure I follow you."

"I understand he wanted to be a writer when he was younger."

"We were all writers back then."

"But you've made a success of it. He never did."

"He took another path. He made a success of *Gray Streets.*"

"It's not the same though, is it?"

"If Tom ever envied me, he kept it to himself."

"How close were you?" she said. "Did you see him often? Did you talk to him on the phone?"

"Sometimes he'd call to ask me how a manuscript was coming along, or if he discovered a new writer. And we would go out to dinner—Tom and Laura, my wife and I."

"There's a Mrs. Hifflyn then?"

"She's traveling in Europe. I could give you a number if you want to talk to her. She's in Venice now. She has family there."

Elizabeth tipped her head to the side. "And here you are in Michigan."

"I'd rather be with her," Hifflyn said, "but I'm trying to finish a book."

"Who do you suppose killed Tom?"

He had been watching the fire, but now he turned to her sharply with a puzzled look. "I don't know."

"That was an abrupt question," she said. "I apologize. I should have eased into the subject. When you found out he'd been killed, what did you make of it?"

"I didn't know what to make of it. It seemed entirely senseless."

"But there must have been a reason. If I went digging around in Tom's past, what would I discover?"

Hifflyn's fingers touched his earlobe. His face made a pained expression. "I don't know if I feel comfortable talking about Tom in this way. It doesn't seem proper."

"I don't mean any disrespect. But I could use your help. Tell me what he was like in school."

"That was twenty years ago."

"Indulge me."

Hifflyn sighed. "He was driven. Dedicated."

"To the magazine?"

"And to fiction writing."

"You were in the creative writing program?"

"The three of us were," he said. "Me and Tom and Laura."

"And Bridget Shellcross, where does she fit in?"

"Bridget was a year ahead of us. But she was studying art history."

"All right," Elizabeth said. "Now, remember, I'm digging. What do I find?"

"I don't know what you're looking for."

"Sure you do. Imagine I was talking to someone less scrupulous, someone willing to pass on tales. What would he tell me?"

Hifflyn folded his hands in his lap. "If I were willing to pass on tales," he said, "I might tell you that Bridget and Tom were once involved."

"You mean romantically."

"Yes. Bridget was . . . open-minded then."

"Was this before or after Tom and Laura got together?"

"It was after they were together, but before they were married. Eventually, Laura found out about Bridget, but she and Tom worked it out."

"And that was the end of it—between Tom and Bridget?"

"I believe it was."

"But in the years since, you don't know what may have happened," Elizabeth said. "They could have started up again."

"I've no reason to think so."

"If they had started up again, would Tom have told you?"

"I don't see why. I wasn't his confessor."

"All right. I'm still digging. What else do I find?"

After a quiet moment Hifflyn got out of his chair and stood staring at the night sky. "Do you like looking at the stars, Detective?"

"Not while I'm digging."

"In the city, it's hard to see anything at all. Artificial light drowns out the real thing. But it's better here, for stargazing." He pointed toward the northern sky. "Those three stars—I believe that's Orion's belt."

Elizabeth joined him. "I think you're right. Look a little to the east and you can see Sirius."

"The bright one there?"

"The brightest. Also known as the Dog Star, part of the constellation Canis Major. Why don't you tell me what I'm digging for?"

Watching his profile, she saw a crow's-foot form at the corner of his eye.

"Laura and me," he said.

"You were involved with Laura?"

"Freshman year. Before she and Tom met. I introduced them. In fact, I believe you would say he stole her away from me."

"I see. And how did that play out?"

"Tom was charming. And I told you he was driven. 'Obsessed' might be a better description. Especially after he got the magazine started. Laura was attracted to that."

"You must have been hurt."

"There were some rough days," he said. "There were even days when I hated Tom. Days when I might have been tempted to push him in front of a bus. Or out an open window."

Hifflyn stood looking down at the ground. With the toe of his shoe he traced the outline of a flagstone.

"I had my reasons then," he said. "If Tom had been killed twenty years ago, I might have been a prime suspect. I don't know what that makes me today."

Chapter 17

IN THE KITCHEN OF SEAN WRENTMORE'S CONDOMINIUM, THE CUPBOARDS were efficiently organized, the surface of the stove was clean. The counter-tops were free of crumbs.

There was a glass in the sink, a few plates in the dishwasher. Then, in the refrigerator, indications of Wrentmore's absence: an expired carton of milk, leftovers beginning to grow mold.

David Loogan closed the refrigerator door and moved on to the living room. He noted a fairly expensive stereo system, a flat-screen television. The furniture seemed to have been purchased as an ensemble: the sofa matched the reclining chair; the coffee table matched the end tables. There were a few photographs hung in metal frames. Most of them were portraits of people in Third World settings: women at a well, young men leaning against a graffitied wall. Their expressions were invariably serious; some-times angry, sometimes resigned.

The photographs had not been taken by Wrentmore. They were matted and signed by the photographer, a woman Loogan had never heard of. There were no personal photographs, no snapshots, no photo albums that Loogan could discover.

He went down a hall and came to the bedroom. It was large and doubled as an office. Desk by the window. Shelves of books. A walk-in closet held dress shirts and turtlenecks, khaki pants and blue jeans—they seemed about the right size for the man Loogan remembered from the floor of Tom Kristoll's study. In a corner of the closet stood a shotgun, barrel pointed toward the ceiling. A box of shells on a shelf above. A smaller box of twenty-two-caliber ammunition. Loogan thought of the nickel-plated pistol in the dead man's ankle holster.

Loogan left the closet and sat at the desk, which was cluttered with empty notepads and scattered pens and pencils. There was no computer, just as Michael Beccanti had said, and Loogan guessed that the clutter was there to disguise the computer's absence.

He made a casual search of the drawers of the desk and came across a few phone bills and utility bills, but no bank statements, no checkbook. There were no journals, no notebooks, nothing to indicate that the owner of the desk was a writer. There were index cards, but they were all blank. Loogan fanned through them idly. He would have liked to find a cryptic word or series of numbers—a password that might unlock the flashdrive that Beccanti had discovered hidden behind the faceplate of an electrical outlet. He found nothing of the kind. But in one of the drawers he turned up a student ID with Sean Wrentmore's name on it. It was ten years out of date, from a community college in Ohio, but the photo was recognizable. Lean face and long, dirty-blond hair. It was a younger version of the man he and Tom had buried in Marshall Park.

The books in Wrentmore's collection were more or less what Loogan would have expected. Most were mystery novels. Raymond Chandler was there, as were Dashiell Hammett and Rex Stout. As for contemporary writers, Wrentmore seemed to favor Michael Connelly, Jeffery Deaver, and Elmore Leonard, but Nathan Hideaway, Bridget Shellcross, and Casimir Hifflyn were also represented.

The non-mystery books were eclectic: science fiction by Robert Heinlein, an anthology of Mark Twain, the plays of Edmond Rostand.

Loogan opened one of Nathan Hideaway's novels and got a hint of Wrentmore's personality. There were passages underlined, notes in the margins. Wrentmore would bracket off sections of dialogue and mark them *stilted*. He would circle a paragraph and write *ugh!* or *god-awful*.

On the last page of one of Bridget Shellcross's books—*Roll Over,* featuring art dealer Linda Lorenger and her golden retriever—Wrentmore had provided a two-sentence review: *Shoot the dog. Run off with Linda.*

One of Casimir Hifflyn's Kendel novels carried a series of blurbs on the opening pages. A *Boston Globe* reviewer had written: *Grabs you by the collar and doesn't let go.* Wrentmore had lined through this and replaced it with: *Punches you in the face and throws you off a moving train.*

There were similar comments in other books. Loogan sampled more of them, but stopped when he realized he was procrastinating. He had gotten what he came for—a sense of Sean Wrentmore. He wasn't likely to learn much more by snooping through the man's books.

He took a last look around and then went out through the front door, the way he had come, into the cool gray of an October afternoon. He turned the key to secure the dead bolt, stripped off the plastic gloves he had been wearing so as not to leave his prints behind. He spotted movement on the sidewalk, a woman coming toward him—young, African-American, wearing what looked like nursing scrubs. She had a purse slung over her shoulder; she might have just come home from work.

Loogan slipped the gloves in the pocket of his jacket, hoped she wouldn't notice. He smiled sheepishly and waved.

She halted a few feet from him, looking uncertain. "Are you a friend of Sean's?"

"I'm his cousin," said Loogan. "Ted Carmady."

"Delia Ross." She nodded a greeting and closed the distance between them. "I live next door."

"I came up from Dayton on business," Loogan said, "and stopped for a visit. But Sean's not home." Wrentmore's bio note in *Gray Streets* said he had grown up in Dayton.

"I haven't seen him for a while," said Delia Ross. "I kind of wonder where he's gone to."

"We haven't heard from him in the last month or so," Loogan said. "Not so long, really, but his mother worries. Otherwise I wouldn't have gone in." She had seen him come out, Loogan thought. No sense denying it.

"Lucky you had a key," she said.

He held it up for her. "Sean keeps a spare outside, hidden under a rock." With a wink, he added, "I probably shouldn't tell."

That elicited a tentative smile. "His secret's safe," she said.

"Do you know Sean well?" he asked her.

"I wonder if anybody does," she said.

"He was always a loner, growing up. Still lives alone, from the look of things in there," Loogan added, nodding toward the door. "Keeps the place neat, though. I wonder if he has a cleaning service come in."

"I've never seen anyone," she said. "I think he's kind of a neatnik."

Loogan put some mischief into his voice. "Any girlfriends? I wouldn't ask, but it's the first thing his mother'll want to know when I see her."

"I couldn't say for sure. But none that I've seen."

"He's still writing, I suppose."

"Yes. That I can vouch for."

"I've read some of his stories," Loogan said. "They're pretty wild. Violent. But I guess that's what people want to read."

"Do you know about his novel?"

A short pause. "I know he talked about writing one. Is it finished?"

"Yes. He's still polishing it. But he let me read it."

Loogan smiled. "He must like you."

"I had to ask him three or four times before he let me see it," she said. "He's shy. I don't know what he'd do if it ever got published. If it was a success. I don't know how he'd manage being famous."

"Is it any good?" Loogan asked. "What's it about?"

"It's wonderful, but it's hard to describe," she said. "The main character is an artist. He's dropped out of school and he's back in the town where he grew up. He falls in love with a woman who writes children's books. But there's also a pickpocket, and the pickpocket is mixed up with a corrupt cop. The cop is blackmailing him—threatening to expose a crime he committed. Only he didn't really commit it—you find that out in the end."

She closed her eyes briefly, recalling. "Anyway, the artist and the pickpocket become friends, and together they steal the children's writer's manuscript so the artist can illustrate it. I know it sounds ridiculous, but in the book it makes sense. There's also a lot of other stuff. The artist's father has just died, and you find out he was an alcoholic, and there are all these scenes that flash back to the artist's childhood and when he was a teenager. And there's a sweet love story, about the artist and his high school crush, and they never quite get together."

"It sounds complicated," Loogan said.

"It is. The manuscript is twelve hundred pages long."

"Wow."

"And there's some violence in it, but you wouldn't call it a crime novel. I don't know how you'd categorize it. I think that's part of the problem. Sean showed me a rejection letter from an agent. She said she loved the writing, but she wouldn't know how to sell it."

"Even so, it sounds like an intriguing book," Loogan said. "What's the title?"

"*Liars* and something," said Delia Ross. "Let me think. . . . *Liars, Thieves, and Innocent Men.*"

"I'd like to read it. Do you still have the manuscript?"

"I've got it on disc." She hesitated. "The thing is, Sean made me promise not to let anyone else see it. I wouldn't feel right about giving it to you without his permission."

"I can understand that. I wouldn't want you to do anything you're not comfortable with." Loogan glanced at his watch. "Well, I guess I'll come back another time. Be nice if I knew where to look for him. Do you know if he's working these days? At a day job, I mean. He must do something to support his writing habit."

"He told me he sells things on the Internet," she said. "Used books, stuff like that. Must do all right with it. I always suspected he was living on a trust fund or something—that his family was secretly wealthy."

"Not us," Loogan said. Though for all he knew it might have been true.

She went quiet and took a step back as if she would leave, then turned her head to stare at the door of Sean Wrentmore's condo.

Loogan said, "Is something on your mind?"

"I don't know," she said slowly. "It's just—well, Sean is kind of an odd character. I guess I don't have to tell you that."

"I guess not."

"You say you haven't heard from him in a month," she said, "and I think it's been almost that long since I've seen him. Do you think he's traveling?"

"I don't know."

"If he's on vacation, he forgot to stop delivery on his mail. His box filled up and the other day I emptied it out. I've got quite a pile of it on my dining-room table."

"It's nice of you to keep it for him."

"I don't want to overreact, but . . . you don't think something happened to him, do you?"

Loogan raised his eyebrows. "Well, I wouldn't want to overreact either."

"I don't want to be paranoid. On the other hand—I don't know if you've noticed this about him, but Sean is kind of a paranoid man."

"Yeah?"

"Only I'm not sure what he's paranoid about." She brought her purse off her shoulder, reached into it, and took out a ring of keys. She held one of them up.

"Would you care to guess what this opens?"

Loogan smiled and shrugged. "What?"

"I'm pretty sure it's for a padlock," she said. "Sean gave it to me a few months ago, after we had become friendly. He gave me the number of a storage unit too, and the address—one of those self-storage places you see along the highway. He said if anything ever happened to him, I should go there and have a look, and I'd know what to do."

"That's . . . cryptic," Loogan said. "You didn't ask him to explain?"

"Of course I did. He wouldn't. Like I said, he's a character."

"You were never tempted to go and see what was there?"

"I was tempted, once or twice," she said. "It didn't seem right. It's silly, but I thought that somehow he'd know, and he'd take it as a betrayal. Then other times I thought, Maybe there is no storage unit. Maybe it's his idea of a joke."

Loogan tilted his head. "There's only one way to find out."

Delia Ross looked doubtful. "Do you think we should?"

"I don't see what harm it could do."

She drove her own car and Loogan followed. They got onto the interstate but got off again after only three or four miles. They drove past a lumberyard and a printing plant, and there was the storage place, surrounded by a chain-link fence. The gate stood open. The buildings were long blocks of concrete with gravel lanes running in between.

The key fit the padlock on unit 401. Delia Ross stood back and let Loogan raise the door. Two feet up and it stuck in the track, and he lowered it and hauled it up again, and when it finally ran up all the way there was a moment absolutely bereft of drama.

"You know, I half expected to find a body," Delia said.

There was an old china cabinet with broken glass in the door. Several wooden straight-back chairs. A number of cardboard boxes labeled BOOKS.

The boxes were closest to the door. Loogan opened one of them and found that "books" was a euphemism. There were girlie magazines inside: copies of *Playboy* and *Penthouse*, five years out of date. Delia stood looking over his shoulder but made no comment. He tried another box and was rewarded with actual books. Philosophy textbooks—*Introduction to Ethics; A Theory of Justice.*

"Those are mine," she said. "I gave them to Sean a while back, thinking he might be able to sell them. I guess he didn't."

"You were a philosophy student?" Loogan said.

"Still am," she said. "Medical ethics. I defend my dissertation next month, and then with any luck I'll get a teaching job. And then it's good-bye nursing."

Loogan looked in each of the boxes, hauling them out onto the gravel in order to get at the ones farther in. There was another box of magazines, but the rest were books, and uninteresting books at that. Textbooks and paperback novels and book club editions. Hardly worth storing.

"Well, I'm here," Delia said, as Loogan moved the last of the boxes back inside. "And I've had a look around. But I haven't a clue about what to do."

"Maybe it was a joke all along. I could believe that."

"I could believe it too," she said. "But did you notice the space over here?"

Loogan had noticed it. In the front of the unit, on the far right, there was an empty space on the floor about two feet square.

"What do you make of it?" he said.

"Looks like there was something here once. Another box, probably." She squatted down. "You can almost see an outline in the dust."

She stood up again. "Maybe there *was* something here—the thing I was supposed to come here and see. Maybe Sean took it away."

It was possible, Loogan thought. Or maybe someone else took it away.

"Well, if he did," Loogan said, "he'll have some explaining to do next time I talk to him. That is, unless you'd rather I didn't mention this to him. Coming here, I mean."

She laughed. "No, I guess you can tell him. I think I'm going to ask him myself. Find out what he had in mind." Her expression grew serious. "He'll turn up, right? He's just gone off somewhere. You don't think anything happened to him."

"He'll turn up eventually," Loogan said. "I'm sure of it."

Chapter 18

ON SATURDAY EVENING THE LOCAL NEWS HAD A THIRTY-SECOND UPDATE on the apparent suicide of Adrian Tully. There was footage of the empty cornfield and the narrow lane where Tully's car had been found. Footage of Tully's parents in their son's apartment—Tully's father expressing the family's grief, his mother holding up a framed portrait of her son.

David Loogan watched it on a small TV in the kitchen of his rented house. He already knew about Tully's death. He had gone to visit Laura Kristoll that morning, to tell her he would accept the job as editor of *Gray Streets* and to ask her for keys to Tom's office. While he was with her she received a call from Tully's parents, who asked her to pass the news along to their son's friends. She hung up the phone and sank into a chair and was dull-eyed and quiet for a long time. Eventually Loogan got the bare details from her: Adrian had shot himself sometime during the night. She would rather not talk about it. Did he mind terribly? She thought she would like to lie down.

He let himself out of the house and drove to a hardware store and had duplicates made of the keys. Then he drove to Saline, to the trailer park where Michael Beccanti's girlfriend lived. Beccanti wasn't there and his girlfriend, Karen, regarded Loogan darkly. But she let him leave the duplicate keys and he went on from there to Sean Wrentmore's condo.

The local news ended at seven o'clock and Loogan switched off the TV and cleared away the remnants of his dinner—takeout Chinese. He spent some time scrubbing dishes, and then built a fire in the fireplace and settled in with a copy of *Gray Streets*. He was reading one of Sean Wrentmore's stories, about a trio of bank robbers who botch their getaway and hole up in

a convenience store with an exotically beautiful Latina clerk and four cus-
tomers as hostages. The police surround the store and there's a standoff—

Loogan heard a knock on his door. He put down the magazine, padded
through the kitchen, turned on the porch light. Michael Beccanti grinned at
him through the small square of glass in the door.

He worked the locks and let Beccanti in.

"Are you on your way to the office?" Loogan said.

"I've already been there," said Beccanti.

"How did it go?"

Beccanti shrugged off his overcoat. Underneath he looked academic:
slacks, dress shirt, houndstooth jacket. He said, "David, your manners. I've
spent hours ransacking an office for you. You could at least invite me to sit."

Loogan drew out a chair for him at the table. He brought him a beer in a
longneck bottle and microwaved the leftover Chinese food.

When half the beer and most of the lo mein noodles were gone, Beccanti
said, "No one's called here then?"

"No," said Loogan. "What do you mean?"

"I had some minor trouble at the office," Beccanti said, and when Loogan
made a sour face, he added: "No need to panic. I didn't expect to see anyone there on a Saturday, but the secretary came in to use the photocopier."

"Maybe you should have gone in later," Loogan said. "That's what I expected you to do."

"Going later would have carried its own risks. If I had the lights on at
two in the morning, someone might have wondered why—especially in *that*
building, given what happened to Tom. I would've had a harder time explaining my presence there. As it was, I stuck close to the truth. I didn't
have much choice, since I'd been to the office before and I had to assume
the secretary might recognize me. I gave her my real name and told her I
was doing some work for you—reading manuscripts."

"The interns usually do that."

"Well, you're in charge now, and you have your own way of doing things,"

Beccanti said. "I didn't let on that I had keys. I told her you'd been there earlier to let me in. I could tell she wasn't convinced. I advised her to call you if she had questions—that's why I asked if anyone had called. I told her I was finished for the night anyway and got out of there. I think she was relieved."

Beccanti paused, turning the beer bottle in a slow circle on the table. "I didn't take anything out with me," he said. "There was nothing to take. If Tom had any more secret hiding places in his office, it's beyond me to find them. I checked everywhere I could think of, riffled the pages of every book on his shelves. Nothing."

Beccanti took a drink and put the bottle down. "You wanted me to look for some connection to Sean Wrentmore, and I went in there with the half-baked idea that I might find he'd been erased—deleted from the files of *Gray Streets*. But there's a folder on him, just like all the other authors. Manuscripts for each of the stories he wrote for the magazine, some routine correspondence. I didn't bring it. You can go in and read it for yourself. I don't think it'll do any good."

"I wouldn't expect the entire file to be gone," Loogan said. "But if something had been removed from the file, we'd really have no way of knowing."

"True enough," Beccanti said. "In any case, Wrentmore's still on the Web site too. I checked it on Tom's computer while I was there. His stories are still up, and his biography. There's no picture, but there might never have been one."

"I don't need a picture," Loogan said. "I found one in his desk. It was a match. Sean Wrentmore was the man Tom and I buried." He filled Beccanti in on the time he had spent at Wrentmore's condo, his conversation with Wrentmore's neighbor Delia Ross. The twelve-hundred-page novel Delia had described—*Liars, Thieves, and Innocent Men*. Their trip to Wrentmore's storage unit, and the mysterious empty space where a box might have been.

"What do you think was in the box?" Beccanti asked.

"Who knows?" Loogan paced between the table and the kitchen counter. "Maybe it was just a copy of Wrentmore's novel, and he wanted Delia Ross to try to get it published if something happened to him."

"You said she read it. Doesn't that mean she already had a copy?"

"He gave it to her on disc. But he couldn't be sure she'd hold on to it. If he wanted her to get it published, he'd want to make sure she had a printed copy."

Beccanti shook his head as if to clear it. "But whatever it was in the box, we're assuming that after Wrentmore was killed, someone went to that storage unit and took it away. Right?"

"Right."

"So who was it? Who knew about the storage unit?"

"Wrentmore himself, and his neighbor. And we don't know who else."

"You're avoiding the obvious, David. You don't want to think ill of the dead. Tom could have gone there. He searched Wrentmore's condo, and then had me search it again for good measure. Maybe something he found in the condo led him to the storage unit. Whatever was in the mystery box, he might have taken it. Just like he took Wrentmore's computer from the condo—and whatever else he took."

Loogan leaned against the counter. "I can think of one other thing Tom must have taken—Wrentmore's manuscript. If you've written a novel, you're going to print at least one copy, and probably more than one. Maybe there was a copy in the storage unit and maybe not. But I'd wager anything that Wrentmore kept a copy at home."

Beccanti slid the beer bottle over the surface of the table. "Do you suppose the manuscript is the MacGuffin?"

"What?"

"The MacGuffin," Beccanti said. "It's Alfred Hitchcock's term. It's the thing that spurs the plot and forces Cary Grant to go on the run—but no one really cares about it, once the story's moving. At first I thought the flashdrive I found was the MacGuffin, but they're probably the same thing.

Wrentmore's novel is probably what's on the flashdrive. Have you had any luck guessing the password?"

Loogan had been carrying the drive with him. He put his hand in his pocket to reassure himself it was still there. "I haven't even tried," he said.

A scowl passed over Beccanti's face. "I don't like the idea that Tom might've been killed because of an oversized novel that no one would even want to publish. What's our next move?"

Loogan shook his head. "I don't know if we have one."

"I'm not going to quit."

"We should think about the risk. You almost got caught tonight. Strike that: You did get caught. Even if there were no consequences this time. And then there's what happened to Adrian Tully."

Beccanti obviously hadn't heard. "Who?" he said.

Loogan summarized what he'd learned from Laura and the local news. As an afterthought he added, "The news report didn't draw a connection between Tully and Tom, but Tully was once an intern at the magazine."

"You don't think he shot himself," Beccanti said.

"I could buy it, but I'd need convincing."

"I'd need convincing too. I'd like to have a look at his car."

"The police have his car."

"And his house. Did he live in a house? No, he was a student. He probably had an apartment."

"You're not going to break into his apartment."

Beccanti got up from the table. "I didn't say I was going to, I said I'd like to. Imagine finding a copy of Wrentmore's manuscript in the trunk of Tully's car, or under his bed. It would make things interesting."

He finished off the beer and brought the bottle and his plate to the sink. "I'm not going to break into Tully's apartment," he said. "I think I'd have better luck with the Kristoll house. We need to know what Tom was up to. If he took the mystery box from Wrentmore's storage unit, maybe it's there in the house. It's time I had a look around in there."

Loogan frowned. "That's a bad idea. It's not like the office. If you get caught breaking into Tom's house, I won't be able to cover for you."

"You worry too much, David. I won't get caught. You're going to help me."

"I can't get you into Tom's house. I don't have a key."

"I don't need you to get me in," Beccanti said. "I need you to make sure Laura Kristoll is out."

Chapter 19

Nathan Hideaway's home was more modest than Elizabeth had expected: a single-story cottage with a garden and a duck pond and a detached garage. Hideaway's crown of white hair was damp when he met Elizabeth at the door on Sunday afternoon. He had just come from his health club, he said. He went every day to swim laps, and today he had worked in a game of tennis with the club's pro.

He deposited Elizabeth in a living room lined with tall bookshelves, disappeared for a minute, and returned with two glasses of lemonade.

He handed one to Elizabeth. "I shouldn't say this," he told her, "but I'm glad to see you."

"Is that right?" she said.

"I heard you've been making the rounds. Talking to writers. If you had waited much longer, I might have had my feelings hurt."

He waved Elizabeth to a seat on a curved sofa and dropped into an armchair across from her. "Bridget Shellcross," he said. "And then Cass Hifflyn. And now you've got around to interviewing old Hideaway. I guess it's only right. If you go strictly by the calendar, I've got twenty years on them, but they've both been in the business longer than I have. I never wrote a word of fiction until I was forty-eight years old."

"Really?" Elizabeth said. "What did you do before?"

He drank some lemonade, lowered the glass to the floor. "I was an insurance adjuster," he said. "If the wind knocked a tree over and it crashed through your roof, I'd come out and tell you what it was worth. On my forty-eighth birthday, my wife gave me a book—a novel about a crew of shady characters who worked together to defraud insurance companies. It was a half-assed thriller. Unrealistic. I thought I could do better. I wrote some opening chapters, just goofing around, then my wife found the manuscript and wouldn't stop pestering me until I finished it. Well, I saw it through to the end, but when I got there what I had was about forty thousand words—too long for a story, too short for a novel. I sent it to some magazines and they sent it right back, and then Tom Kristoll published it in *Gray Streets*.

"A literary agent read it, a bright young thing just out of college. She called me one day and asked what I was working on. I described an idea I had for a novel, and she said she'd like to see it when it was ready. A month later I sent her sixty pages and an outline of the rest. I didn't dare wait any longer. I was afraid she'd forget about me. Somehow she got me a contract based on those sixty pages. That was my first novel, *The Longest Night in June*.

"I've still got the same agent. We didn't meet in person until I delivered the final manuscript of that first book. I think she was surprised. She thought she was dealing with someone close to her own age—not with someone's grandfather, which I was by then. My wife and I had raised two girls, in a split-level house in Huntington, Long Island. The oldest had a three-year-old and another on the way. I had a grandfather's name then too: Nate Henderson."

Elizabeth traced a finger through the condensation on her glass. She said, "Hideaway is a pseudonym then."

"It would have to be, wouldn't it? I'm surprised Cass Hifflyn didn't tell you. He was already established when I was just getting started, and he swears I picked 'Hideaway' so my novels would be shelved next to his in the bookstores." Hideaway grinned. "It's not a bad story, but the truth is more mundane. I opened the dictionary to a page in the H's and scanned down until I came to 'hideaway.' I liked the sound of it."

"How did you end up in Ann Arbor?" Elizabeth asked him.

The grin left him and his mouth went slack. Suddenly he looked very old. "My wife passed on six years ago," he said. "Cancer."

"I'm sorry."

"Bad business," he said heavily. "After that, I was alone in our house. My daughters had both moved to the West Coast. It was just as well. I didn't want to see anybody. Couldn't work. Tom Kristoll got wind of it, and he and Laura arranged a fellowship for me at the university here. Six months to write, an office in the English department, surrounded by students. I almost refused, but it turned out to be just what I needed. When the six months were up, I decided to stay."

"You weren't tempted to move out west," Elizabeth said, "to be closer to your daughters?"

"I was, but I resisted the temptation. Do you have children?"

"I have a daughter."

"She must be young."

"Fifteen."

Hideaway nodded. "Just the age when a girl needs her mother. When they get older, they want some distance. I can fly out to see my girls whenever I like, and I'm always welcome. My grandchildren are always thrilled to see me. It wouldn't be the same if they saw me every day. Here I can be alone when I need to, and I have company when I want it."

"The students must like having you around," Elizabeth said. "A published novelist is a curiosity—that's what Cass Hifflyn told me. They must like spending time with you."

"Some of them do."

"What about Adrian Tully?"

Hideaway leaned forward in his chair. "Now you've managed to steer me around to the point," he said. "Adrian was friendly. A little intense, I would say."

"Cass Hifflyn thought he was meek."

"I don't know about that. Adrian was intelligent, thoughtful." His eyes locked on Elizabeth's. "You believe he was attracted to Laura Kristoll."

"Someone's been gossiping."

"There's never any shortage of that. I think it's true. I think he was in love with Laura."

Elizabeth put her glass aside. "Did he tell you that?"

"Not directly," Hideaway said. "But he spoke about her sometimes—usually about some insight she'd had that had helped him with his work. She was his adviser, of course. There was always a reverence in his voice when he spoke about her. And he would watch her at gatherings, social events. He was careful not to stare, but you got the sense that he always kept track of where she was."

"Sounds like he wasn't careful enough."

"Others might not have noticed," Hideaway said. "I like to observe people. In Adrian's case, you could almost predict he would fall in love with his adviser. He was just that kind of man. He would fall for any beautiful woman he came in close contact with. He fell for that redhead, the one with the Botticelli face."

"Valerie Calnero?"

"Valerie, yes. Some men are like that. And I'm not talking about a superficial attraction. I believe Adrian felt things deeply."

"So if he was in love with Laura Kristoll and he found out she was having an affair with someone else, he would have been jealous."

"Certainly."

"Do you think he might have gone to Tom Kristoll, to tell him about the affair?" Elizabeth asked. "And if Tom didn't believe him, would that have made him angry?"

"I'd be speculating, but I'd say that's possible."

"Do you think Adrian killed Tom?"

"I wouldn't want to go that far. Speculation has its limits."

"But you think it's plausible, as a hypothesis."

Hideaway shrugged. "As a hypothesis."

"And Adrian felt things deeply. So if he killed Tom, it would weigh on him. He would feel guilty."

"Of course."

"Would he feel guilty enough to shoot himself?"

"We've come up against the limits again," said Hideaway. "I understand you have doubts about whether Adrian shot himself."

"There are some things that don't fit."

He made a steeple of his fingers. "I'm curious about the gun. I wouldn't have thought Adrian owned a gun."

"Is that right?"

"We never discussed the subject. But if you had asked me if he was the sort of man to keep a gun, I would have said no."

"The gun was registered to a man in Dearborn," Elizabeth said. "We haven't located him yet. He moved out of state two years ago. His ex-wife says he used to go to gun shows. I have a feeling it'll turn out he sold the gun to somebody in a parking lot somewhere. Sold it for cash, and didn't take down any names. The ex-wife never heard of Adrian Tully."

She waved a hand dismissively. "Tully's parents said he never expressed much interest in guns, though he knew how to use a rifle. His father is a hunter."

"So much for my instincts," Hideaway said. "I wouldn't have imagined Adrian handling a rifle either. Perhaps the simplest explanation is the right one after all—Adrian killed Tom and then killed himself. If not, then someone has gone to an awful lot of trouble."

Hideaway rose from his chair and walked over to a bookcase. "That should make your job easier," he said. "The easiest murder to solve is supposed to be the one somebody tried to get very cute with. The hardest is the one somebody thought of two minutes before he did it. That's something Raymond Chandler said—another old-timer who got a late start as a writer."

"Tom's murder doesn't fit into any easy category," Elizabeth said. She got up and joined Hideaway by the bookcase. "Whoever killed Tom may have decided to do it on the spur of the moment. But once he did it, he tried to get very cute with it. He started by knocking Tom out. A hard blow to the back of the head. We think he used a book. At that point, if he just wanted to finish Tom off, there were simple ways to do it: Smother him or strangle him. Hit him again with the book. But our killer hauls him over to the window, tries to make it look like he jumped. Then it gets even cuter. If it's a suicide, there should be a note. Did you know we found a note?"

"This is the first I've heard of it," said Hideaway.

"We've kept it from the public. I don't think even Laura Kristoll knows. Suppose you were in Tom's office and you needed to fake a suicide note. Fast. How would you do it?"

He rubbed his jaw thoughtfully. "You'd probably type it," he said. "You could open a file on Tom's computer and peck something out. Use the end of a pencil on the keys, not your fingers. Keep it short, keep it general. You wouldn't need to print it, just leave it on the screen."

"That's one way to do it, but not if you wanted to be cute," Elizabeth said. "If you wanted to be cute, you'd leave a book open on the desk. Say, Shakespeare's *Collected Works*. You'd mark a particular line. Would you care to guess which one?"

"Lines from Shakespeare—that's a big field," said Hideaway.

"Remember, it has to suggest suicide."

"Maybe something from the end of *Romeo and Juliet*?"

"Try *Hamlet*."

"Let's see. Ophelia drowned herself, but I don't think she left a note."

"No," said Elizabeth. "The line the killer chose was from the last scene, when Hamlet is dying and Horatio wants to die with him. 'I am more an antique Roman than a Dane.' It's what Horatio says when he reaches for the poisoned cup."

Hideaway let out a long breath. "Cute. Now I see why you've been talking to writers."

"Do you?"

"Whoever killed Tom must have given some thought to the suicide note beforehand."

"Yes," Elizabeth said.

"Suppose he didn't go there with the intention of killing Tom. That means he would have had to improvise quickly. So he was drawing on something he had already thought about."

"Yes."

"He must have come across that line in *Hamlet*—'I am more an antique

Roman'—and he must have thought, *That would make a good suicide note.* Then he finds himself in Tom's office. Tom is on the floor unconscious, or he's already out the window. The killer is in a hurry. Now is not the time to cast around for ideas. He already has the idea. And there's the book. He opens it to the right page, leaves it on the desk, and gets out of there."

Nathan Hideaway turned to face Elizabeth. "So even if he didn't plan the crime in advance, he must have thought about the scenario in advance. He must have thought about suicides and suicide notes. At the very least, that makes him someone with an active imagination. Odds are, it makes him a writer."

Chapter 20

CARTER SHAN SPENT HIS WEEKEND TALKING TO NIGHT OWLS AND insomniacs.

At midday on Saturday, he spoke to a tractor salesman who lived in a refurbished farmhouse about a mile from the narrow lane where Adrian Tully had died. The salesman had been up playing solitaire in the small hours of Saturday morning. At quarter to one he had heard what sounded like a rifle shot. Though the surrounding woods and fields were posted against hunting, he was used to hearing the occasional rifle shot, though not usually at one in the morning. The first shot, he said, had been followed by a second shot a few minutes later.

On Saturday afternoon, Shan spoke to a retired seamstress who had been up tending to a sick cat. She lived three-quarters of a mile from the site of Tully's death. She was certain there had been no gunshots.

On Saturday evening, Shan spoke to a paramedic who had returned home from his shift after midnight. He'd had time to fix a sandwich and carry it into the living room before he heard the shot. He swore there had been only one.

Early Sunday afternoon, Shan spoke to a teenage girl, an amateur photographer, who had stayed up late on Friday night to take pictures of the moon. She had kept a pad and pen with her to record f-stops and exposure times. She had written down the time of the first gunshot: 12:41 A.M. The second, she noted, had come at 12:44. The third, at 12:50. The fourth, at 12:53.

On Sunday evening, a group of detectives met at City Hall in the office of Chief Owen McCaleb. Shan was among them, and Elizabeth too, fresh from her visit with Nathan Hideaway.

McCaleb perched on the corner of his desk. The others arranged themselves in a rough semicircle. Shan summarized his findings first, and came in for some gentle ribbing from his colleagues.

"You should have stopped after the first witness, Carter," said Harvey Mitchum, a jovial black man who had twenty years with the department. "Two shots fired. That's the answer we wanted. The rest of them just confuse things."

Mitchum made his report next. He and Ron Wintergreen had organized the search of the scene of Adrian Tully's death. Tully's car had been removed from the road, but its position had been carefully marked. Mitchum and Wintergreen had blocked out a search area that extended over the fields on either side of the road and into the woods beyond.

A team of patrolmen and academy cadets, equipped with metal detectors borrowed from the university's archaeology and geology departments, had worked in shifts to cover the area systematically over the course of Sunday afternoon.

"We were looking for two bullets," Mitchum noted. "One that killed Tully and punched a hole through the driver's window. And the other—the hypothetical second bullet—that Tully's killer could have fired in order to get gunshot residue on Tully's hand. Ron found the first bullet early on, in the field on the driver's side."

Ron Wintergreen, a gangly thirty-year-old with pale blond hair, looked uncomfortable at the mention of his name. Leaning against a wall, he gazed down at the laces of his hiking boots.

"Unfortunately," Mitchum added, "we had no luck after that. The second bullet, if there was one, could have gone through the same hole in the driver's window, though it would have been a tricky shot. More likely, the killer rolled down the passenger window and fired it that way. We looked on both sides, but couldn't find it."

Kim Reyes spoke next. One of the youngest detectives in the department, she had been given the task of interviewing Adrian Tully's friends and classmates from the university. They tended to describe Tully as shy and moody, she said. None went so far as to call him depressed or suicidal. And none of them had ever seen a gun in his possession, or heard him talk about owning one.

Reyes had also been assigned to the search of Tully's car. Everything in the vehicle had been catalogued, she reported, down to the soda cans and fast-food wrappers that littered the backseat. Every item that might hold a fingerprint would eventually be dusted.

"I found something interesting under the passenger seat," she said. "It was stuck in one of the tracks that allow the seat to slide forward and back."

Casually, she took a manila envelope from under her arm and drew out a plastic evidence bag. Inside was a small triangle of paper. One of the edges was rough, as if the scrap had been torn from a larger piece.

There were fragments of type on the paper. Elizabeth leaned in for a closer look. She could make out the words OXFORD UNIVERSI—

"It's part of a book jacket," Reyes said. "It set bells off when I found it, because the book on Tom Kristoll's desk was missing a dust jacket. Shakespeare's *Collected Works*. I wanted to compare it, so I stopped into Borders to see if they had a copy."

She drew an intact dust jacket from the envelope. Elizabeth glimpsed the publisher's name on the rear flap: OXFORD UNIVERSITY PRESS.

"Cute," she said, half to herself.

"They're a match," Reyes said.

Owen McCaleb reached for the evidence bag and examined the small triangle within.

"You think it's a plant?" he said to Elizabeth.

She was noncommittal. "I don't suppose there's a print on it."

"It's clean," said Reyes. "No prints."

Carter Shan had retired to a chair by the window, but now he got up. "If it's a plant, then it confirms what we've been thinking anyway. Tom

Kristoll's killer used the book to knock him out, then took the dust jacket because it had his fingerprints on it. Later he decided to kill Tully and frame him for Kristoll's murder. He tore this scrap from the jacket, wiped it clean, and left it in Tully's car."

Elizabeth added, "It's clever, leaving just a scrap. Subtle. The alternative would be to leave the entire jacket, but then you'd have to wipe the whole thing down. And then we'd see that it had been wiped down, and we'd wonder why. The jacket connects Tully to the crime. Why would he go to the trouble of wiping it down and then not get rid of it altogether?

"This way we can imagine Tully fleeing the scene of Kristoll's murder. He shoves the jacket under the seat as he drives away. Later, he stops somewhere and pulls the jacket out again to throw it away or burn it or whatever he's going to do. Part of it is caught in the track under the seat and tears off, but he doesn't notice."

McCaleb drummed his fingers on the edge of his desk. "Why couldn't it have happened that way? Tully kills Kristoll, hides the dust jacket under the car seat. Later he burns it—except for the corner that got torn off. The corner stays under the seat until Tully shoots himself, and then we find it. Why not?"

"There's the witness who heard two shots," Shan said.

"And the witnesses who heard one, or four, or none," said McCaleb.

Kim Reyes broke in. "There's another possibility. Suppose Tully did kill Kristoll and that's how the scrap ended up under his car seat. But then someone—a partner, an accomplice—lured Tully out to the cornfield and shot him to keep him quiet."

Harvey Mitchum chuckled. "Aw, don't say that, Kim. It's complicated enough as it is. I'd hate to have to sort it out for a jury."

Reyes started to reply, but McCaleb interrupted her. "Let's move on," he said. "We still need to hear from Elizabeth."

Elizabeth took a breath and then began to outline her conversations with Bridget Shellcross, Casimir Hifflyn, and Nathan Hideaway. The fingers of her right hand went automatically to the string of beads at her neck as she spoke. When she was through, McCaleb asked for her analysis. Did she think any of the three could have been involved in Kristoll's death—or Tully's?

"Hifflyn and Hideaway are both living alone," she said. "Hideaway's wife died six years ago. Hifflyn says his wife is in Europe, though I haven't confirmed that yet. I intend to. I don't want to find out later that she's buried under the flagstones in the backyard."

Her fingers twisted the beads. "So neither one has an alibi for the night of Kristoll's murder, or the night of Tully's. Bridget Shellcross lives with a woman named Rachel Kent and claims to have been home with her on both nights.

"Shellcross is a small woman, and the image of her lifting a body through a window is comical, but the two of them together could have done it, and I think Rachel could have managed it on her own. Cass Hifflyn claims that Shellcross was once involved with Tom Kristoll. That raises the possibility that Shellcross got back together with Kristoll recently. If she did, and if Rachel found out—well, I can see Rachel helping Kristoll out a window.

"Hifflyn also admits to having been involved with Laura Kristoll in college, and says that Tom Kristoll stole her away from him. That gives him a motive for doing Kristoll in—a twenty-year-old motive. If he killed Kristoll for revenge, it may have been the most deliberate, patient act of revenge in history.

"Hideaway had no motive that I can see. Kristoll was his benefactor. For the record, Hideaway is sixty years old, but he's a vigorous sixty. He keeps in shape. I would say he's capable of lifting a body through a window."

She rolled the beads against her skin. "All three of them—Shellcross, Hifflyn, and Hideaway—knew Adrian Tully. Any of them, I think, could have come up with a story to convince him to drive out to a meeting on a lonely road at night."

———

There was more discussion before the meeting wound down. Owen McCaleb wanted to know if there were others who might have been able to lure Tully out to a lonely road. Laura Kristoll's name was added to the list. She would need to be questioned. Other avenues would need to be pursued: the possibility of a recent affair between Tom Kristoll and Bridget Shellcross, or between Laura Kristoll and Casimir Hifflyn. Inquiries would be made; photographs would be shown to hotel clerks.

It was well after seven when Elizabeth left City Hall. The sky was blue-black and clear and there was a cool wind. As she turned onto her street a shower of rain began to fall. From a distance she saw her house, the porch light on. Sarah was there in the light, and another figure with her, leaning on the railing. Elizabeth thought at first that it was Sarah's friend from school, Billy Rydell, but Billy, though tall, was very thin. He had dark, unruly hair. The man on the porch was broader in the shoulders. Sarah was talking to him animatedly, her arms gesturing. His hair, when he bent forward into the light, was copper-colored. It was David Loogan.

Elizabeth left the car and came up the walk. Now she could see the meaning of Sarah's gestures. Her daughter was juggling. Three oranges traced their arcs through the air. Sarah saw her and waved reflexively and the pattern was lost and the oranges went bouncing over the floor of the porch. One rolled down the steps and Elizabeth caught it at her feet.

Loogan bent to retrieve the others and then turned to flash Elizabeth a smile. "Hello, Detective."

"Hello. What's this?"

"David's a juggler," Sarah said. "He's been teaching me."

"She's a natural," said Loogan.

"I'm learning. It doesn't feel natural yet. It feels like a parlor trick."

"It *is* a parlor trick," said Loogan.

Elizabeth joined them on the porch. "Let's see it again."

Sarah took the oranges once more and arranged them in her hands. She made practice movements as if to remind herself and then let them fly.

She kept the pattern going for five seconds, for ten. Elizabeth saw the moment when she lost control. Loogan saw it too. He snatched an errant orange from the air, and the next thing Elizabeth knew he had all three. He sent them up to brush the ceiling of the porch, then froze suddenly with two in his right hand and one in his left. He offered them back to Sarah.

"That was good," he said.

Elizabeth smiled. "I'm impressed."

Sarah tossed an orange in the air and caught it. "I've invited David to stay for supper."

"You have, have you?"

"I'm afraid I can't stay," Loogan said.

"He doesn't want to impose," said Sarah. "You'll have to work on him."

"I see."

"I'm going in," Sarah said. With the screen door open, she turned back. "What do you think about oranges in the salad?"

Elizabeth considered the question. "I think three may be too many."

"I'll see how one looks."

As the screen door clapped shut, Loogan said in a low voice, "I hope it was all right for me to come here." He seemed deliberately casual. Stubble on his chin, darker than the copper of his hair. Weathered coat, flannel shirt, denim, sturdy hiking boots. But his eyes glinted, his mouth was a long ironic line.

"It's all right," Elizabeth said.

"Your address is in the phone book," he said.

"That's practically an invitation."

"Your daughter is charming."

"Yes."

"You're not going to ask me why I'm here."

Elizabeth leaned her back against a column and listened to the rain falling on the porch roof. "Sometimes I find that if I don't say anything, people will tell me what they want to tell me, all on their own."

"I heard about Adrian Tully," Loogan said. "I wondered what the story was."

"Is that right?"

"I suppose I shouldn't show too much interest. You'll start thinking I'm guilty of something."

Elizabeth put a hand out to feel the rain. "We had a meeting today to consider who might be guilty of killing Adrian Tully. Your name didn't come up."

"That's good."

"It should have. Did you know we were looking at Tully as a suspect in the murder of Tom Kristoll?"

"No," Loogan said. "Is that true?"

"It's true. We believe Tully was the one who vandalized your car. He knew about your affair with Laura Kristoll. It's possible he went to tell Tom and they got into an argument about it. You haven't heard any of this? Laura didn't tell you?"

"No. You're saying she knew?"

"At the very least, she knew Tully was a suspect. I'm surprised she didn't tell you."

"She didn't."

"If she did—if you believed that Tully killed Tom Kristoll—it would have given you a motive. Tom was your friend. You wanted his killer caught. If this were a story in *Gray Streets*, you'd catch him yourself. Isn't that what you told me?"

"It is."

"You've even been playing detective," Elizabeth said. "Have you found Michael Beccanti yet?"

Loogan showed her his palms. "I haven't been looking for him."

"If this were a story in *Gray Streets*," she said, "you might want to do more than catch Tom's killer. You might want to punish him. Have you ever been to a gun show, Mr. Loogan?"

He looked puzzled. "No. Why?"

"Have you ever owned a gun?"

"No."

"I'm sorry to be so abrupt," Elizabeth said. "It's been a long day and sometimes I get tired of dealing with this nonsense. Did you lure Adrian Tully out to a cornfield and blow his brains out?"

Quietly, firmly, he said, "No."

She came close to him under the porch light and studied his face. There was no sign of deception in it. He returned her gaze curiously. Though she didn't study him for long, she had time to think about when she had seen him last: only two days before, at the funeral of Tom Kristoll. She had time to recognize that she was pleased to see him now.

Other thoughts occurred to her, all on their own: David Loogan had an interesting mouth. She could probably convince him to stay for supper.

If he stayed, he would linger for a while afterward. Sarah would go off to do her homework. He would want to help with the cleaning up; it was consistent with the persona, with the flannel and the denim and the broadbacked sturdiness. He would volunteer to wash the dishes. He would stand at the sink and she would stand behind him—she was nearly as tall as he was—and his collar would smell freshly laundered and she would put her hands on his shoulders.

Strange thoughts.

And if he had something to do with Adrian Tully's death, or Tom Kristoll's, she would have to testify against him. She would be cross-examined. She would have to explain why she'd had a murder suspect as a guest in her home. She would have to account for every move.

And did there come a time, Detective Waishkey, when you smelled the defendant's collar?

Under the porch light with David Loogan, she was able to find it amusing. She turned away from him to hide her smile. In reality, it would not be amusing.

She managed to get the screen door open. Loogan stayed where he was.

"I believe you," she said. "About Tully."

He was still regarding her curiously. He didn't answer.

"I should go in," she said. "I hope you won't mind if I don't invite you to stay."

Chapter 21

Ann Arbor has the street life of a much larger city. When the weather is fair, and sometimes when it's not, the sidewalks along State Street and Liberty and Main bustle with people: hip, arty, confident people who walk to theaters and shops, bookstores and coffeehouses, who gather at sidewalk tables that spill out of restaurants.

David Loogan found them fascinating. He thought it must be the university that produced them. The university made the city more prosperous and young and good-looking. It gathered all these people to itself and then it sent them out into the city where they ate fine meals, and attended plays, and greeted one another on the street with hugs and cheery shouts and back-slapping.

On Monday night he watched them from a distance, from the top of a parking garage on Main Street. Laura Kristoll stood beside him. She wore a long, dark green coat and kept it hugged tight around her.

"Ten days," she said.

Loogan looked down along the canyon of the street. At people gathering on corners at an intersection. At the streetlights reflecting off the hoods of passing cars.

"Tom's been gone for ten days now," Laura said. "It seems longer. Does it seem longer to you?"

"Yes," said Loogan.

It had taken some convincing to get Laura out of the house. She had declined his invitation to dinner on Sunday night, saying she was exhausted. He decided to try for Monday. He suggested a jazz bar called the Firefly

Club—it was sure to have live music, even on a Monday night. He would pick her up at seven.

He got to the house early, while she was working on her makeup and her hair. He waited for her downstairs. When they left, she turned her key in the dead bolt of the front door. Loogan wondered if Michael Beccanti could get past a dead bolt. He wouldn't need to; Loogan had unlocked the patio door.

They stopped at a café for a light dinner and then went on to the Firefly. A blues trio on the stage. The crowd was low-key. Loogan brought Laura to a table in the corner farthest from the bar, and she leaned against him and they were quiet in the dark.

Later they walked to the garage where they had left his car. Waiting for the elevator, she put her arms around him and kissed him and started to cry. The car was on the fourth level, but they took the elevator all the way to the top and stood looking out over the concrete wall in the cool night and talking about Tom.

"Do you think he was frightened?" she said.

Loogan knew what she meant. From where they were standing they could see the building that housed *Gray Streets*; they could see the distance from the sixth floor to the sidewalk below.

"No," he said. "I don't think he was aware of anything by then."

She lifted her shoulders, buried her hands in the pockets of her coat. "I don't know what I'm doing, David. I had a class I should have taught today, but I didn't go. The chair of the department is an old friend. He insisted I take at least two weeks off. He wanted me to take the rest of the semester."

"Maybe you should."

"What's the point?" she said. "I'd rather be doing something. It's just me in the house, and every minute I spend there reminds me of Tom—"

The words seemed to catch in her throat. She bowed her head and looked away and Loogan watched her. He thought she would cry; she didn't cry. She stood quiet and small and Loogan would have liked to comfort her, but he felt like a heel. He had lured her from her home and Michael

Beccanti was there now, rummaging through her possessions. He and Beccanti had worked out a plan—a plan with a secret signal, with cloak-and-dagger nonsense. Loogan had a cell phone in his pocket; he had bought it earlier that day. He would keep Laura out as long as he could, and before he took her home he would dial Beccanti's cell phone number and let it ring twice. He would need to be out of Laura's sight to place the call, but he had worked that out too; he had made sure the gas in his car was low, so he had an excuse to stop at a filling station. He would be able to dial the number when he went inside to pay.

He stood looking down at the street with his hands in the pockets of his black leather coat. He breathed the cool air. His right hand closed around a folded paper in his pocket. That was part of the plan too. He hadn't mentioned it to Beccanti; it was a small touch of his own. He thought he should question Laura as long as he had her to himself. Two birds with one stone. The paper was a prop, a way of broaching the subject.

He crumpled the paper in his pocket. The plan was ridiculous. He should take Laura home now and forget all about it. Call Beccanti and warn him and then have nothing to do with him again. He watched a green light turn to amber down on the street below. He felt Laura beside him, her hand slipping into his pocket, her palm warm against the back of his hand.

She looked up at him, her face close to his own. Her fingers touched the paper. "What's this?" she said.

"Nothing," he said.

"It's something."

"We should go," he said. "We've been up here too long."

"You've gotten very serious, David. What are you afraid of?"

Without hesitating he said, "Parking garages."

"Really?"

"They're dangerous. Forty percent of all violent crimes take place on the top levels of parking garages."

She smiled and looked over her shoulder. "There's no one here but us."

"That's the way it starts," he said. "You think you're safe and you drop your guard, and when you're not paying attention someone sneaks up on you."

Her fingers gripped the paper in his pocket. "I'll protect you, David. I won't let anyone sneak up on you."

He watched the upturned corners of her mouth. She tugged at the paper and he slowly relinquished it. With her eyes locked on his, she brought it out and opened it and smoothed it against the top of the concrete wall.

Finally she looked down. "What is this?"

He shrugged. "Just some notes I made, a few weeks ago."

She read the first sentence aloud: " 'Someone Tom Kristoll identifies as Michael Beccanti was killed on the night of October seventh in the study of Tom's house on the Huron River.' Well, that's a promising beginning. You've got my attention, right out of the block."

Loogan leaned against the wall. "I can improve on it," he said. "It wasn't Michael Beccanti who died. It was Sean Wrentmore."

"Ah," she said. "Well, let's go on. 'The dead man had a pistol strapped to his ankle—why?' That's a good question. 'He had traces of blood and skin under his nails, indicating a struggle with his killer.' A valid inference."

She brushed a strand of hair away from her eyes. " 'Most likely he would have scratched his killer on the face, neck, arms, or hands. Tom has no scratches in any of these places. . . . Laura Kristoll has no scratches anywhere on her body.' Well, that's good detective work, isn't it? Remind me to question your motives the next time you ask me to strip naked in my office."

Loogan watched her read through the rest silently. He focused on the last line he had written: *I know next to nothing about Tom and Laura Kristoll.*

"David," she said. "You could have asked me about this before. I would have told you." She passed the paper back to him. "Do you want me to tell you now?"

"You don't have to," he said.

"Let's go back to the car," she said. "It's getting cold up here. And it's dangerous."

———

"Sean Wrentmore wrote a novel," Laura said.

The parking spaces on either side of them were empty. Loogan had the engine running and had switched on the heat.

He said, *"Liars, Thieves, and Innocent Men."*

"That's right," said Laura. "Did Tom tell you that?"

"Not Tom. I have my sources."

"It was somewhere in the neighborhood of three hundred fifty thousand words," she said. "That made it three or four times longer than it should have been. Sean sent it to some agents. They praised the quality of the writing. But they told him what he should have known already—no one was going to publish it. A first novel, by an unknown writer? At that length? It wasn't going to happen.

"Sean gave Tom a copy of the manuscript. Tom liked it. That was early this year, before we met you. I read it too; it was a good book. But Tom didn't let it go. I think he was smitten with it. He thought he could find a way to fix it. Do you know what it's about?"

Loogan gave a vague nod. "Roughly. I've heard a summary."

"Then you have an idea of how complicated it was," Laura said. "There were too many characters, multiple story lines, long flashbacks. It was a love story. And a mystery novel. And a coming-of-age story."

She stared out through the windshield, though there was nothing to see but a bare concrete wall. "Tom worked on the manuscript for months. Editing it, reshaping it. By the first week of October, he had pared it down to a hundred thousand words. He was ready to show it to Sean. He hadn't told Sean what he was doing. I think that was his first mistake. By then, Tom was thinking of the book as his own. In a way, it was; he had been laboring over it.

"He wanted to meet with Sean in person, to explain what he had done. So he arranged for Sean to come to our house. He told him only that he had some ideas for cutting the manuscript, for making it publishable. That was his second mistake."

She turned toward Loogan. "I wasn't there when Tom met with Sean. He didn't tell me about it beforehand. He told me everything after. But there was someone else there: Adrian Tully."

Loogan had been sitting with his head back, his eyes closed. Now he opened them. "Why would Tully be there?"

"Adrian was a good copy editor," Laura said. "Working with a manuscript of that size is a huge undertaking. Adrian was Tom's second pair of eyes. If Tom made a cut in one chapter, it would have repercussions for the others. He needed someone to go over what he'd done, to see that it made sense.

"So he had Adrian there, at the meeting with Sean. By then, Adrian knew the manuscript almost as well as Tom did. He could help convince Sean to go along with the cuts Tom had made. Or so Tom thought. That was his third mistake.

"Because Sean didn't like the cuts. Tom had dropped whole story lines; he had eliminated half the characters. It was necessary; there was no other way to get the length down to where it had to be. But Sean didn't like any of it. The very idea that Tom had been editing his manuscript in secret made him furious. And then there was Adrian; he was part of it."

She paused and Loogan thought he could hear her breathing over the hum of the engine. "It might have gone differently if it had been only Tom," she said. "Sean admired Tom, respected him. But Adrian was something else. Here was this graduate student telling Sean how his book should be written. Sean was thirty-two. He had dropped out of college, but he had learned some things. He thought of himself as an accomplished writer, and not without reason. Now this kid was critiquing him.

"It set him off. The fight started when Adrian mentioned that some character or other was inessential to the plot. His tone must have been a little too casual. Sean didn't like it. Adrian had the manuscript on one of those low tables in Tom's study. Sean got fed up and kicked the table over. Then he was out of his chair, and Adrian was on his feet too. The pages were scattered over the floor. Adrian was annoyed. Sean took a swing at him.

"Tom got between them and broke it up. It was a pretty feeble fight, to hear Tom tell it. Slapping and scratching. Tom got them to calm down, and Adrian started picking up the pages, and it seemed like that was the end of it. It wasn't, not for Sean. That's when he went for his gun.

"Sean was the sort of person who liked to go to the shooting range on a Saturday afternoon. I don't think he ever shot anything other than a paper target. Why he had the gun that day, I can only guess. Tom had invited him over to talk about cutting his manuscript. That was a serious matter, from Sean's point of view. He was going into what he thought of as a hostile situation. Maybe he intended to take the gun out at just the right moment, a dramatic gesture to remind Tom that his work was not to be trifled with. 'I'll shoot us both before I'll let you ruin my book.' That sort of thing. Sean was a little odd. I could just about see him doing something like that.

"But I don't know what he intended. What I know is that after his tussle with Adrian he went for the gun. Tom wasn't paying attention. He had scooped up some pages from the floor and had gone to his desk to sort them out. But Adrian saw Sean groping around at his ankle and realized what he was doing. The bottle of Scotch was there at hand. It had gone over with the table. Adrian picked it up from the floor. Sean got the gun free of the holster. I don't know if he meant to shoot or just to show the gun. But Adrian didn't wait to find out. He hit Sean with the bottle. Struck him on the temple. Hit him again after he went down. Before Tom could react, it was over. Sean was dead."

Loogan drove south in the cool night, then west, then aimlessly past rows of tranquil houses. Laura rested her head against the passenger window and Loogan thought she might fall asleep, but after a while she sat up and closed the vent in the dash and unbuttoned her coat.

He thumbed a lever to scale back the heat, switched on the radio, and scanned through some channels before switching it off.

"There are things I need to ask you," he said.

"You sound very solemn, David," she said. "Is that the way it's going to be?"

"There are things I need to understand, so I can figure out what to do."

Loogan steered the car around a corner. The streets were dark with old rain.

"Adrian killed Sean Wrentmore," he said. "Did he kill Tom too?"

Laura fiddled with the hem of her coat. "He said he didn't. He swore he had nothing to do with it. I believed him at the time. But now I think he must have done it."

"Because he shot himself?"

"It makes sense, in retrospect. That detective—Waishkey—she thinks Adrian and Tom might have gotten into an argument. I don't think Adrian would have killed Tom deliberately, but if it were an accident . . ." She let the thought trail off. "And afterward Adrian would have been troubled. He had a conscience. He was in bad shape the night Sean died. Tom said he sat on the floor with his knees up and stared. Couldn't speak. Tom had to send him home."

Loogan knew very well what had happened next. Tom had called him for a favor. Asked him to bring a shovel.

"Do you know where Sean Wrentmore ended up?" Loogan said.

"I know Tom buried the body. I know you helped him."

"What was the point?" he said. "Why not call the police?"

"Tom didn't see any sense in ruining Adrian's life. It was all a mistake. Adrian was defending himself, or thought he was. No one meant for Sean to die."

"That's just it. The police could have been persuaded to see it that way. But Tom covered it up. And even after Tom died, you didn't tell the police about Sean. Why not?"

"I had my reasons, David."

Loogan felt an anger that tightened his chest, roughened his voice. "You're just like your husband. He told me the same thing."

"It's true."

"That's not going to do it. I'm going to need more than that."

Her fingers were still fussing at her coat. He reached over and seized hold of them.

She drew back, startled. He returned his hand to the wheel and slowed and brought the car to a stop along the curb. "You're going to tell me the truth," he said.

"It's not simple, David. It's not easy to explain."

"Take as long as you want. I think I've been patient so far."

Loogan had parked under a burned-out streetlight. The car idled in the dark.

Laura was silent for a time and then said, "Tom wanted to be a writer."

"I know," said Loogan. "He told me once."

"He thought he wasn't good enough."

"He told me that too."

"I think that's wrong," Laura said. "I think things could have gone differently. But he sank too much energy into *Gray Streets*. I don't think he meant to. That wasn't the plan, when we were younger. We both wanted to be writers, but both of us went off track, somewhere."

She reached for the hem of her coat, caught herself, and folded her arms across her middle. "Plans go wrong," she said. "That's something Tom used to say. I remember when we were starting out, when the magazine was first beginning to catch on. A reporter came to interview us. I think he was expecting a typical literary journal, but we were publishing mysteries and crime stories. What was the theme? he wanted to know. If we had to describe a *Gray Streets* story in one sentence, what would it be? Tom had an answer ready, almost as if he had expected the question: 'Plans go wrong, bad things happen, people die.'"

A car passed on the street, tires hissing like static on the pavement. Laura had paused and Loogan was watching her in profile. Her lips pressed tight together, her chin came up. She was a woman trying not to cry.

"Tom had a plan for Sean's manuscript," she said quietly. "He worked on it for a long time, and he wanted it published. The plan didn't go the way he expected, but that wasn't his fault. A bad thing happened to Sean Wrentmore, but when it was done, it was done. There was no reversing it. Whether Tom told the police or not, it couldn't make any difference to Sean. But if Tom told the police, he would have to tell them the whole story."

Head bowed, her hair obscured her face. "I don't know what the legal consequences would have been, or what the newspapers would have made of it," she said. "But I know that Tom wanted the manuscript published—his version of the manuscript. And if he had gone to the police, that would never have happened. Sean wasn't close to his family. I don't think he shared his writing with them. But they would have had to agree, if the book was going to be published. And why would they agree, once they found out how much Sean hated what had been done to his manuscript?

"So Tom didn't go to the police. I don't know if he thought about what it would mean to Sean's family. They would never know what had happened to Sean. As for the manuscript, a handful of people may have read Sean's version, but memories fade. And the edited version was very different. I think Tom would have waited a few years and then published it under his own name, or under a pseudonym."

She brought her palms up to rub the weariness from her eyes. Loogan focused on the delicate lines of her fingers as they passed down along her cheek. "But plans go wrong," she said. "Bad things happen. Tom died, and then it was up to me to decide what to do. Maybe I should have told the police about Sean, maybe I should tell them now. But none of that can make a bit of difference to Tom.

"Tom wanted to be a writer," she said. "The closest he came to what he wanted was when he edited Sean Wrentmore's novel. I've got the manuscript. I'm going to keep it in a trunk in the attic, and in a few years I'm going to discover it—a forgotten work by Tom Kristoll. And one way or another, I'm going to get it published, because that's what he wanted."

Chapter 22

IT WAS NEARLY ELEVEN-THIRTY WHEN LOOGAN DROVE LAURA KRISTOLL home. He stopped for gas along the way and made his call to Michael Beccanti. Cloak-and-dagger.

When they reached the house, Laura invited him in for a drink. She embraced him before he left, and held on to him for a long time. She didn't ask him to stay.

He was back on his street, at his rented house, at around quarter to one. He got out and locked the car. The driver's door gleamed in the streetlight. The graffiti that Adrian Tully had scratched there had been smoothed away and painted over.

He looked up at the porch and there was the X that Beccanti had cut in his window screen. He would have to attend to that.

Inside, he left his coat on a kitchen chair. He ran the tap until the water was cold and drank two glasses. He kicked off his shoes at the foot of the stairs. Got his cell phone out of his pocket: no messages. He could call Beccanti now, he knew the man would be awake, but he didn't feel up to a conversation. Tomorrow would be soon enough.

He went upstairs and brushed his teeth. His eyes in the mirror looked weary. He set the alarm on his night table for nine in the morning, hung up his shirt, folded his pants on the dresser, and crawled into bed.

When he woke, it was from a dream. He and Tom Kristoll were in the woods of Marshall Park. A flashlight tied to a branch shone down into Sean Wrentmore's grave. Tom had cast aside the shovel and from somewhere had produced a thick sheaf of pages. He pressed them on Loogan. *Tell me this isn't brilliant,* he said. The title page was streaked with dirt from Tom's hands. Loogan tried to brush the dirt away and only made it worse.

Suddenly a ragged hole, the size of a dime, appeared in the page. A circle with black edges. Loogan, bewildered, brought the manuscript closer to his face. The hole went straight through; it pierced every page of the manuscript. Through it, Loogan could see the figure of Sean Wrentmore standing in his grave, smoke rising from the barrel of his nickel-plated gun.

Only then did Loogan hear the shot. It startled him awake and he sat up sharply in his bed. He heard his alarm go off, but it was dark outside the window. The clock read 2:09. Then Loogan realized it wasn't the alarm. His cell phone was ringing; he had left it on the night table.

He answered it and heard Michael Beccanti's voice. "David, it's me. Don't panic."

He propped a pillow at his back and leaned against the headboard. "I'm not panicking."

"Were you asleep?" Beccanti said. "I keep forgetting how you sleep."

"I'm awake now."

"Good, because I got in through the window again and I'm coming up the stairs. I'm going to switch on the hall light. Don't let it startle you."

The light came on. Beccanti appeared in the doorway, folding his cell phone and slipping it into his pocket. He wore blue jeans, a loose black dress shirt with the tails out, a heavy black blazer over all.

"Hello, David," he said cheerfully.

Loogan closed his phone and turned on the lamp on his night table. He had a T-shirt on, and his boxers, and the blanket pulled up to his waist. He stayed where he was, determined to be unfazed by Beccanti's sudden appearance.

"Pull up a chair," he said. "Where have you been?"

There was a straight-back chair by the dresser. Beccanti brought it over to the bed, spun it around, and sat with his arms resting on the back.

"I'm sorry to come so late," he said. "I lost track of time. I've been reading."

He brought a CD out of a pocket of his blazer and held it up for Loogan to see. It gleamed gold in the lamplight.

"What is it?" Loogan asked.

"It's what I've been reading. I found it in the closet in Tom and Laura's bedroom. There's a space in the wall, behind a clever little panel. There was five hundred in cash in there, and this. Well, not this exactly. This is a copy. I burned it on the computer in Tom's study. I wonder if you can guess what's on it."

Loogan reached to take the disc. It was unlabeled. He spun it on the end of his finger.

He said, "It's Sean Wrentmore's manuscript. *Liars, Thieves, and Innocent Men.*"

Beccanti grinned. "That's a good guess, but not quite right."

Loogan tapped the edge of the disc against his forehead. "I should have been more specific," he said. "It's an edited version of Wrentmore's manuscript, pared down to something like a hundred thousand words."

Beccanti's grin faded, but he recovered quickly. "How did you know that? You've been holding out on me, David."

Loogan handed the disc back to him. "I just found out about it tonight." Briefly he passed along Laura's account of Tom's work on the manuscript and Sean Wrentmore's death. Beccanti listened silently, his arms resting on the chair-back, his chin resting on his arms.

"Where does that leave us?" he said when Loogan finished.

"I think we're done," Loogan said. "I think we've learned everything we're going to learn."

"We still don't know who killed Tom."

Loogan studied the shadows on the ceiling. "I think Tully may have killed Tom."

"Yeah?"

"I think Tom planned to go to the police," said Loogan. "It didn't sit well with him—covering up Wrentmore's death. He wanted to tell the truth. I think Tully disagreed and they argued and Tom wound up dead."

"And then what? Tully shot himself? You weren't ready to believe that before."

"It could have happened that way."

"We're supposed to believe that Tully didn't mind killing Wrentmore, but killing Tom pushed him over the edge?"

"Why not?"

Beccanti trailed his thumb across his chin. "That would be nice. We wouldn't have to look for Tom's killer anymore. Tully's the killer and Tully's conveniently dead. It makes for a tidy story. I could almost believe it. But the CD isn't the only thing I found in Tom and Laura's house."

He reached again into the pocket of his blazer and drew out a white envelope. "The desk in Tom's study had a drawer with a false bottom," he said, "just like the one in his office at *Gray Streets*. I found this inside."

He tossed the envelope on the bed. Tom's address was on the front, no return address. The top edge had been sliced open. Loogan took out the letter, a single printed page. *Dear Mr. Kristoll,* it began. *I know about Sean Wrentmore.*

There were a few more lines. A demand for fifty thousand dollars in cash, instructions on how to package it and where to send it—to "M. L. Black" at an address in Chicago.

"M. L. Black," Loogan said aloud.

"I know," Beccanti said. "It's cute. I imagine there's no one named Black at that address. It's probably a storefront, one of those mailbox rental places."

Loogan turned the page over, as if there might be something more. He looked at the envelope. It bore a Chicago postmark, dated a week after Sean Wrentmore's death.

"Let me ask you this," Beccanti was saying. "Do you think Laura's telling you everything she knows?"

Loogan waved the letter impatiently. "Let me think for a minute. I'm trying to figure out what this means."

Beccanti laughed softly, bitterly. "I can tell you what it means, David. It means we're not done. We haven't learned everything we're going to learn. We need to plan our next move."

He got up from the chair and held out a hand for the letter and the envelope.

"Why don't you get dressed?" he said. "I'll wait for you downstairs."

The man who called himself David Loogan was frequently on the edge of breaking, but he had learned to cover it well. He didn't like going out at night, but he had gone out to buy a shovel when Tom Kristoll asked him to. He didn't like high places, or parking garages, but he had gone with Laura Kristoll to the top level of a parking garage to talk with her about Tom.

He didn't like open doors, because they made him feel vulnerable, but he didn't like closed doors, because you never knew what might be behind them. He left the door to the bathroom half-open when he went in to wash his face after Michael Beccanti had gone downstairs.

He didn't like bending over the sink to splash water on his face, because it made him feel out of control. He had visions of being struck on the back of the head, his face slamming into the faucet, blood streaming from his nose.

Nevertheless, he looked in the mirror—he was dressed now in the same shirt and pants he had worn earlier—and told himself he was being ridiculous, and he ran the water and felt the cool of it on his face. He endured the sound of it running, even though the sound of running water can drown out other sounds—can cover the approach of an attacker, for instance. Still, he washed, and no one attacked him, though for a second he thought he heard something other than the sound of the water. He thought he heard someone cry out.

He turned off the faucet and reached for a towel and the cry was not repeated. He took the towel into the hall with him, walking slowly, drying his hands and listening, and when he got to the top of the stairs he called Beccanti's name.

There was no answer.

Descending the stairs, he had the towel with him still. It was cool at the bottom of the stairs. The living-room window, the one that looked out on the porch, was open wide. The curtains fluttered. No lights on in the living room, only the diffuse light that came down from the hallway above. In the dim, he could see Beccanti sitting on the sofa. He spoke the man's name again; he could hear him breathing.

Outside on the street, a car engine started. The car drove away.

Loogan turned the switch of the floor lamp. He saw the blood first on the carpet: splotches of it where Beccanti had fallen. He must have dragged himself, pulled himself up onto the sofa. The blood on his shirt was harder to detect; it was a wet sheen on the black fabric. Beccanti's right hand was pressed against his stomach, slick crimson between the fingers. The knife lay beside him on the sofa. Loogan recognized the long blade; it was a knife from the kitchen.

He saw the wound on Beccanti's throat last: a dark line and the blood ran under the collar of his shirt. Loogan had the towel; he rushed forward and pressed it to Beccanti's throat—too hard and Beccanti gasped. He eased the pressure.

The phone was across the room. With his free hand, Loogan dug Beccanti's cell phone from his pocket, dialed 911, and got a dispatcher.

"I need an ambulance," he said. "My father's having a heart attack." The lie came to him easily. His voice held the appropriate note of urgency.

"Please give me your name and location, sir."

"David Loogan," he said, and gave her the address.

She asked him to hold on and he didn't know what to expect—maybe music while he waited—but there was only silence and she was back on the line a moment later.

"EMTs are on their way, sir. Is your father alert?"

"I don't think he's going to be for long. Ask them to hurry, will you?"

She began to say something more and he closed the phone. Beccanti's brow, under his dark, tangled hair, was damp and pale. His eyes were unfocused. His mouth worked but it made no words.

"It's not bad," Loogan said to him. Idiotic. "Sometimes it's not as bad as it looks."

Beccanti's eyes squeezed shut and Loogan swore under his breath, but after a few seconds Beccanti's eyes fluttered open again.

Blood was coming through the towel. Loogan doubled it over. He was bending over Beccanti, one knee on the sofa cushion. He could see the stomach wound, blood trickling over the back of Beccanti's fingers. The stomach wound might be the worst of it, he thought.

He swore again and tucked the ends of the towel behind Beccanti's shoulders. "Back in a second," he said.

His shoes were at the bottom of the stairs. He stepped into them and dashed into the kitchen, turned on the overhead light, the porch light, unbolted the front door and threw it open wide. He grabbed dish towels from a drawer, grabbed his coat, back in the living room, tossed the coat halfway up the stairs. At the sofa again, bowing over Beccanti, he peeled the man's hand away from his stomach, gingerly, and pressed dish towels to the wound. He unclasped Beccanti's belt, tugged it free, threaded it behind the man's back—this brought a gasp—and fastened it tight over the towels.

Light pressure on the neck, pressure on the stomach, Loogan kept watch over Michael Beccanti. Beccanti's eyes had closed, his breathing was shallow as a sleeping child's.

The flashing lights showed up on the wall behind the sofa. Loogan hadn't measured the time, but it hadn't been long. He looked over his shoulder and saw the ambulance through the front window. Lights, no sirens. No police yet, no patrol car. He didn't think they would send a car for a heart attack.

Doors slamming outside. Voices. Loogan said good-bye to Michael Beccanti. Laid his palm on the tangle of dark hair.

He took his coat, careful to grasp it by the inner lining, and vanished up the stairs. He hit the switch of the hallway light.

Bathroom first, water over his hands, pink as it spun down the drain.

Blood on his shirt, and on the knee of his pants. The pants weren't bad. Into his bedroom. He got a fresh shirt.

Voices from below, a man's and a woman's. They had found their way to Beccanti. Loogan listened in as he stuffed clothes into a duffel bag from the closet.

A bit of gallows humor first. "That's no heart attack," the man said. The woman called for a patrol car, on what must have been a handheld radio. She got a reply; a unit was on its way.

"Can you hear me, sir? What's your name?"

"I don't think he can hear you," the woman said.

They got down to work, talking quietly to each other. From the bedroom Loogan heard snatches.

"Pulse is weak."

"Got an airway, but I don't like it much."

They remarked on Loogan's work with the towels and the belt.

"Who do you suppose did this?"

"And are they still here?"

"Not sure I want to find out."

Quiet, and then one of them must have run out to the ambulance. Loogan heard the clatter of a gurney rolling in over the kitchen floor, subdued when it hit the carpet of the living room.

Moving Beccanti must have posed a tricky problem. They strategized it first, then counted three.

Sounds of effort. The gurney creaked under the weight of the body.

"Start an I.V.?" the man's voice said.

"Do it in the rig. We've got to move him now."

Rapid steps, wheels running again over the kitchen tiles. Loogan zipped the duffel bag. He got his checkbook from the top dresser drawer. He took a hurried inventory: wallet, keys, wristwatch, cell phone. A briefcase in the bottom of the closet held all his important papers—his birth certificate, financial records, the title to his car.

Into his coat and down the stairs with the briefcase and the duffel. He killed the lights in the kitchen, pulled the door shut behind him. The ambulance drove away as he descended the steps of the porch. Across the street, lights were on. He saw silhouettes in windows. Down the block, a white-haired woman stood on the sidewalk, a down jacket over her nightgown. She called out and started walking toward him.

Long strides to the curb with his head down. Loogan's breath was surprisingly even, his heartbeat not too rapid. He expected sirens at any moment, blue and red lights.

He stowed the briefcase and the duffel in the backseat of the car, walked around to the driver's side. The white-haired woman was closer. "What's going on?" she said.

He told her he had to go to the hospital. His father had suffered a heart attack.

She looked unconvinced—maybe she had seen them load Beccanti into the ambulance. But she hung back from Loogan and he paid her no further attention.

The engine turned over; the car had always been reliable. Seat belt on, headlights, he drove south to the end of the block. Stopped for the sign. As he rolled through the intersection he looked right and left, saw the twinkle of a patrol car approaching from the east, still some blocks away. He drove sedately on. David Loogan, nerves of steel. He took the first right he came to. No traffic to speak of. Rows of dark houses, citizens asleep.

For a fevered moment he thought he would drive to Elizabeth Waishkey's house. Tap on her door. He imagined her coming out to the porch in a robe, sleepy, raven hair tousled, bare feet. She would brighten at the sight of him, and then she would be appropriately grave as she listened to him explain. He would tell her that it wasn't him: he hadn't stabbed Michael Beccanti.

Eventually he brought the car around, pointed it east toward Main Street. Then south on Main to the interstate, I-94 eastbound. He got behind a semi and stayed there for five miles. Exited onto Route 23, heading for Ohio.

Chapter 23

Elizabeth Waishkey had never before been involved in three homicide investigations at the same time. And as she stood in the living room of David Loogan's rented house on Tuesday afternoon, it occurred to her that she had never felt a personal connection to a crime scene before. Yet she had been here, in this room, little more than a week ago. She had sat on the sofa where Michael Beccanti's blood had run out of him.

She was alone in the house now. It had seen a swarm of detectives overnight. Beccanti had died in the ambulance, two minutes out from University Hospital. Elizabeth heard the news from Carter Shan a little before three A.M. When she got to Loogan's house, Shan was already there, along with Harvey Mitchum and Ron Wintergreen. Kim Reyes arrived a short time later. Then Owen McCaleb, in a dark blue tracksuit and white running shoes.

They had spoken right away to some of the neighbors, and McCaleb was quietly furious when he learned how casually Loogan had escaped the scene. He directed his anger at the two patrolmen who had responded, too slowly, to the 911 call. Elizabeth witnessed their encounter only from a distance—they were three dark figures on the lawn, beneath a barren elm tree. She couldn't hear what McCaleb said, but the patrolmen sulked off afterward and went to linger timidly by their car, as if they didn't know whether they should stay or leave.

Mitchum and Wintergreen had been the first detectives to arrive. McCaleb put them in charge of the crime scene. He sent Elizabeth and Shan to University Hospital to secure Beccanti's personal effects and interview the EMTs who had answered the call at Loogan's house. They spoke to the pair in the ER waiting room. Neither of the EMTs had seen Loogan in the house, but the woman said she had the feeling that someone might have been lurking upstairs. She went on to describe the efforts someone had made to stanch Beccanti's wounds. "Do you suppose that was him?" she asked.

Afterward, Elizabeth and Shan learned that no one had contacted Michael Beccanti's next of kin. They drove down to Saline to talk to Beccanti's girlfriend, Karen Fenton. The woman's expression darkened as soon as she saw them. She refused to sit, took the news standing in the doorway of her trailer in sweatpants and a long T-shirt, her arms crossed above her bulging stomach. When Elizabeth tried to take her arm, she jerked it away, staggered, then dropped to her knees and wailed. Shan was able to coax her into a chair, where she sat weeping, the heels of her hands pressed to her eyes. They did their best to console her until one of her neighbors appeared, an older woman who wore a woolen coat over a pale blue nightgown. The woman's arrival seemed to calm her. They whispered to each other. The woman put water on for tea and shooed Elizabeth and Shan away.

By sunrise they were back on Loogan's street. They checked in with Harvey Mitchum and the other detectives who had been working the crime scene. There was no news on Loogan. A bulletin had gone out on his car, but there were no leads on where he might have gone.

Elizabeth's morning was taken up with meetings and paperwork. She managed to grab a late breakfast, a shower, and two hours' sleep. In the afternoon she returned to Loogan's house. Mitchum and the others were gone by then; she had the place to herself.

She began with a circuit of the house, starting in the basement, ending on the second floor. She was struck by how little David Loogan had left behind. Clean laundry in the dryer in the basement. A few shirts and a sport jacket in the bedroom closet. Papers in the small office off the living room: bills, half-edited manuscripts for *Gray Streets*.

She knew Loogan had rented the house. The neighbors had supplied the name of the owner, a history professor on sabbatical, doing research at an institute in Frankfurt. Loogan had slept in the man's bed, eaten off his plates, made use of his office; apparently he had brought little of his own into the house. There were no boxes of mementos, no records of his past.

Elizabeth lingered for a moment in Loogan's bedroom. She imagined him there, hurriedly packing as the EMTs worked downstairs. What would he have done if someone had decided to come up and investigate? She looked to the window—a long drop, a sprained ankle at least, maybe a broken leg. Not a good way out. He would have been trapped here. Yet he had stayed in the house with Beccanti, had done his best to bind the man's wounds.

She descended to the living room, where the copper scent of blood hung in the air. She surveyed the room, trying to work out what had happened. Beccanti had driven to Loogan's house; they had found his car parked across the street. He had come in through the window. The sliced screen told its own story—that was Beccanti's M.O.

Where was Loogan when Beccanti climbed through his window? The covers on the bed upstairs were thrown back. Had Loogan been asleep?

She had trouble making sense of it that way. Imagine Loogan awakened by an intruder. He creeps down the stairs. Fine. But when does he acquire the knife? Was he sleeping with it under his pillow?

It made far more sense if she assumed Beccanti's killer had hidden in the downstairs office. She turned a slow circle, letting her gaze pass over the office doorway, the lamp, the chair, the sofa. There was Beccanti's blood, a pattern for her to read. She had seen his body in the hospital morgue; she knew the location of his wounds. Put the killer in the office in the dark, give him a knife, and everything fell into place. Imagine Beccanti climbing through the window, moving to the center of the living room. He's near the floor lamp; maybe he's about to switch it on. His back is to the doorway of the office. The killer seizes Beccanti's hair, runs the blade across his throat.

He misses the carotid arteries; they're harder to find than most people suppose. Beccanti slumps, catches himself against the back of the chair. Leaves some of his blood there. He turns to face his attacker, barely has time to register the knife before it sinks into his abdomen. He doubles over, draws himself up again, bracing himself against the chair. The knife strikes three more times before it lets him be. Retreating, he falls over backward. The knife is in his stomach. He has the strength to draw it out, to roll over, to crawl on hands and knees to the sofa. Somehow he pulls himself up, manages to sit; the knife ends up beside him.

And what about his attacker? There are two possibilities. Loogan is the attacker and he's had a change of heart; he does what he can now to stop the bleeding. Or the attacker is someone else entirely. Someone who was lurking in the office with a knife while Loogan was asleep upstairs.

You want it to be someone else, Elizabeth thought. You don't want to believe that David Loogan would slice a man's throat and stab him four times.

She looked up at the framed photograph over the fireplace: paper leaves, bits of colored glass. She touched the beads of her necklace.

"An unknown subject," she said aloud.

If Beccanti was stabbed by an unknown subject, then his attacker must have fled the house. Did he leave by the front door? No. Why take the long route when there was an open window right there, beckoning him? He would have some of Beccanti's blood on him; it would be a wonder if he didn't. But the curtains were spread wide. He could get past them without leaving blood behind.

What about the screen? Elizabeth crossed to the window. The remnants of the screen were bent inward. They ought to bend outward, if someone had exited that way.

She brought out her phone and dialed Harvey Mitchum's number. There was a strain of weariness in his voice when he answered.

She said, "Something occurred to me, Harv. Wanted to run it by you." Deference in her tone. It was his crime scene.

"What's that?" he said.

"What do you think about sending the window screen to the lab, looking for traces of blood?"

He paused for a second, working it out. "Beccanti's blood? You think the killer went out that way?"

"Could be."

"That doesn't fit with Loogan being the killer."

"No."

"Besides, the screen was bent toward the inside." Mitchum had always had a sharp eye.

"Suppose the killer let himself out," she said, "and then bent the screen back in."

Another pause. "All right, Lizzie. I'll send somebody to collect it."

"Thanks."

She punched the cut-off button on her phone and rounded back toward the center of the room. Her eyes were drawn again to the framed photograph over the fireplace. It was a gift from Tom Kristoll, Loogan had told her. He took the frame apart when Kristoll died, hoping to find a hidden message from his friend.

She stood on tiptoe to take the frame down from the wall. Turned it over in her hands—no secret envelope taped to the back, nothing but the emptiness of the white posterboard backing.

Her phone rang and she answered it absently, holding the framed photograph with one hand. The voice she heard was one she recognized.

"Hello, Detective."

Carefully, she propped the frame against the stone of the fireplace.

"Mr. Loogan."

"I hope this isn't a bad time," he said. "There are things we need to talk about. You've been to my house, I imagine."

She glanced at the window, struck by the sudden thought that he could be watching her.

"Yes," she said.

"Someone stabbed Michael Beccanti in my living room."

"I know."

"I've been trying to decide what I should say to you. I know how it looks. The knife is from my kitchen. You've probably found my fingerprints on it."

She moved closer to the window. No sign of him on the street.

"We'll find them, if they're there," she said.

"It looks like he broke in and I stabbed him. That's not what happened."

"I believe you, Mr. Loogan." She said it quietly, half to herself.

"What's that?"

"I said I believe you. But it doesn't matter what I believe. You need to come in to the department. We'll talk. You can tell me what really happened."

"I don't think so."

"I'll come to you then," she said. "Tell me where you are."

His sigh came clearly over the line. "I'm not really in any one place. I guess you'd say I'm on the move. Did you look in Beccanti's pockets?"

The question caught her by surprise, but she didn't let it show in her reply.

"We always look in their pockets, Mr. Loogan. It's part of the job."

"Did you find a compact disc, or a letter addressed to Tom Kristoll?"

"No. What's this about?"

"I wish I knew. Look, I haven't been completely honest with you."

"Is that right?"

"I told you I stopped looking for Michael Beccanti, and that's true. But the reason I stopped is, he found me. He came to my house on the night of Tom's funeral."

She stood up straight, alert. "Go on."

"He came in through the window that night. That's when the screen got slashed. He knew I'd been looking for him. I think he wanted to meet me on his own terms. We were both friends of Tom. He thought we should do something about Tom's death."

"This isn't a story in *Gray Streets*, Mr. Loogan."

"You keep telling me that. But more and more it's getting to look like one. Beccanti went to Tom's office downtown on Saturday. Just to look around. He didn't turn up anything. Then last night he went to Tom's house. He found a letter and a disc, brought them over to show me. I was in bed. He came in through the window again. I think it amused him. We talked upstairs. He wanted to plan our next move. He went downstairs, and I was supposed to get dressed and join him down there.

"But that's when it happened. Either someone was watching the house, or someone was following him. And whoever it was, he saw Beccanti climb in through the window. He must have climbed in the same way. He must have been downstairs while Beccanti and I talked. Then, when Beccanti went down, he was waiting with the knife."

The energy was draining slowly from Loogan's voice. "By the time I went down he had gone. Beccanti was bleeding on the sofa. I didn't think to look in his pockets; I had other things on my mind. But if you didn't find the disc and the letter, then the killer must have taken them."

Elizabeth heard nothing for a long moment. There were no street sounds to fill the silence, no signature of a car's engine. She imagined him pacing in a barren hotel room.

Then: "He didn't say anything, by the way. Beccanti. I think he was in shock. I remember his eyes focused on me a couple of times. I think he knew he was going to die." She heard him let out a long breath. "I'm sorry. I'm tired. Last night I drove a long way."

He went quiet again and she found herself staring at the leaves in the photograph by the fireplace.

"David," she said. "You should come in. Get a lawyer. Get this cleared up."

"If I come in, can you guarantee I won't be put under arrest?"

She hesitated. "I could, if it were up to me."

"But it's not up to you," he said. "That's what I thought. I know where I stand. Beccanti's dead and I'm a suspect. If this were a story in *Gray*

Streets, I'd have to solve the crime on my own. I'd have to find the killer and clear my name."

She closed her eyes. "David, this isn't a story in *Gray Streets.*"

"That's what you say. Look, there's more I need to tell you, but it's complicated. It starts with the disc and the letter. The disc had a manuscript on it. The letter was from a blackmailer. Do you have a pen? You're going to want to write some of this down."

Chapter 24

ELIZABETH'S EYES OPENED. "DID YOU SAY A BLACKMAILER?"

"I can't remember the text of the letter exactly, but it started with 'Dear Mr. Kristoll, I know about Sean Wrentmore.' Then there was a demand for fifty thousand dollars and an address to send it to in Chicago. The letter was signed, but that won't help you. Whoever wrote it used a pseudonym: M. L. Black."

A few steps took Elizabeth to the kitchen, where she had left her coat.

"Should I know who Sean Wrentmore is?"

"I'm getting to that," Loogan said. "The thing is, there's something more I haven't told you. I suppose I should have. Sean Wrentmore's dead. Have you found a pen?" His tone was matter-of-fact; the energy had returned to his voice.

She pulled her notebook from her coat. "Yes. Go on."

"Sean Wrentmore was a writer. He died on the night of October seventh in Tom Kristoll's study. Wrentmore wrote a novel and Tom edited the manuscript—that's the manuscript that was on the disc, by the way. Adrian Tully helped Tom work on the manuscript. There was an argument over the editing and it turned into a fight and Wrentmore was killed. Tully was the one who killed him. Am I going too fast?"

"I'm keeping up," she said. "How do you know all this? Why didn't you tell me before?"

"Some of it I found out only recently. Some of it I can't be certain of. I know for sure that Wrentmore's dead. I believe Tully killed him. If you want to check my story, you should talk to Laura Kristoll. She told me what happened. She heard it from Tom."

Elizabeth turned a page in her notebook. "You say you know Sean Wrentmore's dead. How? And what happened to the body?"

"Buried in the woods," Loogan said. "Look, there are a few more things. I can save you some time on Wrentmore. He lived in a condo on Carpenter Road." He recited the address for her. "He also rented a storage unit, at a place called Self-Storage USA. I think he kept something important there. Unit 401. He gave his neighbor a key and told her that if anything ever happened to him she should go there. The neighbor's name is Delia Ross. She and I drove out to the storage place on Saturday, but whatever Wrentmore kept there was gone by then. It would be interesting to know if anyone else has gone to that unit recently."

Elizabeth tapped her pen against the page. "Did Tom Kristoll bury Sean Wrentmore's body?"

"Didn't I already say that?"

"Not exactly. Did you help Tom bury the body?"

His silence stretched so long that she thought he had put down the phone.

"That's a question I'd rather not answer," he said finally.

"Mr. Loogan, I need to know where to find Sean Wrentmore's body."

"I liked it better when you called me David," he said. "Look at it from my perspective. If I helped Tom bury the body, I may be the only one alive who knows where it is. That gives me a certain advantage. A certain leverage."

"Listen," she said. "The story you've told me is outlandish. This Wrentmore was killed over a manuscript. Without a body, I don't know how I'll get anyone to take it seriously."

"I've said all I'm going to say for now. I think they'll take it seriously."

"I don't know why *I* should take it seriously."

"Because you believe me."

"I haven't said so. Not about this."

"You believe me, and you want to find out who killed Tom," he said, as if the matter were decided. "I've got to go. You'll do what you think is best."

She tried to come up with something that would keep him on the phone.

"David—" she began.

But the line had already gone dead.

Her phone rang again as she drove to the end of Loogan's block, heading for City Hall. She heard Sarah's voice when she answered.

"Hi, Mom. Did he call you?"

Though she knew what the answer would be, she asked, "Did who call me?"

"David. He called here a while ago, looking for you. I gave him your cell. He said he didn't stab that man."

Elizabeth drove past lines of bare trees. "He said the same thing to me. I think it's probably true."

"Well, no kidding," Sarah said. "He's an editor. He knows how to juggle. It's not like he's dangerous or anything."

Elizabeth didn't have to convince anyone to take Sean Wrentmore's death seriously. Loogan had been right about that.

She arrived at City Hall to find that Laura Kristoll had just left. She and her lawyer, Rex Chatterjee, had met with Owen McCaleb in his office. The purpose of their visit was to deliver a brief statement—three pages, single-spaced. Elizabeth found a copy waiting on her desk. It was Laura Kristoll's description of the circumstances of Wrentmore's death, as they had been related to her by her husband.

Carter Shan had sat in on the meeting. He told Elizabeth all about it. "I asked her why she didn't come in sooner," he said. "But Chatterjee wouldn't let her answer. He said any further questions should be submitted to his office. Apparently we're supposed to be grateful that she came in at all. We're not supposed to notice that she's been withholding knowledge of a homicide for nearly a month."

Elizabeth thought she understood why Laura had decided to make a statement now. Loogan must have warned her that he intended to talk about Sean Wrentmore.

Shan nodded toward McCaleb's office. "The chief's on the phone with the county prosecutor," he said. "Chatterjee's attitude ticked him off. He wants to see if any charges can be brought against Laura Kristoll."

A moment later, McCaleb appeared at his office door and summoned Elizabeth and Shan inside. He shook his head wearily when Shan asked him about his conversation with the prosecutor.

"He wants us to treat Laura Kristoll gently," McCaleb said. "He thinks she's suffered enough already, given the death of her husband." He scowled. "He won't admit it, but I think Chatterjee already talked to him. The two of them went to the same law school."

As he sank into the chair behind his desk, Elizabeth began to tell him about the phone call she had received from David Loogan. She passed along Loogan's version of what had happened at his house the night before. She saved the part about the blackmail letter for last.

"So someone was blackmailing Tom Kristoll," McCaleb said. "Someone who knew Sean Wrentmore was dead."

"Apparently."

Shan picked up the pages of Laura Kristoll's statement from McCaleb's desk. "There's nothing in here about blackmail," he said.

"No," McCaleb said mildly. "Mrs. Kristoll neglected to mention it."

"Do we think it's possible she didn't know?"

"It's possible," said McCaleb. "We'll have to ask her."

Pointedly, Elizabeth said, "Are we allowed to ask her?"

McCaleb gave her a bitter smile. "We'll ask her gently, through her lawyer. In the meantime, we'll act on the information we've been given. Let's see what we can find out about Sean Wrentmore."

The bedroom of Wrentmore's condominium had a set of vertical blinds along one wall. The blinds covered a sliding glass door opening onto a rectangle of cement that served as a patio.

Elizabeth stepped out onto the cement. The sun had set and the grass beyond the edge of the patio looked sickly in the dark. A few pine trees made a broken row at the border of Wrentmore's yard. Beyond those trees, the ground sloped down to the parking lot of a franchise restaurant. The sign above the restaurant's entrance was a bright half-circle, like an enormous moon hanging low in the sky.

Elizabeth was beginning to form an image of Sean Wrentmore. This was his view, the circumscribed world he lived in. Sitting at the desk in his bedroom, he would have looked out at that artificial half-moon, the same every night.

He had been thirty-two years old, quiet, disciplined, slightly eccentric. Elizabeth had interviewed his neighbor, Delia Ross, and these were the words the woman had used to describe him. The photograph on his old college ID showed a plain, lean face, blond hair, eyes that seemed determined to stare down the camera.

According to Laura Kristoll's statement, Wrentmore had owned a laptop computer. Tom Kristoll had taken it and disposed of it after Wrentmore's death. A laptop would have allowed Wrentmore the freedom to write anywhere, out in public or in any room of the house, but Elizabeth imagined him sitting at his desk, facing off against a white screen night after night.

And when he rose from his desk, he would wander to the other rooms. He would look around his walls and see strangers in black-and-white photographs, people from Third World countries, their expressions intense, their eyes, like Wrentmore's, staring down the camera. He would see their faces, not the faces of family members or friends. There were no snapshots that Elizabeth could find, no photographs of old girlfriends tucked away. No evidence that any woman had ever entered Wrentmore's home.

But Wrentmore had not been completely solitary. He had turned outward and had found Delia Ross. He had given her his manuscript to read, and he had shared with her an odd secret. He had given her a key to a padlock.

The next morning Elizabeth drove out to Sean Wrentmore's storage unit: number 401 at Self-Storage USA. Carter Shan accompanied her and when the metal door rolled up they looked together on Wrentmore's sad belongings. Boxes of books and girlie magazines, scraps of furniture not worth keeping.

Under a cloud-gray sky they crunched across the gravel lane to a tiny rental office. The attendant on duty was a muscular young man in his twenties, tattoos covering his arms and curling around his neck from under his collar. He leaned his thick forearms on a Formica counter and studied Wrentmore's photograph.

"Yeah, I've seen him before," he said. "Are you really cops?"

His face was animated, his voice enthusiastic.

"We're really cops," Shan told him.

"So if I tell you what I know about this guy—Sean Wrentmore of unit 401—that makes me a solid citizen, right?"

Shan nodded. "Sure."

"It earns me credit," the attendant said with a sly grin. "Like if I ran a red light, you'd cut me some slack."

"We'd let you off with a warning," Elizabeth said.

"Awesome," the attendant said. "Get ready to be dazzled then, because I'm going to tell you everything I know about Sean Wrentmore. Starting at the beginning." He turned to the computer on the counter beside him and tapped at the keyboard. "Sean Wrentmore has had unit 401 for five years now. Since before my time."

"How long have you worked here?" asked Shan.

"About two years. But like I said, I've seen him around. I talked to him once. We have the same tattoo." The attendant raised his left arm to show them a series of linked rings, drawn in black ink, that circled his wrist. "He showed me his, asked me where I got mine. That, I'm afraid, was the extent of my conversation with Sean Wrentmore."

Elizabeth exchanged a weary look with Shan. "We're not dazzled," she said.

The attendant's grin returned. "I'm not finished. I haven't told you about the girl."

"What girl?" Shan asked.

"The girl from unit 401. She came here two or three weeks ago. Drove up in a Chevrolet—gray, or light green. Parked in front of 401. Rolled the door up. She was in there for a while. I wandered over. It was a slow day. Besides, she was a hot girl. I thought I might help her out, like if she needed to load something in her car."

"And did you—help her out?"

"I lifted a box for her, put it in her trunk. That's all she ended up taking. It was heavy, one of those fireproof file boxes."

"Did you see what was in it?"

"I didn't see inside," the attendant said. "But I think she had it open before I came around. There was a key in the lock." He braced himself against the counter and lowered his voice a notch. "Now I'd like to be able to tell you I got her name and number, and Lord knows I tried. But the number she gave me, when I called it, turned out to be a Chinese restaurant. The name is probably a dud too. Mary-Louise."

The name caught Elizabeth's attention. She thought of the letter Loogan had described—the letter signed M. L. Black.

"What did she look like?"

"Hot, like I said. Tall, but not too tall. Maybe twenty-four years old. Her nose wasn't quite straight, but who cares? Great skin. Long hair—not quite red and not quite brown."

"Auburn," Elizabeth said softly.

Shan turned to her. "It's Valerie Calnero. What does Valerie Calnero have to do with Sean Wrentmore?"

Elizabeth closed the cover of her notebook. "Let's go ask her."

"So that's good, right?" the attendant said eagerly. "That earns me some credit."

"It does," Elizabeth said. "You've been a big help. We appreciate it." She turned away from the counter. Shan was already at the door.

"Cool," said the attendant. "But where are you going? I haven't covered everything."

She stopped and turned back. "What do you mean?"

"I still have to tell you about the guy I talked to yesterday. You're not the only ones interested in unit 401."

Chapter 25

FROM WHERE HE HAD PARKED ON THE STREET, DAVID LOOGAN HAD A clear view of a modest apartment building: three stories, glass doors at the entryway, bricks the color of sand. He watched Valerie Calnero walk down the steps with a small suitcase in one hand and a garment bag over her shoulder. She took these to a light green Chevrolet parked in the horseshoe drive in front of the building, where they joined the items she had already stowed away—more suitcases, cardboard boxes, a wicker laundry basket full of books.

It was Wednesday morning. He would have gone to her sooner, but he'd had some trouble finding her. Her address was not in the phone book. It was on the *Gray Streets* list, but he had left the list behind at his house.

He had it now, folded and tucked away in his glove compartment. He had retrieved it earlier in the morning—a calculated risk, based on the assumption that the police, with all they had to do, wouldn't keep someone stationed at his house.

Still, he had been cautious. He had parked around the block, walked through an alley, climbed the low chain-link fence that enclosed the backyard. Entered through the back door that opened into the utility room behind the kitchen. The *Gray Streets* list was in the office, among the papers in the deep drawer of the desk.

With the list in hand he risked a detour upstairs. There was a guitar in a solid black case in the spare bedroom. He remembered seeing it when he first moved into the house. The guitar itself was glossy and unworn, as if it had never been played. Loogan left it in the bedroom. He took the case.

Valerie Calnero slammed the trunk of her car and headed back into the building. Loogan watched her through his windshield, a slim figure in a lightweight, tapered jacket and blue jeans. He got out of his car, grabbed the guitar case from the backseat, and jogged to the horseshoe drive, up the steps. The entrance door was wedged open with a folded newspaper.

The hallway on the second floor was deserted. Valerie lived in number 203. Loogan had a moment of doubt as he reached for the doorknob. If you were loading a car, going in and out repeatedly, you might leave the lock disengaged. Then again, you might not.

The knob turned. Loogan opened the door an inch, held it with his foot. Laying the guitar case against the hallway wall, he worked the snaps, opened the lid. Sean Wrentmore's shotgun was inside.

Loogan still had the key to Wrentmore's condo. He had picked up the gun there the day before.

Passing through the foyer of Valerie's apartment, Loogan kept the shotgun aimed at the floor. The door closed behind him. The rooms looked abandoned. The furniture remained, but there were open cupboards, empty cardboard boxes. On the counter that separated the kitchen from the living room stood a plastic pet carrier. A gray and white cat peered out at Loogan from behind the carrier's wire door. It whined at him softly.

There was a purse on the counter too, and, on the floor below, a briefcase and several small travel bags piled together—and a fireproof file box, the size of an ottoman, with a key resting in its lock.

Down a short hallway Loogan heard water running, a door opening. Valerie stepped into the hall, froze when she saw him. He knelt by the file box, turned the key, opened it. There was nothing inside.

Valerie stepped closer. "Mr. Loogan," she said.

He drew himself up. "Miss Calnero."

"You can take the box if you want," she said. "You'll save me the trouble of getting rid of it."

She regarded him coolly. Eyes remote behind glasses with black plastic frames, auburn hair drawn tight in a ponytail.

Loogan thought, just then, of something Michael Beccanti had said to him. *Some people, you break into their house, they get hysterical.* Valerie Calnero wasn't one of them.

He matched her bland tone. "Will you sit with me for a minute?"

"I'm pressed for time," she said.

The barrel of the shotgun swayed like a pendulum at Loogan's side. With his free hand he waved her into the living room. "It shouldn't take long."

He stepped back so she could pass, and she waded through empty cardboard boxes and bubble wrap and settled onto the sofa. Loogan took a chair.

"I know what you want," she said. "I can't help you."

A single line of worry appeared in her smooth brow. Loogan studied it.

"I think you can," he said. "You can tell me about the box. I know it came from Sean Wrentmore's storage unit. You can tell me what was in it. And what it has to do with Tom's death."

She looked at him sidelong. "Does it have something to do with Tom's death?"

"You were blackmailing Tom about Sean. The two things can't be entirely unrelated."

"Do you think I wrestled Tom out his office window, Mr. Loogan?"

"I think you know who did. Or you have suspicions."

"And if I did—have suspicions—why would I share them with you?"

He made a point of not looking at the shotgun that lay across the arms of his chair. "Because you want to leave," he said, "and I can't let you leave until you tell me what you know."

"Suppose I told you Sean was a friend of mine," she said. "He let me keep some things in his storage unit. Keepsakes. Chapters from my dissertation. When I was a child, my grandmother's house burned down. I'm paranoid about losing things in a fire."

"I don't believe you."

"But it's not a bad story, and the part about my grandmother's house is true."

"I don't think the police would be convinced."

"They may never get a chance to ask. I intend to be out of their jurisdiction soon."

Loogan crossed one leg over the other, resting his ankle on his knee. The barrel of the shotgun fell across the instep of his shoe.

He said, "Do you think that's smart, leaving town right now, after all that's happened? It makes you look guilty."

"I don't see why," Valerie said. "If anyone looks into why I left, they'll find that I've requested a leave of absence from the university. If they talk to Laura Kristoll, they'll learn that I've been unhappy for the past few months about how my dissertation's going. You try keeping up your enthusiasm for the Scottish Chaucerian poets of the fifteenth century. Then with Tom's death, and Adrian's suicide, it was just too much to bear. Sometimes you have to take a break, step back, regain your perspective."

"And what about the blackmail?" he said. "Suppose someone investigates that? Suppose they talk to the clerk who rented you a mailbox in Chicago?"

The faintest of smiles played at the corners of her mouth. "I wish them luck. Sometimes those clerks are careless. I dealt with one once—he didn't go by the book at all. They're supposed to check your driver's license and take down the number, but I had forgotten mine that day. So he did me a favor. He thought I looked like a nice person. Some men are sweet that way. But if he ever had to pick me out of a lineup—well, maybe if he was allowed to look down my blouse. I don't think he'd remember my face."

Her body leaned forward and her fingers rose reflexively to the open collar of her shirt. Loogan watched them touch the hollow at the base of her throat.

"Look, I think it's admirable," she said softly. "You want to find out who killed Tom. I wish he were alive. I wish Adrian were alive. I wish none of this had happened. But there's nothing I can do about it now. I can't help you."

He uncrossed his legs. The muzzle of the shotgun grazed the carpet.

"That's not good enough. If you won't tell me what was in that file box, I'll have to go looking for it on my own."

"You won't find it," she said. "Whatever was in that box is long gone."

"We'll see. We can start here, with those." He pointed to the bags on the floor below the counter. "Then we'll go down and look in the car. I'm willing to spend all day."

"I'm not," she said. "I need to leave."

She started to rise from the sofa, but he sprang to his feet, grabbed her shoulder, pushed her back down.

Her glasses had slipped down her nose, and he saw her eyes clearly for the first time as she looked up at him. They were hard and dark and steady.

"That's better," she said. "You were much too genteel before, but now I can see you're just a brute."

"Stay there." He retrieved the briefcase from among the other bags and set it on a cardboard box between them.

"Start with this," he said. "It needs a key. Where is it?"

"In my pocket," she said.

"Let me have it."

"Why?"

"I have a gun."

"You're not even pointing it at me."

Holding the shotgun one-handed, he leveled the barrel at her knees.

"That's more like it," she said, "but you wouldn't really shoot me, would you?"

"I'm a dangerous lunatic," he said. "Two nights ago, I stabbed a man."

She reached into her jacket pocket, drew out a ring of keys.

"Toss them here," he said.

Her fist closed around a small black cylinder attached to the key chain. Her thumb found the end of it.

"Pepper spray," she said. "Now we have a standoff."

He made a grim mask of his face and leveled the shotgun at her chest, holding it with two hands now. "Give me the keys," he said.

Valerie Calnero stood up slowly from the sofa, her dark eyes fixed on him. The muzzle hovered inches away from her chest. Off to the side, the cat whined plaintively from its carrier.

With no particular urgency, Valerie said, "Do you think no one ever aimed a gun at me before? I had a stepfather once. At least that's what my mother wanted me to call him. They weren't married. He had a pistol, a souvenir from his days in the army. He used to bring it out, when my mother wasn't home, when he'd had a few beers. He'd aim it at my head and make me take off my clothes. I was eleven. He never touched me. He thought men who did that were sick. He had scruples. I was safe with him, he said. Then in a couple years, when I started to fill out, he lost hold of his scruples and I wasn't safe anymore."

Without taking her eyes from Loogan's, she reached for the briefcase with her left hand. Her right hand gripped the pepper spray. "You'll have to shoot me or let me go," she said. "I'm willing to use mine."

He stepped back from her, lowering the shotgun. He watched her gather the straps and handles of the remaining bags on the floor. The black cylinder remained in her right hand. The pet carrier was still on the counter when she headed for the door.

"Are you coming back for the cat?" Loogan asked her.

She looked at him over her shoulder from the doorway. "I think the cat's on her own. This is the one and only exit I plan to make."

The cat mewed quietly in the hallway as Loogan restored Wrentmore's shotgun to the guitar case. The animal was purring softly when he placed the pet carrier on the front passenger seat of Valerie Calnero's car.

The sun came out from behind a cloud as Valerie piled her bags in the backseat. She turned to Loogan and the sunlight illuminated her face.

"I'm off," she said. "It's a good day for driving."

She held the pepper spray discreetly at her side.

"Where to?" Loogan asked her.

Her laugh came involuntarily. It tossed her head back. "You're a ridiculous man," she said.

He squared his shoulders against the weight of the guitar case. "Was it true what you said, about your stepfather?"

Taking off her glasses, she looked at him keenly. "Ridiculous," she said again. "And you make a terrible gunman. But I can see why Laura likes you."

She raised her chin and stood on tiptoe and with her eyes open she gave him a kiss that lingered on his lower lip.

He got his phone out as she drove away. Turned it on and punched a number as he crossed the street. Three rings and then he heard Elizabeth Waishkey's voice.

"Mr. Loogan. Where are you?" She sounded slightly amused.

"You need to talk to Valerie Calnero," he said.

"We're on our way to do that. We've been delayed, listening to the story of your visit to Self-Storage USA."

"She's skipping town," he said evenly. "If you want to catch her, now's the time. She just left her apartment."

All amusement vanished. "Is that where you are? Stay put. We'll be there in a few minutes."

"She's heading east in a light green Chevy sedan." He recited the license number from memory. "You'll want to hurry."

"We're hurrying. Don't go anywhere, Mr. Loogan. Stay right there."

He reached his car, popped the trunk, and lifted the guitar case inside.

"I'm already gone," he said.

Chapter 26

In the quiet of Wednesday evening, Elizabeth found herself alone in her living room. Sarah had gone to the library to work on a project for school. Elizabeth sat on the sofa, a glass of wine on the coffee table nearby, files and reports arranged on the cushions beside her. A Chopin étude played softly on the stereo.

The flight of Valerie Calnero had set the tone for Elizabeth's day. Chief Owen McCaleb had taken the news stoically, standing for once perfectly still in the center of his office. He had offered no reproach to Elizabeth or Shan, saying only, "Let's find her, and let's find Loogan while we're at it."

The problem of finding David Loogan had occupied much of Elizabeth's thought. Throughout the afternoon, she had experienced the growing realization that she knew very little about him. Where was he from? Where had he lived before coming to Ann Arbor? What work had he done before Tom Kristoll hired him as an editor?

The one link she had to his past was the history professor from whom he had rented his house. The professor was in Frankfurt, and Elizabeth had spoken with him on the phone. But the man didn't know Loogan personally; Loogan had rented the house through an ad on the Internet. The only lead the professor could give her was Loogan's previous address—an apartment in Cleveland—and the name of his landlord there.

She'd had no luck yet contacting the landlord, and had delegated the task to Alice Marrowicz. "If we know where Loogan's been," she said to her, "and if we can find someone who knew him there, it might help us convince him to come in." It sounded weak to Elizabeth even as she said it, but Alice seemed eager to help.

Carter Shan had suggested tracking Loogan through his cell phone. Elizabeth knew it was possible in theory. Any cell phone that's turned on sends out signals periodically, whether or not it's being used to make a call. The signals are picked up by cell towers and allow phone companies to determine how to route incoming calls. But they can also be used to estimate a phone's location. Any given signal is likely to reach two or more towers, and if it does, the relative signal strength at each tower can be used to triangulate the phone's position—narrowing it down, in some cases, to an area of a few square blocks. If the phone is equipped with a global positioning chip, its location can be determined even more precisely.

That was the theory. In practice, things were more complicated. They had subpoenaed Loogan's cell phone records, and his phone turned out to be an inexpensive prepaid model, without GPS. And he had been keeping it turned off when he wasn't using it—he seemed to realize the danger that it posed.

As long as the phone was off, he was invisible. The only option was to wait and see if he would use it again. Shan had spoken with a technician at Loogan's cell phone provider, and the technician had flagged Loogan's number in the company's computer system. If Loogan turned on his phone, the company would notify the department and attempt to triangulate his position. But it would take time, and then it would take more time to send patrol cars to look for him, and when they arrived at the search area he might already have moved on.

"I don't think it'll work," Elizabeth had told Shan that afternoon. "He's not going to linger long enough to be found."

Shan had merely shrugged. "Maybe not. We're just covering the bases. He could decide to ditch the phone altogether. Maybe he's done making calls."

But whatever doubts Elizabeth had about tracking Loogan's phone, she didn't believe he was done making calls. She expected to hear from him again. He would want to talk. She had dialed his number and left a message on his voice mail, encouraging him to call her.

Now, in the evening, she was home catching up on reports, going over the files on Kristoll and Tully and Beccanti. A draft of cool November air came through a partly open window. Chopin's piano notes ambled along sadly on the stereo.

Her cell phone rang around eight o'clock, and even before she read his number on the display she knew it would be Loogan.

"Where are you?" she said to him.

"You ask that as if you expect me to answer."

"I do."

"Let's say I'm at a rest stop on the Ohio Turnpike. I figured I'd be safe calling you from here. How fast can you organize a manhunt in Ohio?"

She couldn't help smiling at that. "I'm not sure," she said, "but I'll get right on it."

"Did you catch up with Valerie Calnero?"

She debated whether to answer him, decided it would do no harm. "Valerie slipped away from us. We had people watching for her on the interstates, all the main routes out of the city. I think she may have stuck to the back roads."

"What will you do now?"

"We've got a bulletin out on her, and we've contacted the police in Milwaukee. That's where she grew up. She might go back there."

"I doubt it. She's smarter than that."

"We'll see."

"Did you find the file box at her apartment?"

Elizabeth got up and turned down the volume on the stereo.

"We found it," she said. "I'm not sure how much good it does us. There was nothing else of interest in the apartment. We talked to some witnesses on the scene though."

"Witnesses?"

"People who saw her leave," Elizabeth said. "They saw you with her. Saw you put something in her car."

"That was her cat."

"Then they saw you kiss her."

"Technically, she kissed me."

"Is that right?" Elizabeth stood by the window and rested her palm against the cool glass. "Are you really such a passive man? Blackmailers kiss you. Publishers' wives seduce you. Maybe you need to take some initiative." She drew her fingertips down along the glass. "The witnesses said you were carrying a guitar case. That's a nice touch."

He laughed. "The thing is, I needed some way to threaten Valerie. I told her if she didn't talk, I'd beat her with my guitar. But in the end, I couldn't bring myself to do it."

"No wonder she kissed you. Mr. Loogan, I should advise you that carrying a concealed weapon is a crime. I should also advise you that there are now two warrants out for your arrest—one as a material witness to the death of Michael Beccanti, one for obstructing a police investigation. I recommend you find a lawyer and turn yourself in."

"You said that before."

"I'm going to keep on saying it."

He went quiet for a few seconds. Then: "Have you worked out the connection yet between Valerie Calnero and Sean Wrentmore?"

"More or less," Elizabeth said. "We know Wrentmore left a key to his storage unit with Delia Ross, in case something happened to him. He must have done the same with Valerie. She copyedited one of his stories when she was an intern at *Gray Streets*. I'm not sure why he wanted two people to have access to his storage unit. Maybe he thought one of them was unreliable."

"Delia Ross is close to finishing her degree and plans to leave Ann Arbor," Loogan said. "If Wrentmore knew that, he might've chosen Valerie as a replacement."

"That's possible."

"Also, Sean Wrentmore was a solitary man, and Valerie Calnero is a beautiful woman. He might have seen it as a way of getting close to her."

"You've given this some thought."

"I've had time on my hands," he said drily. "That reminds me. I've been thinking about Michael Beccanti. Whoever killed him was either waiting at my house, or followed him there. I think they must have followed him."

"Why would they follow him?"

"Because they knew he was looking into Tom Kristoll's murder. I told you Beccanti searched Tom's office on Saturday. I forgot to mention that someone caught him at it. The secretary, Sandy Vogel. She might have told someone else. That's worth investigating, isn't it?"

"Yes, it is."

"I'd talk to her myself, but I'm afraid you wouldn't approve."

"I wouldn't. Don't try to contact Sandy Vogel."

"I won't. How are you holding up?"

Elizabeth turned away from the window. "I'm fine," she said.

"Four murders now," he said. "It must be a lot of work."

"I have colleagues, Mr. Loogan. I'm not expected to solve four murders on my own."

"Still, you must be busy."

"A lot of it is paperwork," she said, returning to the sofa. "Forms, notes, reports. That's what an investigation comes down to—papers in a file. I've got some of them here." She picked up one of the folders beside her. "We've made a timeline of your actions, for instance. When you called me yesterday, you implied you were somewhere far away, but that was a bit of deception. You must have been in Ann Arbor, or at least nearby, because a short time later you went to Self-Storage USA. Then you may have left town for all I know, but you came back this morning for your tête-à-tête with Valerie Calnero. In the meantime, you acquired a guitar case. To anyone else, this might seem like trivia, but yesterday I happened to walk through every room of your rented house. There was a guitar case in the spare bedroom. I went back today, and there was a guitar but no case. Do you know what that means?"

"What?"

"It means now I've made a note in the file about the guitar case. You're making more work for me."

"Sorry."

"If you were sorry, you'd turn yourself in." She reached for a different folder. "Here's another report—on the knife that killed Michael Beccanti. Most of the fingerprints we found on the knife belonged to Beccanti himself. That's not surprising. He was the last one to touch it—he pulled the knife out of his stomach. But we found a partial thumbprint that didn't belong to him, and we compared it to yours. You gave us a set of prints after Tom died, as I'm sure you recall. We fingerprinted everyone who had access to Tom's office, for purposes of elimination. The thumbprint on the knife was yours."

"That can be explained," Loogan said mildly. "I told you the knife came from my kitchen."

"That's true. You told me," Elizabeth said. "But your prints also turned up in Adrian Tully's car. What do you think of that?"

This was something she herself had learned earlier in the day. She could tell from the way he paused that it had caught him by surprise.

"If I didn't know better," he said softly, "I'd think you were trying to trick me."

"I'll take that as a compliment," she said.

"My prints have no business being in Adrian Tully's car."

"That's what I would have thought. Yet there they are."

"Where? Where exactly did you find them?"

She put the folder aside and stood. "There was a box of ammunition in Tully's glove compartment. The box was wrapped in a plastic grocery bag. We found your prints on the bag."

Another pause. She paced across the room, listening to the static on the line.

"Are you still with me, Mr. Loogan?"

"I'm here," he said. "Let me ask you something. Did Tully drive a Honda Civic, sky blue, rust on the fenders?"

She stopped her pacing. "That's a good description."

"I've been in that car."

"Some of the people I work with believe you were in that car the night Adrian Tully died."

"No, it was before that," he said. "It was the night Sean Wrentmore died. Look, it's a little complicated."

She felt herself smile. "Let's see if I can follow along."

"Tom called and asked me to come over, to help him with the body. But he didn't tell me it was Wrentmore. He said it was a thief he had caught breaking into his house. He wanted to conceal Wrentmore's identity. That car, the blue Civic, was in Tom's garage. It was Tully's car, Tully had been there that night, but Tom didn't want me to know that either. He let me think it was the dead thief's car. When we got rid of the body, we got rid of the car too. Tom drove his Ford, and I drove the Civic, and we left it on the street in a bad neighborhood. It must have been a charade on Tom's part, to keep me from knowing that Tully had been there."

"And why would Tully leave his car behind?" she asked him.

"I can only assume he drove off in Wrentmore's car, planning to get rid of it."

"That's fine," she said. "But you haven't accounted for the fingerprints on the bag of ammunition."

The static seemed to clear from the line. "I stopped at a store on the way to Tom's that night," he said. "I bought a few things—a shovel, bottled water, leather gardening gloves. I transferred all this stuff from my car to Tully's and then, later on, from Tully's car to Tom's. But I must have left a plastic bag behind in Tully's car. It must still have been there on the night he was killed. Say it was on the floor of the backseat; Tully's killer snatched it up, maybe he thought Tully's prints would be on it; he put the box of ammo inside and stashed it in the glove compartment. That's plausible, isn't it?"

"It's not bad," Elizabeth said. "I'm inclined to believe you. But my opinion doesn't matter. You've ticked a lot of people off. Fleeing the scene the night Beccanti died. Showing up at Valerie Calnero's apartment, then just letting her drive away. My boss looks darkly on these things. He's a genial man, mild-tempered, soft-spoken, but he believes it reflects poorly on us when an inordinate number of people die. You're not helping. There are people I work with who suspect you stabbed Beccanti and then staged it to look like a break-in. There are others who are convinced you shot Tully. Some think you did both. The fact that you haven't turned yourself in makes it worse. The longer you wait, the more they think you're guilty. You need to come in."

"I can't do that."

"I don't want to be misunderstood, Mr. Loogan. I think you believe you're doing the right thing—that there's something you can accomplish by running around on your own—that somehow you're going to discover who killed your friend. Maybe you think I'm urging you to come in because it's my job, because it's the official line I have to take—but secretly I'm on your side, I'm rooting for you. That's not the case. I don't approve of you. I don't think you're going to accomplish anything."

"I understand."

"I hope you do," she said. "Look, I shouldn't tell you this, but your picture will be in the paper tomorrow. Probably on the news too. It would have been in today, but we had trouble finding a photograph. There's no photo of you on file at *Gray Streets.*"

"They never got around to taking one."

"We wound up using your driver's license photo. Those are stored electronically. We had to doctor it a little. You had a mustache and a beard when it was taken."

"It was winter."

"We had someone Photoshop it. You'll see the result tomorrow. You should come in now, voluntarily. Things will go better for you."

"I wish I could." He seemed to waver for a moment, and she tried to read his silence. "But it's not something I'm willing to do."

"I'm having trouble understanding that," she said.

"Is it really so hard to understand?"

She sensed him slipping away. "Why don't you explain it to me?"

"I'd like to, but I can't."

"Why not?"

"You already don't approve of me," he said.

Then he was gone. He had broken off the call.

She dialed his number, hoping to catch him before he turned off his phone. But after a single ring she got shuffled to his voice mail. She called in to the department next and learned that Shan had been in contact with Loogan's cell phone provider—and was on the line now with the state police. Shan called her back a few minutes later.

"He's in Livonia," Shan told her.

Elizabeth had to suppress a laugh. "He said he was in Ohio." Livonia was a suburb of Detroit.

"He's somewhere around Newburgh Road and Six Mile. There's a shopping mall there—Laurel Park Place. Lots of cars. He'd blend right in."

"He knows what he's doing."

"The Livonia police have a cruiser there now, and they're sending another. But he could be out of there already."

"I'm sure he is," Elizabeth said.

"He's right next to I-275 and I-96," said Shan. "From there he can go anywhere he wants. I talked to the state police and the Wayne County sheriff's department. They've got his description and a description of his car. They'll look for him." He didn't sound optimistic.

"They're not going to find him," she said.

Chapter 27

SARAH ARRIVED HOME FROM THE LIBRARY AROUND NINE O'CLOCK, AND Elizabeth put away her files. The two of them ate a late supper, then watched part of a documentary on PBS—people suffering injustice in foreign lands.

No word came in about David Loogan. Elizabeth tried to put him out of her mind, though there were echoes of him in her house. Once, as the night wore on, she looked in on Sarah and caught the girl standing in the middle of her bedroom, juggling three tennis balls with a look of fierce concentration.

Later, when Sarah was asleep, Elizabeth puttered around downstairs. She piled magazines, gathered stray dishes. She moved Sarah's school books from the coffee table to the dining room. With a casual curiosity she opened a notebook and saw a drawing of Loogan's face: rough-feather pencil strokes outlined his jaw; his gray eyes were clear and free of shadow. A good likeness, she thought—far better than the image they had released to the press.

In the morning, she decided to follow up on something Loogan had told her about: Michael Beccanti's visit to the offices of *Gray Streets*. She drove to the *Gray Streets* building, rode the elevator up, tapped on the pebbled glass of the door. Sandy Vogel let her in. Elizabeth thought she seemed subdued. She leaned against a filing cabinet with her arms crossed, a slender brown-haired woman in her early forties, dressed crisply in a matching skirt and jacket.

"He was here," she said when Elizabeth asked her about Beccanti. "I came in to use the copier Saturday night, around eight. The lights were on. The door to Tom's office was open. Beccanti was in there."

"You recognized him?" Elizabeth asked her.

"Yes. He used to visit Tom. I didn't remember his name, but he came out and introduced himself. I think he realized he had startled me. He served time in prison, you know."

"I know."

"He told me David Loogan had hired him to do editorial work. I didn't know anything about it. He left quickly after that. It seemed a little strange."

"Did you tell anyone?"

"Just the brain trust."

"Pardon?"

"Things have changed here, with Tom gone," Sandy Vogel explained. "David Loogan was supposed to take over, but there doesn't seem much chance of that now, does there? In the meantime, there's still a magazine to run. Most of the work has fallen to me, so far, but I'm not who's in charge. That would be the brain trust. Laura Kristoll, Bridget Shellcross, Nathan Hideaway, Casimir Hifflyn. Officially, they're a board of directors, though we never had a board when Tom was alive. I'm supposed to keep them informed about what goes on here."

"So you told them Beccanti was here Saturday."

"I sent them an e-mail that night."

"Did you get any response?"

"Nathan Hideaway sent a reply Monday. He said it was fine, Loogan could hire who he liked."

"And when you found out Beccanti had been stabbed?"

Sandy Vogel frowned. "I suppose I should have called you, though I don't see what his being here had to do with his death. Except in the obvious sense."

"What sense would that be?"

"David Loogan hired him to work here, and then David Loogan stabbed him. From what I've read in the papers, you don't need me to work that out." The woman's frown deepened. "The truth is, I don't care much for drama, or for mysteries. I like the stories we publish as much as anybody, but as for actual murders, real people dying—I'd like to stay as far away from that as I can. So you'll forgive me for not rushing to the phone when Michael Beccanti died."

Later in the morning, Elizabeth drove to Bridget Shellcross's townhouse. She found herself less welcome than on her previous visit.

It started with Rachel Kent, who was doing stretches on the sidewalk in front of the house. She wore spandex and a loose-fitting T-shirt. She had obviously just come from a run.

"Is Bridget in?" Elizabeth asked her.

"She's in. She's not going to want to talk to you."

"Why not?"

"Not for me to say."

Elizabeth went past her and up the steps and rang the bell. Bridget Shellcross let her into the foyer, but invited her no farther.

"I hope this isn't a bad time," Elizabeth said, trying to get a read on the woman's mood. "I'm here about Michael Beccanti."

"Of course," said Bridget tonelessly.

"Did you know him?"

Bridget stood with her hands on her hips and her feet apart on the tiles of the foyer. The light from the windows cast her diminutive shadow across the floor.

"I'm surprised you would come around here," she said. "I've seen the news. Beccanti was stabbed in David Loogan's living room, and now Loogan's disappeared. You don't need to look for suspects. You already have one."

"We still need to talk to people who might have known Mr. Beccanti," Elizabeth said. "It's routine. Did you ever meet him?"

"I wish I was in a position to help you," said Bridget, her tone suddenly grave.

"He was a friend of Tom Kristoll. You might have met him through Tom."

"I wish I had some vital piece of information, something that could lead you straight to Michael Beccanti's killer," Bridget said. "Because then I would have the pleasure of withholding it from you."

Her pixie hair seemed to bristle in the sunlight. "I've lived in this city for more than half my life," she said. "I have friends here. One of them is a hostess at a restaurant downtown. She tells me that someone from the police came by with a picture of me and a picture of Tom, asking if we'd been seen together."

Her gaze was piercing. Elizabeth made herself meet it. "I'm sorry. That wasn't me."

"No. She said it was a man. She didn't describe him, but when I imagine him he's stout, slightly greasy, with a yellow shirt collar. He smells of cigar smoke. And there are others like him, scurrying around in cheap hotels, flashing my picture at desk clerks."

"I'm sorry."

"I suppose you found out that Tom and I dated in college, and that gave you license to root around a little, see what you could dig up," Bridget said. "Well, so it goes. But now, if you want to learn something about Michael Beccanti, I suggest you find a good picture of him and start making the rounds. You'll get nothing from me."

Her voice fell on the last words and then she turned and vanished through a doorway, leaving Elizabeth alone.

Outside, Rachel Kent was still stretching. An ornamental fence ran between the sidewalk and the house, and the fence had a metal rail along the top. Rachel had a leg up on the rail like a ballet dancer. She nodded as Elizabeth walked by.

"I told you she wouldn't want to talk to you."

In the early afternoon, Elizabeth called on Casimir Hifflyn. He invited her into his workroom, a large space, sparely furnished. He had a bookcase and a divan, a computer with a flat-panel monitor set up on an antique writing table, and behind that a pair of French windows looking out on the terraced lawn.

"Rex Chatterjee warned me about talking to you," he said lightly.

"Is that right?" said Elizabeth.

"He and Laura sat me down last night. Rex mistrusts the Ann Arbor police. I suppose that's a common affliction among lawyers. He seems to think I'm in danger of being framed. You've got four murders to account for. If I'm not careful, you'll have me running around at night stabbing people, and shooting them, and throwing them out of windows. And, I suppose, clobbering them with liquor bottles. That would make me rather eclectic."

"It would," said Elizabeth.

"But I don't mind answering your question about Michael Beccanti," Hifflyn said. "I got the e-mail about him from the Vogel woman. I glanced at it and deleted it. That's what I tend to do with most of her e-mails. If I did much more I'd never get anything done. When someone renews their subscription to *Gray Streets,* Sandy Vogel sends me an e-mail."

"Did you know Beccanti?" Elizabeth asked.

Hifflyn rubbed his bearded chin. "I've been trying to remember if we were ever introduced. I don't think so. But I remember someone pointing him out to me at a party once. 'Don't look now, but there's Tom's burglar'—something along those lines. Tom had some unusual friends."

"What about Sean Wrentmore? Did you ever meet him?"

"Yes. He cornered me at one of Tom's barbecues, years ago. Gave me a lengthy synopsis of the novel he was working on. I gather it's the one Tom edited, the one Wrentmore got killed over. A great convoluted thing. I believe he was hoping I'd offer to read it."

"I take it you didn't."

"I like to be generous with my time, but not that generous." Hifflyn glanced at his writing table and smiled apologetically. "In fact, I'm rather pressed at the moment. Need to put more words on more pages. I'm sorry to rush you out. I wish there were more I could tell you."

"That's fine."

"I have to keep up a certain pace, or I'd never get through a book," Hifflyn said as he led her to the front door. "Then I'd be in trouble. Nate Hideaway knocks out a novel every couple years, and his publisher is happy. Same with Bridget. But if I don't manage a book a year, my agent looks at me like I kicked his puppy."

Nathan Hideaway told Elizabeth he wanted to get out into the air. He took her along a path behind his cottage that led down to a wooden dock on the shore of the pond. They watched a trio of ducks glide slowly across the surface of the water.

"I tried to have a conversation once with Michael Beccanti," Hideaway said. "This was last year, and if memory serves, he had just been released from prison. I did a reading at a bookstore downtown, and Tom showed up, Beccanti with him. They stayed afterward and Tom made introductions. The three of us went for a drink. I was thinking then of doing a book about a burglar, and I thought I might get some insight into the character. What does it feel like to climb through someone's window, to know you could be caught at any moment? What would motivate someone to do that, again and again the way Beccanti had? I'm sure he could have told some stories. But I never got anything out of him."

Hideaway fell silent and a leaf twisted through the autumn air and landed on the dock at his feet.

"Were you surprised when Sandy Vogel told you that he had been in Tom's office?" Elizabeth asked. "That Loogan had hired him to work on *Gray Streets*?"

"It was unexpected, certainly. But I knew if we were going to put David Loogan in charge of the magazine, we would have to give him some latitude. Beccanti wrote for *Gray Streets*; maybe he had some talent as an editor that I was unaware of."

"Suppose I told you Michael Beccanti didn't go to Tom's office to do editorial work," Elizabeth said. "Suppose I told you he went there to snoop around, hoping to find something out about Tom's death?"

"Is that true?"

"That's my understanding. He and Loogan were working together, conducting their own investigation."

Hideaway looked down at the water. "That should surprise me, but it doesn't. Last week, when we offered Mr. Loogan the *Gray Streets* job, I spoke to him in private. He suggested I should hire him to investigate Tom's death. I didn't take the idea seriously. Apparently he did."

He walked out to the end of the dock and then turned back. "And now Beccanti's dead. The news reports take it for granted that Loogan stabbed him. What do you suppose happened? Did the two of them have a falling-out?"

"Not according to Loogan," Elizabeth said.

"You've talked to him? I thought he was missing."

"He is. We've been in touch by phone. He denies stabbing Beccanti, says someone else did it. Presumably the same person who killed Tom."

"Remarkable," said Hideaway. "Do you believe him?"

"It's possible he's telling the truth. What do you think?"

Hideaway scuffed his boot along a plank of the dock. "I think David Loogan is an unusual man. But Tom saw fit to trust him, so it doesn't seem right to think ill of him. Last week I got an uneasy feeling about him, but it was nothing solid. And it still isn't."

"What do you mean?" Elizabeth said.

"I wonder if any of us really know who David Loogan is," Hideaway said thoughtfully. "Laura doesn't know anything about his past. Tom didn't seem to care. And I suppose it could be a coincidence."

"What could be a coincidence?"

"His name," said Hideaway. "I've done a very unscientific search—in the Detroit phone book. There are almost a million people living in Detroit, and none of them are named Loogan. Maybe it means nothing. Maybe there are Loogans in California, maybe Texas is rife with them. Or maybe there are no Loogans in the United States, in North America, except for our David."

A breeze came over the water and ruffled Hideaway's white hair. "The thing is," he said, "I've heard the name Loogan before. Only it's not a name. It's a piece of slang. Raymond Chandler used it in *The Big Sleep*. He probably invented it; he was known for inventing his own slang. Philip Marlowe used it, talking to Vivian Sternwood. A 'loogan' is a gunman, someone on the wrong side of the law."

When Elizabeth left Hideaway's cottage, she drove north and west, following along the course of the Huron River. Her phone rang as she crested a hill. It was Carter Shan.

"Where are you?" he asked her.

"About three minutes away from Laura Kristoll's house," she said.

"We're not supposed to question Laura Kristoll."

"I thought I'd risk it. I'll be gentle."

"You should get back here fast," he said. "Something's happened."

"What are you talking about?"

"The matter of David Loogan has taken an interesting turn."

"Have you found him?"

"No, but you should come in. You'll want to hear this."

Chapter 28

ELIZABETH WAS THE LAST TO ARRIVE FOR THE BRIEFING. CARTER SHAN met her at the door of the chief's office; Harvey Mitchum and Ron Wintergreen were already inside. Owen McCaleb was leaning against his desk, talking quietly with an older man in a rumpled suit.

Shan passed Elizabeth a photograph as she came through the door—a mug shot of a man she recognized as a younger David Loogan. In the photo, Loogan's hair was longer and curlier. He had a close-trimmed beard. He wore the expression of a man who has lost patience—the victim of a practical joke that has gone on too long. He held a small placard under his chin: a string of numbers and a name. The name was Darrell Malone.

Elizabeth was still studying the photo when the briefing got under way. She half listened as McCaleb introduced the man in the rumpled suit. She caught the man's name—Roy Denham—and that he was a detective, retired, from a city called Nossos in upstate New York.

She put the photo aside and focused on Denham as he began to tell his story. He had weary eyes and the rough voice of a longtime smoker, but he spoke with assurance, without consulting any notes.

He said, "Darrell Malone—the man who calls himself David Loogan—was indicted nine years ago on a charge of second-degree murder. The charge stemmed from an incident that took place on a night in June, on the top level of a parking garage in the center of Nossos. Patrolmen responded to a 911 call placed from one of the garage's emergency phones. They arrived on the scene to find a man dead from multiple stab wounds, a woman seriously injured, and Darrell Malone holding the knife.

"The dead man turned out to be a twenty-five-year-old named Jimmy Wade Peltier. He had a long list of prior arrests, from assault to auto theft, and had been released from prison only six weeks earlier. The injured woman was a dental hygienist named Charlotte Rittenour, a pretty girl, blond, twenty-eight years old.

"We got the story out of Malone. He was very cooperative. He had a minor injury, a superficial cut to his arm, and after that had been treated he was brought to the station house and my partner and I questioned him. He waived his right to counsel; he was eager to talk.

"It turned out he and the girl had been on a date. Dinner and a movie, and then they had gone up to the top of the parking garage to look at the stars. Jimmy Peltier caught them up there and tried to steal their car. The problem was, their car—both their cars—were parked on a different level of the garage. They were standing next to a car when Peltier approached them, but the car wasn't theirs. They tried to explain that to him, but it only made him more agitated. Later, when we tested his blood, it came back positive for both alcohol and methamphetamine.

"Peltier had a knife. He had grabbed hold of the girl's wrist. Malone tried to reach for the knife, but Peltier slashed him. At that moment the girl, Charlotte, managed to struggle free. She ran toward the elevator, and Peltier followed her, caught hold of her hair, put the knife to her neck. Malone chased after them, but before he could do anything, he watched Peltier draw the blade across the girl's throat and push her to the ground.

"There was a struggle after that, and Malone managed to get the knife away from Peltier. The coroner found seventeen separate wounds on Peltier's body. From the position of the wounds, it was clear that some of them had been delivered after the man was down. Malone never tried to deny it. He told us he had left Peltier bleeding on the ground, had gone to call 911— he found an emergency phone on the next level down—and when he came back he found Peltier moving, so he stabbed him some more.

"The girl, Charlotte Rittenour, survived. Her wounds, though serious, weren't as bad as they first appeared. She had tucked her chin down toward her chest as Peltier slashed her with the knife, so most of the damage was to her chin and her cheek. She needed extensive surgery, and her face was never the same, but when she had recovered enough to talk to us, she confirmed Malone's version of events. She was grateful for what he'd done.

"Malone always maintained that he had been defending her, and himself. He said he had done what any reasonable man would have done, and there were plenty of people who agreed with him. My partner and I were tempted to help him out with his story, but there are limits to what you can do, no matter how much sympathy you feel for a man. And there was the physical evidence, the seventeen wounds. The coroner said that if it was self-defense, it was the most thorough case of self-defense he had ever seen.

"The county prosecutor had to make a decision—and he had to think about Jimmy Peltier too. Peltier was a louse, but he had a mother and a father, and no matter what crimes he had committed, on that night or before, he deserved some consideration. No jury had sentenced him to death; Darrell Malone had made that decision on his own. The prosecutor decided to charge Malone with second-degree murder, thinking he would plead to manslaughter and serve minimal jail time.

"But Malone wouldn't plead, and the case was scheduled for trial. In the meantime, Malone was a free man; a sympathetic judge had granted him bail. Malone had his own business. He was trained as a structural engineer, and he worked as a consultant on building sites. He earned good money and had put a lot of it away. Some of it he paid to his lawyer, and some he took with him when he vanished.

"Because of course he did vanish. The day of his trial came up, and he was nowhere to be found. He hadn't confided in anyone. His parents were deceased and he had no siblings. His friends, such as he had, turned out to be not very close friends. None of them could give us a clue. His lawyer was baffled.

"The search for Darrell Malone went nowhere. His car turned up in Newark, sold for cash to a private buyer. There were sightings in Baltimore that never panned out. Then, a few weeks ago, he was spotted at a discount store here in Ann Arbor—the Value Mart on Oak Valley Drive. He bought a shovel and some other items there, and the cashier thought he looked familiar. Her name is Allison Wick and she grew up in Nossos and went to high school with Malone. When she saw him at the Value Mart, he gave her a false name, but the encounter stayed with her and later on she realized who he was.

"She had no idea he was a fugitive, but the next time she talked to her sister she mentioned seeing him. The sister knew his story and got in touch with the Nossos police. It was a slim lead and people in the department weren't inclined to act on it. It had been years since they'd thought about Darrell Malone. But one of my friends in the department mentioned it to me, because he knew I had worked on the Malone case.

"I decided to drive out here and see what I could discover. Blame it on the fact that I've been retired for two years now and have already had my fill of fishing and golf. I arrived here on Friday and drove around, walked through downtown. It struck me as the kind of place Malone would like; it reminded me of Nossos. That didn't bring me any closer to finding him. The name I had for him was the one he had given to the cashier—Ted Carmady. But that didn't lead me anywhere. I didn't pay much attention to the news, though I gather you've had some excitement here in the past couple weeks. I didn't connect Malone with that. If I was going to find him at all, I expected to find him living a quiet, anonymous life. I've spent the last three days driving around to engineering firms, on the theory that Malone might have gone back to what he knew. I must have shown his picture at every firm between here and Detroit. Then today I picked up a newspaper and saw his face on the front page. And here I am."

At home that night Elizabeth read up on the killing of Jimmy Wade Peltier by Darrell Malone. She had a copy of the case file, transmitted by fax from the Nossos P.D. She sat on the sofa with a pillow at her back, a quilt over her legs, and sorted through the pages. There were autopsy pictures of Peltier, gruesome even in their grainy fax versions. She tucked them away when Sarah came over to see what she was reading.

She had struggled a little over whether to tell her daughter what she had learned about David Loogan, but now she gave the girl a bare-bones account of Loogan's crime. Sarah listened, staring all the while at the young Loogan in the mug shot.

"We ought to help him," she said when Elizabeth came to the end of the story. "It sounds like Jimmy Peltier had it coming."

"I'll do what I can for him," Elizabeth said. "But there's nothing for you to do. If he comes here, you're not to let him in."

"I don't think he'll come here."

"I don't either. But if he does, call 911. Then call me. And keep the doors locked."

Sarah gave her an impatient look. "The doors are always locked."

"Then we won't have any trouble. Promise me you'll do what I've asked you."

"I promise," said Sarah firmly. "But I'm not going to be afraid of David Loogan."

The case file included a copy of Denham's notes on his conversation with the cashier Allison Wick. Elizabeth underlined the alias Loogan had used with Wick: Ted Carmady. He had used the same name when he talked to Sean Wrentmore's neighbor, Delia Ross. Elizabeth wondered if the name held some significance. She thought of calling Denham to ask him about it. He was still in town; she had his cell phone number and the number of his hotel. But his notes were thorough and she reasoned that if he had any insights about the alias he would have recorded them.

She didn't know how long Denham would be in town. Owen McCaleb had talked to the man's former chief at the Nossos P.D.—a woman who, according to McCaleb, sounded like "a tough old dame" on the phone. She had given Denham her endorsement.

"She says he's solid," McCaleb told Elizabeth. "Reliable, a team player. A little restless. She thinks he wasn't ready to retire, but their department rules encouraged it. He won't be any trouble, she says, but if he is we should send him packing. It sounds like he wants to stick around, see what happens with Loogan."

Putting the case file aside, Elizabeth got up and fixed herself a cup of tea. When she came back she dug through her notes and found Nathan Hideaway's number. On an impulse she dialed it, and when he answered she said, "I hope I'm not calling too late."

"Detective," Hideaway said. "Not at all. It's a pleasure to hear from you."

"I have a question. Does the name Ted Carmady mean anything to you?"

She listened to his breathing. "Let me think," he said. "I believe that's a literary reference. In some of Raymond Chandler's early short stories, the protagonist was named Ted Carmady."

"I see."

"I wonder, does this have something to do with our friend Mr. Loogan?"

She answered him in a half-amused tone. "I really shouldn't say. Police business. Thanks for your help."

"How awfully enigmatic. Very well. Good night, Detective."

Sipping tea, Elizabeth wondered how attached Loogan might be to the name Ted Carmady. Would he be careless enough to register at a hotel under that name? It might be worth checking around. She made a note to put Alice Marrowicz on it in the morning.

She picked up the phone again and dialed Loogan's number, knowing he wouldn't answer. His phone would be turned off. Even if he did answer, she wasn't sure what she would say. Should she let him know what she had learned about his past? She had discussed the matter with McCaleb and the others after the briefing. They had agreed that they should keep

Loogan's history from the press for the time being. But as for how to handle him, McCaleb had told Elizabeth to use her discretion. She was the one in contact with the man; she would have to make the decision.

But she wouldn't have to make it yet. She got Loogan's voice mail and left a message asking him to call, then finished her tea, and went up to bed.

Chapter 29

On Friday morning Elizabeth put aside the file on the killing of Jimmy Wade Peltier. She had not yet heard from Loogan, and she thought about leaving him another message, but decided against it. He would call her when he was ready.

Loogan was a distraction, she thought. What she needed was to start over, to return to the beginning. From a drawer of her desk in the squad room, she took out a sheet of paper and a pencil. In the middle of the page she wrote Tom Kristoll's name and the date of his death: October 23. But that was not the beginning. If Loogan and Laura Kristoll were to be believed, Sean Wrentmore had died on October 7.

She wrote Wrentmore's name and date above Tom Kristoll's. Below Kristoll's, she added two more names: *Adrian Tully, October 31; Michael Beccanti, November 3.*

In the space between Wrentmore and Kristoll, she added: *Valerie Calnero visits Wrentmore's storage unit; Calnero sends blackmail letter to Tom Kristoll.*

She filled in some other details at the top of the page: *Wrentmore writes novel—Liars, Thieves, and Innocent Men. Tom Kristoll edits Wrentmore's manuscript.* But Wrentmore's death was the key event. Everything that followed was connected to it somehow. If she understood Sean Wrentmore, she could understand the rest.

She believed Loogan when he told her that Wrentmore was dead. But she had more than Loogan's word. Traces of blood had been recovered from between the floorboards in Tom Kristoll's study—Laura Kristoll and her lawyer had consented to the search.

They had also consented to a search of the woods around the Kristolls'
house. Ron Wintergreen had gone in first with a police dog; afterward, cadets from the academy had trudged through the woods in a widening spiral.
But no remains had been found, no signs of a grave.

Wrentmore's family lived in Dayton. Carter Shan had driven down
Wednesday afternoon to meet with them, returning on Thursday morning.
Wrentmore's father had died when he was young. His mother had remar-
ried. Her second husband worked as a carpet salesman, and they had two
daughters together, both in their early twenties, both still living at home.

None of them had heard from Wrentmore in the past eight weeks. They
were used to long silences from him. Wrentmore's mother, a heavy woman
with graying hair, was at first bewildered when Shan related Laura Kristoll's
account of her son's death. Later she broke down in sobs. Her daughters
did what they could to soothe her. Eventually they took her upstairs and got
her to lie down.

The woman's husband questioned Shan in weary tones. Would it do
any good if he drove up to Ann Arbor? Maybe he could help search for
Sean's grave. He thought he should be doing something. Shan discouraged
him gently and left him with the promise that he would be in touch if there
were any developments.

Now, on Friday morning, as Elizabeth sat at her desk penciling in the
details of her timeline, Shan sat across from her sorting through Wrentmore's mail. Wrentmore's neighbor had turned over stacks of it: mostly junk,
a few bills, some magazines, a form-letter rejection from a literary agent who
thanked him for submitting a sample chapter from his novel.

Shan looked up from the mail and said, "How much do you think *Gray
Streets* pays when they publish a story?"

Elizabeth tapped her pencil on the desktop. "I don't know. I imagine it's
not much."

"Wrentmore published stories in there, right? But it's safe to say he
didn't make a living that way."

"Right."

"And his opus, his twelve-hundred-page novel, that was a bust. So it would be fair to describe Sean Wrentmore as a failed writer."

"I suppose it depends on your standards," Elizabeth said. "Tom Kristoll thought he was good."

"He may have been brilliant," said Shan. "He may have been a neglected genius. Literarily. But financially, he was a dud. You'd expect a guy like that to be living in a garret, suffering for his art. But Wrentmore owned a condo."

"Maybe his family helped him out."

"They didn't. They were in the dark about the condo. They had his address, of course, but they assumed he was renting. Last they knew, he had a job at a bookstore."

Elizabeth got out her notebook, found the notes on her conversation with Delia Ross. "Wrentmore told his neighbor he made a living selling used books on the Internet."

"But we didn't find a ton of books at his condo," said Shan. "Just his personal collection. There were books in his storage unit, but if he were selling them—"

"If he were selling them, it would be all wrong. He'd have to drive out to the storage unit every time he needed to fill an order." Elizabeth closed the cover of her notebook. "Where was Wrentmore's money coming from?"

Shan held up Wrentmore's bank statement. "There's only one deposit for the whole month. Five thousand dollars. Direct deposit from something called InnMan, Limited."

He picked up his phone and Elizabeth listened as he flirted with a teller at Wrentmore's bank. InnMan turned out to be an abbreviation for Innocent Man. The direct deposits occurred monthly and went back several years, though the amount had increased over time: from four thousand to forty-five hundred to five thousand.

Shan's second call was to the office of Michigan's secretary of state. He learned that Innocent Man was a single-owner limited liability company—with Sean Wrentmore as the single owner. The same call netted him the name of the lawyer who had filed the company's articles of organization.

As Shan hung up the phone, Elizabeth already had the yellow pages open.

"Who's driving?" he asked her.

She found the lawyer's address. "It's close," she said. "We can walk."

Todd Barstow, Esquire, had a soft, unanimated face. His forehead was unlined, his pale blond hair slicked back, immobile. The walls of his office were paneled in dark wood and the carpet was tan, and the suit he wore was a shade of brown that fell somewhere between the walls and the carpet.

He held three stapled pages in his thin fingers and his lips drew tight together as he read them. The pages were Laura Kristoll's statement on the death of Sean Wrentmore. Elizabeth and Shan sat silently until he was finished with them.

He laid the pages on his desk and said, "I agreed to talk to you only out of courtesy, and with great reluctance."

"We appreciate that," Elizabeth said. "The courtesy."

"Not the reluctance," added Shan.

"This document"—Barstow pointed to the statement—"is hearsay. Mrs. Kristoll relates events described to her by her late husband. Yet you're asking me to take it as evidence of Mr. Wrentmore's death. I'm not inclined to. Do you have any other evidence? Physical evidence?"

Shan nodded. "We have a blood sample from the floor of the Kristolls' study. The blood type is the same as Sean Wrentmore's."

"That's far from conclusive," said Barstow.

Elizabeth watched a spider crawl along the rim of the lawyer's in-box.

She said, "We also have a statement from a friend of Tom Kristoll's—a man named David Loogan—saying that he helped dispose of Sean Wrentmore's body."

"Would this be the David Loogan whose picture was on the front page of the *News* yesterday, the David Loogan currently being sought in connection with another homicide?"

"That's right."

"Then he's hardly a reliable witness."

The spider found the edge of the desk and began to descend.

Elizabeth said, "Do you have reason to believe that Sean Wrentmore is alive, Mr. Barstow?"

"You've given me no solid reason to believe he's dead."

"When was the last time you spoke to him?" asked Shan.

"Several weeks ago, I'm sure. Eight weeks? Twelve? Something on that order. But that's not unusual. We have no need to be in constant contact."

"Well, his neighbors haven't seen him for a month," said Shan. "His parents haven't spoken to him for longer than that."

"Sean Wrentmore is a competent adult. He can come and go as he likes, and doesn't have to answer to his parents." Barstow held up his open palms. "But let's leave that aside. You believe he's dead. I have no knowledge of his alleged death. There's nothing helpful I could tell you."

Shan shifted in his chair. "What can you tell us about Innocent Man, Limited?"

"I can tell you nothing at all about Innocent Man, Limited," said Barstow.

"You prepared the paperwork that created the company. It's a matter of public record."

"That's true."

"What sort of work does Innocent Man do?"

The lawyer's small mouth made a frown. "Mr. Wrentmore is my client. I'm not at liberty to discuss these matters."

"The paperwork describes it as a consulting firm," Shan said.

"Then you can be sure that's what it is."

"What sort of consulting did Sean Wrentmore do? Who did he consult with?"

"I've already said I'm not going to discuss my client's business."

"Innocent Man paid Sean Wrentmore five thousand dollars a month. Where did that money come from?"

"I'm not at liberty to say."

Elizabeth broke in. "Did any of it come from Tom Kristoll?"

Barstow's face was unreadable. "I'm not at liberty to say."

Elizabeth got out of her chair and crossed to the room's lone window. The blinds were thick with dust and cobwebs.

She said, "Mr. Barstow, are you aware that Sean Wrentmore has been renting a storage unit for the last five years?"

He looked at her blankly. "No."

"So you have no idea what he might have kept in that storage unit?"

"No."

"Do you think it's just a coincidence—that he formed a company and started renting a storage unit at about the same time?"

"What else would it be?"

"Are you aware of any relationship between Wrentmore and a woman named Valerie Calnero?"

"I'm not privy to Mr. Wrentmore's personal relationships."

"What if I told you that after he died—"

"Allegedly died."

"After he died, Valerie Calnero took something from his storage unit. And shortly after that, she attempted to blackmail Tom Kristoll."

Barstow shot her a condescending look. "In that case, I would say that this Calnero woman is in need of a lawyer. But I fail to see how her actions reflect on Mr. Wrentmore."

"I'm sure you can look at it from our point of view," said Shan. "Sean Wrentmore has this mysterious company, and an unexplained income. Then if we toss in the idea of blackmail—"

"You should be careful what you toss in," Barstow said sharply. "Do you have evidence that Mr. Wrentmore is guilty of blackmail, or any other crime?"

Elizabeth shook her head slowly. "No. And we'd like to be able to eliminate it as a possibility, so we can move on to other matters."

Barstow rose behind the desk, picked up Laura Kristoll's statement, and held it out. "You should move on then," he said. "Mr. Wrentmore's income is from entirely legitimate sources. You have my assurance."

Shan was silent on the elevator and through the lobby of Barstow's building. When they hit the street he said, "Well, if we have his assurance . . ."

They were within sight of City Hall when Elizabeth's cell phone rang.

"Where are you?" Harvey Mitchum asked her.

When she told him he said, "Do you have time to do me a favor? Run by Sean Wrentmore's place?"

"What for?"

"I need to know his shoe size."

Chapter 30

MITCHUM HAD CALLED FROM THE NICHOLS ARBORETUM, A PARK ON THE shore of the Huron River. Elizabeth and Shan drove there together, left their car in a lot by the water, and walked along a broad dirt path to a spot at the foot of a hill where Mitchum stood with a tall, thin black woman in her fifties.

The woman had a dog on a leash, a mixed breed that was mostly greyhound. For the benefit of Elizabeth and Shan, she explained that she had let the dog off his leash and he had run up the hill and into the woods. He had been gone a long time. He had returned with a shoe in his mouth—a white running shoe covered in dirt and stained with something that looked like blood.

The shoe was a size ten. Wrentmore had worn a nine-and-a-half—too close to rule out a match. Still, Elizabeth had her doubts. According to Laura Kristoll, Wrentmore had been struck on the head; it wasn't clear how his blood would have ended up on his shoe. A call to David Loogan could have resolved the matter, if she could reach him and if he were willing to talk, but when she tried his number she got connected to his voice mail as usual.

In the end, there was nothing to do but have a look around. She and Mitchum and Shan climbed the trail up the hillside and fanned out into the woods. After an hour or so Ron Wintergreen joined them, bringing along one of the department's police dogs. At three o'clock Elizabeth and Shan departed. Shan had been called away on another case. He dropped Elizabeth at City Hall.

Back at her desk, she worked up a report on their conversation with Wrentmore's lawyer, then gathered Wrentmore's mail from Shan's desk and began to sort through it piece by piece. She was still at it when Alice Marrowicz came by, wearing a flowered dress like faded curtains.

"I've been calling hotels," Alice said. "We already sent out a fax with David Loogan's photo and description, but I've been following up like you suggested—asking if they've had anyone registered under the name Ted Carmady. I've gone through every hotel in town and a bunch in Detroit and the surrounding area. No luck yet. I'll keep trying."

"Thanks, Alice. But he's smart enough to come up with a fresh alias. Don't let this keep you from other work you have to do."

"It's no problem. I wish there were some other way I could help."

Elizabeth combed her fingers through her hair. "You can help me with Wrentmore's mail if you want." She picked up one of his credit card bills. "About all I've uncovered is that the man bought gas and groceries and occasionally went to a restaurant—where, from the looks of things, he ate alone."

She had the mail in two piles. She transferred one of them to Shan's desk. "This is the stuff I've already gone through," she said. "See if anything jumps out at you."

Alice settled into Shan's chair and set to work, poring over each piece of mail as if it might lead her to a buried treasure. She was still there when Elizabeth left at five o'clock.

Under a deep blue sky Elizabeth descended the steps of City Hall. As she walked to the parking lot, she thought about picking up groceries, getting home to her daughter.

She got her car out of the lot and aimed it south on Main Street. There were banners hung from lampposts. College students smoking in front of downtown shops. She crawled along for a while in rush hour traffic, and then, without intending to, found herself driving west toward David Loogan's neighborhood. She found his street and drew up before his rented house. An X of yellow police tape marked the front door.

She left the car and drifted up the walk. Made her way onto the porch— slow, hollow footsteps on the wooden planks. She stood by the porch swing and got out her phone. Entered Loogan's number, expecting to get his voice mail again.

He answered on the second ring. "Detective Waishkey," he said. "You startled me. I was just about to check my messages."

Now that she'd reached him, she wasn't sure what she would say. She sat on the porch swing, leaned back, put one foot up on the railing.

"Where are you?" she asked him.

"Always the optimist," he said. "One of these times I might tell you."

"I wish you would."

"I wonder what would happen," he said. "Would you send squad cars screaming down on me? Suppose I told you I was at the cemetery, standing by the fence where you and I talked the day of Tom's funeral—"

The smallest pressure of her foot on the railing set the porch swing in motion. "I wouldn't send squad cars. But I don't think that's where you are."

"No, it's not. How are things going? Did you talk to Sandy Vogel? Did you ask her if she told anyone about seeing Beccanti in Tom Kristoll's office?"

"Yes."

"What did she say?"

She relaxed into the motion of the swing. "I'm afraid that's part of an ongoing investigation. I'd like to tell you, but technically I'm not supposed to. I might be willing to bend the rules, but only if you told me something in return."

"Like what?"

"Like where Sean Wrentmore's buried."

"That's a big something."

"Let's start smaller then. Is he buried in the Nichols Arboretum?"

"No. Where'd you get that idea?"

"Someone found a shoe in the woods there today. It was roughly his size."

"He's not in the Arboretum. You shouldn't waste your time there."

"I already did," she said. "A good part of the afternoon. Me and three other detectives and a police dog. That's the way it's going to be from now on, whenever anyone finds a scrap of clothing in the woods, or a patch of dirt that looks like it's been disturbed. You need to tell me where to find Sean Wrentmore."

"I'm not ready to do that yet," he said.

She listened as the wind stirred the branches of a forsythia bush beside the porch.

"I know," she said. "Wrentmore is your leverage. You know where he is, and you think you might use the information as a bargaining chip later on." The bare forsythia branches scratched the wooden railing. "You're wrongly suspected of stabbing Michael Beccanti, and you think you're going to figure out who really killed him, and maybe you'll solve Tom Kristoll's murder too, while you're at it. But none of that is going to happen. Do you know why?"

"Yes," he said, without hesitation.

"Because this isn't a story in *Gray Streets*," she said. "Listen, you know I'm right. You should come in now, and tell me where Wrentmore is, and we'll go from there."

"I'll think about it. Give me a few more days."

"Don't think about it. Do it. I'm at your house right now. I'll wait for you here. We'll figure out what to do."

He paused, and the pause gave her hope, but only for a moment.

"It's tempting," he said, "but I'm not ready yet. A few more days."

Less than three miles away, Loogan turned off his phone and slipped it into a pocket. He looked down at the headstone of Tom Kristoll's grave, then turned and jogged across the cemetery lawn to his car. He drove along the winding road to the gate and headed east toward downtown Ann Arbor.

A few minutes later, he managed to find a metered parking space on a side street. He walked two blocks to Main, slipped into a café, found a table in front by the window. From there, he could look out at the building that housed the offices of *Gray Streets*.

His own face stared up at him from a discarded copy of the *Ann Arbor News*. He folded the paper over and smiled at a girl reading Kafka at another table. The corners of her mouth turned up briefly before she went back to her book. The photo in the paper had been a poor one to begin with, and he hardly resembled it now. He had shaved his head and bought a pair of drugstore reading glasses—black plastic frames and the weakest prescription he could find. He looked very much like every other man with a shaved head and glasses.

A moment later, the lobby door of the *Gray Streets* building opened, and a woman emerged. Sandy Vogel wore a long navy blue coat and had a handbag slung over her shoulder. She walked south along Main Street and when she was out of sight Loogan stood up. He smiled again at the girl reading Kafka, pushed through the door to the sound of a tinkling bell, and jogged across the street.

Elizabeth closed her phone and got up from the porch swing. She had called in to the department and talked to McCaleb. She had learned that Loogan's cell phone company had traced his call to an area on the west side of Ann Arbor, near the intersection of Wagner and Jackson. Tom Kristoll had been buried in a cemetery off Jackson Road. Loogan had been telling her the truth. She thought of driving there to look for him, but he would be gone by now. And McCaleb had already dispatched patrol cars to search the area.

As she descended the steps of Loogan's porch, she noticed a car parked across the street, partway down the block. The driver's door opened and a man climbed out—for a moment she had the crazy sense that it was Loogan. Then she saw that it was an old man in a rumpled suit, a man with gray, comb-over hair: Roy Denham, the detective from Nossos, New York.

Closing the door, he leaned wearily against the car. He smiled as she approached, and the smile transformed his loose-jowled face. He said, "Detective Waishkey, isn't it?"

"Detective Denham," she said. "How long have you been here?"

He checked his watch. "Nearly four hours," he said. "I wanted to be of some use, and yet stay out of everyone's way. Seemed like a good idea to watch Malone's house."

Elizabeth blinked at hearing Loogan's real name. She looked through the driver's window at the front seat and saw the usual detritus of a stake-out: a tall thermos and a half-eaten sandwich, a folded newspaper with a crossword mostly filled in. No sign of a weapon, and Denham didn't seem to be wearing a holster under his suit jacket.

"You don't have to worry," he said, as if he could read her thoughts. "I don't have a gun. Haven't carried one since I retired. I don't plan to try any cowboy stunts. If I see Malone I'll call it in." He flashed a cell phone and slipped it back in his pocket. "Technology," he said. "When I was young we had radios and nightsticks. Now you've got Tasers and cell phones."

He tipped his chin up at Loogan's porch. "Who were you talking to there, if you don't mind my asking?"

"Chief McCaleb," Elizabeth said. "And before that, Loogan—or Malone, if you like. I'm trying to lure him in. But he's got his own agenda. He thinks he's going to find out who really stabbed Michael Beccanti, and he thinks that's going to tell him who killed Tom Kristoll."

"You think he's telling the truth—he's not the one who stabbed this fellow Beccanti?"

"Yes. Though that puts me in the minority around the department, especially since you showed up and we found out about Jimmy Wade Peltier."

Denham produced a pack of cigarettes from a shirt pocket. Shook one loose, but didn't light it. "It may surprise you," he said, "but I tend to agree.

Like I said yesterday, I never expected to find Darrell Malone mixed up in something like this. I don't think he's a violent man, not at the root of him. What happened that night—up there on that parking deck—it was a fluke. Peltier provoked him."

Elizabeth watched him roll the cigarette between his finger and thumb, consider it, and slip it back in his pocket.

"Do you think you got the real story?" she said. "About what happened that night?"

"What do you mean?"

"I listened to your briefing, and I read the file. Loogan—Malone—stabbed Peltier, and Peltier went down. He was no longer a threat. Malone went to call for help. Then came back and stabbed Peltier a few more times for good measure. Do you think that's really what happened?"

Denham turned his face up to the dark sky, considering the question. "That's the story Malone told, and the wounds were consistent with it. What's the alternative?"

"It occurs to me that it wasn't just the two of them up there," said Elizabeth. "There was the woman—Charlotte Rittenour. She was unconscious for a time, but suppose she came to while Malone was calling for help. And there's Peltier lying right nearby, the knife in him. She's disoriented, terrified. Maybe he moves. She grabs the knife and stabs him."

"And then Malone takes the blame for it?"

"He's being noble," Elizabeth said. "He figures she's gone through enough."

Denham set his weary eyes on her. "It might be easier to take, if it happened that way. But we interviewed Charlotte Rittenour, and we questioned Malone every which way. His story was always the same. There's no reason to think it didn't happen the way he told us."

His smoker's voice dropped low. Elizabeth heard sympathy in it.

He said, "You like him—Malone. It's all right. There's no shame in it. I got to like him too. I think he's an honorable man, in his way. But there's no question about what he did to Jimmy Peltier."

———

Loogan crossed through the empty lobby and rode the elevator to the sixth floor. The doors opened and a man with a briefcase stood waiting. For a second Loogan froze, but the man gave him a bored look and stood aside to let him pass.

Loogan had the key ready when he reached the *Gray Streets* door. He listened for a moment with his ear close to the pebbled glass. No sound, no light inside.

He turned the key, went in, and locked the door behind him. Sliding his glasses into his pocket, he made his way to Sandy Vogel's desk and switched on her lamp. A stack of envelopes rested on her blotter: stories from eager writers, unsolicited and probably unpublishable.

At the edge of the blotter lay a leather-bound notebook: Sandy's day planner. Loogan opened it and glanced through some of the entries. Many of them were personal—a meeting at her daughter's middle school, a reminder to pick up her son from band practice. Out of curiosity, Loogan paged back to the day Tom Kristoll died. No dark secrets were revealed to him. He paged forward and spotted an entry for Saturday, November 7. Tomorrow. *Brunch at 11 with board at LK's.*

He closed the book, rolled the chair back from the desk, and spun slowly in a circle, thinking. After a moment he tapped the space bar on the keyboard of Sandy Vogel's computer and watched the monitor come to life. Ten minutes later he had what he needed and was back in his car heading out of town.

The moon glowed full overhead as Elizabeth made the turn onto her street.

She had spent a while with Denham, trading stories, and then she had left him behind at David Loogan's house. He promised her he wouldn't stay much longer; he would get something to eat and get some rest.

She had her window rolled down a few inches as she coasted along her street, barely touching the gas. A cool current of wind took her hair. She saw her house from a distance: the silhouette of the elm out front, the light of the porch, framed by the eaves and the posts and the railing. There were figures in the light. One of them was Sarah, the other was distinctly male. She knew at once it was not Loogan. It was a tall, skinny sixteen-year-old boy with unruly hair. Billy Rydell.

The two figures leaned into each other. Sarah put her arms up, clasped her hands at the back of the boy's neck. It was a practiced gesture; this was not the first time. A second later, when they kissed, Elizabeth knew that it was not their first kiss.

She eased her foot onto the brake. This needed thought. It was better not to overreact. Teenage girls had boyfriends. She had joked with Sarah about having an affair with Billy Rydell. She should have seen this coming.

She looked away for a moment, because it was awkward, watching. But she wasn't sure how she felt about not watching either. She knew all the theories about parenting, about respecting a child's privacy, trusting her to make good decisions. But there were limits, and sitting in a car at night and waiting patiently while your daughter made out with her boyfriend on the porch was somewhere on the far side of the limits. It was over the border and past the minefield and beyond the razor-wire fence.

Time to move then. She would drive on, let them see she was home, and sort it out from there. She looked up and Billy Rydell had his hand on her daughter's waist. They were still kissing. Elizabeth released the brake and the car rolled along and Billy's hand went under her daughter's shirt. He walked her a step backward until she was against the screen door. Sarah broke the kiss and wriggled sideways. She grabbed his wrist and pushed it down and away.

He moved in for another kiss and she braced her hands against his chest and shoved him away. He spread his arms in a gesture that said, *What's the big deal?*

Both of them turned then. Elizabeth had borne down on the accelerator and then the brake. The car screeched to a stop at an angle to the curb. The headlights washed over the lawn. She had the presence of mind to put the car in park, but not to cut the engine. Then she was out of the car. Billy Rydell saw her coming. He understood his situation. He thought about running—Elizabeth could read it in his face.

To his credit, he didn't run. He came down the porch steps, palms out, mouthing apologies. He tried to skirt her only at the last moment, when she reached for him. She got hold of his shirtfront, used his own momentum to spin him around. Walked him backward three paces and slammed him into the trunk of the elm tree.

The impact knocked the wind out of him. His eyes stared. The fist of her left hand clutched the fabric of his shirt. Her right hand was down at her side. Her pistol was in it. It took an act of will to keep herself from pressing the muzzle into Billy Rydell's ribs.

There ought to be shouting, she thought. There ought to be neighbors coming out of doors. There was nothing but Billy whispering, "Sorry, sorry, sorry, sorry, sorry."

Her own voice was scarcely louder.

"What are you doing?" she said. "What do you think you're doing?"

Chapter 31

ON A YELLOW LEGAL PAD, WITH A CHEAP BALLPOINT PEN, DAVID LOOGAN composed a story.

An ocean of cars surrounded him. He had parked in the lot of a cineplex south of Lansing, sixty miles from Ann Arbor. Behind him, on the backseat, lay his duffel bag and his leather coat. The guitar case and Wrentmore's shotgun were in the trunk.

On the passenger seat beside him there were three small items arranged in a row. The first was his cell phone; the second, a thin canister of pepper spray. The third was the flashdrive that Michael Beccanti had recovered from Sean Wrentmore's condominium. The flashdrive figured into the story Loogan was writing.

He had looked through Sandy Vogel's e-mail and read the memo she'd written about finding Beccanti in Tom Kristoll's office. The memo had gone to Laura Kristoll, Nathan Hideaway, Casimir Hifflyn, and Bridget Shellcross—the members of the *Gray Streets* board. He knew the board would meet for brunch tomorrow at Laura's house. He planned to join them there and tell them his story.

The story was a simple one, but Loogan was a fastidious writer. He drafted and redrafted and edited. He tore pages from the notepad and tossed them over his shoulder into the backseat.

Shortly after eleven, he produced a final draft. He read through it one last time, put the pad aside, and thought about settling in for the night. He had a reservation at a bed-and-breakfast in Okemos, east of Lansing, fifteen minutes away.

He had stayed away from hotels. There were bed-and-breakfasts everywhere, and their owners were glad to take cash and didn't require a lot of paperwork. He had searched for listings on a computer at an Internet café, and had made his reservations from pay phones, using the names of his old high school teachers. His pattern was to arrive late and leave early and never stay at the same place twice.

The owner of the place in Okemos had assured Loogan that he and his wife would be up at least until midnight. That gave Loogan some leeway. He glanced at his cell phone, lying dormant on the seat beside him. He could turn it on and check his messages, and then turn it off again and be on his way. He debated for a few seconds and then pressed the power button.

The screen showed him two missed calls, both from Elizabeth Waishkey, both within the last hour. He considered the wisdom of calling her back, and his curiosity got the better of him. She answered on the third ring.

"Mr. Loogan," she said. "Where are you?"

"I like hearing you say that," he told her. "It reassures me that you haven't caught up with me yet. If you didn't say it, I'd have to assume you had me surrounded."

"You're not surrounded. Why don't you tell me where you are?"

He opened the car door and got out to stretch his legs. "I'm standing in a parking lot," he said, "an undistinguished parking lot, in an unspecified city."

"Do you see lights flashing, red and blue?"

"Not yet."

"Then you're safe for now."

He walked along the side of the car. The marquee of the cineplex hung suspended in the distance.

"You called me twice," he said. "You must be working late."

"I couldn't sleep. Tell me what you were doing in Ann Arbor today."

"I already told you, I went to the cemetery. I visited Tom's grave. Are you all right?"

"Sure. Why?"

"You said you couldn't sleep. Is something wrong?"

"Nothing's wrong," she said. "Why did you visit Tom's grave?"

"It's been a week since Tom was buried. I'm a sentimental man. Did you know there's a headstone already? A thick chunk of granite. I don't know why that surprised me, but it did."

"So you risked a trip to Ann Arbor just to visit Tom's grave," she said. "Because you're sentimental."

"Yes."

"I don't think you're telling me the truth," she said.

"I don't think you're telling me the truth when you say nothing's wrong." He stared at the marquee and listened to her silence.

Eventually she let out a long breath. "I almost shot a sixteen-year-old today."

Elizabeth paced in her bedroom with the phone to her ear. She stopped at the window, pressed her fingers against the glass. Moonlight came from behind a cloud.

She heard Loogan ask, "What happened?"

The glass cooled her fingertips. "He's a friend of Sarah's," she said. "Her boyfriend, though I didn't know that for sure until today. I came home tonight and saw them making out on the porch. He got a little aggressive."

"Is she all right?" said Loogan. Sharply, fiercely.

"She's fine. She handled him—told him no, pushed him away. He was a little slow getting the message, and I overreacted. Before I knew what I was doing, I had him pinned against a tree, my nine-millimeter in my hand. It was a close thing."

It had been closer than Elizabeth would have liked. Sarah had been the one to bring it to an end. She could have panicked, she certainly had cause, but she never raised her voice. She came down from the porch and put her palm against her mother's back. Elizabeth felt it there, a soft touch between her shoulder blades. She heard her daughter say, "Okay. I'm okay. Let him go."

And she holstered the gun and let Billy Rydell loose and sent him home.

She went inside with Sarah and calmed down enough to talk. The talk was reassuring. Billy had never done anything like that before, Sarah told her. He had never tried to force her.

They had talked for an hour and then fixed a late supper. Sarah had gone to bed. Elizabeth had been unable to sleep. And now she stood at the window in her room, in a T-shirt and sweats, her raven hair tied up. And now she said to David Loogan, "I wanted to shoot him."

"I know," he said.

"That wouldn't have gone over well. There's a term for it: disproportionate force."

"You didn't shoot him," Loogan said.

"If I'd shot him, I might not have stopped with one bullet."

"It's over now."

She left the window and paced across the room. "That's what I keep telling myself, and it's comforting to think so. But it isn't really over, is it? Because I know how close I came. This time I'm safe. I got through it. But what happens next time?"

"You controlled yourself this time," he said. "You'll do the same thing next time."

"How do I know that?"

"Because you're an honorable person."

"Is that enough?"

"It should be."

"But you can be an honorable person and still do the wrong thing. Isn't that right?"

The question echoed in the confines of her room. Silence on the line. She imagined him standing perfectly still.

"Do you know why I wanted to talk to you tonight, David?"

The smallest of delays before he answered. "Yes."

"I shouldn't say David. I should say Darrell. Darrell Malone." She braced her back against the bedroom door. "I like David better."

"So do I."

"We've heard from the Nossos police," she said. "We know about Jimmy Wade Peltier."

No response to that. She realized she had been hoping for puzzlement—*Who's Jimmy Wade Peltier?*—or a denial.

"I've talked to Roy Denham," she added after a moment. "Do you know what he said about you?"

"What?"

"He said he thought you were an honorable man."

"That was nice of him."

"He also said you stabbed Jimmy Peltier seventeen times."

David Loogan, who had once been Darrell Malone, leaned against the fender of the car.

"That sounds about right," he said.

"Denham said you stabbed Peltier until he went down, then came back and stabbed him some more. I didn't want to believe that."

He tipped his head back and looked up at the sky. "Elizabeth—"

"I came up with an alternative," she said. "The woman you were with—Charlotte Rittenour. She could have played a part. You started the job, and then went off to call for help. And while you were gone, she finished it."

Loogan watched the blinking light of an airplane passing overhead. Slow progress, east to west. "It could have gone like that," he said. "I'm sure it would have—if it was a story in *Gray Streets*."

"But it wasn't a story in *Gray Streets*," she said.

He reached for the handle of the car door, feeling suddenly cold and tired. He got in and dragged the door shut after him.

"I wish I could give you what you're looking for," he said. "But there's no mistake. I did what I did to Jimmy Peltier. I'm not going to try to make excuses now."

Quiet on the line. He was about to turn off the phone when she said, "Are you getting ready to leave?"

He touched the key in the ignition. "I'll have to, soon. I can't stay here all night."

"I mean *leave* leave," she said. "You went to Tom's grave. That's the action of a man who's moving on—who's not sure when he'll come this way again."

"I'm not leaving yet," he said. "There are one or two more things I want to do."

"Like what?"

"I can't tell you," he said lightly. "You wouldn't approve."

He expected protest—the familiar admonition to turn himself in. But he heard her laugh softly, and then she added two words: "Be careful."

Chapter 32

A BRIGHT YELLOW LEAF BROKE FREE OF A HIGH BRANCH AND DRIFTED down, spinning slowly through the autumn air. David Loogan followed its descent and at the last moment reached out and caught it on his palm.

From his vantage point at the edge of the woods, he could see the Kristoll house: the lines of the slate roof, the broad windows, the path of crushed stone that led to the front door. He had watched the four guests arrive. Nathan Hideaway first, then Casimir Hifflyn and Bridget Shellcross in Hifflyn's Lexus. Sandy Vogel had shown up last, and had parked her minivan away from the other vehicles. Laura Kristoll had come to the door to greet each of her guests.

Loogan held the stem of the yellow leaf between his finger and thumb and spun it slowly. His car was parked on the side of an unpaved road about a mile away. He had left it there and had hiked up the side of a hill and through the woods. After a while he broke onto a path that he remembered— he and Tom had used it once to walk down to the river. He followed it up to the Kristolls' backyard, then skirted around to the front.

He had been waiting for more than two hours now. He wasn't sure how long they would be. A leisurely brunch, he thought, and then a discussion of *Gray Streets* business. He spun the leaf side to side and let it go and watched it drift to the ground. Yawning, he stood on his toes and stretched his arms over his head.

He had not slept well at the bed-and-breakfast in Okemos. His dreams had been troubled. In one of them, he had stood shoulder deep in Sean Wrentmore's grave, holding Wrentmore's pistol up to the moonlight.

Now he leaned his back against the trunk of a birch and watched as the front door of the Kristoll house opened. He had assumed and hoped that Sandy Vogel would be the first to depart. She was the outsider, the employee. The other four were old friends.

He was right. Sandy came out; Laura waved her good-bye and went back in. Sandy, in her navy blue coat, walked down the crushed-stone path and got into her minivan.

Loogan watched her drive away and then crossed quickly to the front door of the house. The knob turned and he slipped inside, through the entry hall, into the living room. He heard voices from the back of the house. He made his way past Tom's study—empty. A right turn at the stairs and there was the dining room. Casimir Hifflyn was coming through the doorway. He saw Loogan and stopped short.

Loogan put on a friendly smile. "You're not leaving, are you, Cass?" he said. "You can't leave. I just got here."

The curtains in the dining room had been drawn back, and the windows were panes of glass over canvases of autumn leaves, dots and strokes of orange and yellow and red. The plates from brunch had been cleared away to a sideboard, and the main table held a smattering of papers and copies of the latest issue of *Gray Streets*.

"Don't get up," Loogan said, but they were already rising. Laura rushed forward to embrace him. He felt her fingers on the bare skin of his scalp. "David, are you all right?" she whispered. Nathan Hideaway clapped him on the shoulder. "The remarkable Mr. Loogan," he said.

"We've been discussing you," said Hifflyn. "Where's David Loogan? we've been asking ourselves. And how will we find someone to replace him?"

"Don't tell him that," said Bridget Shellcross. "He's back now. We won't need to replace him." She stood on tiptoe to peck him on the cheek. "We've mostly been talking about how ridiculous it is—that anyone could think you stabbed Michael Beccanti."

"Of course it's ridiculous," said Laura.

"But now you're back," said Bridget. "I hope that means you've been cleared."

"I'm afraid not."

"Well, it's a lot of nonsense," Hideaway said. "We need to get you a lawyer, someone who knows how to handle the police."

"Nate's right," said Hifflyn. "Laura, why don't you get Rex Chatterjee on the phone?"

"I didn't come here for a lawyer," Loogan said. "Why don't we all sit down."

Laura slipped her hand into his. "David, I'd be happy to call him."

"I don't have much time," Loogan said. "My car's parked not that far away. If the police see it, they'll be able to guess where I am. But there's something—"

Hideaway interrupted him. "That's more nonsense: having to skulk around like a criminal."

"There's something I need to tell you," Loogan continued. "It's the only reason I came here. To warn you."

He drew a wooden chair out from the table and settled into it. The rest of them followed suit, returning to their places.

"To warn us about what?" asked Casimir Hifflyn. "What are you talking about?"

"I'm talking about what's been going on in plain sight for the past two weeks. Tom, and Adrian Tully, and Michael Beccanti. Someone is murdering people associated with *Gray Streets*."

Loogan spoke the words to the tabletop, then looked up to see Laura's blue eyes regarding him intently.

"And I don't think it's over yet," he said. "All of us are at risk." He let his gaze shift to each of the others. "The police are on the wrong track. They're focusing on Sean Wrentmore. I thought he was part of it too, at first. But I've come to realize I was wrong. Wrentmore was an isolated case. Adrian Tully killed him, and Tom covered it up. But Wrentmore's death has nothing to do with the other three: Tom's and Tully's and Beccanti's. Those three were all killed by the same person, and it's somebody no one suspects."

Hideaway spoke up. "Are you saying you know who killed them?"

"Yes," Loogan said. "I figured it out yesterday."

He let the words hover in the air. Waited for someone to ask the obvious question.

Laura obliged him. "Who?"

Loogan turned to her. "It's someone you just ate brunch with," he said.

Hifflyn's chair creaked as he leaned forward. "That's in poor taste, Mr. Loogan—suggesting that one of us is a murderer."

"No," said Loogan, waving the idea away. "It's not one of you. It's Sandy Vogel."

Chapter 33

Looks were exchanged around the table. Heads wagged from side to side. Indulgent smiles appeared. Hifflyn seemed about to speak, but Bridget Shellcross cut him off.

"You can't really expect us to believe that Sandy Vogel is a serial killer."

"I know how it sounds," Loogan said.

"Sandy is the mother of two teenagers," Hifflyn observed.

"On the night Tom died," said Loogan seriously, "he and Sandy Vogel were alone in the office together. As far as anyone knows, she was the last person to see Tom alive."

Laura frowned. "She left at five o'clock. It was after seven when Tom died."

"She says she left at five. I'm not sure the police even bothered to check her alibi." Loogan shrugged the issue away. "And consider Adrian Tully. Someone convinced him to drive out to a cornfield late at night. Sandy Vogel is a good-looking woman. I don't think she would have had any trouble luring him to a secluded spot."

"That's awfully thin," said Nathan Hideaway. "Just because she could have lured him out there, that doesn't mean she did."

Loogan continued as though Hideaway hadn't spoken. "And then there's Michael Beccanti. He's the clincher. Because Sandy had a motive to kill Michael Beccanti. It's one of the oldest motives there is. They were lovers, and he left her for another woman."

"I admit I'm speculating about Tom and about Tully," he said. "But Sandy's affair with Beccanti is a fact. I went to the *Gray Streets* office last night and I got onto Sandy's computer. The evidence is there. Tom told me the story once of how he met Beccanti. Beccanti was in prison, and he sent a fan letter to the magazine, and later he submitted stories. Sandy handled Tom's correspondence. And at some point she struck up a relationship with Beccanti. It's all there on her computer: the letters she wrote to him while he was in prison, then the e-mails they exchanged after he got out."

Loogan looked around the table—at Hideaway on his left, Laura across from him, Bridget and Hifflyn on his right. He had their attention. Casually he reached into the pocket of his leather coat. His canister of pepper spray was there, and Sean Wrentmore's flashdrive. He would need them in a moment.

"The relationship turned physical after Beccanti got out," he said. "That's clear from the e-mails. But gradually it went sour. Sandy began to suspect that Beccanti was seeing other women. He denied it at first, but she kept after him. Finally he confessed. He was seeing a woman named Karen, and it was serious. He broke things off with Sandy."

Loogan brought his hand out of his coat pocket and rested it on the tabletop—the flashdrive and the pepper spray beneath his cupped palm.

"She took it hard," he said. "She was especially angry when she found out that Karen was a much younger woman—and that Beccanti had gotten her pregnant. Sandy felt betrayed. She wrote him a long note about that. The language was telling. 'You wounded me,' she said. 'You might as well have stabbed me with a knife.'"

Bridget Shellcross shot him a skeptical look. "And that's your proof? That's why you think she stabbed him?"

"If anyone has a better explanation, I'm eager to hear it."

"Come now, Mr. Loogan," said Hideaway. "Sandy's not exactly a trained assassin. She's a secretary."

"She's a secretary now," Loogan acknowledged. "Who knows what she might have been before? A Navy SEAL, or a Hollywood stuntwoman. What do any of us really know about her past?"

Hifflyn sat back in his chair with his arms crossed. "Even if she had a motive for killing Beccanti," he said, "why would she kill Tom, or Adrian Tully?"

"That's the ingenious part," Loogan said. "I think she planned this very carefully. She had been discreet about her affair with Beccanti. But she couldn't be sure who Beccanti might have told. Someone might be able to connect them. If he turned up dead, she might be a suspect. So she found a way to disguise his murder—to make it look like part of a series."

Loogan reached for a saltshaker and stood it on the table in front of him. He stood the flashdrive beside it, and then the canister of pepper spray.

He pointed to each item in turn. "Tom was first," he said. "Then Tully. She had no motive to kill either of them, and no one suspected her. Then it was safe to go after her real target—Beccanti. No one would suspect her of that either."

He paused and looked at the pepper spray as if noticing it for the first time. He picked it up and a sheepish grin passed across his face.

"I brought this along in case one of you decided you had a duty to call the police and turn me in. But you're such a well-mannered bunch. I should have known I wouldn't need it."

He slipped the canister back into his coat pocket. Then he picked up the flashdrive.

"This is something Beccanti found in Sean Wrentmore's condo. I still don't know what's on it—it's password protected. Doesn't matter. It's a red herring." The drive went into his pocket. "Like I said, Wrentmore's death has nothing to do with the other three."

Laura stared at him from across the table. "David, do you really expect us to believe this—this wild theory of yours?"

He looked off at the autumn colors beyond the windows. "I've done what I came for: I've warned you," he said. "You can believe what you like. But if you think the killing is over, maybe you should think twice. If Sandy Vogel committed a series of murders in order to disguise her murder of Michael Beccanti, then who's to say she's finished?"

He pushed his chair back slowly and stood. "I'm not worried about my-self. I'm going to walk out of here, and that'll be the end of it for me. I've been staying in a place where no one's thought to look yet, and tomorrow I'll be gone. But the rest of you are vulnerable. She knows where to find you."

He took a last look around the table. None of them had risen with him.

"Maybe I'm wrong," he said. "But if I'm not, one of you may be next."

When Elizabeth dropped by the squad room on Saturday afternoon, she found Sean Wrentmore's mail in an orderly pile on her desk. At the top of the pile was a cryptic note from Alice Marrowicz: *Looking into Wrentmore— Art Studio.*

She tossed her coat onto a filing cabinet and sat down. Beside Wrent-more's mail she found a copy of a report that Shan had written up for the file on David Loogan. It told her something she already knew: Loogan's cell phone company had traced his Friday-night call to an area south of Lan-sing. Loogan had left the phone turned on when he ended the call, and after a long search the Lansing police had recovered it from a movie-theater parking lot. They'd been unsuccessful in locating Loogan himself.

Beneath Shan's report, she found a note from Harvey Mitchum, telling her that the sneaker from the Nichols Arboretum wasn't likely to lead any-where. Mitchum had left it at the county lab for testing, and the techni-cian he had spoken with thought the stain looked more like motor oil than blood.

As she was reading Mitchum's note, Alice Marrowicz came in. She seemed reluctant to approach until Elizabeth waved her over.

"Alice. Sit down. Tell me what you've been up to."

Alice slipped into Shan's chair. "I've done some investigating. Maybe I shouldn't have. You only asked me to look at Sean Wrentmore's mail."

"It's all right," said Elizabeth. "What did you find?"

"A charge on his MasterCard bill—from the Art Studio. You may have missed it."

"No, I remember that. I assumed he bought something to hang on his wall. He had a fondness for arty black-and-white photographs."

"The Art Studio is a tattoo parlor on Cross Street in Ypsilanti."

Ypsilanti bordered Ann Arbor on the east—the city's rougher cousin. Elizabeth felt mild surprise at the thought that Alice was familiar with tattoo parlors there. Then she considered the woman's penchant for long sleeves and sweaters and high-necked dresses, and realized how little she knew about what might lie underneath.

She put the thought aside. "Wrentmore had a tattoo on his wrist," she said. "A series of interlocking rings."

"He had another one besides," said Alice. "He got it in September. I called the Art Studio last night, but the guy I talked to wasn't the one who worked on Wrentmore. And they're not big on record-keeping, so he couldn't tell me anything. I tried again today, and Wrentmore's artist was there, but he was reluctant to answer questions on the phone.

"Tattoo artists are like shrinks, I guess. They believe in confidentiality. Only they're not so strict about it, because when I drove out there he agreed to talk to me. I guess I look like a trustworthy person."

"What did he tell you?" Elizabeth asked.

"Sean Wrentmore got a freehand. That means a unique design, not some standard thing you pick off the wall. It was two words in black ink, on his left arm just below the shoulder. But the words were reversed, so you could read them in a mirror. That made it tricky, having to write backwards."

"I imagine it did," said Elizabeth. "Were the two words 'Adrian Tully'?"

Alice looked momentarily confused. "No. Why would you say that?"

"Because that's supposed to be who killed him. It would be clever if he had the name of his killer tattooed on his arm."

Alice considered the idea solemnly. "No, it wasn't that," she said, and then went quiet, seemingly lost in thought. As the silence drew itself out, Elizabeth had to smile.

"What were the words, Alice?"

Chapter 34

THE HEADSTONE OF TOM KRISTOLL'S GRAVE WAS A SLAB OF GRANITE, rough-hewn at the edges. But its face had been polished smooth and his name and dates engraved there. A clutch of roses lay before it on the grass, their petals dark and withered. And on a lip of granite at the base of the stone was another offering: a small bottle of Glenfiddich Scotch. David Loogan's work, Elizabeth thought.

The late-afternoon sun sent the headstone's shadow long across the grass. Elizabeth looked up and saw Carter Shan lingering a dozen yards away, studying an inscription above the door of a mausoleum. She saw a pair of cars winding their way along the cemetery road and watched their progress until they reached the spot where she had left her car. Rex Chatterjee was the first to emerge. He took up a position at the edge of the road and folded his arms, and a breeze mussed his thick gray hair.

Casimir Hifflyn got out of the second car, stopped for a few words with Chatterjee, and then began to make his way across the grass. He wore a suit of black wool and the wind caught the open front of his jacket. He wore a pale gray shirt underneath with no tie.

He grinned shyly as he got close, and bowed his head, but when he stood before Elizabeth he met her eyes. "Hello, Detective."

"Mr. Hifflyn. Thanks for coming." She looked past him at Chatterjee. "Your lawyer can come closer, if you want him. You don't have to leave him way over there."

"He'd rather I didn't talk to you at all, but we worked out an agreement. If it gets to the point where you read me my rights, I have to call him over here."

"Then I'll try not to read you your rights," Elizabeth said.

"This is better. Talking one-on-one. It's more dramatic." Hifflyn looked down at the roses on the ground. "You must have a sense of drama, or you wouldn't have asked me to meet you at a cemetery—at the site of my friend's grave, no less—without explaining why."

He looked up again and his smile made crow's-feet at the corners of his eyes. "Well, now I'm here. What will we talk about?"

"Kendel's Fortune," Elizabeth said.

He nodded thoughtfully. "That's a dramatic subject."

"Kendel's Fortune is the title of your latest book. It comes out in hardcover at the end of the month."

"Just in time for holiday shoppers."

"Last month Sean Wrentmore had the words 'Kendel's Fortune' tattooed on his left arm," Elizabeth said. "Why do you suppose he would do that?"

Hifflyn smoothed the palm of his right hand over his close-cropped beard.

"I imagine you won't be satisfied if I tell you he was a really big fan."

"No."

"Then the alternative is obvious," he said. "Sean Wrentmore was a writer."

Elizabeth nodded. "He was an obscure writer with an unexplained source of income. And you're a famous writer with a demanding schedule. Book signings, speaking engagements, and you're expected to crank out at least one new novel every year. And that's what you've done—eighteen books over the last seventeen years. Ten stand-alone novels and eight Kendel mysteries. How many of those did Sean Wrentmore write?"

"Just three," Hifflyn said, with a little lift of his shoulders. "The last three Kendel books."

"How much did you pay him?"

"We split the money, half-and-half. Maybe he deserved more—he put the words on the pages. But I created the character, and my name on the cover sold the books. I think he was happy with what he got. It was more money than he had ever seen."

"But he never got any recognition."

The wind sent stray leaves tumbling over the grass. Hifflyn followed them with his eyes.

"I'm not sure he wanted it. Sean was a classic introvert. I think he would have been out of his element at a reading or a book signing."

"Still, it must have bothered him," said Elizabeth. "He wrote novels that made the best-seller lists, and he couldn't tell anyone. That was part of the deal, right?"

"Of course."

"All he had was empty gestures—like tattooing the title of his novel on his arm. Did you know about that?"

Hifflyn looked up from watching the leaves. "No."

"He had it put on backwards. It was something for him to look at in the mirror. That reveals something about his character, don't you think?"

"I suppose it does."

"Maybe you're wrong, when you say he didn't want recognition. I think he wanted it—even if he felt ambivalent about it."

"That may be true."

"I think we both know it's true," Elizabeth said. "And it's the reason Tom Kristoll died."

She studied his reaction. He looked away, at the grave. She thought she saw one of his eyelids flutter—a sign of tension, but hardly enough to convict a man on. When he looked back to her, his features were composed. His mouth set itself in a pleasant line. He asked, "Am I going to need my lawyer?"

"That's up to you," she said. "I haven't read you your rights. I'm not going to ask you questions. I'm going to spin you a tale. All you have to do is listen."

He spread his arms. "Go ahead."

Elizabeth's fingers touched the beaded necklace at her throat. "Some of this is speculation," she said. "Suppose Sean Wrentmore did care about recognition. He was the author of three Kendel books, and he wanted it to be known. But he liked the money he was earning, the deal he had made. He wanted it to go on, and that meant keeping quiet. But Wrentmore thought of himself as a serious writer. Serious writers take a long view. At some point—whether at the end of his life, or after his death—the deal wouldn't matter anymore. Then he would want people to know who he was.

"How could he make that happen? First he would need proof. Suppose he kept the original manuscripts of his Kendel novels—the working copies, with his own handwritten edits. Suppose he sealed them in envelopes and sent them to himself by registered mail. That would fix the dates. It would prove he hadn't copied them from published sources. It wasn't a hoax; he was the real author.

"Then he would need to keep the manuscripts in a safe place. He decided not to keep them in his condo—I can only guess about the reason. If he died, his family would control access to his condo, and he wasn't close to his family. Maybe he didn't want to trust them with his secret.

"The hiding place he settled on was a fireproof box in unit 401 of a place called Self-Storage USA. Now he needed an accomplice, someone to carry out his wishes after he was gone. In the end, he chose two accomplices. Neither one knew about the other. He gave them each a key to the storage unit, asked them each to go there if anything ever happened to him. They would know what to do when they got there, because he had left instructions in the box with the manuscripts. It's easy enough to guess what the instructions were: Alert the press. Call *Publishers Weekly*, or whoever you'd call to report that the real author of the most recent Kendel books was Sean Wrentmore."

Hifflyn smiled at that, but said nothing.

Elizabeth continued. "So his accomplices take the keys and agree to Wrentmore's request. Maybe they're curious, but they're not curious enough to actually drive out to Self-Storage USA and see what's there. Sean has his strange ways, and it does no harm to indulge him. Nothing's going to happen to him anyway.

"But something does happen. Wrentmore's got this manuscript—this ungainly thing he's been working on for years. *Liars, Thieves, and Innocent Men*. He shows it to Tom Kristoll and Tom tries to do him a favor. He edits the novel down to a realistic length. Adrian Tully helps him. But Wrentmore doesn't take well to being edited. It's a matter of pride—and he's earned some pride, hasn't he? He's the author of two published novels, with a third one coming out soon. Tom's editing—all these drastic cuts—it ticks him off. There's an argument, and it goes farther than anyone could have predicted. Wrentmore ends up dead.

"But his death is kept secret. Tom covers it up. Adrian Tully knows about it, because he's the one who knocked Wrentmore over the head with the Scotch bottle. Laura Kristoll knows because Tom tells her. David Loogan doesn't know—even though he helps Tom dispose of the body. Tom decides to keep him in the dark."

Elizabeth paused. She watched Carter Shan strolling along behind a row of headstones. Rex Chatterjee slouching against the fender of his car.

She returned her gaze to Hifflyn. "So that's three people who knew, not counting Loogan," she said. "But that's not all. Tom told you, didn't he?"

"Yes," Hifflyn said.

"Because he knew about your arrangement with Sean Wrentmore."

"Tom's the one who brought us together," Hifflyn said. "It was his idea to get Sean to take over the Kendel series."

"How did you react when he told you Sean was dead?"

Hifflyn put his hands in the pockets of his black wool jacket, drew his chin down to the collar as if to escape a chill.

"I thought it was horrible, naturally," he said. "But I'm afraid I reacted less than honorably. Tom had made the decision to conceal Sean's death. It was done. I thought reversing that decision could only make things worse.

I told him I didn't want to hear anything more about it. I didn't want to discuss Sean Wrentmore ever again."

"But that wasn't the end of it," said Elizabeth.

"No."

"Because Wrentmore still had his two accomplices. His death was a secret, but one of them found out."

Hifflyn cocked his head to the side. "You might as well say her name—Valerie Calnero."

"All right."

"I don't know why you'd want to hide her identity from me, unless you think I intend to do her harm."

"Well, she's given you reason to wish her harm, hasn't she?"

Hifflyn shrugged the question away.

Elizabeth went on. "Wrentmore made a bad judgment when he chose Valerie. David Loogan thinks he chose her because he wanted to get close to her. But whatever affection he may have had for her, it only went one way. Wrentmore had everything planned, he knew what he wanted, but Valerie didn't follow the plan. She found out he had been killed—I imagine she found out from Adrian Tully. He would have needed someone to confess to.

"She heard his confession and then remembered the key Wrentmore had given her. She drove to his storage unit and found his Kendel manuscripts and his instructions, but she didn't call the newspaper or *Publishers Weekly*. From what I can gather, she was unhappy at the university. She may have been looking for a way out. Now she had one. She knew Tom Kristoll had covered up Wrentmore's death. He might pay to keep her quiet. And she knew Sean had been writing your Kendel novels—and she was sure you'd pay to keep that quiet."

A cloud drifted across the sun. Elizabeth watched the change in the color of the grass.

"So you and Tom each got a letter," she said to Hifflyn. "Valerie asked him for fifty thousand dollars. I assume she asked you for considerably more."

"She did."

"What was the deal? You were supposed to send the money to a mail drop in Chicago, and she would send you the manuscripts?"

"She wanted me to buy them one at a time," Hifflyn said. "A hundred thousand apiece. She thought I'd be more willing to go along that way. I wouldn't have to send all the cash at once and then hope I'd get the manuscripts."

"Is that the way it worked? Did you decide to give her what she wanted?"

Hifflyn skimmed the sole of one of his shoes over the grass. He nudged the withered roses, then bent to pick one up.

"I know you think I did," he said. "That's the only way your theory makes sense."

"My theory?"

He held the stem of the rose in two hands. "Your theory of the crime," he said. "The murder of Tom Kristoll. Tom and I are being blackmailed, and I decide to pay. But Tom balks at paying fifty thousand. Or he develops a conscience and decides he has to go to the police and tell them everything. But I can't let him do that, because if the truth comes out about Sean, my reputation will be ruined. So I go to Tom's office and knock him out and push him through the window. Is that the story?"

"That's part of it," Elizabeth allowed.

"What's the rest?"

"Adrian Tully."

"Sure," Hifflyn said. "Adrian knows about Sean's death, and he's a suspect in Tom's murder. So I get him to drive out to the middle of nowhere one night, and I shoot him in the head. I make it seem like a suicide. Sean's death remains a secret, and you assume that Adrian shot himself out of remorse. So you can stop looking for Tom's killer."

He touched a petal of the rose and it broke free and drifted in the wind. "But I'm still not done," he said. "David Loogan and Michael Beccanti won't let things rest. Beccanti starts to poke around in Tom's office. So one night I follow him to Loogan's house and stab him. And now you've found me out, because Sean Wrentmore got a tattoo."

He plucked at another petal and it crumbled between his fingers.

"Is that about right?" he said. "Is that your theory?"

"More or less," she said.

"Shall I tell you what's wrong with it?"

"Go ahead."

He drew out a petal and set it loose on the wind. "I never responded to the blackmail letter."

"I find that hard to believe."

"I never talked to Tom about it. We never argued." Another petal took flight. "I never paid Valerie Calnero a dime. Put yourself in my place. One day I found out Sean was dead. A few days later I received the letter. I didn't know it was from Valerie. It was signed with a pseudonym. But whoever wrote it knew that Sean was dead. I assumed it was from Adrian Tully."

"When did you realize it was from Valerie?"

"I started to wonder earlier this week," he said, "when she suddenly left town. I wasn't sure until you confirmed it just now. But the letter had to be from Tom or Laura or Adrian—or from someone they confided in. Adrian seemed to be the likeliest candidate. And if the letter came from him, it was a bluff. He wasn't going to carry out his threat. If he revealed that Sean wrote my Kendel books, people would go looking for Sean. Sooner or later they'd find out he was dead. Adrian couldn't risk that, since he was the one who killed him."

He plucked the remaining petals all at once and tossed them away. "But even if the letter wasn't a bluff, it wasn't worth paying. The deal I made with Sean wasn't illegal. It used to be a common practice: An author would originate a character, and others would come in and continue the series under the same byline. My agent knew about Sean. So did my publisher.

"I'm not ashamed of my arrangement with Sean," Hifflyn said. "I didn't pay ransoms to keep it secret. I certainly didn't kill anyone." He dropped the stem of the rose on the ground. "If you really thought I was a killer, why would you meet with me out here alone?"

"We're not alone," said Elizabeth. "You brought your lawyer."

"You didn't know he'd be here."

She nodded toward Shan, who had walked to the cemetery fence. "My partner's here too. He's been keeping an eye on you." She smoothed a strand of hair that the wind had pushed across her forehead. "But the reason I asked you to come here is simple," she said. "I was hoping you'd confess."

"I'm sorry to disappoint you."

She looked thoughtfully at the gray stone that marked Tom Kristoll's grave. "The story you've told isn't bad," she said to Hifflyn. "You never paid off Valerie Calnero. You might be able to stick with that and get away with it. It will be difficult to prove either way, unless we get a chance to talk to Valerie. You're a resourceful man—I think you're capable of paying off a blackmailer without leaving a paper trail."

She turned away from the stone and stepped closer to Hifflyn. "But you're not invulnerable," she said. "I think you regret what happened between you and Tom."

His brow furrowed. "Nothing happened between me and Tom."

"With the others—Tully, Beccanti—you did what the logic of the situation required," she said softly. "You weren't attached to them. But Tom was your friend. Never mind what happened twenty years ago—he stole Laura away from you. That was in the past. Or maybe not. Maybe that made it easier.

"I'm sure you didn't go to his office intending to kill him. You thought he'd be reasonable. Both of you would pay and Sean's death would remain a secret. Then suddenly Tom tells you he wants to go to the police. I'm sure you tried to talk him out of it. But at some point it became clear he was serious. And then things happened fast. You hit him—it was a spur-of-the-moment decision. Maybe you hit him harder than you meant to. Then he was on the floor. And there was the window. You did it without thinking, and you regretted it as soon as it was done. I think you've been obsessing about it ever since. You've been trying to figure out just how it went wrong, and whether there was something you could have said to him to change his mind."

"It sounds like I've been tormented," said Hifflyn dryly.

"And now you've got your lawyer. You'll try to ride it out. You think there's no possible advantage in confessing. Maybe you think it's all or nothing: If you admit to killing Tom, you'll be charged with killing the others—Tully and Beccanti. But that's not true. No one's going to make a case against you for killing Tully, not with the evidence as muddled as it is. Tully looks like a suicide. You could argue he killed himself because Laura Kristoll rejected him, or his mother didn't love him, or the world never gave him a chance."

She softened her voice further. A tone for sharing confidences. "As for Beccanti, he got stabbed in David Loogan's house, and Loogan disappeared the same night. Any public defender could get reasonable doubt out of that. Rex Chatterjee could do it with the sun in his eyes. So put Beccanti out of your mind, and Tully too. Focus on Tom. You were friends, you had an argument, it spun out of control. A situation like this, it's what plea bargains were made for. There are people in the prosecutor's office who'd be glad to work out a deal, just to have some resolution. They'd be willing to make allowances. You wouldn't have to say what you and Tom argued about. You could leave Sean Wrentmore out of it. The books he wrote, the blackmail—none of that would have to come out."

Hifflyn frowned. "I told you, I don't care if that comes out."

"Of course," she said. "You're not ashamed of your arrangement with Sean Wrentmore. It used to be a common practice. But these days you never know how readers are going to react, do you? They might decide they want their money back. If you really didn't care, you'd put out a press release, get out ahead of the story. But I think you're still hoping to keep your secret. Maybe you still can."

He locked his eyes on hers. "If I confess to a crime I didn't commit."

"No," she said. "I would never advise an innocent man to confess."

"But you don't believe I'm innocent."

She put on her best neutral expression and said nothing at all.

They regarded each other, and if it was a contest of wills, she was the victor. He turned away first. He paced to the foot of Tom Kristoll's grave, rubbing the hair at the nape of his neck.

"Suppose I could offer you an alternative theory of the crime, and a new suspect?"

This was something she hadn't anticipated. "Who would that be?"

He turned around to face her. "Sandy Vogel," he said. "Don't laugh. Hear me out. Suppose Tom's murder had nothing to do with Sean. Suppose Sandy killed Tom, and Adrian, and Beccanti too. Suppose she had a motive for killing Beccanti—they had an affair, and he threw her over for a younger woman. She killed the others to disguise the fact that Beccanti was her real target."

Elizabeth looked past Hifflyn at a far-off willow, at the branches swaying with the wind.

"Did you come up with that just now?" she asked.

"No."

"It sounds like something Tom might have printed in *Gray Streets*."

"I think he did, more than once," said Hifflyn. "It's a variant of a standard scenario: covering up a murder by making it look like part of a random series."

"You don't really think it's plausible."

"It's as plausible as the idea that I killed Tom because he wanted to tell the police about Sean. You've got as much hard evidence against Sandy Vogel as you have against me. None."

Elizabeth shrugged. "You'll have to do better than that, Mr. Hifflyn. You're not going to help yourself by making up stories about Sandy Vogel."

"I didn't make it up," he said, lifting the sleeve of his jacket to look at his watch. "Listen, where does this leave us? Am I under arrest?"

"No."

"In that case I need to go, much as I'd like to stay and convince you I didn't kill Tom Kristoll." He got out his keys. "My wife is back from her trip to Europe. She flew into New York last night, and she arrives in Detroit today. I need to pick her up."

"Is that right?"

"I mention it in case you've decided I have to be followed. I don't want to alarm you when I drive to the airport."

His tone was light, detached. His composure had returned to him—if it had ever really left.

Elizabeth mimicked his detachment. "You're not planning to flee the country then?"

"I don't think I'll need to. And I've left my passport at home anyway."

He turned to walk back toward his car. She walked with him.

"My wife is flying on Northwest," he said casually. "Flight 1479, in case you'd care to check my story. I'd just as soon you didn't follow me. But you'll do as you like. I think your time might be better spent on other things." He tossed his keys in the air and caught them. "You might look into that story about Sandy Vogel, for instance. I didn't make it up. I heard it from David Loogan."

Chapter 35

THE THREE CARS MADE A SLOW TRAIN ROLLING ALONG THE CEMETERY road: Rex Chatterjee in the lead, then Hifflyn, then Elizabeth and Shan. At the end of the road Chatterjee turned left, heading toward downtown. Hifflyn turned right.

Shan followed him, tapping out a leisurely rhythm on the steering wheel. In the passenger seat, Elizabeth went over what Hifflyn had told her about Loogan's visit to the Kristoll house earlier in the day.

They got on the interstate with Hifflyn and drove east. Shan listened skeptically to the details of Loogan's peculiar story about Sandy Vogel.

"She and Beccanti were supposed to have had an affair?" Shan said.

"According to Loogan," said Elizabeth.

"And he said he had proof—letters and e-mails from her office computer."

"Right."

"But Loogan didn't show any letters," Shan said. "If there really were letters, you'd think he would print out copies. To prove he was telling the truth."

"I don't think there are any letters, Carter."

"No. So what's Loogan up to?"

"He's trying to draw out Tom Kristoll's killer," Elizabeth said. "He goes to see Hifflyn and the others, thinking one of them could be the killer. He tells them a far-fetched story about Sandy Vogel. He doesn't expect them to believe it.

"But telling the story achieves a couple of purposes. In the first place, it reminds everyone that Loogan is still around. Michael Beccanti was stabbed for getting too curious about Tom Kristoll's death, but Loogan's still kicking. And the details of the story aren't accidental. Loogan tells them he's been on Sandy Vogel's computer. That's his way of reminding them he still has access to the *Gray Streets* office, he has a key. And Hifflyn remembered two other things Loogan said: He's been staying someplace no one's thought to look, and he intends to leave town tomorrow."

"He was putting the killer on notice," Shan said.

"Right. He was saying: If you want me, come get me at *Gray Streets*. And if you're going to do it, do it tonight."

Shan's fingers ceased their tapping on the wheel. "But it's not going to work, is it? It would be foolish for the killer to show up there tonight. That's just what Loogan wants."

"He's counting on the killer to be overconfident. It doesn't matter." Elizabeth flipped open her cell phone and started to dial a number. "The killer may not show up. But I think Loogan will."

Two hours later, Elizabeth stood alone on the porch of Loogan's rented house. Black stillness behind the windows. Both doors locked. His street was quiet.

Twelve blocks away, Harvey Mitchum sat in a café across from the *Gray Streets* building. He had a clear view of the lobby doors. Kim Reyes was watching the service entrance in the back. Ron Wintergreen had gone up to Tom Kristoll's office on the sixth floor. None of them had seen any sign of Loogan yet.

Elizabeth and Shan had followed Casimir Hifflyn all the way to the Detroit Metropolitan Airport. They had seen his wife, a slim woman with exotic, Mediterranean features, waiting with her bags in front of one of the terminals. They had watched him greet her, lifting her off her feet and spinning her around. Elizabeth thought about following the pair home. She considered sending a patrol car to watch Hifflyn's house. But she wasn't sure what good it would do. As Rex Chatterjee would have reminded her, Hifflyn had the right to go wherever he wanted.

She returned with Shan to City Hall, where arrangements for the *Gray Streets* surveillance were under way. She told Owen McCaleb she would like to join in, and he said she would have her chance.

"Harvey, Kim, and Ron will handle it for now," he told her, "but I don't intend to make them stay there all night. If Loogan doesn't put in an appearance by one A.M., there'll be a second shift. You're on it." He glanced at Shan. "You too. I suggest you go home and rest up."

But Elizabeth had gone to Loogan's house instead. It had been an impulse. And now, standing on his porch in the mild night air, she began to doubt that he would show up at *Gray Streets*. She realized that part of her didn't want him to. Didn't want him to be caught in the trap she had helped set.

She walked down his steps and got into her car and started the engine. She circled his block and aimed the car toward home, but when she got there she kept on driving. The house looked fine. Lights on in the kitchen. She dialed her own number and talked to Sarah. All was well. She told her daughter she would be home in a little while. She had errands.

South and east, she cut across Ann Arbor to Carpenter Road. She passed the restaurant with the half-moon sign and found the turn that would take her to Sean Wrentmore's condominium. Ash trees flanked the entrance, their bark peeling. She coasted along, cleared a speed bump. A couple, well dressed, climbed into an SUV: sharp young professionals off to revel with other sharp young professionals on a Saturday night.

Elizabeth rolled slowly through a long curve of parking lot and when she drew near to Wrentmore's condo she saw a familiar car.

David Loogan watched a figure approaching in his rearview mirror. He turned his head in time to see the passenger door opening.

A soft voice said, "If you knew what you were doing, you would have disconnected the dome light. Now we're bound to attract all kinds of attention."

"Hurry up then," he said, "and shut the door."

The dome light went out. Laura Kristoll leaned toward him, her breath sweet in the semi-dark. She closed her eyes and he kissed her. He got his arms around her inside her open coat, ran his hands over her body, down her legs.

"David," she said, sounding injured. "You're a romantic bastard, aren't you? I don't have a gun."

"You shouldn't have come here," he said, drawing back from her. "How did you find me?"

"You wanted to be found. That line about staying somewhere no one's thought to look yet. That was a clue. It had to be somewhere they *should* have thought to look, and there are only so many places that could be."

She gazed through the windshield pointedly. There, up a short slope, beyond some pine trees, they could see the sliding glass door at the back of Sean Wrentmore's condo.

"It's been empty for the past month," she said. "A perfect hiding place. Is it really where you've been staying?"

"No."

"But you wanted them to think so," she said. "Nate and Cass and Bridget. You wanted to lure one of them out here, and now you're watching to see if anyone takes the bait. You don't really think one of them killed Tom, do you?"

"I intend to find out."

"What if someone comes, but decides not to use the back entrance? What if they knock on Sean's front door?"

"Then they'll find that nobody's home. What do you want here, Laura?"

"I want to help you. I've got some money with me. I thought you could use it if you're leaving town." From a pocket of her coat she took an envelope and laid it on the dash.

"There's two thousand there," she said. "I can send you more later."

He didn't reach for it. "What do you want, in exchange for two thousand dollars?"

The wounded tone again. "Bastard. The money's yours. You don't have to give me anything."

He tried to study her face in the dimness. "I don't have Sean Wrentmore's flashdrive here. It's hidden somewhere safe. I couldn't give it to you now even if I wanted to."

"Meaning you don't want to," she said mildly. "But that's all right. I trust you to hold on to it."

"What do you think it's got on it?"

"It must be Sean's manuscript."

"Sure," said Loogan. "What else could it be? But it's Sean's drive, so it would be Sean's version. Not the edited one."

"I don't want any copies of that manuscript floating around," she said. "Not in any version."

"You still think you can publish it?"

"In a few years. When things cool down."

"But you gave a statement to the police about Sean's death. Did you tell them the truth?"

"Of course."

"And they weren't curious about the manuscript? It's the reason Sean died. They didn't want a copy?"

"They haven't asked for one. Not yet."

Loogan said nothing for a moment. Then: "If they ask, what are you going to give them?"

"I'll figure something out," Laura said. "People have sent a lot of manuscripts to *Gray Streets* over the years. We only publish short stories, but they send us novels anyway. The discs pile up, and we don't always get around to sending them back."

He let her have a long, appreciative stare, and she laid a hand on his shoulder. "I'm telling you this because I trust you, David. And to show you I'm serious. Sean's novel—the edited version, Tom's version—is going to be published in a few years. I'm going to make sure of it. For Tom's sake."

A van cruised through the parking lot. Loogan watched it in the rearview mirror. He watched a family approach the entrance of the restaurant with the half-moon sign. He heard a snatch of distant music as the restaurant door opened.

"I believe you," he said, turning back to Laura. "Mostly. I'd believe you all the way, except for one thing. The police found my fingerprints in Adrian Tully's car."

"What are you talking about?"

He reached over to brush his fingertips against her golden hair. "Tully was at your house, the night Sean Wrentmore died. But he left before I got there to help Tom with the body. So far so good. But Tully didn't leave in his own car. It stayed behind. A blue Civic hatchback. Tom put it out of sight in your garage, and it would have stayed there if I hadn't asked so many questions. Tom didn't want to tell me that the body in his study was Wrentmore; he said it was a thief who had broken into the house. *How did the thief get there?* I wanted to know. *Did he have a car?* He did have a car, naturally, but Tully had driven away in it. Tully took Wrentmore's car to dispose of it. Isn't that right?"

"I guess it must be. I don't really know all these details, David."

"Of course not," he said. "You weren't there. Well, Tom didn't want to explain everything to me, but he had to account for how this thief had gotten to his house. So he improvised. Tully's blue Civic became the thief's car, and Tom and I would have to get rid of it, along with the body. I drove the Civic, and we left it in front of a run-down apartment building, assuming it would be stolen. I wiped my fingerprints off the steering wheel, but I left a plastic shopping bag in the backseat. Just carelessness. That's how the police found my prints."

He drew his hand back from her hair. "Here's the funny part. The other day I looked up Adrian Tully's address and drove by there—it's a run-down apartment building. It's where Tom and I left the blue Civic. Tom chose the spot; he drove ahead of me in his own car." He waited a beat. "We delivered Tully's Civic right to his doorstep."

"Tom had a sense of humor," Laura said. "But I'm not sure what your point is."

"Maybe I'm the only one who's interested in all these little details. But I've been mulling them over. Think about Sean Wrentmore's car, for instance. It hasn't been found. Where did Tully leave it?"

She looked away. "I don't know. I guess he would have picked a run-down neighborhood, just like you did."

"You can do better than that. Dumping a car is a two-person job. You helped him do it."

A few seconds ticked by while she sat unmoving. Nothing to read in her profile. Then she turned to him and gave him a sorrowful look up from under her brow.

"I'm not going to deny it, David. I came home from the university that night and found the three of them in the study: Sean dead on the floor. Adrian in a corner, hugging his knees, and Tom pouring himself a drink. I did what needed to be done."

"No," said Loogan crisply. "You were never at the university that night. You were in the study, with Adrian and Sean. I don't know where Tom was. But you were there, because you were the one who edited Sean's manuscript. You were the one trying to convince him to accept the changes."

She almost wavered then, he thought. But she said, "No. Tom was the editor."

"Anyone can be an editor," Loogan said. "You don't have to go to school for it. It's something that happens to you, like falling down a well. Tom told me that. I have a good memory for these things. You and I talked about editing once. You said you like it when a manuscript needs work. When you can see right away what's wrong and how to fix it. You make the changes and they're so obviously right that the author can't argue, not if he has any sense.

But Sean Wrentmore didn't have any sense. He argued. Are you the one who hit him with the bottle?'"

Laura shrank away from him, sat facing forward with her coat tight around her.

"I suppose I deserve that," she said in a hollow voice. "You have grounds to think the worst of me. But I'm not that bad. Adrian's the one who hit him. It happened fast. I couldn't stop it."

She faced him again and he thought he could see tears welling in her eyes. "I'm sorry, David. I was wrong to lie to you—to say I wanted Sean's novel published for Tom's sake. I want it for myself. I know I handled things badly, but I never meant for anything to happen to Sean. And the work I did on his manuscript—I don't regret that. You can't tell me that was wrong. I know what I accomplished. I won't apologize for wanting to see it published."

"I wouldn't ask you to," he said. "Go home, Laura. Keep your two thousand dollars. Publish your novel, if you think you can. I won't try to stop you."

The envelope still rested on the dash. Neither of them looked at it.

But she said, "Take the money, David. You need it."

"I don't want it," he said. "There's only one thing I want from you, but I don't hold out any hope of getting it. So let it go."

She leaned close to him. "What? What do you want?"

"A straight answer to a straight question. Do you know who killed Tom?"

In the gray shadow-light of the car, her eyes narrowed and a pulse beat at her temple. Her lips parted but no words came from her. Loogan watched her open the car door, and the dome light blazed white on the cool, smooth porcelain of her skin. Before she got out, she turned to him again and drew back her right hand very deliberately and slapped him hard across the face.

Chapter 36

A HUNDRED YARDS AWAY, ON THE OTHER SIDE OF SEAN WRENTMORE'S condo, Elizabeth approached a car parked off by itself beneath a crab-apple tree. The man in the car saw her and pushed a button to unlock the passenger door.

Roy Denham grinned as he cleared his thermos and his newspaper from the seat.

"Detective Waishkey," he said, brushing crumbs onto the floor.

"Detective Denham," she said. "Any sign of our friend?"

"None at all. But I've only been here an hour or so."

Elizabeth settled in and pulled the door shut. The car's interior smelled of smoke, and stubs of cigarettes filled the ashtray. Denham lowered his window to clear the air.

"I just came from Loogan's house," Elizabeth said. "I half expected to see you over there. What brought you here?"

Denham pointed to a paperback lying on the dashboard. *Kendel's Key*, by Casimir Hifflyn.

"I picked it up in a secondhand store to pass the time," he said. "The detective, Kendel, travels across country to investigate a woman's murder. She lived alone, and her apartment is sitting empty, so he decides to sleep there instead of staying at a hotel."

He touched his temple with an aged hand. "So then a light went off and I figured there must be at least a couple empty places here in town. Sean Wrentmore lived alone, and so did Adrian Tully. I thought I'd try here first."

He nodded toward Wrentmore's condo, a single-story unit at the end of a long brick building. The blinds were closed behind the two front windows. No glow from the porch lamp above the door.

"Nothing stirring," he said, and turned back to Elizabeth. "What about you? You're working late on a Saturday night. Anything new?"

"Our friend's been on the move," she said. Briefly, she sketched Loogan's strange visit to the Kristoll house, and the stakeout currently under way at the *Gray Streets* building.

"I'll take my turn there later," she said. "But I got to thinking about where else Loogan might be. He came here last weekend and talked to Wrentmore's neighbor. She saw him coming out of Wrentmore's place. He had a key. I should have thought of it before."

"It's a long shot anyway," said Denham. "He might not turn up here."

"Wrentmore's involved in this though. He may be at the heart of it." Elizabeth picked up the Hifflyn book from the dash.

"I talked to him today," she said. "Cass Hifflyn. He's a man with a secret." She dropped the book on the seat between them. "He didn't write this."

Denham looked puzzled.

"Sean Wrentmore wrote it," Elizabeth explained. "He and Hifflyn had an arrangement." With Denham listening intently, she described her encounter with Hifflyn at the cemetery. She went over her theory of Tom Kristoll's murder: how Kristoll had covered up Wrentmore's death; how he and Hifflyn had been blackmailed; how Kristoll had decided to go to the police; how Hifflyn had murdered him to keep him silent.

"Hifflyn denies it," she said. "He insists his arrangement with Wrentmore was no big deal. Not something he would kill to keep secret. Either I'm right and he's lying, or he's telling the truth and I'm way off base."

Denham stared off thoughtfully into the night. "But those aren't the only alternatives," he said. "There's a third way, isn't there?"

The words caught Elizabeth by surprise. A third way. She looked at Denham keenly. "What do you mean?"

"Say you're right about why Kristoll was killed, but you're wrong about the killer. Hifflyn's telling the truth. Someone else killed Kristoll." Denham raised his bristly eyebrows. "Who else was Wrentmore writing books for?"

David Loogan crept up the slope behind Wrentmore's condo. He had a canister of pepper spray in his pocket and Wrentmore's shotgun at his side, pointed at the ground. He slipped through the sliding glass door and closed it behind him.

Quiet in Wrentmore's bedroom. Loogan made his way through in the dark. Reconnoitered the empty house and then doubled back to the bathroom. He had been sitting in his car a long time.

Two minutes later he stood in Wrentmore's living room before one of the two front windows. He had closed the blinds earlier but now he turned the rod to open them so he could scan the parking lot. He knew Hifflyn's car, and Hideaway's, and Shellcross's. He saw none of them. Off out of the way, beneath the bare gnarled branches of a tree, he saw a nondescript sedan with someone sitting behind the wheel. After a while he made out a second form in the passenger seat. He couldn't make out faces.

"Nathan Hideaway," Elizabeth said.

Her mind worked, putting together the details. She spoke them aloud to Roy Denham.

"Hideaway lost his wife six years ago. Cancer. He couldn't work after that. He told me so. Then Tom Kristoll brought him to Ann Arbor, got him a fellowship at the university. And his writer's block was cured. Tom was the one who introduced Hifflyn to Sean Wrentmore. He could have done the same for Hideaway."

Denham nodded, listening. He got out a pack of cigarettes, started to shake one loose, and then thought better of it.

"The timing is right," Elizabeth said. "It was about five years ago when

Wrentmore's fortunes started looking up. He wrote three books for Hifflyn. He could've written one or two more for Hideaway. I should have thought of that before."

"You're awfully hard on yourself," said Denham. "You can't think of everything."

Elizabeth frowned. "He's a charming old rogue. Hideaway. White-haired. Grandfatherly. That's what threw me off, I think."

"The old ones are the ones you have to watch out for," Denham said with a wink. "But if he's guilty you still need proof. How will you get it?"

She had been asking herself the same question. "Tattoos, for starters," she said. "Wrentmore had the words 'Kendel's Fortune' tattooed on his arm. That's one of the novels he wrote for Hifflyn. He may have had other tattoos. We need to recover his body. And Loogan's the one who can lead us to it."

Denham leaned forward suddenly, staring at the front of Wrentmore's condo. "I think he's in there. That window on the left—the blinds are open. They were closed before. I've been waiting for him to go in through the door. Maybe he's been in there all the time."

"He might have just gone in," Elizabeth said. "There's an entrance in the back, a sliding patio door."

Denham's hands fidgeted on the steering wheel. "I could watch the back if you want. You and I could pick him up right now."

"Easy, Roy," she said. "Let me call in for backup. Do this by the book. You'll have to sit it out, I'm afraid."

Denham flashed her a self-deprecating grin. "I guess you're right." He sighed and his right hand went to an inner pocket of his rumpled jacket. "Do you want to use my phone?"

"I've got mine." It was in her coat pocket. As her fingers closed around it, it began to ring.

At the same moment, Denham's hand came out of his jacket, gripping something that was not a cell phone. Elizabeth had time to register colors: yellow and black. She had time to think: *Taser*. Then the current leaped to her body and her phone slipped away from her and a searing pain made her cry out.

Carter Shan jerked awake. He had lingered at City Hall to catch up on paperwork and then had settled in for a nap in the Investigation Division's break room. Now he bolted up on the cushions of the tattered couch and swung his feet onto the floor.

Alice Marrowicz, who had only touched his shoulder, stumbled backward, startled. She should have turned on the light, she thought. Not the wisest thing, to wake an armed man in the dark. "Sorry," she said.

She faded back to the wall and flipped the switch. Fluorescents buzzed overhead.

Shan blinked. "What's the matter?"

"I'm not sure."

"Is it one o'clock?"

"What happens at one o'clock?"

"Alice," he said impatiently, "what can I do for you?"

She turned shy for a moment, searching for the right words. "I tried calling Detective Waishkey. She didn't answer her cell. And she's not home— her daughter answered there."

"What do you need her for?"

"It's about David Loogan—Darrell Malone."

Shan became alert then. "I'm listening."

"On Wednesday," Alice said, "Detective Waishkey asked me to do some research on Loogan. This was before that New York detective showed up— Roy Denham. We had an address for Loogan in Cleveland, and the name of his landlord there.

"I got through to the landlord Thursday morning and learned that Loogan had moved to Cleveland from Philadelphia. The landlord was able to give me Loogan's Philadelphia address and the name of the woman he rented from there. So I tried calling her, but I only got her voice mail."

She was watching Shan's face, and his impatience seemed to be growing. She hurried on. "Then Denham came in on Thursday afternoon and we knew who Loogan was, and where he was from originally—Nossos, New York. So I never followed up with the woman in Philadelphia. I figured it didn't matter anymore—"

He interrupted her. "Where's this going, Alice?"

"She called me today. She'd been on a trip and just got my message. She was intrigued to hear from the police about Loogan. She was hoping for some juicy gossip, I think. Anyway, she told me something odd about him—he changed his name."

Shan relaxed into the tattered cushions. "Well, we knew that. He was Darrell Malone when he lived in New York, and at some point he started using the name David Loogan."

"It was while he was renting from her," Alice said. "He signed his first lease as Darrell Malone. His second, as David Loogan. He changed his name. Legally."

Shan's eyes narrowed. "That can't be right."

"He gave her proof," Alice said. "A certified copy of the petition, approved by the court. She's going to look for it in her files and fax me a copy."

"Oh, hell."

"He shouldn't have been able to do that, should he? If he was really a fugitive?"

The Nossos *Tribune* had a Web site, but no archives online. Carter Shan called the city desk and got a number for the paper's crime reporter. She had covered the Malone case when she was just starting out, and after some cajoling—he had interrupted her Saturday-night dinner date—she told him what he needed to know about Darrell Malone.

Malone had been indicted nine years earlier in the stabbing death of Jimmy Wade Peltier. That much was true. But he had never fled. He had been put on trial for murder in the second degree, and the jury had been unable to reach a unanimous verdict. The reporter claimed to know that they had been split nine to three in favor of acquittal. The prosecutor had declined to retry the case. Darrell Malone was a free man.

Owen McCaleb received the news stoically. He stood at his office window, looking out into the dark.

"Is there a Detective Roy Denham in the Nossos Police Department?" he asked Shan.

"There was. He died year before last. Stroke."

"So the Denham we talked to—"

"James Peltier," Shan said. "Jimmy Wade's father. The reporter gave me a description. She interviewed him a few times, before and after Malone's trial. He wasn't happy with the outcome."

The weight of the situation descended on McCaleb. It showed in his posture—the energy seemed to drain out of him.

"He showed me an ID card," McCaleb said faintly.

"According to the reporter, he owned a printing shop for thirty years," said Shan. "He could manage a fake ID."

"I imagine he has a wife. A tough old broad. Does a good impersonation of a chief of police."

"They planned this well. She calls to let you know he's coming. He appears right on cue. The faxed case file seals it. What is there to doubt? The file was probably more or less authentic. The reporter told me the real Denham befriended James Peltier. It wouldn't be the first time a detective felt sorry for a grieving father. Peltier could have asked for a copy of the file and held on to it. It would only require a few alterations, to make it look like Malone had skipped out before his trial. Probably the wife handled that, after Peltier told her what he needed."

"What led them to Loogan in the first place?" asked McCaleb. "How did they know he was here?"

"I haven't checked on that yet, but it probably happened just about the way Denham—Peltier—described. Loogan goes shopping for a shovel. The cashier recognizes him, because she went to school with him. She mentions him to her sister—who, instead of passing it along to the police, passes it along to the Peltiers."

McCaleb gathered himself and turned away from the window. "All right," he said. "I'll send a patrol car around to James Peltier's hotel. See if we can pick him up. You should call Elizabeth in. She'll want to hear about this."

Shan took out his cell phone and dialed Elizabeth's number. His call cycled through to her voice mail, and he began to feel uneasy as he remembered that Alice too had tried to reach her earlier and had gotten no answer. He left a message and then tried Elizabeth's home number. His conversation with Sarah did nothing to reassure him.

He turned to McCaleb. "Lizzie's not answering her phone. She called her daughter around seven-fifteen, said she had errands to run. No word from her since."

McCaleb frowned. They both knew that Elizabeth kept her phone close. It wasn't like her to be out of touch.

"Maybe nothing's wrong," McCaleb said, "but I'm not willing to make that assumption. Not tonight. We need to find her. I want you to work with Harvey Mitchum on that. I'll call him and tell him to pull everyone off the *Gray Streets* stakeout."

"Right."

McCaleb sank into the chair behind his desk. "Maybe her phone isn't working," he said wistfully. "Maybe she really is running errands. Do you think she's running errands?"

Shan was already on his way out. Without breaking stride he said, "No."

"Neither do I."

Chapter 37

ELIZABETH WAISHKEY FELT TREMORS PASS THROUGH HER. THE MUSCLES of her back twitched as she leaned against the wall of Sean Wrentmore's living room. Her wrists tingled within the circles of handcuffs. Her legs, extended straight along the carpeted floor and bound at the ankles with electrical tape, jerked and trembled with minor aftershocks.

A single lamp lit the room, a table lamp with a shade like parchment. It gave off a golden light and the light seemed to flicker, but after a time Elizabeth realized it was steady. The flickering was in her mind.

There were things she remembered. A glimpse of black and yellow in Roy Denham's hand. The cry that escaped her when she felt the current. Her fists clenching uselessly and Denham tugging her pistol from her holster.

Denham's voice. "My dear lady, forgive me."

Then her feet on the ground. Knees wobbly. Tightness in her arms. The cuffs were on by then. Her own cuffs, from the leather case at her belt. A drunken march across the parking lot with Denham at her back, his fingers like talons in the flesh of her arm.

The porch light shining suddenly over the door of Wrentmore's condo. David Loogan in the doorway, a shotgun leveled, wavering.

Denham holding the muzzle of her pistol to her temple. Cool steel. Loogan bending slowly to lay the shotgun on the step, retreating into the house with his palms open, fingers spread wide.

"Take it easy, Mr. Peltier," he said.

She would have slapped her forehead then, if her mind had been less addled, if her hands had been free. Instead, the realization sank in slowly, as Peltier's fingers dug into her biceps. As he guided her up the steps.

You're awfully hard on yourself, she remembered him saying. *You can't think of everything.*

Passing through the doorway, she heard his voice again, a whisper at her ear: "Keep quiet and do what I say. You're going to survive this."

Now, in the flickering golden light, she saw David Loogan in the center of the room, in a straight-back chair from Wrentmore's kitchen. He had shaved his head. She hadn't noticed it before.

His hands were behind his back—Peltier had produced a second set of cuffs.

Loogan regarded her calmly. She looked at his mouth. She had always thought he had an interesting mouth. His lips were moving. "Elizabeth," he said.

James Peltier—the man who called himself Roy Denham—extended his arm casually. The Taser, black and yellow, touched Loogan's chest and made a spark. Loogan grimaced and his body stiffened, but only for a moment.

"Shut up," Peltier snapped, and returned the Taser to the pocket of his jacket.

He got his cigarettes out and fired one up. Blew smoke at Sean Wrentmore's ceiling. Another drag and he switched the cigarette to his other hand, reached into a trouser pocket, and came out with Elizabeth's nine-millimeter.

"Mr. Peltier," she said, "you don't want to do this." Her voice sounded odd, as if it were flickering like the light.

Peltier didn't look at her. "I asked you to keep quiet."

"If you really wanted to," she said, "you would have done it by now. And you would have brought a gun of your own."

Peltier still didn't take his eyes off Loogan, but he took the cigarette from his lips and ground it into the carpet with his shoe. He tucked the nine-millimeter into his waistband and rooted in an inside pocket of his jacket. When he drew his hand out he held a metal object six inches long. A snap of his wrist and the thing unfolded as if by magic—a butterfly knife with a polished blade like a mirror.

He held it up for Elizabeth to see, but his eyes remained on Loogan. "He killed my son with a knife like this, and he ought to die the same way. That would be justice. But I guess I don't have the stomach for it." He tossed the knife onto the sofa behind him.

"It'll have to be a gun," he said.

His hand went to the grip of the nine-millimeter, but he didn't draw it out. Elizabeth took that as a positive sign. She might be able to talk him down. She had precious few other options. She could yell at the top of her lungs and hope someone heard. But if Peltier panicked, that might get her shot—no matter what assurance he had given her about surviving.

She scanned the room and didn't see Loogan's shotgun. Peltier might have left it outside on the steps. Someone might see it and get suspicious and call the police. Or they might not. If the porch light was off—and Elizabeth thought it was—the shotgun might go unnoticed. And the blinds were all closed now. No one would be able to see in.

She would try to reason with him, stall him. It was the best she could do.

"Mr. Peltier."

He took a step back from Loogan and turned to look at her.

"Think about what you're doing," she said.

David Loogan chuckled then. An unexpected sound.

"Oh, he's thought about it," Loogan said. "He's been thinking about it for years. He's been working up the nerve."

Peltier stood impassively. The golden light cast half his face into shadow.

"He used to throw rocks through my windows," Loogan said. "Used to call me in the middle of the night. Always from a public phone, always untraceable. And he never said a word. The police could do nothing about it. After a while, I moved away. I changed my name. I'm almost grateful to him for that. I never much liked being Darrell Malone."

Elizabeth studied the easy set of Loogan's shoulders. He looked relaxed for a man with his hands cuffed behind his back. She allowed herself to hope that he might have a plan. He was a juggler. Dexterous. Perhaps he had other skills. Perhaps, somehow, he was picking the locks of the handcuffs even now.

He was still talking: "Mr. Peltier and I have been out of touch for six years. I thought maybe he had mellowed. He'd come to grips with what happened. But I guess not. Here he is, primed to shoot me. That's a far cry from prank phone calls. But I think I understand. You got old, Jim. Time's running out. If you don't do it now, you might never do it."

"If I were you, I'd keep still," Peltier said in his gruff smoker's voice. "I'd think about the state of my soul. I'd try to get myself right with God."

"I feel like talking, Jim. When are we going to have a chance to talk again?"

"I've heard enough of you talking. I sat through two days of it at the trial." Peltier drew the gun from his waistband and glanced at Elizabeth. "He testified at his trial. He told them exactly what he did to my son. He didn't even try to deny it. And they let him go anyway."

"I'd like to hear about it, Mr. Peltier," she said calmly. "Why don't you sit, and we'll talk about it?"

His expression showed his disappointment. "That's not going to work. You're not going to talk me out of it. And I don't care to listen to him."

"You and I can talk," she said. "I'd like to hear what you have to say."

"Talking won't do any good."

Loogan broke in. "You heard him, Elizabeth. He doesn't want to talk. And he doesn't want to listen. I killed his son. Jimmy Wade. I was there in his last moments. I heard his last words. But Jim here's not interested."

Peltier pointed the gun at him accusingly. "That's a lie. Jimmy didn't say any last words."

"Of course he did."

"You're trying to buy yourself time. You never said anything about last words at the trial."

"It's something I kept quiet about at the trial. Because what he said wouldn't have helped my case."

Peltier aimed the gun at Loogan's heart. "What did he say?"

"That's not how it's going to work," said Loogan. "I'll tell the story my own way, from the beginning."

"Tell me now, or I'll shoot you."

Loogan sat very still and said in a low voice, "You'll shoot me anyway. I know I'm going to die. But so are you, Jim. Both of us are dying men. Do you want to die without hearing your son's last words?"

The nine-millimeter held steady. Peltier's face was impossible to read.

"What harm can it do to hear him out?" Elizabeth said. "You're in control here. You can show some mercy."

"He doesn't deserve mercy."

"Justice then," she said. "That's what this is about, isn't it? You're not a killer. You're an executioner. He deserves to die."

"That's right. He does."

"But even a condemned man has the right to make a statement. That's the law."

Without looking at her Peltier said, "I know what you're doing. You're trying to save him. He's not worth saving." The gun stayed steady, then fell a fraction of an inch, then dropped gradually to Peltier's side. "You can listen to him if you like. It won't change anything. When he's done, I'm going to shoot him. You can arrest me after. I don't really care what happens to me, so long as he's dead."

In the next moments, as Loogan began to tell his story, Elizabeth knew for certain that there was no grand plan. He didn't have the skill to pick a handcuff lock, and he had nothing to pick it with anyway. He could only play for time, try to draw out the last minutes of his life.

"It happened in the summer," he said. "Nine years ago. June twenty-first. I went out that night with Charlotte Rittenour. Charlotte had a beautiful face. People have done studies about what makes faces beautiful. It's mostly symmetry and proportion. High cheekbones and wide-set eyes and just the right distance between the mouth and the bottom of the chin. Charlotte's face was perfect. That's not opinion. I think it could be proven mathematically."

James Peltier stood back by the sofa, well out of reach of either Loogan or Elizabeth. He held the gun down by his side, but his finger rested on the trigger.

There were frames behind him on the wall—rectangles of glass. Sean Wrentmore's black-and-white photographs. Grim, sober, defiant faces.

"Charlotte met me for dinner at an Italian restaurant," Loogan said. "It was our first date. The waitress put a basket of rolls on the table and when Charlotte and I threatened to run out of conversation I picked out three and started juggling them. My one trick. It went over well, and later on the waitress brought three little bottles of Perrier and I did it again. I made kind of a stir. Darrell Malone, entertainer. Charlotte seemed amused.

"We went to a movie after, but I couldn't tell you the plot. What I remember is sitting close to her in the dark and waiting for something bright to come on the screen so I could turn and look at her face.

"It was late when the movie let out. I walked her to her car—we were parked in the same garage. But when we got there she wanted to go to the top and look at the stars. We got up there and she pointed out a radio tower in the distance. It wasn't far from the house where she lived as a kid. She talked about her family then, and growing up, and I talked a little about my work. I was a structural engineer. I had consulted on the construction of the parking garage we were standing on. She was interested in that, miraculously, and I spent a few minutes explaining to her what kept the garage from collapsing beneath our feet.

"I'm not sure how that led to kissing. It was a fine night, and clear, and we were alone in a high place under the stars. We got carried away, I guess. Lost track of our surroundings. And that's the way Jimmy Wade Peltier found us."

Loogan turned suddenly toward Elizabeth. "I don't know what Jim told you about his son—"

"I told her what she needed to know."

"He wasn't exactly a Boy Scout—"

"You're on thin ice," Peltier said, tapping the barrel of the gun against his side. "You better get along to the end. You don't have much time left."

Loogan took a long breath before resuming. "He'd been raising hell, before he ever got to us. Jimmy Wade. The police went back and retraced his movements afterward. He clocked in and out of five bars that night. Got into a scuffle with a college student, chipped the kid's tooth. Tried to pick up at least two waitresses, and struck out with both. By midnight, when he broke in on us at the top of the parking garage, he was drunk, and high on crystal meth."

"I told her that," Peltier snapped. "I never pretended Jimmy was perfect."

"No, I think you'd have to say he was slightly imperfect. Also, he was stranded. He had hitched a ride into town with a friend of a friend, who had promptly abandoned him. So when he found Charlotte and me, he was looking for a car.

"There happened to be a single car on the top level of the parking garage. It didn't belong to either one of us, but we were standing near it so Jimmy made an assumption. The first words out of his mouth were a demand: He wanted our keys. He startled us out of the clinch we were in, and as soon as I got a look at him I didn't like him. I took a step forward to get between him and Charlotte.

"He was thin and pallid and his shirt had a tear from the fight he'd been in. His hand came out of his pocket and there was a flash and a twist of metal and suddenly he was holding a knife.

"'Car keys,' he said again. 'Right now.'

"I made the mistake of trying to reason with him. 'That's not our car,' I said.

"'Don't fuck with me,' he said. 'Gimme the keys.'

"Charlotte was more sensible. She got her key ring out of her handbag and stepped around me. 'The man wants keys,' she said. 'Give him keys.'

"He didn't take the keys. He grabbed her wrist and yanked her toward him.

"'Smart girl,' he said to her. 'Too smart for this bozo you're with. You should take a ride with me.'"

Loogan had been talking with his eyes held shut, as if to remember better. Now he opened them. "Several things happened then. She tried to pull away, but he kept his grip. Without thinking, I reached for his right hand, the one that held the knife. I felt a sting and drew my arm back. Charlotte stomped a heel hard on his foot and broke away from him and took off running across the parking deck. He let out a yell and chased after her. I froze for a second. There was a six-inch slash along my forearm. It wasn't deep and didn't even hurt that much, but as I looked at it blood started to well up along the length of it.

"Charlotte might have made it if she had gone for the stairs, but she didn't feel right about abandoning me. There was a phone in the elevator alcove—an emergency phone—and she snatched up the receiver. She realized too late that the cord had been cut. The line was dead in her hand. She spun around and Peltier was on her. She swung the receiver at his face, but he caught it on his shoulder. It hurt him enough to make him angry. He shoved her into the wall, yanked her hair, put his knife to her throat.

"By then I had come to my senses. I had lost a few seconds, mesmerized by the sight of my own blood. But now I approached him, cautiously. I called out to him—I'm not sure I even used words. It was like trying to get the attention of a wild animal. He turned around warily, put Charlotte between us. The knife at her throat.

"I stopped a few feet away from him, showed him my empty hands.

" 'Back off,' he said.

"I took a step back.

" 'I'm taking the car,' he said.

" 'Take it,' I said.

" 'And the girl,' he said.

"I shook my head. 'You can't expect us to go along with that.'

"I watched his fingers flutter as he loosened and tightened his grip on the handle of the knife. Charlotte strained against him, trying to tuck her chin down toward her chest.

" 'I guess you're right,' he said. Then his knuckles went white and he slashed with the knife and she screamed and he pushed her roughly to the ground.

"Next thing I remember I was on my knees beside her. Blood on my hands and her eyes were closed. Her head had struck the pavement hard. But when I put my cheek next to her mouth I could feel her breath. I got a handkerchief out of my pocket and tried to stanch the bleeding. That didn't get me very far.

"I had my jacket off when Jimmy Wade reappeared. He had figured out that Charlotte's keys wouldn't open the car. He stood over me with his knife.

" 'I'm only going to ask this once more,' he said. 'Give me your keys.'

"I reached into my pocket and tossed them up to him without thinking. I hoped he would go away. But he singled out the key to my car and said, 'This is for a Toyota. That car's a Mazda. Do you think I'm stupid?'

"I had an answer for that, but it wouldn't have calmed him. So I explained to him once more that the car wasn't mine. I handed him my wallet, hoping he would take it and go. I reached for Charlotte's handbag, which was on the ground beside me, thinking I would give Peltier her wallet too.

"I reached in and felt something wet, and for a moment I thought that blood had somehow gotten into her handbag. But it wasn't that. She had taken a bottle of Perrier from the restaurant—one of the three I had juggled—and the bottle had broken when she fell.

"I got out her wallet and passed it to Jimmy Wade, and while he was looking it over I wrapped my fist around the neck of the broken bottle and brought it out and jammed the jagged edge of it into his thigh.

"He sank to his knees then and let loose the knife. I left the bottle in his thigh and looked down at the silver blade where it had fallen. I saw the shape of him reflected in it. Then my own face. I picked up the knife and drove it into his stomach and drew it out again and I swear it came out clean. He gasped and fell toward me and I drove it into him again and he wrapped his arms around me in a weak embrace and I could feel his breathing on my neck. I kept at it until I could feel all his weight against me and then I got out from under him and eased him to the pavement. The knife stayed where it was.

"I staggered up to my feet. Charlotte was still unconscious. There was a good deal of blood and I didn't know then if she would live. She needed help, so I had to go look for a phone. My clothes were stained with Peltier's blood and if anyone had seen me on the stairs I don't know what they would have thought. But no one saw me. I found a phone one level down and got through right away to a 911 operator. She promised an ambulance. I left the receiver dangling and went back up to the top.

"Charlotte was awake when I returned. She had managed to sit up and had her back against the wall near the elevator. One hand rested at the base of her throat, the other at her cheek. Blood trickled down her wrist. The sight of me must have frightened her—she slid herself sideways along the wall. I crouched down, told her help was coming.

"After a few seconds she got over the shock of seeing me. Slowly she peeled her hand away from her face. The knife had missed her throat. It had sliced a long curve that started below her ear and passed over her cheek and along her jaw. I found out later that Peltier had cut her clear to the bone. Her face had already begun to swell. She kept her hand away and lifted her chin and whispered a question. 'How bad?'

"I didn't expect it. I should have. If I had been prepared I might have handled it better. But she saw something in my eyes. I got the words right. 'It's not bad,' I told her. 'You'll be fine.' But my eyes betrayed me, because I knew it *was* bad, and I wasn't at all sure that she would be fine. She turned her face away from me then and I knew that something good was gone. Whatever we had gained that night was lost, it was over, and nothing would be the same.

"I heard the sirens then, the police and the ambulance, faintly at first but growing closer. I stood up, half intending to go watch for them, but just then Jimmy Wade Peltier stirred. If he had stayed still, he might have lived, they might have saved him. But as I watched, he planted his palms, he dragged his knees along the hard concrete until he was up on all fours. The palm of his right hand separated itself from the ground and hovered in the air, trembling. He got control of it slowly and sent it trailing along his chest, along his stomach, until it found the knife.

"The fingers closed around the handle and his breath caught and the blade began to slide free of his flesh. I got down beside him and our eyes met and he adjusted his grip on the knife and drew the last slow inches out of him. His knuckles dragged along the concrete and his fingers went slack and there was a click of metal on stone. He closed his eyes and I reached for the knife. I looked at Charlotte but she had turned away from me. There was no one watching.

"Then the sirens suddenly went quiet and patiently with my fingers I hunted for a space between his ribs. And Jimmy Wade's eyes came open and I found what I was searching for and sank the blade in."

Sometime in the course of Loogan's story, Elizabeth found that the light of the table lamp had ceased to flicker, her muscles had ceased to twitch. A mild ache remained in her shoulders, the consequence of having her hands cuffed behind her back. With the end of the story, in the silence that followed, she had a strange thought: He would be feeling the same ache.

She looked up and saw that James Peltier hadn't moved. He was still there by the sofa, with the picture frames behind him. He still held her nine-millimeter. She saw his heavy-lidded eyes and thought for a second that Loogan's story had somehow put him to sleep. But it wasn't so. He was awake. The story had done nothing to him, unless it had borne down upon his body, bowed his head, bent his back.

Loogan himself sat patiently. His words had gained him time, but nothing more. They hadn't saved his life. It would be different, Elizabeth thought, if this were a story in *Gray Streets*. She thought again of the shotgun that Loogan had laid on the front steps, that Peltier had left there. If this were a story, some conscientious passerby would have seen the shotgun and called the police. They would have come, and they would have recognized the address—Sean Wrentmore's condo. They would have seen her car in the parking lot.

Carter Shan would have come, and Harvey Mitchum, and all her colleagues. Owen McCaleb himself. They would have cordoned the place off and surrounded it. All without sirens or lights, without tipping James Peltier off. And one of them would have come in—it would be Carter. He would have come in through the sliding glass door of Wrentmore's bedroom. He would have stalked through to the hallway without a sound and he would have come down the hallway toward the living room, and he would be there now, with a clear shot at Peltier. He would be behind Peltier and off to the side, and Peltier wouldn't see him. And Carter would wait until Peltier raised the gun, and then he would take the shot.

If this were a story in *Gray Streets*.

James Peltier came sluggishly to life and unbent his back and looked at Elizabeth sadly. He gestured at Loogan with the gun. "You see how he is. A liar on top of everything else. He said he would tell me my son's final words. And I let him talk, and you see what good it did me."

"Mr. Peltier—" she began.

"Give me one good reason why I shouldn't shoot him. Just one. I'd like to hear it."

She searched for an answer that might restrain him.

"It won't bring Jimmy Wade back," she said finally.

"That's true," he said, "but it's not a good reason."

He raised the gun.

Elizabeth bent her knees, braced her shoulder blades against the wall, tried to get her feet under her. At the same time, Loogan shifted his feet and leaned forward in his chair as if he would try to lunge at Peltier.

Peltier's finger began to squeeze the trigger and there was an explosion of sound and a burst of red mist and Peltier's scalp peeled away from his skull. Great gaping pits opened in his cheek and the loose skin of his neck was torn away in ragged chunks. On the wall behind him, the glass shattered in the picture frames.

His body gave way at the knees and dropped and slumped against the sofa. The nine-millimeter bounced a little bounce on the carpet.

Elizabeth went tumbling sideways and Loogan, free of the chair, dove to the floor and rolled in front of her to shield her with his body.

From the hallway a tall figure stepped into the living room. He held the shotgun aloft like a scepter. His hair was a tangled white crown. He wore a trench coat and black leather gloves. Nathan Hideaway.

He stood over the body of James Peltier for a moment, a black snub-nosed revolver in his fist. He dropped the shotgun onto the sofa. A final shudder passed through Peltier's body and then it went still.

Hideaway lowered the black revolver. He stooped to dig through Peltier's pocket for his key ring. He collected Elizabeth's nine-millimeter from the carpet. Both went into a pocket of his trench coat.

Only then did he speak. "Detective Waishkey," he said, "and the remarkable Mr. Loogan." His tone was jovial.

Elizabeth started to say his name, but he silenced her with a gloved finger raised to his lips.

"Not yet," he said.

He grabbed Loogan by the collar and dragged him away from her. Stood over him with the revolver at the back of his neck and patted him down. He tugged a canister of pepper spray from Loogan's coat pocket and tossed it casually aside.

He gave Elizabeth the same treatment, then took the butterfly knife from the sofa and slashed through the tape binding her legs.

He seized the handcuff chain and hauled her to her knees.

"On your feet now," he said. "You too, Mr. Loogan."

Chapter 38

WHEN THE 911 CALL CAME IN, CARTER SHAN WAS ALREADY ON HIS WAY TO Sean Wrentmore's condominium.

He had contacted Elizabeth's cell phone provider and had run a trace on her phone. It was easy enough to do, once he convinced the operator that it was an emergency. Elizabeth's phone had a GPS chip; there was no need to triangulate the signal. When the operator gave him the location, he recognized it at once. All he needed were the words "Carpenter Road."

He tore a jagged path across Ann Arbor, weaving in and out of traffic, and was first to arrive at the scene. He saw Elizabeth's car in the lot, went through Wrentmore's front door with his gun drawn.

He found Wrentmore's neighbor there with Peltier's body. The nurse, Delia Ross. She had placed the 911 call. She had come off a long shift at the hospital and had been drifting on the edge of sleep when she heard the shot. She convinced herself at first it was a car backfiring in the restaurant parking lot nearby. She turned over and pulled the blanket up and drifted some more until it occurred to her that backfiring cars were something she had mostly read about in books; she had rarely encountered one in real life.

By the time she rose and went to the window, there was nothing to see, but she got her coat and went out and stood on the sidewalk under the blue-black sky. She thought of Sean Wrentmore's empty condo, of some mischief that might have happened there. Kids breaking in; teenagers with firecrackers. She walked to Wrentmore's door and the knob turned under her hand, and even before she passed in, she knew that what she'd heard had not been firecrackers.

A single lamp bathed the living room in golden light. James Peltier's body was a still figure of bronze and crimson and shadow. She made the call and waited with him. She knew at once he was beyond her help.

Shan talked to her in Wrentmore's kitchen, then asked her to wait outside. He tried to make sense of the scene. He was sure Elizabeth had been there. He had more to go on than the car outside; he had a broken strand of necklace on the living-room floor, a scattering of glass beads.

He took note of the overturned chair. The sliced remnants of electrical tape. He found the Taser in Peltier's pocket, the shotgun on the sofa, the sliding glass door left ajar in the bedroom. He traced the path that Peltier's killer must have taken. Soon Harvey Mitchum and Ron Wintergreen arrived, and once they'd had a chance to look around, there were other clues: James Peltier's car beneath the crab-apple tree, with Elizabeth's cell phone on the floor on the passenger side. Loogan's car abandoned in the restaurant parking lot.

When Owen McCaleb drove up a few minutes later, Shan and Mitchum had worked out a theory of what had happened, one that came very close to the truth. They huddled with the chief on Wrentmore's front lawn and sketched it out. It seemed clear enough that Elizabeth had come here looking for Loogan. She found Peltier instead and got into his car. Peltier caught her by surprise, used the Taser to subdue her, and hustled her into the condo. There was no sign of forced entry, because Loogan was already inside.

"Suppose Loogan cooperated, he let Peltier in, because Peltier was threatening Lizzie," Shan said. "Once Peltier had them both under control, he could relax a little. He planned to kill Loogan, because Loogan killed his son. But he couldn't resist taunting him first. He wanted Loogan to know exactly what was coming."

"But he delayed too long," Mitchum added. "Long enough for someone else to show up. Someone with a shotgun."

Owen McCaleb stood with his arms crossed, his head bowed. "And this someone would be Tom Kristoll's killer," he said. "And he showed up here because Loogan went to a lot of trouble this afternoon to make himself a target."

"Right."

McCaleb looked up. "So why isn't Loogan lying dead in there with Peltier? What am I missing?"

"Maybe the killer wants something else from Loogan," Shan offered. "Maybe there's unfinished business between them."

Shan watched McCaleb shift his weight from one foot to the other, thinking it over.

"All right," McCaleb said at last. "Loogan talked to four people this afternoon. Laura Kristoll, Bridget Shellcross, Casimir Hifflyn, Nathan Hideaway. I want to know where each of them is right now, and where they've been. That'll do for a start."

Just then Ron Wintergreen came loping up. He had been canvassing some of Sean Wrentmore's neighbors. "I don't know if this is important," he began.

"What is it?" the chief asked him.

"I talked to a woman four doors down. Lady in her sixties. Retired. She says she didn't hear anything or see anything. She's been watching TV all night."

McCaleb frowned. Harvey Mitchum made a gesture to hurry his partner along.

Wintergreen went on at his own pace. "She only came outside after we showed up. She mostly wanted to make sure no one trampled her lawn. She's protective of her landscaping, and her garden."

Mitchum started to interrupt, but Wintergreen raised a hand to show he had come to his point.

"She had a shovel out by her front steps. She says someone stole it."

A twig is a poor implement for picking a handcuff lock. She had hoped it might be otherwise, but twenty minutes of patient experimentation had convinced her.

Elizabeth relaxed her hands, slowly flexing her fingers. She kept her movements small, and Nathan Hideaway seemed not to notice.

He stood a little way off, at the edge of the clearing, in a thick woolen sweater and corduroy slacks. He had shed his trench coat and his gloves. Too warm, perhaps. He had kept his black revolver.

He had pressed the muzzle of the revolver to the back of her neck as he took her out of Sean Wrentmore's condominium. He made sure Loogan saw the muzzle at her neck, and the sight of it was enough. The threat didn't have to be put into words.

They walked out in a line, with Loogan in the lead. When they got to Hideaway's car—a sleek black Lincoln—Hideaway used James Peltier's key to unlock one of Loogan's cuffs. The left hand. Loogan would do the driving; Elizabeth and Hideaway would travel in the backseat.

The shovel was a last-minute acquisition. It appeared in the spotlight glow of the Lincoln's headlights, standing upright beside the front door of one of Wrentmore's neighbors. Hideaway sent Loogan to fetch it. Stowed it in the trunk.

They crept through the parking lot to Carpenter Road, Loogan with his wrist cuffed to the steering wheel. She could see his eyes—dark, colorless— in the rearview mirror.

When they reached the road he said, "Where to?"

Hideaway said, "Take me to Sean Wrentmore's body."

The dark eyes narrowed to slits. "What for?"

Elizabeth felt the muzzle hard against her neck. Hideaway said nothing.

Loogan turned north onto Carpenter and rolled along with the traffic. "I'll take you," he said. "But I don't know why you'd want to go."

Beside Elizabeth, Hideaway smiled. "Detective Waishkey knows."

She thought for a moment and realized he was right. She did know.

"Tattoos," she said.

They stopped at a light, a car full of college kids beside them. Hideaway brought the revolver down from her neck and pressed it against her side.

"You talked to Cass Hifflyn today," she said to him.

"We had quite a visit, yes."

For Loogan's benefit she added, "Sean Wrentmore wrote novels for both of them. He tattooed the titles on his skin."

She watched Loogan nodding in the mirror.

"Valerie Calnero found out about it after Wrentmore died," Elizabeth said. "She blackmailed them. Blackmailed Tom Kristoll too. Tom decided not to go along. That's what got him killed."

The light changed and they started moving again. Hideaway silenced her with a nudge from the revolver. "That'll do, Detective."

He leaned toward Loogan and asked, "How far is it?"

It wasn't far. North for a few miles on Route 23. East on Plymouth Road. A left turn, a gravel drive. A row of parking spaces marked with old railroad ties. A sign at the base of a path leading up into the woods. MARSHALL PARK.

Loogan led them up the hill, then off the path and through the trees. They ended in the clearing. Through a break in the clouds, the light of the full moon cast thin shadows at the edges of the fallen leaves. Loogan was at work now, at the clearing's center, the blade of the shovel biting into the earth. One circlet of steel around the wrist of his right hand, the other dangling. Hideaway had brought a flashlight from the car; it hung from a branch, secured with a knotted handkerchief. The branch moved with the wind, and an oval of light played itself over the ground at Loogan's feet.

Elizabeth sat on a bed of moss, her back against the trunk of a birch, and considered her situation. Her nine-millimeter was in the pocket of Hideaway's trench coat, in the backseat of his car at the bottom of the hill. Her legs were free, but her hands remained cuffed behind her. She had failed to open the lock of the cuffs, but she still had the twig between her fingers and she would try again.

Someone would have heard the shot at Sean Wrentmore's condo; someone would have called it in. That would do her little good out here, but the thought of it encouraged her.

The presence of her car would place her at the scene, along with the beads of her necklace in Wrentmore's living room. Carter Shan would recognize the beads. Elizabeth had broken the necklace intentionally—tucked her chin inside it and then pushed outward until the string snapped. She had picked up two of the beads with her teeth, and deposited them later in Hideaway's car. She was fairly sure Hideaway hadn't seen. Those beads, if they were ever found, would tie him to her disappearance.

Not much encouragement there. She was already thinking of this as her disappearance. But what else could it be? Her chances of walking away from the clearing seemed slim. No reason to suppose Nathan Hideaway would let her leave, once his errand was done.

She listened to the sound of the shovel slicing the earth. David Loogan had sunk into the excavation to his knees, and little mounds were growing all around him. Nathan Hideaway prowled at the edge of the clearing, the black revolver ever-present in his oversized hand. A meager rain had begun to fall, specks of it passing between the branches of the trees. Loogan turned his face up to it.

Hideaway came to sit on a fallen tree trunk a few feet away from Elizabeth. He kept his eyes on Loogan, held the revolver between his knees. The rain seemed to glitter in his hair.

"A few years ago," he said, to either one of them, or both, "a tourist went hiking on a glacier in the Austrian Alps. He found a body that had been almost perfectly preserved. Perhaps you heard about it. The body was dressed in leather clothes. It had an axe in its belt and a quiver of arrows. It was a Stone Age hunter who had fallen into a crevasse. He'd been there for more than five thousand years. His skin was intact, and so were the elaborate tattoos that covered his back."

Hideaway used his sleeve to wipe the rain from the revolver.

"Poor Sean would never last that long," he said. "Still, his skin might take years to decompose. Burying a body delays things—it keeps the animals and the insects away. If Tom had dumped him in a field, the tattoos might be gone by now, picked away by scavengers. But here we are. I wish it hadn't come to this."

At the center of the clearing Loogan laughed, shaking his head.

A smile passed over Hideaway's face. "Mr. Loogan finds me amusing," he said to Elizabeth. "I can hardly blame him. He imagines I've killed three people already—Tom and Adrian Tully and Michael Beccanti—so why should I balk at digging Sean up and slicing away chunks of his hide? That would be the least of my sins."

Hideaway's expression turned serious. "But as it happens, I haven't killed three people. Mr. Loogan would realize that if he gave it some thought. Consider Michael Beccanti. I'm supposed to have killed him because he was looking into Tom's death. But he and Mr. Loogan were working together, and they were both there in Mr. Loogan's house that night. Why would I kill one of them and let the other live?"

The simple logic of the question caught Elizabeth off guard. She looked at Hideaway curiously, wondering if he might be telling the truth.

He continued: "Mr. Loogan told a tall tale about Michael Beccanti's murder this afternoon. But he may have been closer to the truth than he realized. He said Sandy Vogel killed Beccanti because they were having an affair and he left her for another woman. Beccanti was stabbed, of course, and some might wonder whether a secretary in her forties would make a good suspect in a crime like that. But Mr. Loogan had an answer for that too. What do we really know about Sandy Vogel? Maybe she used to be a stuntwoman, or a Navy SEAL."

No reaction from Loogan. Only the steady rhythm of the shovel.

Hideaway said, "I happen to know that Sandy has never been anything but a secretary, and I have no reason to believe she ever had an affair with Michael Beccanti. But I know Bridget Shellcross did."

That caught Loogan's attention. He paused for a moment to glare at Hideaway.

"I saw them together once, at a coffeehouse downtown," Hideaway said. "Later I asked her about it, and she told me. Bridget trusts my discretion. Some people mistake age for virtue."

Elizabeth tipped her head back against the trunk of the birch. "So you're saying Bridget stabbed Michael Beccanti? Do I have to point out the obvious? Bridget Shellcross was never a stuntwoman or a Navy SEAL either."

Hideaway smiled, acknowledging the point. "No, Bridget wouldn't know what to do with a knife. But you're forgetting the Amazon she lives with. Rachel Kent used to be a martial arts instructor."

He turned to watch Loogan. "I think she found out about Bridget's affair with Beccanti by accident. Tom's death was what triggered it. Bridget took it hard. She and Tom had been involved in their college days. Rachel knew about that, and I think she wondered if there was something more to it—if they had been involved more recently."

Elizabeth thought suddenly of her last conversation with Bridget Shellcross. She remembered the cool reception the woman had given her. Shellcross had learned about a detective who'd been showing her picture at restaurants, asking questions. She had been offended. Elizabeth had assumed that the detective was one of her colleagues from the Investigations Division. But there was another possibility.

"Rachel Kent hired a private detective," she said aloud.

Hideaway nodded. "I think so. And I think the detective found out that Bridget hadn't been running around with Tom, but she had been running around with Michael Beccanti."

With a small shrug Hideaway went on. "It would be natural for Rachel to go looking for Beccanti, and then to start following him. Late one night he goes to Mr. Loogan's house. She follows him in. It's a charged situation, sneaking into someone's house. The senses are heightened, the adrenaline's flowing. She's been fantasizing about killing Beccanti all along. Now she sees her chance, and she takes it."

Loogan spoke up from the center of the clearing, where he stood braced against the handle of the shovel. "You're lying."

Hideaway shook his head. "As it happens, I'm not."

"You're the one who followed Beccanti into my house. You're the one who stabbed him."

"No."

"You stabbed him," Loogan said, "and you took the disc he was holding, and the letter. The blackmail letter. Rachel Kent would have no reason to take those."

Hideaway turned to Elizabeth. "You see how desperate he is to paint me as a villain." He pointed casually at Loogan with the black revolver. "I don't know about Beccanti having a disc, or a letter. If he had them, if Rachel saw them, who can say what she might do? She would have to make a quick decision—take them or leave them behind. She would need to get away."

Loogan said nothing and went back to his digging. Hideaway waved the revolver dismissively.

"That accounts for Michael Beccanti," he said. "Not my work, I'm pleased to say. Then there's Adrian Tully. I'm supposed to have tricked him into driving out to a cornfield so I could shoot him in the head. A murder made to look like a suicide. One shot to kill him. Then a second shot, out into the field, to get gunshot residue on his hand." He looked intently at Elizabeth. "How much luck have you had, finding that mysterious second bullet?"

She lifted her shoulders a fraction of an inch. "We haven't found it."

"Because it's not there," said Hideaway. "I certainly didn't fire it. Adrian Tully was a troubled young man. Guilty over killing Sean Wrentmore. Despondent because he loved Laura Kristoll and Laura wanted nothing to do with him. Nobody murdered Adrian. He got a gun and drove himself out to a lonely place and made an end of it."

Hideaway gazed thoughtfully into the dark woods. He turned the cylinder of the revolver absently and the clicks sounded out slowly in the quiet of the clearing.

"That leaves Tom," he said after a while. "Tom can't be explained away. I wouldn't want to try. I killed him, of course."

Chapter 39

"SEAN WRENTMORE WAS THE CAUSE OF IT," HIDEAWAY SAID. "TOM WAS wobbly about Sean from the start. Second-guessing himself. Maybe he should never have buried the body. Maybe it would have been better to own up to what had happened. Then the blackmail letter arrived and set him spinning. It was too much money and if he paid once he'd be paying for the rest of his life. He could lose *Gray Streets*; he could lose everything. Better to tell the truth now, while he still had a chance."

Elizabeth bent forward, listening eagerly. Loogan stood unmoving in the grave. The rain was no more than a mist in the air.

"I didn't think he could be serious," Hideaway said. "If it was a matter of money, I could have given him a loan. Valerie had only asked him for fifty thousand. I could have given him that outright. I offered to do it, that night at his office. But he'd made up his mind. He'd decided to do the right thing. I found him with a notebook open on his desk.

"He'd been writing it down—what he was going to tell the police. Nothing about me, he said. Nothing about Sean writing my books. He would leave me out of it. As if it wouldn't all come out, once he told his story.

"It was easy to deceive him, to pretend to agree. *Maybe you're right. Maybe that is the only way. Why don't you read me what you've got so far?* I went around behind his desk, as if to read along over his shoulder. The bookshelf was there within reach. A volume of Shakespeare. I'd never noticed it there before. The symbolism appealed to me—the publisher of a pulp magazine, struck down by the Bard himself."

Hideaway turned his head sharply toward Elizabeth. "I thought I'd have to work myself up to it," he said, "but it was easy. Easy to decide that I hated

Tom Kristoll, with his summer parties and his hangers-on. His pretentious magazine, trying to pass off crime stories as literature. And then he discovers a genuine talent, and what does he do? Sean Wrentmore was a great writer. He wrote two books for me—*The Heat of December* and *The February Killers*—and they got better reviews than anything I had ever done. He was the goose that laid the golden eggs, and Tom let some third-rate graduate student beat the goose over the head with a bottle of Scotch.

"How long does it take to reach a book down off a shelf? A second? Two? Long enough to determine that Tom deserved to die. The deed itself didn't take much longer. The first blow wasn't strong enough. It stunned him and he started to shake it off and ask me what the hell I'd done that for. The second put him down. After that it was automatic: Throw open the sash of the window, lift him to the sill, push him out. No time for thinking."

Hideaway raised his free hand, brushed thick fingers through his white hair. "I've thought about it since, though. I regret what happened, but I can't quite manage to feel guilty about it. You could say Tom brought it on himself. When he decided to go to the police, he was putting me at risk. My publisher didn't know about Sean. If the truth came out, my career would be over. So Tom was a threat to my reputation, my livelihood. What I did to him, you could almost call it self-defense."

Elizabeth saw Hideaway watching her, as if to gauge her reaction. "You're deluding yourself," she said quietly. "There was no threat to your life. It wasn't self-defense."

"Perhaps you're right," he said. "But self-defense is a slippery thing. What Mr. Loogan did to that fellow's son—Peltier. Would you call that self-defense?"

She leaned back against the tree, considering the question. But before she could come up with a reply, Loogan answered for himself.

"No," he said.

Hideaway turned toward him. "Then how do you justify it?"

"I don't."

"But you must have had a reason for doing it."

"I wanted him dead."

"A straightforward answer," said Hideaway. "Let's leave it at that then: I wanted Tom dead." He looked candidly at Elizabeth. "I'll make no excuses, just as Mr. Loogan makes no excuses about stabbing that old fellow's son, or about leading the man on, promising to tell him his son's final words. That was a minor lie, surely, but some might call it cruel."

"It wasn't really a lie," said Loogan from the center of the clearing. "Peltier's son did say something before the end. He said quite a piece."

"Really? What did he say?"

"I don't know. He had a mouth full of blood by then and he mumbled. I couldn't make out a word." Loogan paused thoughtfully and leaned against the shovel and in a deadpan tone he added: "Do you think I should have told his father that?"

Nothing but the sound of the night wind in the clearing and the silence of the misty rain, and then Nathan Hideaway tipped his head back and laughed. He laughed softly and for a long while, and then he got up and paced and didn't speak—except once, when he stopped and shook his white-crowned head and laughed again and said, "The remarkable Mr. Loogan."

Elizabeth fitted the end of the twig once more into one of the handcuff locks. But her movements were mechanical and her thoughts were elsewhere. She thought of her daughter waiting for her at home, thought of the possibility that Sarah might never see her again, living or dead. Because it wasn't hard to imagine what Hideaway intended to do. He would let Loogan dig to the bottom of the grave, let him excavate Sean Wrentmore. Then the black revolver—a bullet for Loogan, a bullet for her. After that, Hideaway could deal with Wrentmore's tattoos at his leisure; he had James Peltier's knife. Then cover up the grave again, with three bodies in it this time instead of one. Then walk down the path to his car and drive away, with nothing to tie him to the crime, nothing but a pair of glass beads that no one would ever find.

Elizabeth looked at David Loogan, up to his waist in the earth. She watched the motion of his arms and shoulders, the blade of the shovel rising. She felt the twig break in her fingers, because a twig is a poor tool for picking a lock. She squeezed her eyes shut then and let herself feel hope.

Because Loogan had given her a message, just after he had begun to dig. Hideaway had been distracted for a moment; he had gone to investigate a noise, some small animal skittering at the edge of the clearing. And then Loogan had spoken to her. He couldn't risk letting Hideaway hear, he could only mouth the words, but it was enough. The flashlight hung overhead; she could see his lips move.

His words were the same ones James Peltier had said to her earlier that night.

You're going to survive this.

She raised her eyebrows and mouthed back, *I am?*

Then he said something else. She couldn't be certain of the words, but she thought she understood, because the thumb and index finger of his right hand made the shape of a gun.

I might have to shoot him.

There was nothing more, because Hideaway had turned his attention back to the center of the clearing. But Elizabeth believed she understood Loogan's message. She remembered Laura Kristoll's account of the night of Sean Wrentmore's death. Wrentmore had worn a gun that night, a pistol strapped to his ankle. Laura never said what had become of the gun, but Loogan would know. Loogan had helped bury the body.

I might have to shoot him.

Elizabeth let herself hope. The gun was in the grave. Loogan was digging for it, and every shovelful of earth brought him closer to it.

Moonlight fell on the hedges bordering Casimir Hifflyn's front lawn. Raindrops clung to blades of grass. Carter Shan walked up the steps to the house and knocked on the door.

When he got no answer he circled around through the side yard. He came to the terraced lawn in back and heard the chirp of his cell phone.

He thumbed the TALK button. "Shan here."

"Checking in." It was Harvey Mitchum. "I've driven by the Kristoll house and Nathan Hideaway's cottage," he said. "Nobody home at either place."

"Well, it's a Saturday night."

"It surely is," Mitchum said. "What about you? Any luck?"

Shan approached the French windows of Hifflyn's workroom.

"Bridget Shellcross is out," he told Mitchum. "Her townhouse is deserted. Casimir Hifflyn's car is in his driveway and there are lights on in his house, but no one answers the door."

"Is that where you are now?" asked Mitchum. "Maybe I should come out there."

"Hold on a second, will you, Harv?"

"Sure."

With the phone in his left hand, Shan put a white cotton glove on his right and pushed at the French windows. Locked. Through the glass, he could see the figure of a man slouched in the high-backed chair at the writing table, one arm dangling toward the floor. Shan rapped his knuckles on the glass. The figure didn't move.

Shan lifted his right foot and kicked solidly with the heel of his shoe at the seam between the two windows. A splintering of wood as the two halves burst inward. He slipped the open phone into his pocket and drew his pistol. Chambered a round and climbed into the room.

He crossed quickly to the writing table and confirmed that the figure in the chair was Casimir Hifflyn. Shan searched with two fingers for the carotid artery. No pulse. He hadn't expected one. The wound at Hifflyn's temple looked gruesome.

The second body lay near the doorway to the room. The writer's lovely Mediterranean wife. One shot to the midriff and another to the chest. And one more that had punched a hole in the wall beside the door frame.

The muffled sound of Mitchum's voice shouting. Shan drew the phone from his pocket.

"What the hell's happening?"

Shan said, "Sorry about that. I'm afraid I had to break in here. You'd better come. The chief too, and the medical examiner. Hifflyn's dead. He and his wife both."

He gave Mitchum the details and ended the call, and then with his pistol still drawn he cleared the house room by room, turning on lights as he went. No one lurking. By the time he made his way back to Hifflyn's workroom he heard the first faint sirens.

He read the note on the writing table, an uncapped fountain pen beside it.

I'm sorry for all of it—Tom and Tully and Beccanti. There's no future now. I hope I have the courage to go through with this.

Signed with Hifflyn's initials. Streaks of matching blue ink on the fingers of Hifflyn's right hand.

Four shell casings on the floor by Hifflyn's chair. The gun lay beneath the table. Carter Shan knelt to pick it up. A semiautomatic pistol, thirty-two caliber. Nickel-plated. He handled it with white cotton gloves.

The serial number was intact. In a short while Shan would call it in, have it run through the computer. He would learn that the pistol was registered to Sean Wrentmore.

But what he noticed now, as Harvey Mitchum's voice called to him from the front of the house, were the flecks of dirt that came off on the gloves. Dirt from the grooves that ran along the thirty-two's barrel, from the head of the screw that attached the grip. Black specks on the white cotton. As if the pistol had been buried underground.

The broken twig lay somewhere on the bed of moss behind her, and Elizabeth had given up on picking the lock of the handcuffs. She had spent half an hour considering whether it might be possible to work her cuffed hands around to the front of her body. She would have to tuck the chain beneath her bottom, slide it along her thighs, bend her knees just so. She might be able to do it, she thought, if she were a magician, if she had time to practice, if there weren't an armed man watching over her.

Nathan Hideaway had returned to his seat on the fallen tree trunk. He leaned forward, elbows on his knees, the black revolver resting on the palm of his right hand.

David Loogan had sunk into the earth nearly to his shoulders. There were dark mounds of dirt arrayed behind him, on the far side of the grave. He had left the nearer side relatively clear, as if he wanted to keep an unobstructed view of Hideaway, and perhaps of Elizabeth herself. She watched him bend his back, and straighten it, and another shovelful of earth joined the rolling landscape behind him.

Every shovelful brought him closer, she thought.

I might have to shoot him.

She hoped that Loogan would give her a sign when he was ready. Her hands were behind her back, and they were going to stay behind her back, but her legs were free. If she had some warning from Loogan, she could scuttle along the ground or try to stand. She could distract Nathan Hideaway. Give Loogan a chance to aim and fire. She might be of some use. Loogan's plan might work.

She glanced at Hideaway, saw him watching her. His eyes big and dark and unblinking in the dim light. When he spoke to her the flesh crawled at the nape of her neck, because he seemed to have read her mind.

"Hope," he said.

She struggled not to react. "What?"

"Hope," he repeated. "It's a curious thing. Consider Mr. Loogan here. He wants to kill me. I've no illusions about that. Yet I've asked him to dig up a body, and there he is, digging. He must be sore by now, and exhausted, and thirsty, but I can't even offer him a drink. He can take a break if he wants—I can give him that much. Would you like a break, Mr. Loogan?"

Loogan answered without pausing in his work. "No."

"No, he doesn't want a break," said Hideaway. "He's a single-minded man. He could have made a run for it in the woods. I would have shot at him, certainly, but he might have gotten away. Or he could have attacked me with the shovel. He might have had a chance, though a shovel is a poor weapon against a gun. But there he is, digging. As if digging is going to save his life. He has to realize that the grave he's digging could end up being his own. So what motive can he have for going on? There's only one. Hope."

The dim light made wells of Hideaway's eyes. Elizabeth regarded him warily.

"I don't know what you're talking about," she told him.

"I think you do. But never mind. I'll make him the offer again. Take a break, Mr. Loogan. Sean's not going anywhere."

The motion of the shovel stopped then, the blade hovered in the air. Loogan's expression turned grim. "No," he said. "Let's get this over with."

"You see how it is," Hideaway said to Elizabeth. "His hope is leaving him now. Mr. Loogan and I have been playing a game. He's been pretending there's no gun in Sean Wrentmore's grave, and I've been pretending I don't know about the gun. But now it's time to stop pretending. As it turns out, there's no gun in the grave, and no Sean either."

Hideaway rose from the fallen tree trunk and aimed the black revolver at Loogan.

"You can put aside the shovel now," Hideaway said. "We're through digging."

Loogan hesitated for a few seconds, then brought the shovel up and tossed it amid the mounds of earth on the far side of the grave.

Hideaway lowered the revolver, but it remained ready at his side.

He said, "When Tom wrote out his story for the police, he drew a map too. X marks the spot in the clearing in Marshall Park. I took his notes after I sent him out the window. Burned them when I got home. But I made use of the map. I wanted to make sure Sean wasn't found, so I moved him."

Elizabeth had let herself forget the ache in her limbs, the weariness. Now it all flooded back. "Where is he?"

Hideaway made a careless gesture with the revolver. "He's far from here. Perhaps we should leave it at that. But I can tell you he no longer has his tattoos. In fact, his flesh is no longer attached to his bones. I wrote five crime novels before Sean took over. I had to learn something about disposing of a body." He waved the matter away with his free hand. "Forget about Sean."

Elizabeth looked off into the darkness, then back at Hideaway. Her brow furrowed. "What was the point of bringing us here, if not to find Sean? You must have had a motive. If you just wanted to kill us, you could have done that back at Sean's condo."

"I had a motive," Hideaway allowed. "I believe Mr. Loogan knows. Why don't you tell her why I brought you here?"

Loogan leaned back against the far wall of the grave.

"The flashdrive," he said. "That's what all the fuss is about."

Hideaway nodded. "The flashdrive. Mr. Loogan made a point of showing it off this afternoon, while he spun his tale about Sandy Vogel. The tale was a distraction. The real reason for his visit was to make it known he had the flashdrive. He said it came from Sean's condo. Michael Beccanti found it there."

"That's true," said Loogan.

"He said he didn't know what was on it."

"That's true too. It's protected by a password. But there's probably a way to circumvent that. Someone with the right expertise could crack the code and get at the files."

Wind stirred the branches at the edge of the clearing. Hideaway drew a deep breath of night air. "I can hazard a guess about what's on the drive," he said. "The two novels Sean wrote for me, and the Kendel books he wrote for Cass Hifflyn. Probably more than one version of each. Sean had some odd habits. He used to keep working on the books, even after they were published. For him, they were never finished. He sent me a revised manuscript of *The February Killers* once. Told me it was much better than what they were selling in the bookstores. He was right. And the manuscript he sent me—it had his name on the title page. He always did that. It was one of his little jokes.

"So you can see why I need that flashdrive. It could cause me no end of trouble if the wrong people were to find it."

Loogan crossed his arms. "You're out of luck," he said. "I don't have it."

"I know," said Hideaway. "I searched your pockets back at Sean's. But there was no time to ask you about it there. We couldn't linger. So I'm asking you now."

"It's in a safe place. With a friend. If something happens to me, it goes to the police."

Hideaway shook his head. "You're not a smooth liar, Mr. Loogan. Just now you looked up and to the right. That's where we look when we're inventing. No, I don't think you've made any such arrangement. I think you've got the flashdrive hidden away somewhere. You're going to tell me where it is."

Hideaway drew another deep breath. "Some people would suppose I have no leverage, since I plan to kill you whether you tell me or not. But it's a wonder what a man will do sometimes if you threaten something he cares about. Tell a man you're going to shoot his wife, and he'll take responsibility for crimes he had nothing to do with. He'll write out a confession by hand and sign it, just to buy his wife a little time. Minutes."

He regarded Loogan thoughtfully. "You don't have a wife, so I have to work with the materials at hand. Detective Waishkey. You can protest that she means nothing to you, but I know better. I heard your story about Peltier's son—enough of it to know your reason for telling it. It wasn't to stall until help came; you weren't expecting any help. You expected to die and you told that story because you wanted Detective Waishkey to hear it. Because you wanted her to understand you. Because you care about her opinion of you."

Hideaway raised the revolver gradually and leveled it at Elizabeth.

"But even if she meant nothing to you," he said, "even if she were a stranger, you'd still feel responsible for her now. You're that kind of man.

That's why you're going to tell me where to find the flashdrive. If you don't, I'll shoot her."

Elizabeth locked her eyes on Loogan. "Don't tell him anything, David."

"Maybe you're thinking that's not much of a threat," Hideaway said, "because I'll shoot her anyway, whatever you tell me. She'll die no matter what. But there are easy ways to die, and hard ways. I'll make it hard for her, if you don't do as I ask. She'll suffer."

"David—"

"Maybe you think there's a limit to how much she can suffer, but the fact is I can hurt her even after she's dead. She has a daughter. When I'm finished here, I'll be free to go wherever I like. If you don't tell me about the flashdrive, or if you lie to me, her daughter dies too."

At the mention of her daughter, Elizabeth strained against the cuffs that bound her wrists, and for a moment she was sure her anger would break through them. But the steel withstood her. It dug into her flesh. She made an effort to relax.

"Don't listen to him, David," she said. The calm in her voice surprised her. "When he leaves here he'll run, if he has any sense. He's a suspect already, in Tom Kristoll's murder. Not to mention Tully and Beccanti. After tonight the department won't let him out of its sight. They take it seriously when a detective goes missing. He won't have a chance to kill anyone else."

Hideaway glanced at her along the barrel of the revolver. "I wouldn't be too sure," he said. "I think there could be a break in the case tonight. Tom's murder could be resolved, and the others too." He turned his gaze back to Loogan. "But even if Detective Waishkey is right— If I'm a wanted man from now on, a desperate man, then there's no telling what I might do. No one's daughter is safe."

He paused and the air of the woods seemed to thicken. He put his thumb on the hammer of the revolver. "I'll ask you once, Mr. Loogan, and I'll give you one chance to answer. Take your time, and think about the consequences if you lie."

He drew the hammer back. "Where's the flashdrive?"

In the long seconds that followed, Elizabeth took in details: the night wind, the small movement of the flashlight tied to a branch, a tiny alteration in the quality of the light, the shadows cast by the mounds of dirt.

Strands of her own raven hair that hung in her eyes, trembling, reminding her of her daughter's hair.

The smell of fallen rain on the fresh-turned earth.

Nathan Hideaway's posture, the cant of his hips, one leg straight, the other bent. The ridges of the knuckles on his gun hand. The barrel of the revolver aimed at her, foreshortened. The steel ring of the muzzle.

David Loogan's face; the shadows under his eyes. The fractional turn of his head, as if to look for the cast-off shovel behind him. Something draining out of him as he realized the shovel would do him no good. His right hand coming up gradually, fingers parted. She thought it would reach up to touch his chin, to rub his neck. It hovered. His eyes wide, staring at his own palm.

She thought she saw the hand shiver. In the dim light, she couldn't be sure.

Tightness around Loogan's mouth. She was sure of that. His lips parted and she began to say his name. She meant to tell him to stop.

A catch in his breathing at the moment of decision. She knew, as he answered Hideaway's question, that he was telling the truth.

"At my house, in the living room," Loogan said, "there's a framed photograph above the fireplace. A photograph of paper leaves and bits of colored glass. The drive is taped to the back."

Steady voice, but the rest of him breaking. He crossed his arms now and his body twisted, as if to retreat from Nathan Hideaway. His head bowed.

The ring of the muzzle vanished as Hideaway turned the revolver on Loogan.

"That's good," Hideaway said gently. "I believe you."

Elizabeth tried to rise, inching her back along the trunk of the birch. Hideaway turned the gun on her for a moment, warningly, and she slid down again.

The barrel of the revolver in profile now, aimed down at Loogan's heart. She watched Loogan twist, and then his knees must have given out. He vanished into the grave.

The revolver stayed where it was. Hideaway frowned.

"Come now, Mr. Loogan. This won't do."

Hideaway took a tentative step, the sole of his shoe gliding over blades of grass.

"On your feet," he said to Loogan. "Better to face it than to hide."

The edge of the grave was obstructing his line of fire, Elizabeth thought. She watched him move forward cautiously, warily, leading with the gun.

"I can see you, Mr. Loogan."

Hideaway advanced more confidently now. He was still a foot and a half from the grave's edge when the ground gave way beneath him.

Chapter 40

THE GUN WENT OFF AS HIDEAWAY FELL.

The orange spark of the muzzle flash and the hollow sharp sound, loud as a cannon in the clearing. Elizabeth got her feet under her, braced herself up along the bark of the birch. Four fast steps brought her to the open pit of the grave. She glimpsed Nathan Hideaway scrabbling in the dirt of the far wall, the revolver still in his hand. He was on his knees—with Loogan, sitting, half pinned beneath him.

That bare glimpse and then without breaking stride she leaped in, her feet landing squarely on Hideaway's shoulders. Her cuffed hands ruined any hope of keeping her balance and she fell back hard against the ragged earth. She heard a pop, too soft for gunfire: her left shoulder slipping out of joint. Grinding pain.

Black dark in the clearing for a moment and then her vision returned and there beneath her feet Nathan Hideaway clawing at the dirt, trying to push himself up with his arms, trying to make some use of the revolver. He began to twist around to see her and she drew back her right foot and kicked him in the face, and he flinched away from the blow and tried to brace himself on hands and knees. And she lifted her foot again and kicked the back of his frost-white head and his face hit the dirt of the grave wall.

The black revolver sank into the dirt and fired a muffled shot at nothing. Hideaway's broad back began to rise and Elizabeth kicked him again in the back of the head, and Loogan, struggling beneath him, got a leg free and kicked him in the ribs. Elizabeth planted both feet at the back of Hideaway's thick neck and pushed and the soles of her shoes slipped up to his skull and she braced herself against the earth behind her. She pushed his face into the dirt, and his body shook and shuddered. And still she pushed, and his face sank into the black. And overhead the flashlight swayed on the branch and the moon shone, and Nathan Hideaway went down into the black.

Loogan's voice called her, mild as the wind. The wind swept into the grave and cooled her brow. Her shoulder burned, her legs ached. A fragment of a leaf spun down and caught in her hair.

Loogan's voice: "Elizabeth. He's done now."

She moved her legs, lazily, her gaze fixed on the revolver half buried in the dirt. She stepped her feet back along Hideaway's spine. Eased herself backward up the broken slope. When she was clear of Hideaway's body, Loogan was able to free his pinned leg and rise, unsteady. He bent over Hideaway and went through the man's pockets. He found Hideaway's keys, and the keys Hideaway had taken from James Peltier.

From her seat on the slope Elizabeth said, "Take the gun."

"I don't want the gun."

"We're not leaving it in his hand."

Loogan trudged up the slope and tossed the revolver onto a clump of grass beside her. Then he knelt with Peltier's key ring and unlocked her handcuffs.

He reached for her arm to help her up and the pain knifed through her.

"Wait," she told him. "I think I dislocated my shoulder." She felt tears coming and closed her eyes against them. "We can fix it," she said. "Shouldn't be hard."

She heard the clink of keys as he put them in his pocket and knelt again beside her.

"Are you kidding?" he said.

"I'll lie back. You bend the arm at the elbow—I can't move it myself. Ninety degrees. Fingers pointing at the sky. Then you just pull the arm toward you."

Worry in his voice. "That's not a good idea."

"You pull it gently, and you rotate it forward, like I'm throwing a baseball. I've seen it done."

She opened her eyes. He started to get up. "I'll take you to a hospital."

She twisted around and seized his wrist with her right hand. "You're going to turn frail on me now?"

Elizabeth steered Hideaway's Lincoln with one hand and rested the other on her thigh. She lifted her arm to reassure herself that she could. The pain was remote.

She looked over at Loogan in the passenger seat. He had his head back and she could hear his breathing. He sounded exhausted.

"Back there," she said, after a mile had gone by. "The grave—"

She left it at that, the question unformed.

He sat up slowly, took his time answering. "Excavations are tricky. Unstable."

"It didn't collapse on its own."

"I helped it along. Dug underneath." The Lincoln's tires hissed along the surface of the road. "His own fault," Loogan said. "He shouldn't have given me a shovel."

Elizabeth guided the car along a curve. "I didn't know that was the plan. You said you were going to shoot him."

"I said I might have to shoot him."

They came to a traffic light, amber turning red. Elizabeth braked the Lincoln to a stop, though there were no other cars at the intersection.

"It's not far to the hospital, is it?" Loogan asked her.

She watched the steady dot of red light. "I'm not going to the hospital. I can have my shoulder looked at later."

"I think we should go," he said.

The light changed. She looked around at him. He had his arms folded, his hands beneath his armpits.

"I made a mistake," he said.

He unfolded his arms. The fingers of his right hand came out tipped with blood.

"I thought he missed."

David Loogan walked into the emergency room of Saint Joseph Mercy under his own power. As the glass doors swept shut behind him, the overhead fluorescents burned suddenly white. He coughed into his open palm, saw blood, felt his knees give way.

The bullet from Hideaway's revolver had struck a chunk of rock in the wall of the grave. From there, it bounced. It entered Loogan's body on the left side, under his arm; it glanced off a rib, flattened, tumbled through his lung, and came to rest an inch behind his heart.

When the ER doctors got to him, they determined that his left lung had partially collapsed. They inserted a chest tube to relieve the pressure and reinflate it. After that, he needed surgery to repair internal bleeding. His surgeons decided against removing the bullet—it could stay where it was and do him no harm.

In the long hours after his surgery, Loogan drifted in a medicated haze. Nurses came around periodically to test the function of his lungs. They made him blow into tubes. They obsessed over his breathing, ever on guard against the formation of phlegm. They woke him at odd hours to pound on his chest.

He saw Elizabeth for a few minutes on Sunday afternoon, then for a longer visit on Monday evening. She told him about Casimir Hifflyn and his wife, found shot to death in their home in a scene staged to look like a murder-suicide. She described the handwritten note, the false confession. She didn't have to remind him of Hideaway's words: *It's a wonder what a man will do if you threaten something he cares about. Tell him you're going to shoot his wife, and he'll take responsibility for crimes he had nothing to do with.*

The next day Loogan had two visitors. The first was Sarah Waishkey, who came while he was napping in the early afternoon and left behind a present she had made for him: a wristband of braided leather.

The second visitor was a cop named Mitchum. Loogan walked with him up and down the hospital corridors and gave him an account of everything Nathan Hideaway had said and done from the moment he appeared at Sean Wrentmore's condominium. Mitchum scrutinized each move, from the shotgun blast that killed James Peltier to the final sequence of events at the grave site in the clearing in Marshall Park. Loogan emphasized that Hideaway had held on to the revolver even after he fell into the grave. He had been a threat to the very end. Elizabeth had acted in self-defense. Mitchum only nodded. "You'll get no argument from me."

Another full day passed before Loogan saw Elizabeth again. They sat by the window in his room, gray November sky behind the slatted blinds, and she told him about her visit to Nathan Hideaway's cottage. She and Carter Shan had searched Hideaway's belongings and found a blackmail letter similar to the one Tom Kristoll had received. In a cellar beneath the house they found an old cast-iron tub and traces of lye. They theorized that Sean Wrentmore's body had wound up in the tub.

His flesh is no longer attached to his bones, Hideaway had said.

"We may never find the bones," Elizabeth told Loogan. "I thought they might be in a sack weighted down at the bottom of the pond behind the cottage, but we sent a diver in yesterday. He didn't find anything."

She had other news as well. An arrest had been made in the murder of Michael Beccanti.

"It was Rachel Kent," she said. "We found the detective she hired to spy on Bridget Shellcross. He confirmed the affair between Beccanti and Shellcross—and that Kent knew about it.

"There's physical evidence against her too. Tiny traces of blood and skin. She scratched her arm climbing through the slashed screen of the window at your house. The lab recovered a sample from the screen on Friday. The blood type is going to turn out to match hers, and eventually a DNA test will confirm it, but none of that matters because Rachel Kent confessed this afternoon. We went around to ask her to submit a blood sample voluntarily and she refused, and two hours later she showed up at City Hall with her lawyer. She brought along the disc and the blackmail letter that she took from Beccanti after she stabbed him. Her lawyer thought they'd be worth something as bargaining chips. They were. From what I've heard, the prosecutor gave her a pretty good deal."

Loogan stared out at the gray sky. "Rachel Kent," he said.

"Rachel Kent," Elizabeth repeated. "Hideaway had it right."

On the morning of the seventh day after his surgery, David Loogan walked out of Saint Joseph Mercy. He wore a new pair of chinos and a blue Oxford shirt, and a denim jacket against the November chill. He had left his leather coat in the woods of Marshall Park.

The new clothes were a gift from Bridget Shellcross, who had visited him the day before. They had talked about Cass Hifflyn and about Michael Beccanti, whose funeral service she had attended earlier in the week.

She had given Loogan her phone number, made him promise to call when the hospital discharged him. She would drive him home. The number was on a slip of paper in his pocket. He took a cab.

The driver dropped him at his rented house. Yellow tape on the front door. He tore it away and went inside and opened all the windows. Upstairs he stripped the bed and put on fresh sheets and blankets and slept until late afternoon.

He woke hungry, washed, and closed windows. Locked the door behind him and descended the steps with his car keys jingling in his hand, and then realized he had last seen his car in the lot of the restaurant behind Sean Wrentmore's condo.

He walked the twelve blocks downtown, taking it slow. Had an early dinner at a place he had gone to once with Tom Kristoll. Then a movie, something French and allegedly comedic.

It was a little after nine when he came out of the theater. A college crowd on the sidewalks. He strolled west along Liberty Street. Banks, restaurants, galleries. He came to Main, crossed with the light. He would turn south now if he wanted to go home. He turned north.

Outside the café across from the *Gray Streets* building, a clutch of students loitered. Pierced noses, dyed hair, clouds of cigarette smoke. Loogan went by them, out of range of the smoke, and leaned against the frame of the café window. He looked up at the building across the street, at a window on the sixth floor. A rectangle of light. After a minute, a shadow passed across it briefly. It looked to Loogan like the figure of a man wearing a fedora.

David Loogan dashed into the street, dodging through traffic, fumbling for his keys. He heard the long blare of a horn still echoing behind him as he cleared the lobby door, slapped the button of the elevator. He shot down the sixth-floor hallway and hit the *Gray Streets* door hard enough to rattle the pebbled glass. Keyed through and the first thing he saw was the open doorway of Tom Kristoll's office. The desk lamp shining on the blotter, and behind the lamp a figure rising from the chair. Laura Kristoll.

She took off Tom's hat as she came out around the desk. She left his trench coat on. The coat squared her shoulders.

"David, are you all right?"

She met him in the outer office, laid her palm against his chest, lightly, as if her touch could tear him open.

"I'm all right."

"I don't like your breathing," she said.

"Sometimes I don't like it myself."

"I thought you were in the hospital. What are you doing here?"

"I saw your shadow from the street just now and I thought—"

"What?"

"I don't know."

She looked down at the trench coat, then at the fedora she had tossed onto the secretary's desk. "David," she said.

"It's not the first time I've thought it," he said. "I mean, what have I had to go on? What have I really seen, with my own eyes? The body of a man on the sidewalk, covered by a blanket. A closed casket lowered into the ground. If this were a story—"

"David—"

"If this were a story, Tom would show up in the final scene. He would explain everything. We'd go off together for a quiet drink and he would explain—"

Her fingers gripped the collar of his denim jacket.

"David, don't." Her voice fading. "David, Tom's dead."

He went home with her. Both of them silent in the car as she drove alongside the river. They rolled up the long driveway to the house and got out, and he followed her up the crushed-stone walk and through the door. She offered him a drink and he took a glass of plain water and she made him sit on the leather sofa while she built a fire in the antique furnace.

She closed the iron grate and came to sit beside him, silently for a while, her head back, golden hair spread over the black leather. He looked up at the wooden beams that crisscrossed overhead.

After a time she leaned close to him and he moved reflexively to put his arm around her. The effort made him wince.

"Is the pain very bad?" she asked him.

"It's all right. It's more a tightness."

The fire shifted in the furnace, crackling.

"I should have come to see you at the hospital," she said. "I was angry with you, but that's no excuse. I had a hard time getting over what you said to me, that night in the car at Sean's. Asking if I knew who killed Tom."

"I shouldn't have asked you that," he said.

"It hurt me," she said. "But I suppose I deserved it. The way I danced around the truth of what happened to Sean. I should have been thinking more of Tom and less about what I wanted. It seems absurd to me now, to think I could ever publish Sean's manuscript. I'm finished with the whole idea. I want you to know that."

The shadows of the beams flickered on the ceiling.

She said, "I'll give it to you if you want it. It's all here, in a box in Tom's study. The paper manuscript and all the discs, the backup copies. I don't want it anymore."

He let out a long breath. "You don't have to give it up, Laura. You worked on it. It's yours. I won't blame you for wanting to publish it."

"I'm done with it," she said. "You should take it." She nodded toward the furnace. "Or we could burn it."

"We don't have to burn it."

At midnight she put him to bed in a guest room upstairs. He piled his clothes on a chair and slid under the covers and lay in the dark listening to her movements in another room, the clatter of cabinet doors, water running. Then a light from the hall and she came through his doorway in flannel pajamas and climbed in beside him and curled up chastely with a pillow and fell asleep.

He woke in the night and listened to her breathing. Slipped out of bed and found his watch: twenty minutes after three. He went down to the kitchen and let the water run cold from the tap and filled a glass. He drank it outside in the air on the stones of the patio with the half-circle of woods deep around him.

When he came in, he wandered through the downstairs rooms until he came to Tom's study. The square shape on the desk was the box Laura had mentioned. He switched on a lamp and the discs glittered silver in the light. He slid them to one side and they glided one over another and uncovered the topmost page of Sean Wrentmore's manuscript: *Liars, Thieves, and Innocent Men.*

He counted the discs: seven of them. Plenty of backups. But a small voice in his mind told him that if there were seven, there could be eight.

A halfhearted search of the desk turned up the drawer that Michael Beccanti had told him about: the one with the false bottom. The secret compartment held nothing. No incriminating eighth disc.

He turned off the lamp in the study and wandered out to the living room. The fire had gone cold in the furnace. He checked the front door to make sure it was locked, then did the same for the back door and the patio door. All secure in the Kristoll house. Turning toward the stairs, he remembered the door to the garage.

He went to check it, found it unlocked. Some impulse made him open it, made him flip the switch of the overhead light. A stark white bulb illuminated Tom's Ford. On the walls, a motley collection of garden tools. A rake, a weed trimmer. Three shovels, all of them long-handled, none of them suitable for digging a grave.

Other items, half-familiar. A lawn mower in a corner. A painter's easel. The folding cot that he and Tom had used to carry Sean Wrentmore's body. A dartboard.

A glint of metal near the center of the dartboard. A piece of cork had been torn away and the steel backing showed through. Loogan touched the steel with a fingertip and felt an indentation. Shallow, rounded. Like the imprint of a bullet.

Chapter 41

"DAVID."

"She killed Adrian Tully."

Elizabeth Waishkey had braids in her long raven hair. She wore a linen shirt open at the collar, a string of glass beads. Blue jeans torn at the knee. She stood at her front door, kneading a dish towel in her hands, as if he had interrupted her at some domestic chore.

To David Loogan's eyes, she shimmered like an angel. Her shirt was white, as was the towel. Unearthly white, glowing. The glass beads glimmered at her throat.

"David," she said, "you're pale." She came onto the porch and looked out at the street. "You didn't walk here, did you?"

Loogan had passed the restless hours of the night on the leather sofa in the Kristoll house, and in the morning he had let Laura drive him home. They had detoured past Sean Wrentmore's condo, hoping to recover Loogan's car, but it was missing from the restaurant parking lot. At home he made some calls and tracked it down—at the impound lot of the Ann Arbor Police Department. He would need to wait a day to pick it up. The lot was closed on Sundays.

He didn't explain all this to Elizabeth. He waved her question away.

"No car," he said.

"How long have you been walking?"

"I don't know." It seemed like at least two hours, though it shouldn't have taken so long. After the first hour, it had occurred to him that he should have called a cab.

He had gotten lost a little at the end, had gone in circles. He had felt light-headed, and he felt light-headed now. That was probably the reason why Elizabeth Waishkey was shimmering.

"You're not surprised," he said.

She tipped her head sideways. "Actually, I am. I didn't expect you to turn up on my doorstep. But now that you're here, you should come in."

"I mean you weren't surprised when I told you she killed Tully. You didn't ask who I was talking about."

"David—"

"Laura Kristoll," he said. "I saw her last night. I went to her house."

"Yes."

He caught something in her tone. "You already knew that," he said. "You're watching her. You've got her under surveillance."

Elizabeth laid her palm on his shoulder. "David, come in and we'll sit down."

"I don't want to intrude on your Sunday afternoon."

"You should sit. You don't look well."

As a concession to her sensibilities, Loogan leaned against the white railing of the porch. The November sun shone blindingly bright on the railing. It shone even under the roof of the porch, where by rights there should have been shade.

"How long have you been watching her?" he asked.

Elizabeth stepped back from him. She tossed the white towel over the white shoulder of her shirt. "We weren't watching her. We were watching the *Gray Streets* building. The thing is, we had the national media in town for a while. Nathan Hideaway made a good story. There were photographers following Bridget Shellcross, and Laura too, and someone got the bright idea to break into Tom Kristoll's office at *Gray Streets*. He was trying to get pictures to sell to the tabloids—pictures of the scene of one of Hideaway's crimes.

"So we kept an eye on the building after that. A patrolman drove by last night and saw Laura walking out the lobby door. You were with her. He followed you."

Loogan narrowed his eyes. "Why?"

"The department has an interest in Laura Kristoll," Elizabeth said with a shrug. "There are people who resent her for withholding information about Sean Wrentmore's death. There are people who welcomed the news that she took you home with her last night. They saw it as a sign that she's resuming her sordid affair with her late husband's friend. It casts her in a bad light. We had a meeting about it this morning."

"Really? Is that enough to warrant a meeting?"

"It was a short meeting," Elizabeth said. "I told them they were mistaken. They don't understand your motives. You still think you're in a story in *Gray Streets*. If you spent the night at the Kristoll house, you were there to play detective."

Loogan looked down at the railing of the porch. It seemed to glow less intensely. He could see cracks and chips in the paint.

He said, "Is it time for you to remind me that this isn't a story in *Gray Streets*?"

"It's never done any good before."

He ran his thumb along the rough surface of the paint.

"You remember what Hideaway said about Adrian Tully," he said. "That his death was just what it seemed—he shot himself. You don't believe that, do you?"

She came a step closer to him. "You don't believe it, obviously."

"Laura killed him," he said. "I know how she did it. Everything hinges on the second bullet. She convinced Tully to meet her out there, by that field, and she got into his car, and she shot him once in the head. And the second shot—that was to get gunshot residue on his hand. But you never found the second bullet."

"No."

"It didn't end up in the field," Loogan said. "Laura took it with her when she left. That's what I realized last night. There's a dartboard hanging on the wall of her garage, a thick one made of cork set in a metal shell. She took it with her when she drove out to meet Tully, and after she shot him she set the dartboard up by the side of the road. She would have had to prop it on something—something like a painter's easel. There's one of those in the garage too. Then she got back in Tully's car and put the gun in his hand and fired the second shot through the open passenger window at the dartboard. The metal backing stopped the bullet and the cork held it and she took everything with her when she drove away. She got rid of the bullet afterward."

Elizabeth leaned against the railing beside him. She took the towel off her shoulder and busied herself folding it into a square.

She said, "Do you eat chicken, David?"

Time passed as he tried to make sense of the question. The sunlight seemed less intense, but the glass beads still glittered at her throat.

"What are you talking about?" he said.

"Some people won't," she told him. "But you don't strike me as one of those. We're having chicken for dinner. Sarah made it. She does most of the cooking around here. She seasoned it with lemon and pepper, I think. Baked it in a casserole with broccoli and rice. I'm sure there's enough for three."

David Loogan pushed himself up from the railing. He no longer felt light-headed.

"I'm sorry," he said. "I shouldn't have come to your house. I shouldn't have interrupted your meal."

She rose with him. "You're not interrupting. We haven't even started on the salad. You should come in and eat something, and we'll talk. We can talk about anything you like. Even about Adrian Tully, if that's what you want."

"That's why I came here," he said.

"I think you know better."

He looked at her soberly. "I'm not making this up, if that's what you think. It's all there in Laura Kristoll's garage—the easel, the dartboard. She killed him."

Elizabeth stood close to him. "Of course she did. And she's going to get away with killing him. It probably happened exactly the way you described.

But the bullet's long gone now. She'll never go to trial. Even if she did, she wouldn't be convicted. Tully's death looks like a suicide. And if it wasn't, if he was murdered, then Nathan Hideaway is a ready-made suspect. He killed Tom and wanted to deflect suspicion onto someone else. That's his motive for killing Tully. Hideaway is Laura's cover. He's her reasonable doubt."

Loogan listened with growing impatience. "You don't seem to mind that she's going to get away with it. It doesn't seem to bother you."

Her expression told him that he had said the wrong thing. She answered him in a voice empty of emotion. "I hate it."

"What are we going to do about it?" he said.

She looked away. "We're going to eat dinner, David. This isn't a story in *Gray Streets*."

"I don't know if I can accept that."

She opened the door to go in. "I don't know if you can either, but you're going to have to try. And I'm afraid we haven't come to the worst of it yet."

He stepped toward her and the floorboards creaked beneath his feet. "What do you mean?"

"I mean that you're not filled with righteous anger over the death of Adrian Tully. He's not the reason you walked for miles to get here. You don't care whether Laura Kristoll goes to prison for his murder. He's not the one we need to talk about."

Somewhere beyond the porch the sun must have blazed, because the white glow came up again. Loogan put a hand against the door frame to steady himself.

"No, it's Tom," he said. "I think Laura knew Hideaway was going to kill Tom."

When Loogan opened his eyes he found himself lying on a couch beneath a quilt. The gauzy white square of a curtained window floated in his vision.

A girl sat in a chair nearby, her feet on a coffee table, a magazine open in her lap. She twirled a strand of raven hair around her finger. Sarah Waishkey.

Loogan remembered Elizabeth guiding him into the house, sitting him down. He remembered deciding he would rest for a moment. He didn't remember getting out of his denim jacket, but there it was, folded on the coffee table near Sarah's feet.

Loogan turned onto his side. "How long have I been asleep?"

The girl looked up and closed her magazine. It was an issue of *Gray Streets*.

"Not long," she said.

"Where's your mother?"

"Outside. She went to walk Lillian Eakins to her car."

"Lillian Eakins?"

"Mom called her. She lives nearby. She came to take your temperature and listen to your lungs."

"She's a doctor?"

"Technically, she's the medical examiner."

Loogan chuckled and threw off the quilt and sat up. "I'm not dead."

"That's what she determined," Sarah said, putting the magazine aside. "How do you feel?"

"Tired."

She smiled. "You got shot in the heart."

"Not quite."

"Close enough. You ought to take a rest. It's over now."

"I'm not so sure."

"It's over. He's dead—Nathan Hideaway. My mom told me the whole story. You saved her life."

"That's one way to look at it," Loogan said.

"What's the other way?"

"Her life would never have been in danger if not for me."

The girl made an impatient face at him. "You can't be responsible for everything," she said. "Do you want some iced tea?"

He considered the question as he looked around for his shoes.

"Yes," he said.

"Don't get up. I'll bring it to you."

He spotted his shoes beneath the coffee table, decided they could stay where they were. Sarah disappeared into the kitchen and came back a minute later with a tall glass of iced tea. Elizabeth came with her.

"How are you feeling?" she asked Loogan.

"He's fine," Sarah said. "I broke the news to him that he's alive."

The girl left the glass on the table and went out again to the kitchen. Elizabeth settled into the chair by Loogan. Her fingers went to the glass beads at her neck.

"We were talking about Tom Kristoll," she said.

"I've taken up enough of your time," he said. "You've got dinner waiting."

She crossed one leg over the other. "We're going to talk about Tom. You've got to get it out of your system."

Loogan reached for the iced tea. Took a sip. Elizabeth watched him patiently.

"Laura came to see me the night Tom died," he said.

"Yes."

"It wasn't a coincidence."

Her fingers worried at a bead. "It could have been," she said.

"Tom and I were supposed to meet that night," Loogan said. "If Laura hadn't come to see me, I would have been at Tom's office when Nathan Hideaway got there."

"It could still have been a coincidence. Did Laura know you were supposed to meet Tom?"

"Not from me. But Tom could have told her. Even if he didn't, she knew Tom and I had a habit of meeting for a drink in the evening—usually at his office. She wanted to make sure I stayed away that night. She knew what Hideaway was going to do."

"It's still possible she thought Hideaway was only going to talk to Tom."

"She knew what was at stake," Loogan said. "She knew what might happen if persuasion didn't work. I think she wanted Tom silenced, one way or another. Her motive was the same as Hideaway's. She didn't want Tom to go to the police about Sean Wrentmore. Laura was the one who edited Wrentmore's manuscript. She put a lot of work into it. She thinks of it as her own, wants to publish it. She killed Adrian Tully because he knew about Wrentmore and she didn't trust him to keep quiet. She let Hideaway kill Tom for the same reason."

Loogan studied the rim of his glass. "She lied to me at every turn," he said. "She still pretends she didn't know it was Hideaway who killed Tom. The worst thing is, part of me still wants to believe her. I'd like to believe she shot Adrian Tully out of revenge—because she honestly thought he was the one who killed Tom. That's one of the reasons I came here. Part of me was hoping you'd convince me I was wrong about her."

Elizabeth shifted in her chair. "I wish I could. But Laura didn't shoot Tully out of revenge."

"I know," Loogan said softly.

"She knew he didn't kill Tom. There's no doubt about that. Hideaway hit Tom with a copy of Shakespeare's *Collected Works*. He took the dust jacket away with him so he wouldn't leave fingerprints behind. Later we found a scrap of a dust jacket from the *Collected Works* under a seat in Tully's car. It had to have been put there to frame him."

"Laura put it there," said Loogan.

Elizabeth was nodding. "If it was a piece of the same dust jacket, then she got it from Hideaway. If it was from a similar dust jacket, then Hideaway told her what book he used to knock Tom out—and that he took the jacket. That detail is one I never discussed with her, and it was never reported in the press. Either way, Laura knew that Hideaway killed Tom—at least she knew after the fact."

"Not just after," Loogan said. "She knew before. She knew what was going to happen to Tom."

"You may be right. She and Hideaway may have been working together all along. But no one's going to prove it to a jury. Because Laura has a good lawyer, and even if she had a bad one he would argue that Hideaway killed Tom without her knowledge, and then killed Tully and framed him, and she had nothing to do with any of it."

Loogan sat back against the cushions of the couch. "I don't suppose it matters that Hideaway denied killing Tully. That night in the clearing, he said Tully was a suicide."

Elizabeth rubbed beads of glass against her chin. "It would be better for us if he had ratted Laura out," she said. "I guess it's possible he didn't know. Maybe he told her the details of how he killed Tom, and she decided on her own to frame Tully. When Hideaway found out about Tully's death, he might have suspected Laura without being sure. But I think the truth is simpler. He knew what she had done, but he felt a kind of odd loyalty to her. So he was discreet that night in the clearing—he confessed to his own crime and kept quiet about hers."

The light outside the window faded and the colors in the room seemed to dim. David Loogan let his head tip back against the cushions.

"So Laura's not going to suffer any consequences."

"She's going to have to live for a long time with her husband's ghost," Elizabeth said quietly. "That's something. As for the manuscript she edited, I think I can make sure it's never published. We've got it on the disc Rachel Kent gave us. I'll see that Sean Wrentmore's family gets a copy. They can block its publication."

"It's not enough."

"It might be all there is."

Loogan closed his eyes. "You and I know she killed Adrian Tully. Maybe I could get her to talk about it. I could wear a wire."

"She's not going to confess, David."

"There has to be something I can do."

"You can let it go. It's not your problem to solve."

Slowly he opened his eyes. Elizabeth had gotten up. She stood with her hands in the pockets of her jeans. The sleeves of her white shirt were rolled to her elbows.

He said, "Are you going to tell me I can't be responsible for everything?"

"You already know that," she said. She took her right hand from her pocket and held it out to him. "I'm going to eat dinner with my daughter. Are you going to join us?"

At one in the morning a gust of wind set a branch scraping against a pane of glass and the sound woke David Loogan from a doze. He sat up on the couch and the light from a lamp in the corner showed him he was alone in the room. A blanket and pillow lay on one arm of the chair beside him, a towel and a toothbrush on the other.

He made his way upstairs and found the bathroom by the glow of a night-light. There he made use of the toothbrush and took care of other business. In the hallway after, he passed a half-open door, caught a glimpse of moonlight on the folds of a blanket.

Down in the kitchen he poured himself a glass of milk and stood drinking it in the light of the refrigerator. The remains of the chicken casserole occupied a small covered dish on the top shelf.

Three apples stood in a row on the counter. After dinner, there had been juggling—Sarah Waishkey demonstrating her skill. Then there had been several games of Scrabble. There had been a movie, a Western on a cable channel. There had been popcorn. No one had said anything about Loogan staying. No one had said anything about him leaving.

Loogan drank the last of the milk and drifted into the living room. He spread the blanket on the couch, arranged the pillow. He heard a sound from the window, the branch scraping again. He pulled the curtain back and checked the window lock. All secure.

He made a circuit of the downstairs rooms, checking every window. The kitchen came last. Two windows facing the street. He had grown careless by then; he almost missed the movement on the lawn. He looked again and saw two figures on the sidewalk beneath the elm tree.

He turned the bolt on the front door and went out onto the porch without thinking. The night air was absolutely still and there was no sound. Even his footsteps on the floorboards were silent.

A streetlight cast the shadow of the elm over the lawn, and in the shadow stood two men he recognized. Neither of them seemed quite right. Jimmy Wade Peltier was thinner than Loogan remembered, and paler. The contours of his skull showed through the flesh of his face. Nathan Hideaway had diminished somehow too, though he was still tall. He had the same wide mouth and square jaw, the same crown of white curls, but there was something insubstantial about him. It was difficult to distinguish him from the shadow of the elm.

Neither of them made a sound, but there was something between them, some debate going on. Jimmy Peltier gestured with his butterfly knife. Hideaway had his black revolver. Loogan thought he was witnessing the prelude to a fight, but it turned out to be something else. A bargaining session. It ended with an exchange: Peltier took possession of the revolver; Hideaway accepted the knife.

As Peltier began to back away, he seemed to notice Loogan for the first time. A grin took hold of his mouth and he raised the black revolver triumphantly, the muscles of his arms tense beneath his torn shirt. He spun on his heel and darted soundlessly across the empty street. Nathan Hideaway saw Loogan at the same time. He stood still on the lawn and let Loogan approach him. He wore the same woolen sweater and corduroy slacks he had worn in the clearing.

The two of them watched Jimmy Wade Peltier jog down the sidewalk on the other side of the street. Loogan lost sight of him, but Hideaway stayed focused on him for a long while.

"He's a graceless fellow, and not very bright," Hideaway said eventually. "If I were you, I wouldn't lose any sleep over killing him."

There was an undercurrent in his voice, like the rustling of dried leaves.

"You shouldn't have given him a gun," Loogan heard himself saying. "He was bad enough with a knife."

Hideaway turned to Loogan and fixed him with his piercing eyes. "It won't do him any good," he said. He raised Peltier's knife and slashed at a branch of the elm. The blade passed through harmlessly.

Looking through Hideaway's body, Loogan could see the porch light of one of the houses across the street.

Hideaway held up the knife and examined his reflection in the mirror of the blade.

"If I can see myself," he said, "then I must still exist in some sense. Wouldn't you say that's true?"

Loogan ignored the question. He turned to look up and down the street, alert for any sign of movement. But nothing stirred. Overhead, a wisp of cloud hung frozen before the moon.

"What are you doing here?" he said to Hideaway.

The man folded and pocketed the knife. "I came to haunt you," he said, "but I'm having second thoughts. I get the feeling it would be tedious work."

"Have you seen Tom?"

Hideaway let out a hollow sigh. "Definitely tedious. Why don't you ask me if I've seen the face of God?"

"Have you?"

"Not yet."

"What about Tom then?"

"I don't think he and I are in the same place."

Loogan leaned forward eagerly. "You mean he's still alive?"

"It'd be a neat trick if he was," said Hideaway. He lifted his right hand over his head and mimed a body falling several stories. His left hand stood in for the sidewalk below. There was no sound when the two met. "What do you want with him?"

"You know the answer to that."

"Tedious," Hideaway said again. He looked over Loogan's shoulder at the Waishkey house. "Go back inside," he said. "If I see Tom, I'll send him around. I wouldn't hold my breath." He shooed Loogan away. "Go on. Those two in there have absolved you. You're not going to do better than that out here."

With that, he turned and began to stroll down the sidewalk. The knife came out of his pocket and he held it up, admiring his reflection.

"Wait," Loogan said, but he made no move to follow.

Hideaway strolled on without responding. He started to fade almost immediately, and before he reached the end of the block he was gone.

Sound and movement returned with his passing: The branches of the elm swaying in the wind. A car's engine puttering in the distance. A cat prowling among garbage cans across the street.

Loogan heard a door opening behind him, the creak of a floorboard, soft footsteps.

Elizabeth Waishkey saying, "Are you all right?"

He turned and looked up at her. She wore a long robe hugged tight around her. She tilted her head curiously and her hair was sleek and black under the porch light. Her feet were bare.

"Did something happen?" she asked him. "Was someone out here?"

He hesitated, but not for long.

"No," he said.

"Come in then," she said. "Get some sleep."

ACKNOWLEDGMENTS

I would like to offer thanks to Amy Einhorn and Victoria Skurnick, who conspired to make good things happen for me and the mysterious Mr. Loogan.

For their support and encouragement, I'm grateful to my family in New York: my parents, Carolyn and Mike, my brother, Terry, and my sister, Michelle. And to Linda Randolph, my family in Michigan.

Thanks also to Ellen Paul, Tamara Sharp, Elizabeth Carter, Monika Verma, Jan Ollila, and Mark Fowler.

ABOUT THE AUTHOR

HARRY DOLAN graduated from Colgate University, where he majored in philosophy and studied fiction writing with the novelist Frederick Busch. He earned a master's degree in philosophy from the University of North Carolina at Chapel Hill and worked for several years as a freelance editor. He grew up in Rome, New York, and now lives in Ann Arbor, Michigan, with his partner, Linda Randolph.